Friends and Enemies

BERYL MATTHEWS

Allison & Busby Limited
11 Wardour Mews
London W1F 8AN
allisonandbusby.com

First published in Great Britain by Allison & Busby in 2019.
This paperback edition published by Allison & Busby in 2019.

Copyright © 2019 by BERYL MATTHEWS

A CIP catalogue record for this book is available from
the British Library.

10 9 8 7 6 5 4 3 2 1

ISBN 978-0-7490-2421-5

Typeset in 11/16 pt Sabon LT Pro by
Allison & Busby Ltd.

The paper used for this Allison & Busby publication
has been produced from trees that have been legally sourced
from well-managed and credibly certified forests.

Printed and bound by
CPI Group (UK) Ltd, Croydon, CR0 4YY

Chapter One

Poplar, London, March 1941

'Here they come again.' Katherine Hammond's mother picked up the bag containing a thermos flask and sandwiches ready for another long night in the shelter. 'Put on something warm, Kathy. It's a cold night.'

Winding a scarf around her neck and slipping on gloves, she followed her mother the short distance along the road to the shelter. It would be lovely to sleep undisturbed in her own bed, but her mother always insisted they took cover when the air raid sirens sounded.

The shelter was filling up as the drone of bombers approaching could be heard. Making sure her mother was well inside, she took a seat right by the door. Everyone was talking, and it wouldn't be long before a sing-song started. It was always the same and the singing helped to comfort people, especially the children. The whistle of bombs falling could already be heard above the noise of chatter. They sounded close.

A man arrived late and sat opposite them. 'Looks like they've picked us tonight. They are right overhead and there are hundreds of the buggers.'

An explosion shook the shelter, making cement dust fall from the roof. Then almost immediately there was another crash, and Kathy was flying through the air. She hit the ground with a force that knocked all the breath out of her, and for a while she was confused, not able to grasp why she was in the road covered in dust and debris. There was an eerie quietness, which was broken all of a sudden by people running and shouting.

'This one's alive!' someone called out.

'Can you move?'

Kathy looked up at the man bending over her and struggled to sit up, glancing at the devastation surrounding her. Then the realisation hit her. The shelter was no longer there. Surging to her feet, she shook off the man's restraining hand and lurched to where the shelter had been. Then she fell onto her hands and knees, and began to pull at the rubble, frantic now.

The man was beside her again. 'Come away, miss. There's nothing you can do here.'

'My mother's in there,' she shouted at him. 'I've got to find her.'

'Where was she sitting?' he asked, helping by pulling away some of the larger pieces.

'About here. I think it's about here. Help me!'

The next two hours were a nightmare as body after body was pulled from the debris, and she inspected every one in the desperate need to find her mother.

She was finally found, and Kathy knelt beside her, knowing instantly that she was dead. After finding out where they were taking the dead, she stood up and tried to take a step forward, but for some reason her body wasn't obeying the command.

'You'd better go to the hospital,' a warden told her. 'You're in shock and need medical help.'

Kathy shook her head. 'They have enough to do this night, and I must find my aunt.'

'The all-clear hasn't sounded yet. You should take cover.'

She gave him a pitying look and pointed to the rubble. 'I did take cover – in that!'

'I'm sorry. It's a bad night.'

'Bad?' Anger raced through her like a wildfire out of control and she looked up at the sky, illuminated by the many fires burning all around. 'Tell that to those bloody men up there. My mother never hurt anyone in her life and now she's dead. None of the people in there deserved to die like this. It's senseless murder!'

'If you won't take cover, go home and try to get some rest.'

Her laugh was almost hysterical as she pointed along the road. 'That great hole is where my home used to be.'

The man swore as she turned, finally able to make

herself move away from the devastation that had just torn her life apart.

On her way to her aunt's house Kathy scrambled over the rubble, dazed and oblivious to the chaos and noise. What was going on around her meant nothing at this moment. She was not even aware of the drone of aeroplanes and the whistle of bombs as they hurtled down.

'You can't go down there, miss.'

She glanced at the air raid warden holding her arm. 'My aunt lives there.'

'I'm sorry, but that row of houses took a direct hit. What are you doing wandering around here? The all-clear hasn't sounded yet. You should be in a shelter.'

'I was. That was hit as well.' Kathy gazed at the devastation around her, unable to put into words what had happened to her. 'Have they found any survivors in there?'

'Not yet, but your aunt might be in one of the centres set up, or in a shelter.'

She shook her head. 'No, she always said she was going to sleep in her own bed, no matter what.'

'Well, we won't know if anyone has survived for a while yet, so why don't you go home and try to get some sleep. Dawn isn't far away, and this raid can't go on much longer now.'

'My house isn't there any more.'

The warden sighed wearily. 'You'd better go to one of the centres, lass. Where's the rest of your family?'

'My dad's in the navy . . .' With a massive effort Kathy dredged up the words she had been trying to deny.

'There's only my mum and she was just killed when the shelter blew apart.'

'Oh, I'm sorry, lass. Go to the hall along the road and get some help. You look as if you need it. You're in a terrible mess.'

Kathy turned and stumbled back the way she had come. When the road was reasonably passable she stood up straight and paused, trying to clear her head so she could think straight. She was lost, not knowing what to do or where to go. In one vicious night her world had been torn from under her feet and there was an emptiness inside her that was like a black void.

Another loud explosion jolted her, and the void was filled with raging anger, blanking out all other emotions. All grief and horror were instantly trampled underfoot, leaving behind a fury that man should unleash such cruelty on its own kind.

With fists clenched she straightened up. Well, if that's the way it was going to be, then she wasn't going to let them get away with this. Somehow, she would make them pay for this night, and all the other nights when people had suffered and died. They wanted a fight and they would bloody well get one. For the first time in her life Kathy regretted being a girl and so unable to join a fighting unit, but she would find a way to get involved in the fight!

'Come inside, dearie, you look as if you need a strong cup of tea and someone to deal with your injuries. Then we'll find you some clothes. Yours are torn to shreds.'

'Are they? I hadn't noticed.' Kathy looked at the woman who had taken her arm and allowed her to lead her into the church hall. It was packed, mostly with women and children, as the men were out there frantically digging in the rubble in the hope of finding anyone alive. There were a couple of nurses and a man who was clearly a doctor, dealing with the injured, and women from the Women's Voluntary Service giving tea and comfort to as many as they could. Kathy noticed the various expressions on the faces of those inside: stunned, sadness, grief and, on many, anger. Oh yes, she thought, this madness would be avenged! The appalling thing was this country was going to have to meet like with like if it was going to survive. It was now a case of fighting or going under, and that was unthinkable.

'Let me have a look at your injuries, miss.'

'Hmm?'

'I'm a doctor, and you've got blood on your clothes, face and hands. I need to dress your injuries.'

Kathy looked down at herself and noticed the mess she was in for the first time. 'I'm all right.'

'Let me be the judge of that.' He took hold of her arm to lead her into another room that had been set up to tend to the injured.

She shook his hand off. 'I said I'm all right!'

'Don't waste my time, young lady. I have plenty of other people who need my help.'

He spoke softly, although was clearly irritated by her attitude, and when Kathy looked into his eyes she saw the strain he had been under during this long night. 'I apologise, Doctor, but at the moment I am so angry, and I am sure the blood on me isn't mine. Please see to your other patients while I try to calm my thoughts and gain some kind of control over what has happened.'

He inclined his head. 'That is something we are all struggling with at the moment, but don't leave here without seeing me. I do believe you have injuries that need attention.'

Kathy watched him walk away, knowing the strain all the rescue workers were under. She mustn't vent her fury on any of them, or anyone here. They weren't to blame for this senseless carnage.

'She's in shock,' Kathy heard the doctor tell someone. 'Keep an eye on her and call me if she needs help.'

'I'll do that, Doctor.'

Kathy gazed around the crowded room and studied the faces. A few were shedding quiet tears and she knew it was something she should be doing but supposed that would come later when the numbness wore off. It was as if her mind had switched off and was refusing to look at the horror she had just experienced. The anger that was surging through her had obliterated all other emotions.

'Come and wash your face and hands, dear, and then we will find you a nice strong cup of tea and a sandwich.' The woman who appeared at her side looked bone-weary, but still managed a faint smile. 'My name's Doris. What's yours?'

'Kathy.'

'Come with me, Kathy, and let's get you cleaned up, shall we?'

She nodded and allowed Doris to take her to a small bathroom.

'We're lucky because we've still got water here. The firemen managed to get it flowing again for us. The doctors need it, you see, and so do they.' She chatted away while she put water in the sink.

As Kathy placed her hands in the sink the water turned pink and she shuddered violently.

'Easy, my dear. You'll feel better when you get that off you.' Doris wet a cloth and wiped the mess from Kathy's face when she was trembling too much to do it for herself. 'There, that's better. I'll see if I can find you some clothes. People have been generous bringing in all kinds of things we might need, so we should be able to find you something.'

'Thank you.' Kathy grabbed hold of the sink for support. The sight of blood colouring the water had brought back the full horror of what had happened, and she knew where the blood had come from. She had tried to revive her mother although she had known she was dead, and that picture had caused her to nearly fall apart. That was something she wasn't going to do, she vowed, and gathered the rage around her again like a blanket of protection.

Back in the hall with a cup of tea and a slice of bread with a thin spread of something on it, she struggled to think clearly. After a tremendous inner fight, control came, and the cup was steady in her hand. Kathy nibbled on the bread, grateful for the small victory. Somehow, she had to get through this night and the days to come. She didn't seriously expect her aunt had survived a direct hit, and she would have to deal with the aftermath of this night. Her father was at sea, so she was alone, without any family or even a home to return to.

'Where were you, dear?' Doris asked gently.

'In the shelter on the corner of Benson Street. It was bombed.'

'How many survived?'

'A few.'

'Were you with anyone?'

Her mouth set in a grim line as she glared at the woman, rage flashing in her dark eyes, but she managed to bite back the sharp reply of telling her to mind her own business. 'I thank you for your kindness, but I'm all right now, and there are many more people who need your help.'

'I understand you don't want to talk about it, dear.' Doris stood up and patted her shoulder. 'You call if you need anything.'

Kathy didn't know how long she sat there, or what was happening around her. It was as if a film was running in her head, showing herself and many others digging in the rubble, and as each of the dead was brought out she could see their faces clearly. When she became aware of someone's hands on her she pushed them away.

'Don't you think she should be in hospital, Doctor?' she heard a woman ask.

'They are already overcrowded, and as far as I can see she isn't injured. She's in shock, so we'll keep her here until she comes out of it. I see you've managed to change her clothes, but has she had anything to drink and eat?'

'Yes, we gave her a strong cup of tea and a slice of bread, and her cup and plate are empty.'

'Good. We must see if we can get her to talk. It might help.'

The woman sighed deeply. 'What a terrible night. So much pain, loss and suffering. Goodness knows what this girl has seen. When we changed her clothes, we saw that none of the blood on her was hers.'

'By the look of her torn fingernails I would say she has been digging in the rubble looking for someone.'

Someone grasped her hands tightly and demanded in a firm tone, 'Look at me!'

Kathy raised her head and looked into a face drawn with fatigue, but the blue eyes were still clear and alert.

'Tell me who you are and what happened to you.'

Such a kind face, she thought, as she formed the words, 'Kathy Hammond.'

'And where were you during the raid?' he prompted, still gripping her hands firmly.

'In a shelter. It blew up.'

'Were you on your own?'

She shook her head and looked away.

'Tell me who you were with. Were they family?' He

gently turned her head back to look at him again. 'Don't keep it all inside, Kathy. All the hurt and grief has got to be released. Talk to me.'

Suddenly, fury erupted. 'What the hell do you think happened on a night like this? Everyone was in that shelter for safety, and those devils blew it up. There were children in there – and my mother.' Her tone was bitter. 'I tried to help, but it was no use. My home was also just a pile of rubble, so I came here to find my aunt. Her house has been flattened as well, and they haven't found anyone alive yet.'

'Do you have any other family you can go to?'

'There's only my dad now, and he's in the navy.' Kathy could hear herself saying these things, but it seemed as if she was talking about someone else.

The doctor unwound himself from his crouched position in front of her, his expression grim. 'Stay here tonight and see what the situation is in the morning. You'll have to sleep on the floor, but we've managed to get some blankets. I'll be here if you need me.'

She looked up at the weary face and reached out in compassion. 'You need rest, Doctor. We are in a world gone crazy and you can't save everyone.'

'Maybe not.' He shrugged. 'But I can have a damned good try.'

Kathy watched him walk away to see what he could do for more people. There was activity all around her. Women were doing their best to supply survivors and rescuers with tea and sandwiches. A baker had just arrived from somewhere with loaves of bread; someone else was bringing in milk and other supplies. Others were hauling in bedding for those who had lost their homes, and there was even an elderly man entertaining the frightened children with card tricks and, miraculously, bringing smiles to their faces. It was an astonishing scene, and one she knew she would never forget.

Rising quickly to her feet she marched over to a group of WVS women who were making sandwiches as fast as they could. 'Give me something to do,' she demanded.

The woman who was clearly in charge nodded, picked up a tray full of mugs and handed it to her. 'Take that to the men outside and tell them there's food here for them when they can take a break. And thanks, dear, we need all the help we can get tonight.'

Someone opened the door for her and she stepped into something resembling Dante's 'Inferno'. The destruction was shocking and the fires from the docks had turned the sky a bright orange. The planes were no longer overhead, but they could be heard as they wreaked havoc in another area of London. There were people everywhere, men, women, some in uniform and many in ordinary clothes, but all were tearing at the rubble in a desperate effort to find anyone buried there. As Kathy gazed at the horrific scene she was certain that it was something she would never be able to forgive.

'That for us, lass?' There was a brief flash of white teeth in the grime-covered face.

'Yes, and there's food inside when you're ready.'

'Thanks.' He gazed at the devastation all around them and beckoned to others to come and get the tea. 'It will be a while, though.'

The tray was quickly emptied by weary and thirsty rescuers. 'I'll get some more. Have you found anyone alive where that house was?' She pointed to the large hole where her aunt's house had stood.

'We've found two people, but they were dead, I'm sorry to say.' He sighed deeply. 'Was that your home?'

Kathy shook her head. 'That was my aunt's house. Mine was in the next street – and that's gone as well.'

'Ah, I'm sorry.'

'I'll get more tea,' she said quickly. The last thing she wanted was sympathy. She was only holding herself together with anger, and that was hanging by a slender thread. If she let that go she didn't know what would happen to her. Everyone around her was suffering in some way or another, and help was needed, not hysterical females making the rescuers' job even more distressing. Kathy gritted her teeth as she made her way back to the hall, determined to stay strong if she could. At the back of her mind she knew this was important if she was going to function well enough to cope with the aftermath of this raid.

She continued to do anything asked of her, and when dawn arrived the rescuers were still everywhere. Exhausted firemen, police, medical staff, military and civilians were sitting on rubble or propped up against anything they could find to support them.

'We've run out of everything,' Betty, one of the WVS women said, coming to stand beside Kathy. 'We've appealed for more and we are going to need it, because these poor devils won't get any rest today.'

'Neither will you or anyone else, and tonight it will all start again.' Kathy fought to keep the tears from her eyes. 'How can anyone do this to innocent people?'

'It's all-out war, dear, and they are trying to break our spirit.' Betty gave a strained smile. 'That won't happen. Just look around you. People are picking their way around the mess in an effort to get to work, and there's even a bus running. We aren't beaten yet!'

Kathy couldn't believe her eyes. People were clambering on the bus and many others were walking, determined to get to work any way they could. She brushed the dust from her clothes. 'I must go as well.'

'Where do you work, dear?'

'Cartwright's, an engineering firm near the docks.'

'Cartwright's, you say?' A fireman had overheard her and was shaking his head. 'I was there during the raid and it's burnt to the ground. No point you going down there, because the whole area is unsafe and fires are still burning.'

Kathy nodded and took a deep breath, trying to clear her mind. There was a funeral to arrange – two if she could find out what had happened to her aunt. Then there was the problem of somewhere to stay, and a decision had to be made about what she was going to do. It was a struggle to grasp the situation she was now facing. In one night, she had lost everything – her mother, almost certainly her aunt, her home and job. All she had were the clothes she stood up in, and even those had been given to her. The list of things to do was daunting, but she was the only one left who could sort everything out, so she had better get on with it. Her first task would be to find lodgings of some sort, then tackle the other distressing things, and she sincerely hoped the meagre amount of her savings in the bank would pay for everything.

Her mind was spinning, threatening to throw her into confusion, but she recognised the feelings as shock, and balled her hands into fists, knowing she must keep functioning. Another thing missing when the shelter blew apart was her handbag containing all her personal details, so that was something else she had better sort out.

It was going to be one of the toughest days she had ever faced!

Chapter Two

The number of people needing help was huge and the authorities were struggling to cope, but everywhere Kathy was directed to go she found kindness and understanding. Fortunately, while she was explaining she couldn't identify herself because she had lost everything, a woman who knew her was able to vouch for her and even offered a room in her house. It had lost most of its windows, but they were going to be boarded up to make the place habitable again. The woman even gave her some more clothes and another pair of shoes, so she felt reasonably dressed.

With those things settled she was able to set about sorting out the many other things to be dealt with. Her dad wasn't here so it was up to her to see her dear mother received a proper funeral. She knew where her mother had been taken so she went there first, and after making enquiries she found out where the dead had been taken from her aunt's row of houses. The only thing keeping her on her feet was the sheer fury surging through her – not only for herself, but for the many others trying to cope with the distressing task of identifying loved ones.

'Have you found your relative?' the man beside her asked.

It was only then she realised she was standing still, gazing at the body in front of her and not saying a word. 'That's my aunt,' she told him, finally managing to get the words out. 'I'll arrange for the funeral.'

He nodded. 'Come with me. I will need your aunt's details.'

'Of course.' She turned away too sharply and swayed.

The man caught hold of her arm and steadied her but said nothing. That didn't surprise her because she knew this poor man was doing this all day. Words were useless after such a dreadful night that had left so many people suffering. The anger bubbled through her with force.

Another man hurried over. 'You all right, miss?'

'That's a daft question,' she snapped. 'My mother and aunt have been killed, and my home is just a pile of rubble. How the hell do you think I feel?'

'I can't imagine.' He spoke softly and gently, not seeming at all offended by her outburst.

She was immediately ashamed of herself for speaking so rudely to the young man. Everyone was dealing with this day in the best way they could, and she had no right to make their job harder than it was. 'I'm sorry to have spoken to you like that. You don't deserve to be on the end of my fury. Please forgive me.'

'There's nothing to forgive, miss.' He gave a tired smile. 'I have seen every emotion possible today, and if I was in your position I would be shouting in fury as well. But remember, as bad as it is now, our turn will come.'

'Yes, I am sure it will, but the thought of unleashing destruction on other innocent people does not bring me any comfort. The only way I can get through this is to hang on to my anger. For some odd reason it seems to give me some kind of strength. Now, can I get this over with and get a cup of tea somewhere?'

'There's tea ready for anyone through the door on the left. Good luck, miss,' he called as he walked away.

'Who was that?' she asked the other man.

'A medical student. We have had to rope in as many people as we could to help out, but everyone is willing to pitch in any way they can. We are all getting used to little sleep.'

She walked beside him to the office and sat down, weary beyond belief. 'How long do you think they will keep up these night raids?'

'I expect Hitler intends to do this until we are on our knees begging to surrender.'

She gave an inelegant snort. 'That will never happen. Churchill said we would never surrender, and I believe that.'

'So do we all, and I believe Hitler will eventually recognise that, but in the meantime we have to deal with each night as it comes.' He pushed a form across the desk. 'Fill that in, please.'

She did so and handed it back.

'You said your mother had been killed as well, so do you know where they have taken her?'

'Yes, she was taken to another centre and I've already dealt with that. Now I have two funerals to arrange.'

'Go and get yourself a cup of tea first,' he said kindly.

It took nearly two weeks before the funerals could take place, and that time was a blur to Kathy. She had written to her father but didn't know if he had received the sad news yet, because he was at sea somewhere. Her fervent hope was that he had, and at the time of the funerals he could give his thoughts to his wife and sister-in-law, both of whom he had loved very much, as she had. He was out there somewhere, coping with the constant threat from U-boats, and now he had to deal with the grief of losing the wife he loved. 'I'm so sorry, Dad,' she whispered, 'but I'll see everything is done properly. I promise.'

The day of the funerals arrived, a cold and dreary day, and the pain she felt as her aunt and mother were laid to rest was beyond belief. The violence of their deaths was a terrible memory to have and weighed heavily on her. During the service she did her best to hold on to happier times they had spent together, for that was the only way she could get through the funeral.

It hadn't been possible to get headstones, and she didn't have enough money for them anyway, but she had found a carpenter who had made two wooden plaques and carved the names on them. They would do for the time being, but they would get proper headstones later, and that choice would be her father's.

The emotional strain had taken its toll on her, and she returned to her lodgings drained and exhausted.

'What are you going to do now?' the woman who had given her a bed asked the day after the funerals.

'I am going to the Women's War Work Enquiry Office to see if I can join the Wrens. The factory I worked in has been completely destroyed, and after what has happened I can't go back to that kind of work or sit on the sidelines. If I was a man I would join a fighting force, but as a girl I will have to get involved in any way I can.'

'I've been told they are not easy to get into.'

'So I believe, but I'll try them first. Dad's a sailor so I thought it would be good to be connected to the navy.'

'Well, good luck. You've had a decent education, so you might stand a chance.'

'Let's hope so.'

After her visit to the War Work Enquiry Office, Kathy had put in her application to enlist in the Wrens and the next step was an interview. The recruitment hall was crowded with other hopefuls and she knew this was going to take some time.

'Busy, isn't it?' the young girl next to her remarked. 'I've been here for over an hour already, and by the look on some faces they are sending quite a few away. Why do you want to join the Wrens?'

Kathy didn't feel like talking but couldn't be rude to the pretty girl. 'My dad's in the navy. He's a captain on a destroyer.'

'Gosh, that's good, because you might stand a better chance of being accepted.'

'Maybe. Why do you want to join?'

She grinned. 'I like the uniform and think the hats are fantastic.'

From the look of devilment on her face Kathy didn't know whether to believe her or not. 'You're joking.'

The grin spread. 'Nope. My name's Joyce, by the way. What's yours?'

'Kathy.'

'Nice to meet you.' She stood up the moment her name was called and winked at Kathy. 'You never know, we might meet up again both wearing those saucy hats.'

Another hour passed, which didn't do anything for her fragile emotions. Finally, her name was called, and she was shown to a small office, which surprised her because the interviews were taking place in the hall. *Still*, she thought, *I expect they have to use every available space to cope with this volume of applicants.* The man sitting the other side of the desk stood up politely when she entered and indicated she should sit down. Then he settled back in his chair. He was a man in his forties, she guessed, and when he looked up from studying the form she had filled in she felt a jolt as if those dark-brown eyes could see her every thought. She was immediately on the defensive.

The questions started gently enough but became more probing as he made brief notes on a pad. After a while he threw down the pen and sat back.

'Tell me in your own words why you want to join the service.'

'My father is in the navy.'

'I already know that. I want to hear your real reason for coming here today.'

She bristled at his tone and her anger rose to the surface. 'I came here because they killed my mother, my aunt and destroyed my home. What other bloody reason do you want?'

He studied her intently for a moment, then picked up the pen and put a line through her application form, then turned his gaze back to her. 'I felt that fury the moment you walked in here, Miss Hammond, but I needed to bring it to the surface, so I could see how bad it was. I understand your distress, but you will not be any use to us, or anyone else until you sort out your emotions.'

That hit her with force. He was turning her down! 'Surely the thing that matters is that I want to do something to help defeat the enemy?'

'That is important, I agree, but we need people who will remain calm in a crisis. If they can't, then mistakes will be made, and that could cause all manner of disasters, and perhaps an unnecessary loss of life. You have a good education, and in all ways are the kind of recruit we are looking for, except for one – your emotions. You are clearly suffering from the ordeal you have gone through, but until you can banish the hatred bubbling through you we cannot accept your application. I am truly sorry.'

She surged to her feet and he also stood as she glared at him, incensed with his assessment of her. She had every right to be angry – didn't she? Of course she did, and she wasn't going to let this drop. 'What is your name?'

'Commander William Jackson.'

With one final glare at him she turned on her heel and stormed out of the building, hurting so badly it was difficult not to cry out in frustration. She had come here with high hopes, knowing that her qualifications were good enough, but not only had she been turned down, she had been given a lecture by that man. How dare he! He had admitted that she was the kind they were looking for. Her education was excellent, and at twenty-one years of age her experience as a secretary was good. He had no right to turn her away!

Without realising where she was going she ended up in a nearby park and found a seat where she could think quietly, well aware that she needed to calm down. Every word of that interview was etched in her memory and she went over it again and again. Ever so slowly she began to see the wisdom in his words. Of course they couldn't have anyone flying into a rage when things got bad. Anger clouds the mind and could result in chaos. What would happen to her father if he acted in that way when they were under attack? The consequences would be too terrible to contemplate.

She drew in a deep, ragged breath and she turned her thoughts back to the raid. In one night, she had lost so much, and surely her fury was justified. Suddenly the word 'No' hit her. For some reason she had survived, and that gift of life had to be put to good use. Allowing herself to be consumed with hatred was wrong and it would achieve nothing. That man was right again. With such an attitude she would be no use to anyone, not even herself. As her mind cleared, one emotion she had not allowed to surface crept up on her: grief for the loss of those she loved, and the many she didn't even know. There was also the loss of her home with all its happy memories. All gone!

The tears she had denied began to run down her cheeks unchecked as she allowed the grief to surface for the first time.

'Are you all right?' An elderly woman sat beside her.

Kathy nodded. 'I am now.'

'Is there anything I can do for you?'

'No, thank you, but I appreciate your kindness.'

The woman stood up. 'You take care, dear.'

'I will.' She watched the woman walk away and wiped the tears from her face. Even though the world had gone mad there was still kindness everywhere – you just had to look for it. That woman had offered help to a stranger, and so had Commander Jackson by being firm in an effort to break through the wall of anger she had built around her. She stood up and marched resolutely back to the recruitment hall.

Just inside the door she stopped, and her gaze swept around the hall, disappointed when she didn't see the imposing man she was looking for. Perhaps he was still in the office.

A sailor came up to her. 'You'll need to take a seat, miss, but it's doubtful anyone will be able to see you today unless you have an appointment.'

'I've already been interviewed,' she told him. 'I was hoping to have a word with Commander Jackson. Is he still here?'

'I'll check. What's your name?'

'Katherine Hammond.'

He quickly disappeared through the door at the end of the hall and she waited anxiously. Her interview had been a disaster and she desperately wanted to put things right with this man. He had dealt with her bluntly and firmly, doing her a huge favour by bringing her to her senses. She could at least thank him for that, but even if he was here would he bother to see her again?

After several minutes the sailor returned and when he said that the commander would see her, she breathed a sigh of relief. Kathy followed him, her shoulders back in determination. She had made a big mistake and was going to apologise for that – it was the least she could do, and she was truly sorry for her bad behaviour. She didn't want news getting back to her father, telling him what a disagreeable daughter he had. She had always been considered kind and understanding to other people, and she mustn't allow anyone to make her act out of character – no matter what the provocation.

When she was announced she stepped into the room and Commander Jackson rose politely to his feet. 'What can I do for you, Miss Hammond?'

'Thank you for seeing me, sir. I want to apologise for my rudeness during our interview. What you said made me go away and take a good look at myself, and you were absolutely right when you pointed out that I would be no use to myself or anyone else if I couldn't control the fury. I want you to know that it is not usually in my nature to be so hateful.'

Having made her apology she turned to leave, but in two easy strides he was beside her and smiled. 'I know how difficult it is to keep your mind clear when you have suffered such terrible losses. You look as if you could do with a strong cup of tea. Please sit down.'

She did as he asked and waited while he ordered the tea and sat behind the desk again. The tea arrived almost immediately, obviously arranged earlier.

'I didn't expect you to return so soon. I thought it would take you a while longer to clear your mind.'

'You knew I would come back?'

He nodded. 'If you had an ounce of Jack Hammond's determination you wouldn't give up so easily, no matter how dreadful an ordeal you have had to cope with.'

Kathy sat bolt upright, immediately alert. 'You know my father?'

'I do. We served together in the past.'

'Do you know where he is? I've written to him with the awful news about Mum and my aunt, but I don't know if he's received the letter yet. I haven't heard from him for quite a while.'

'You know I can't answer that.'

'No, of course not. Forgive me for asking.' She stood up to pour the tea and handed him a cup.

'You are used to doing that,' he said as he took the cup from her.

'Force of habit. I'm a secretary. At least I was before the war started. My boss went into the army and I went to an engineering factory to do my bit for the war effort.' She hesitated for a moment. 'Will you forgive my earlier rudeness and allow me to fill in another form?'

'There is no need.' He removed a paper from a folder in front of him. 'I still have your application here.'

She stared at it in amazement. 'But I saw you draw a line right through it.'

'You saw me draw a line across a form, but you were too angry to notice that it was a blank piece of paper. Your emotions clouded your judgement and you assumed it was your application.'

'And I saw what I believed!' Kathy lifted her hands and puffed out a small breath, shocked by this. 'You were right. I would be no use if I allowed my emotions to be ruled by anger.'

'Absolutely, and that was what I was hoping you would soon see for yourself.'

When she looked at him he was laughing quietly. 'You find that funny?'

'That gesture you just made amused me. I've seen your father do that many times.'

'Oh.' She grinned the first time since that terrible night and it felt good – so normal. 'I didn't realise I had done it. Will you submit my application now, please?'

'I will.' He pushed the form towards her. 'We need a full list of your talents – no matter how trivial you consider some to be – so you can be placed where you can do the most good. You have left that section devoid of details.'

'I can play the violin a bit,' she joked. 'Is that any use?'

'Put it down,' he told her with a serious expression, only the glint in his eyes betraying his amusement. 'Your father said you were good at languages, and you haven't mentioned that either.'

'I can manage in French and Italian, but not well enough to state as a skill.'

'Nevertheless, put it down. What about German?'

Kathy glanced up and her eyes flashed with anger for a moment, then it was gone. 'Certainly not!'

'If you have ability with languages you might be ordered to learn. Could you put aside your anger if you had to?' When she opened her mouth to reply he held up his hand to stop her. 'I know the fury is still there, so don't deny it. What I need to know is can you control it enough to take orders – even if unpalatable?'

That took a little thought but not much, and she answered confidently, 'Yes, I can.'

'I believe you, or I would not have even considered sending your application through. The past is gone, and we can't change it, but now we need to keep our mind on what we have to do to win this war. Don't look back.'

'I understand what you're saying, but that is going to be damned difficult.' She looked him straight in the eyes. 'However, I will promise to do the very best I can.'

'No one can ask for more than that.'

When she had completed the required section of the form she pushed it back to him, studying the impressive man carefully. 'May I ask what you are doing interviewing would-be recruits?'

'I'm not.'

'Pardon?'

'I came along to see how the recruitment was going when I saw your form and decided to interview you myself.'

'Because you know my father?'

'Yes.'

'Well, I'm very pleased you did. You made me go away and think things through calmly. Thank you.'

'It has been my pleasure and I'm glad I came today.'

'You won't be here tomorrow?'

'No. My new ship is nearly ready for sea trials.'

'Oh, you are getting one of the latest ships? That must be exciting for you. Were you sad to leave your last ship?

I know from my father how attached men become to their ship.'

'That's true, but I didn't leave my last ship – she left us. She's at the bottom of the ocean.'

'Oh, I'm so sorry.' Kathy was well aware of the implications of that statement and he was very good at hiding his feelings, but she still caught a glimpse of pain that flashed across his face. How many of his crew did he lose? What pain and anguish did he suffer? She knew better than to ask, but one thing was clear to her now: this man and so many like him had faced unimaginable horrors, and yet they could still smile and carry on with their lives – and that was what she must do.

Her gaze met his and she smiled. 'This will be a lucky ship for you, Commander.'

'I'm sure she will be.' He stood up. 'And until you are in the service, my name is Bill. The pub across the road should be open so would you join me for a drink? Your father will be pleased to know we have met.'

'I'd love a drink. Thank you, Bill.'

Chapter Three

The next week passed slowly while Kathy waited for the official letter to tell her whether she had been accepted or not. She was also desperate to hear from her father, and when they both arrived together she opened her father's letter first. As she read it tears came in torrents. Her parents had had a happy marriage and she could feel his pain in the words on the page; also evident was the worry he felt at not being with her at this time.

She started on a reply straight away to assure him that she was all right and that he must not worry about her. She then gave him a brief account of her meeting with Bill Jackson, telling him that he had taken her out for a drink after the interview, making it as amusing as possible in the hope it would bring a smile to her father's face.

She left out the bit about her being so furious that he had turned her down at first. That would have worried him. Putting the unfinished letter aside she slit open the other envelope, praying she could add a piece of good news as well. Her heart was thudding as she removed the letter – she wanted this so much. After all that had happened she needed a purpose to her life. Losing so much in one night had left her rudderless, unable to see how she could steer a straight course again. The navy was her father's life and if she could become even a small part of it as well it would make her feel useful again. She was no longer prepared to stand on the sidelines, and just had to get involved.

The letter was open and in her hands when she realised that her eyes were closed. Reprimanding herself for such stupidity she forced her eyes open and looked down. At first the words were a jumble and after forcing herself to concentrate they became clear. She had been accepted and had to report to Westfield College, Hampstead in seven days' time to train as a writer, which meant office work. She had hoped for something else, but as she was already an experienced secretary it hadn't surprised her. The important thing was that she had been accepted. Once she was in and the training over that would be the time to see what other jobs were available.

Relief swept through her as she eagerly added the good news to her father's letter, knowing it would give him a measure of comfort to know she had enlisted and was getting on with her life. The last thing she wanted was for him to be worried about her. He had a difficult enough task dodging U-boats as they tried to safeguard the vital supplies being brought in by the Merchant Navy. She didn't know exactly what he was doing, of course, but he was on a destroyer, so it didn't take a genius to know he would be right in the thick of things. So would Bill again by now, she expected. Strange she had only met him once, but in her mind, she had adopted him as part of her family.

After sealing the letter for her father, she hurried out to the nearest postbox, and then returned to the room she was renting. As she gazed around one thing was abundantly clear, it wasn't going to take long to pack. She had only replaced essential clothing in the hope that she would soon be wearing a uniform.

Kathy packed her spare clothing into a shopping bag, which zipped up at the top. She was a bit disappointed she was staying in London and not going to somewhere like Portsmouth. That was a place she knew well as she had waited many times with her mother to watch her father's ship glide into the dock. The memory brought a lump to her throat knowing that the two of them would never stand there again waiting excitedly for him to disembark.

Those days belonged to the past, and she remembered Bill's advice not to look back. He was right – it was too painful. A different time had been forced upon everyone, and what the future held no one knew, but whatever it was she was determined to do anything she could to help end this madness.

When Kathy arrived at the college she was shown to her cabin – a small room with two beds in it and a girl already there putting her clothes away in a little chest of drawers.

'I've saved the bottom two drawers for you,' she told Kathy, smiling broadly. 'I hope that will be all right?'

'That's fine. I haven't got much.' She held out her hand. 'I'm Katherine Hammond.'

'I'm Alice Turnbull.' She shook Kathy's hand. 'Isn't this exciting?'

Kathy smiled back at the animated girl's expression, but there wasn't time to say anything much, because they were rounded up and marched to another part of the building.

There was an air of anticipation among the girls who were having difficulty keeping quiet as they were led to a classroom in the college.

'Stop talking!' a voice bellowed. 'You're in the navy now, but you sound like a bunch of hysterical females.'

'Oops!' Alice grinned again. 'I suppose we are going to have to get used to being ordered around.'

Kathy chuckled quietly to herself. The command to be quiet hadn't had much effect, but they would soon learn. She had grown up listening to her father's accounts of life in the service and knew what to expect.

The rest of the day was a whirl of activity as they were ordered from one place to another, and it wasn't until they were queuing up for their evening meal that they had time to talk to each other.

'Ah, there you are.'

Alice pushed in beside her. It was clear that the hectic day hadn't dampened the girl's spirit one bit. The huge smile was still in place and it helped to lift Kathy's lingering sadness somewhat.

'We haven't had a chance to talk much today, so can we sit together now and get to know each other better?' Alice leant forward and whispered, 'A lot of the girls seem to have come from posh homes and are a bit stuck-up, but I don't think you are like that. I come from a council house estate and it's rough there, but I got in because I'm clever,' she explained, without the slightest hint of boasting.

They collected their meal and found a table to themselves, and when they sat down Alice studied Kathy curiously. 'I watched you today and you looked as if you knew what we had to do before being told.'

'My father's in the navy and I had a drink with a friend of his who told me what to expect.'

'Ah, that accounts for it. Did your dad join up straight away?'

Kathy shook her head. 'He's a career sailor and a captain now.'

'Wow! No wonder you look as if you belong here. Is his friend a captain as well?'

'He's a commander.'

'Gosh.' Alice jiggled in her seat excitedly. 'You're related to gold braid. Can we be friends? You can point me in the right direction if I start acting out of line. I can forget myself at times and say the wrong things. I get a little overexcited now and again.'

'Really? I would never have guessed. I've had to nudge you more than once to make you address officers in the proper manner.'

Alice pulled a comical face. 'That's something I'm not going to be very good at. Where I come from you have to show that you're as good as anyone else, or you get picked on. I ain't used to being subservient.'

'Do your best.'

'I'll try, but you keep giving me a nudge as a reminder.'

Both girls burst into laughter and shook hands to seal their friendship.

'I suppose you come from a posh home as well, then?'

'No, just an ordinary one.' Kathy took a deep breath and managed a smile with difficulty as the anger raced through her again. *Control it*, she told herself severely, *remember what you have to do*.

They talked for a long time that evening, and Kathy found Alice's chatter quite soothing. It helped to take her mind off that terrible air raid, and when they retired she felt reasonably relaxed, making her hope the vivid dreams of that raid would stay away. It had been a good day, and tomorrow their instruction would begin. The first chance she had she would write to her father and Commander Jackson. She felt she had to think of him in that way now, rather than as Bill, as she was a lowly rating in the navy.

The training began with instruction of the naval terminology, and although they were not on a ship the rooms were to be referred to as cabins, kitchens as galleys and when going on leave they were going ashore. They also had to do a lot of scrubbing, much to the disgust of some of the girls. None of this dampened Alice's good humour, though, and she took everything in her stride, even the constant reprimands for not addressing the officers as she should.

One day Kathy couldn't find Alice anywhere. Her bed hadn't been slept in, and she rushed to the next cabin and asked the girl there, 'Have you seen Alice?'

'I was talking to her yesterday when the first officer came and took her away, and I haven't seen her since.'

'Oh dear, that doesn't sound too good.' Kathy was worried now. Had they thrown her out for insubordination?

It was not until the next day that Alice sauntered back, looking completely untroubled.

'Where have you been?' Kathy asked. 'I've been so worried about you.'

'Oh, they just wanted to check and see if my memory is as good as they'd been told. They gave me some tests, that's all.'

'It took all this time?'

Alice grinned. 'They kept running the tests, because they didn't believe I was genuine. I convinced them in the end.'

'That's a relief. I thought they might have thrown you out for not obeying the rules.'

'Not yet.' Alice burst into laughter.

* * *

Towards the end of the two weeks of instruction, Kathy was on her knees scrubbing a long passage with Alice when a woman first officer appeared and stopped beside them.

'Rating Hammond! Step forward.'

Kathy scrambled to her feet.

'Come with me.'

The officer marched along the passage and Kathy fell into step beside her, hoping she didn't look too much of a mess. She was patting her hair in place when they stopped by a door.

Before opening the door, the officer gave a hint of a smile. 'You look quite presentable.'

The door swung open and there were four officers in there making Kathy wonder what on earth they were doing here and what they wanted with her. Had she done something wrong?

'Don't let the gold braid dazzle you,' the officer said quietly. 'In you go.'

It was only when she stepped inside that she looked at the faces and almost cried out in joy. Standing behind the group were two faces she recognised: her father and Commander Jackson. The urge to rush up and hug both of them was almost overwhelming, but she couldn't do that. Not here, not with other high-ranking officers present.

'Ah, Rating Hammond.' An officer she didn't know faced her. 'There are two officers here who would like to see you. You may greet them.'

'Thank you, sir.' She rushed over and hugged her father, so delighted to see him, and then turned to Bill, a huge smile on her face. 'It's so good to see you again, Commander Jackson.'

'Rating Hammond.'

She turned smartly to face the officer who had spoken. 'Sir.'

'You have been given two days' special leave and may go ashore with your father.'

'Thank you, sir.' She knew her father would want to see the graves and she was filled with gratitude for this act of kindness to both of them.

'Go and tidy yourself up and we will go to lunch first.'

'Of course.' She grinned at her father. 'I wouldn't dare be seen with an officer in my working clothes. Are you coming with us, Commander?'

'No, I have to get back to my ship, but I wanted to come and see how you were getting on. Do you think you are going to like it in the navy?'

'Without a doubt.' She gave a saucy grin. 'I never realised I was so good at scrubbing floors.'

An amused glint shone in his shrewd eyes. 'I understand your training is nearly over, so now you will be given something more interesting to do.'

She nodded. 'I can't wait to be of use.'

'How about that other thing we talked about?'

She knew he was referring to her anger. 'It's still there, but under control. I won't allow it to dim my judgement, Commander.'

'I believe you. Now, if you will all excuse me, I must be on my way.'

When he had taken his leave of them she turned to her father. 'Give me half an hour to wash and dress in my uniform.'

'Take your time. I have some business to attend to first.'

Back in her cabin she set about making herself into a smart Wren. They had only just been issued with uniforms and this was her first chance to wear it. She wanted her father to be proud of her in the hope it would give him some comfort while they visited the graves. It was going to be upsetting for both of them, but it was something that had to be done before her father went back to sea.

In no time at all she was immaculately turned out and walking proudly beside her father. Out of the corner of her eye she saw the other girls watching in amazement as she went by. Kathy gave Alice a sly wink when she saw the huge grin on her face.

They had lunch in a pub, and then went straight to the cemetery to put flowers on both graves. Kathy put hers on her aunt's grave and then stood back to allow her father to say goodbye to the woman he had loved.

After a while he turned away and they walked silently out of the graveyard.

'Let's get a drink.' He led her towards a pub where they found a quiet corner.

When they were settled with a small beer each, her father sighed. 'Thank you for everything you did, my dear. I'm sorry I wasn't here for you. It must have been hard for you to deal with everything on your own.'

'It was the hardest and most distressing thing I have ever had to cope with,' she admitted. 'I didn't have enough money to buy headstones so had the plaques made to mark the graves. I thought you might want to choose them yourself when there's time. I hope that's all right?'

'You did exactly the right thing, and we will see to it later – both of us. Now, I would like you to tell me exactly what happened.'

This was the request she had been dreading, but as painful as it was to talk about, he had a right to know. 'The shelter we were in was blown up and Mum was killed. Then I went to find Aunt Emma. Her house was just a pile of rubble and I knew she would have been in it. She wouldn't take shelter, as you know.'

'You gave me that brief account in your letter. I want to know what you did then and how you felt.' He reached across and placed his hand gently over her closed fist. 'I know you don't want to talk about this, my darling girl, but I need to know – and you need to talk about it.'

Opening her curled fingers, she grasped her father's hand. 'She didn't suffer, Dad. It was all over in a flash. I was near the entrance and the next thing I knew I was flying through the air and landed a few feet away from where the shelter had been. I scrambled back and began to move debris looking for Mum and anyone else who might be buried there. There were other people doing the same thing – they seemed to be coming from everywhere, running to help. It took quite a while and when I saw Mum I began to try and revive her, like you taught me when I was a child, but it was no use, she must have died instantly.'

'That's a comfort to know. I was afraid she might have suffered.'

Kathy shook her head. 'I don't suppose she even knew what had happened. I stayed there for a while trying to help until all the injured and dead were taken away. I saw terrible things that night,' she said quietly. 'Once I knew where they were being taken I went in search of Emma. I saw where our house should have been, but it was gone – so was her house. The next day I identified her and arranged for the two funerals.'

'You have been brave and handled everything very well.' He gave a tired smile. 'This is only what I would expect from my courageous daughter. Thank you for taking care of everything for me.'

She took a sip of her beer, relieved she had at least been able to put his mind at rest by knowing that his wife hadn't suffered. He would soon be back at sea and she didn't want him to be troubled or distracted in any way. To lose him as well would be more than she could cope with. Her life had been literally blown apart that night and he was all she had left now.

'I was puzzled when Bill asked you how you were dealing with something you had talked about. It seemed important to him, so will you tell me what he meant? He told me he had met you at the recruitment but didn't go into details.'

She pulled a face. 'I went there filled with fury for the devils that had caused such destruction upon defenceless people and it showed.' She went on to explain in detail about the interview with Bill. 'I owe him a debt of gratitude for what he did. It brought me to my senses.'

'He's always been an astute judge of people. You told him your anger was under control, so I assume it's still there.'

'Yes, and it will be, but I won't let it interfere with anything I have to do in this war. How can one ever forgive?'

'It is difficult, but it is something we are all going to have to learn to do – eventually. We will do things in this war which are anathema to us, and the time will come when we have to forgive not only the enemy but ourselves as well.'

She thought about that carefully for a moment, and could see what her father meant, but with the memory of what had happened still vivid in her mind, she was not at that point yet. Perhaps she never would be. Only time would tell.

Chapter Four

'Did you enjoy your short leave?' Alice asked the moment Kathy walked into the cabin.

'Yes, thank you,' she replied, and began unpacking her bag.

'That was a handsome man you were with. Was it your father?'

She nodded. 'It was a lovely surprise, and they were kind to let me have some time with him.'

'Some of the girls were speculating who you were with, and I told them I thought it was your father. You are so like him, you know: both tall and elegant with dark hair and eyes.'

'My word, you did notice a lot as we walked by.' Kathy grinned at her friend.

'I've got a photographic memory. Anyone I meet is imprinted in my mind in detail. I can recognise all sorts of things, even if I've only seen them once before.'

'You're serious?' Kathy sat on the edge of the bed and studied Alice. She was a pretty girl with lovely dark auburn hair and blue eyes. 'You mentioned having a good memory before, but you never said it was photographic.'

'Well, I don't broadcast that fact because it makes some people uncomfortable, though I've never understood why.'

'So that's why you disappeared for two days.'

'They wanted to make sure, because that's the reason they took me in. Anyway, tell me what you did on your leave,' she said, dismissing the subject.

'We had lunch, and then booked in to a hotel until Dad had to return to his ship. He is sailing again soon.'

'Why a hotel? Your home is in London, isn't it?'

Kathy had never mentioned that terrible night to anyone, but she had faced it again with her father, and talking about it was a little easier. 'We haven't got a home any more. It was bombed.'

'Oh, I'm so sorry. Where is your family living now, then?'

'There is only the two of us now. Mum and my aunt were killed in the raid that night. I took Dad to see the graves before he goes back to sea.'

Without a word, Alice hugged Kathy. 'Well, you've got a big family now – us.'

'Thanks, that's comforting to know, and I hope we are sent to the same place.'

'Me too. We'll find out tomorrow.'

She thought it unlikely they would be able to stay together. Alice had very different talents and with her marvellous memory it would obviously be put to good use. As for herself, Kathy had little doubt she would be classified as a writer, meaning clerical work. Still, she would try to keep in touch with Alice.

Kathy was one of the first to be called the next day and was told to report to Dover. There was a lorry leaving in an hour, so it was a mad scramble to gather her belongings and say goodbye to the other girls.

'Didn't they say what you would be doing?' Alice asked, clearly disappointed she wasn't going there as well.

'No, but I expect it will be as someone's secretary. It's what I have been trained for, and I don't have any other talents – apart from speaking a couple of languages moderately well.'

'Well, that sounds like plenty of talents to me.' Alice grinned. 'I bet they've got something special for you, and anyway, you are related to gold braid,' she teased. 'That's bound to be taken into consideration.'

'What about you? Do you have any idea what you will be doing wherever you are being sent?'

Her friend shrugged. 'I haven't any idea. It was all very vague, and I was told not to talk about it.'

'Ah, they are interested in that memory of yours. I must go, but we'll write, and I bet we'll meet up again sometime.' Giving a wave to everyone, Kathy turned and ran out to the lorry just pulling up outside.

They made a brief stop and collected two more Wrens and several sailors. The rest of the journey was lively, with a lot of teasing and flirting going on.

'What are you girls going to be doing in Dover?' one of the men asked.

'You know we can't answer that, and you shouldn't be asking.' The girl who answered was blonde with clear-blue eyes and the men had been paying her a lot of attention.

Kathy watched the banter but didn't join in; her mind was too occupied with what she would find at the end of the journey. Driving through London had brought that terrible night to the surface again and ignited the anger she had felt and was still struggling with. She had worked hard to keep it under control, but it was still there, and she damned well hoped they were going to give her something useful to do. If not, she would keep on asking for transfers until they allocated her a worthwhile job. She had vowed that night to make a vital contribution to end this war and would not be satisfied with anything less. The young men on the lorry were destined to go to sea to fight and Kathy wished she could do the same. That was impossible, of course, but she did hope for something more challenging than taking dictation and typing letters.

The moment they arrived in Dover a sailor strode up to the lorry and waited for them to jump down. Kathy's feet had hardly touched the ground when he said, 'Hammond?'

'That's me,' she replied, hastily straightening her skirt.

'Come with me.' He turned and began to walk away.

She glanced at the other girls and shrugged.

'We're going to the castle, I think,' one whispered.

Well, the man striding away wasn't going there and was in a hurry, so Kathy broke into a run to catch up with him. 'Where are we going?' she asked, falling into step beside him.

'I've been told to take you to the operations room.'

Ah, that sounds promising, she thought, lengthening her stride to keep up with him. She had been sure they would assign her to the 'writers' section' because of her training as a secretary, but perhaps not.

They entered what she could only describe as a tunnel and walked down steps for quite a way, then along a passage. They were underground now, and it was an extraordinary place. He stopped by a door, opened it and ushered her into a room.

Kathy gazed around in wonder. There were blackboards on the walls, and Wrens were chalking up information on them. In the middle of the room was a large table surrounded by more Wrens, who were watching over a model of a convoy, and the room was full of officers. One of them was an admiral, she noted immediately. She had never seen so much gold braid in one place before. It was fascinating.

The sailor who had escorted her went up to one of the officers and spoke quietly to him. He nodded but didn't look round. The sailor then left without saying another word to Kathy.

She waited – and waited, quite happy to do so as the

men were in deep conversation and it gave her time to take in the activity of this room. She turned her attention to the convoy and soon picked up the escort ships. Were her father and Bill on one of them? She didn't know the names of either of their ships, because that was something that was not talked about. Overcome with curiosity, Kathy edged a little closer to get a better look, careful not to get in anyone's way.

After a while she looked up and saw one of the officers studying her intently. He was younger than the others – no more than late twenties or early thirties, she guessed. He had light-brown hair and piercing grey eyes that seemed to go right through her. She had always been quite a good judge of character and immediately recognised that this was a man not to be underestimated. When he took a step forward, Kathy straightened up and watched him warily.

'I'm Commander Evans.'

'Sir.'

'Are you good at puzzles, Hammond?'

For a moment she was thrown by the odd question. 'I like crosswords, sir.'

'Hmm. I noticed you were interested in that convoy.'

'Yes, sir.' Kathy knew at once she hadn't given him the answer he had been looking for.

'A U-boat has just sunk a merchant ship and the escorts are on the hunt for him. If you were in command of the U-boat, what would you do to keep out of the way of their depth charges?'

When he stepped up to the table she followed him and studied the table carefully, then began speaking quietly, as if to herself. 'If I turn tail and run they will have a chance to find me. I could sit on the bottom and hope they will miss me . . .' She shook her head slightly and then pointed to a ship in the middle of the convoy. 'Is that a tanker?'

One of the girls nodded.

'Then I'd tuck myself under her. They wouldn't dare drop depth charges anywhere near a tanker filled with fuel, then at night I'd try and slip away.'

'And if you were an escort ship what would you do?'

Now she was enjoying herself. This was just like the strategy games she'd played with her father while she had been growing up. She pointed to a place. 'Providing I had some inkling where he was, I'd wait there, hoping to catch him as he moved away. After all he can't stay under the surface for ever. He's got to surface sometime, and I'd make sure I was damned well waiting for him.'

Evans actually smiled. 'Do you think that's what Captain Hammond would do?'

'I can't answer for my father, sir, but I do know he wouldn't give up, no matter how cunning the submarine had been.'

He didn't give an opinion one way or the other, and she had no idea if her answer was what he was looking for, but there was no doubt he had been assessing her suitability for something. Whatever it was, she hoped she had passed his scrutiny.

'Come with me.'

Kathy followed him out of the room and along the passage, needing to quicken her steps to keep up with him. At the end was a door marked SO(I) and she knew it meant senior officer intelligence. Her heart skipped a beat. Was she going to get an interesting assignment after all?

Once inside, he pointed to a desk and her excitement plummeted. It contained a telephone, typewriter and piles of paper.

'You can use that desk.'

She put her bag beside it. 'What are my duties, sir?'

'To do as I say.'

Well that was succinct enough. 'And where is my cabin, sir?'

He frowned. 'Hasn't anyone taken you there?'

'No, sir. I was brought straight to you.'

He sighed. 'I'll take you there later. Are you hungry?'

'Yes, sir.'

'Right, let's feed both of us before we get started.'

He disappeared out of the door and she hurried after him. Damn! This man moved so quickly she was going to spend all her time running after him. They had only just met, and she was already finding him irritating. She fell into step beside him.

'David!' someone called, making him stop abruptly. He turned to face the officer hurrying towards them.

Kathy had already taken a few steps forward and she stayed there so they could talk in private. She had at least learnt one thing: his Christian name was David. After a few minutes he tipped his head back and laughed as he looked over at her. So, they thought it was funny she was here. The look she gave both of them was withering, making them chuckle even more.

David stepped up to her and turned to his companion. 'I'd like you to meet Captain Hammond's daughter.'

'Ah, that accounts for the stern expression, and I can see the likeness. I'm Commander Douglas and I'm pleased to meet you. If you are going to work for this man you will need a good pair of running shoes. He never stands still.'

'I have discovered that already, sir.'

He smiled and spoke to David again. 'Hope those people manage to decipher that message. We are losing too many ships.'

'The boffins at Bletchley Park will do their best.'

The commander shot a concerned glance at Kathy.

'It's all right to speak freely in front of Hammond. She has top-security clearance.'

She knew she had been given security clearance, but top clearance surprised her. Since joining she had been bombarded with questions until they knew everything about her life and family, but she just assumed this was because of her father's position as a serving captain on a destroyer.

'I requested an intelligent female to work with me. One who wasn't frightened to face difficult situations and would be willing to go anywhere and do anything asked of her. We considered Hammond the most likely candidate.'

'Surely a man would be better suited to your line of work?' The commander cast Kathy an apologetic look. 'Sorry about this, but I have to say it.'

She nodded but said nothing.

'David, a girl as young as this could fall apart, leaving you in a mess.'

'I've thought long and hard about this and have had a talk with Bill Jackson, who has met her. He's convinced she has a sound character and wouldn't let me down, but of course, only time will tell.'

'Ah, Bill has an uncanny knack of summing up people. He should be in your line of work.'

'We've tried, but he won't leave the sea, even more so since he had his last ship blown apart by a torpedo.'

Kathy looked from one man to the other, now thoroughly confused. What the devil was going on, and just what had she been sent here to do? And she objected to the way they were talking about her as if she wasn't here. It was blasted rude.

The two men spoke quietly together for a few minutes, and then David stepped up to her. 'Let's get something to eat, so we can get to work.'

'Right, sir. I'll be as quick as I can and meet you back at the office.'

He stopped walking and frowned down at her. 'Why? Where are you going?'

'I can't eat in the officers' mess, sir. I'll have to find out where the ratings eat.'

'Oh, good heavens!' he exploded. 'You are with me and where I go you go, Leading Wren Hammond.'

'I'm not a Leading Wren,' she pointed out, falling in to step beside him as he charged off again.

'You are now. I've just promoted you.'

She couldn't help laughing then. 'You can't do that, sir. I have to sit an exam.'

'I can do whatever I damned well like. Stop arguing with me or I'll have you replaced.'

'I haven't even started yet,' she muttered under her breath.

'My hearing is acute, so don't push your luck,' he warned as he opened a door and ushered her through.

'I wouldn't dream of it, sir,' she replied and smiled sweetly at him, while thinking that working for him was going to be a trifle difficult. That was even if she lasted for more than a day, which as far as she could see was unlikely.

She was even more convinced of that when they sat down and he ordered their meal without asking what she wanted. She was so hungry, though, she let that go.

'Have you had many assistants?' she asked, making polite conversation.

'A few, but they didn't stay long.'

'And why would that be, sir?'

'They weren't suited to the work.'

'I see, and you think I might be?'

He shrugged. 'If you're not, then you will go the same way.'

Great! When she looked up he had a grin on his face and that transformed him. He was not just handsome – he could be devastating.

'Is something amusing you, sir?'

'Your expression broadcasts your feelings. I must teach you to control that, because in our line of work that could be a drawback.'

'I haven't been told exactly what my line of work will be, sir.'

'I've already told you. You do as I say. Now eat your food and let us start to get some work done, shall we?'

Taking a mouthful of food to stop herself from speaking, she wondered how long it would be before she was dismissed for insubordination.

He was impossible.

Chapter Five

Back in the office Kathy waited, and when he didn't say anything, she asked, 'What would you like me to do first, sir?'

'Get that mess in to some sort of order.'

Kathy thought 'mess' was being kind – 'chaos' would be a better description. She started on what would be her desk, when she could get anywhere near it, and the first discovery was a pile of reports waiting to be typed up. 'Couldn't any of your other assistants type, sir?' She dumped the heap in a pending file she had found under the desk.

'Nope.' The phone rang, and he snatched it up, listened for a moment, then replaced it and swept out of the room.

She watched the door close and sighed. It looked as if she was in the 'writers' section', after all. He clearly needed someone with secretarial skills, but she had hoped for something else. Ah well, it was no good moaning about it, she had better get on with it.

There were soon two clear desks and a pile of documents for filing, but the cabinet was locked, and a thorough search of the office did not produce a key. He probably had it with him.

Suddenly the door opened, and the intelligence officer swept in. 'Where is the key to the filing cabinet, sir?'

'Key? What do you want a key for?'

'It is locked, sir,' she replied as patiently as she could.

He walked over to the cabinet, kicked the side and all the drawers shot open, then he picked up something from a shelf and strode out again, slamming the door closed behind him.

Kathy stared at the door in disbelief. He was gone again! She sat down and rested her head in her hands, wondering what the devil she was doing here. Then, seeing the funny side of it, she began to laugh, not sure whether it was hysteria or amusement. Well, the cabinet was open, so she might as well get the filing out of the way. She had no idea what he was working on, so if papers he needed were filed he would just have to ask her where she had put them. When she had finished she closed the drawers and they locked tight again. Copying what he had done she gave the cabinet a sharp kick – nothing happened, so she tried a different spot and the drawers all opened. She nodded in satisfaction – you had to kick in the right spot. What a way to run an office, but it obviously came low on his list of priorities.

There was no sign of the officer, so she settled down to the typing, hoping she would learn something about his work and find it more interesting. It wasn't. The reports were ordinary stuff about meetings, and certainly nothing of a classified nature.

An hour later he returned, picked up the pile of finished reports and sat down to read through them. After a while he glanced at his watch. 'You can go now, but be back here by eight o'clock tomorrow.'

'Go where, sir?'

He frowned. 'To the Wrennery they've set up in the college, of course.'

'I haven't been told where that is, sir. If you remember, I told you that they brought me straight here.'

Muttering under his breath he stood up and stormed out of the office, and she groaned. This was turning into a pantomime. No wonder his other assistants didn't last long.

Five minutes later he was back. 'Have you got any trousers in your bag?'

'Yes, sir.'

'Put them on.'

'What, now?'

'That's what I said.' He gazed up at the ceiling. 'What on earth possessed me to ask for a female? I'll wait outside. Hurry! I haven't got time to waste running around after you. It's supposed to be the other way around.'

When the door slammed behind him she dug in her bag and changed in a flash. Whatever this job was supposed to be it certainly didn't appear to be something she was hoping to do in the navy.

He was leaning against the wall smoking a cigarette when she came out, and his gaze swept over her, then he spun on his heel and she was rushing after him again as they made their way outside. It was dark, and she hadn't realised so much time had passed since she had arrived.

'Give me your kit.'

She did as ordered and watched as he stuffed it in a side pannier of a motorcycle.

He got on and turned his head. 'Well, get on.'

Kathy had never been on one of these before, and having some idea about this man now, she doubted he would be safe in charge of anything mechanical.

'Hammond!' he snapped when she hesitated. 'The ferry has already left for the day, so if you don't want to walk to the Wrennery, I suggest you get on.'

Not wanting to make him even more irritable Kathy sat on the pillion, fearing she would never reach her destination, and sincerely prayed that it wasn't far.

'Hold on to me.'

'Sir?'

'Put your arms around me, woman, or you'll fall off.' The machine burst into life with a roar.

She grabbed hold of him as the bike leapt and began to speed up the road. Fortunately, it was only a short ride and she breathed a sigh of relief when he stopped. Her legs were shaking when she got off the machine. Her first ride on a motorbike had been quite an experience – especially the way he drove!

'This is it,' he told her, handing over her bag. 'You catch the ferry in the morning.'

'Thank you, sir.' Her words were drowned out as he roared away into the night. She walked inside and gave her name.

'Who was that noisy devil?' the Wren at the desk asked her.

'Commander Evans, the Senior Intelligence Officer.'

'Oh, of course. I might have guessed. He has quite a reputation around here for rushing around on that bike. You should have checked in here this morning. Where have you been?'

'In the tunnel with Commander Evans.'

A slow smile appeared on the girl's face. 'Handsome devil, isn't he?'

'I'd describe him as exasperating.'

'So I've heard. You look a bit shaken up, so I'll show you to your cabin, then you can go and have something to eat.'

'Thank you. I was told to catch the ferry in the morning. What on earth is that? I didn't like to ask. He was already irritable enough.'

'They use navy terms for everything. It's a lorry and comes here at eight o'clock in the morning.'

'Of course. I should have realised that.'

Kathy dumped her kit and went for some food. There were three girls there who were newly trained telegraphers awaiting deployment to one of the many listening stations. She heard their stories about the training with interest, wondering if this was something she could apply for. The thought of learning Morse was intriguing, so she might make enquiries if this posting didn't work out. If today was anything to go by, then her stay here was going to be short. She didn't think she had made a very good impression on that man, and he certainly hadn't endeared himself to her.

She only spent an hour with them before retiring and wished Alice was here, but she wasn't sure if they would ever meet again. War was like that. People came and disappeared from your life as everyone in the services moved around constantly.

Worn out by the odd day she had just endured, she fell asleep immediately, but was awake and ready for the ferry on time in the morning. Remembering the day before, she put a pair of trousers in her bag – just in case they were needed – and clambered on to the lorry.

There wasn't a sign of the officer when she arrived, and Kathy wondered what she should do. There wasn't anything on her desk she could be getting on with. The question was soon answered when a young sailor opened the door and looked in.

'Come with me, please.'

'Where are we going?' she asked as they made their way along the passage.

'I've been told to take you to Commander Evans.'

There were four men in the room he took her to. They were sitting around a table littered with cups, glasses and empty plates. The small room was filled with smoke from their cigarettes and all of them were unshaven and bleary-eyed. It didn't take a genius to realise they had been there all night.

Evans glanced up. 'Hammond, clear up this mess and get us more tea.'

'Yes, sir.' She quickly set to work and studied the men as she moved around them. Three were navy officers, but the other one was in civilian clothes. There was a sink in the corner of the room and a small table containing the necessary things for making tea. The men continued their discussion in quiet tones while she washed the dishes and then boiled the kettle of water to make fresh tea for them.

She wasn't paying much attention to what was being said until suddenly something registered and she spun round to study the man in civilian clothes more closely. He was German – she was sure of it! But what was he doing here?

The fury she had controlled quite successfully erupted to the surface and she glared at him. She was expected to serve him with tea?

Her fury hadn't gone unnoticed by one person – her boss.

'Hammond!' he said sharply, making her jump to attention. 'Go to the galley and get us something to eat, then you can return to the office and wait for me there.'

'Yes, sir.' She marched out, and on the way to get the food she berated herself for being so stupid. When was she going to learn to keep her emotions hidden? The instant she had recognised who the man was, all her good intentions had melted away as the fury rushed back. Bill had told her to let the past go and concentrate on what had to be done now. *Don't look back*, he had advised her, and she had tried – she really had – but obviously not enough. She was still seething when she reached the galley, and knew she had to gain control of her feelings before she went back into that room.

'Commander Evans wants breakfast for four,' she told the cook. 'And I'll need someone to help me.'

'Are they still in the same room?'

She nodded. 'I think they've been there all night.'

'Then they'll be hungry. It's some time since we took anything to them.' He barked out orders and everyone sprang into action.

Kathy watched the activity and couldn't help admiring the efficiency and the speed with which the food was prepared and loaded onto trays. 'My goodness, they will never eat all that,' she exclaimed.

'Commander Evans is highly respected around here, and if he wants food, then he'll get it in plenty.'

She was quite taken aback by that remark. 'Is he? I only arrived yesterday and haven't had time to get to know him.'

'Don't be fooled by the young man you see dashing about, seeming to accomplish nothing. That's just a front. Underneath there is a highly efficient intelligence officer who is determined to win this war, even if he has to do it by himself.'

Now she was intrigued, and her anger began to fade. An officer didn't receive that kind of respect without earning it. For the first time since arriving she wanted this assignment and prayed he wouldn't dismiss her now.

Three sailors were lined up with trays full of food and taking one herself she led the way. Once inside the room she expertly served each man, dismissed the sailors, made another pot of tea, and then stood by her officer. 'Do you need anything else, sir?'

The men were obviously ravenous and when the German smiled at her and thanked her in good English, she said politely, 'Enjoy your breakfast, sir.'

'You may go now, and if anyone wants me I won't be available for a while yet.'

She looked at the intelligence officer with fresh eyes, stepped back and saluted. 'I'll do that, sir.'

'Thank you, Hammond,' he said softly.

Worry gnawed her as she made her way back to the office. The tone of his voice made her hope he had forgiven her for that lapse of self-control. She would soon find out when he was finished with this strategy meeting, for it was evident to her that they were planning something of importance.

Kathy fended off six calls in the next two hours, and when he appeared in the doorway of the office she jumped to her feet and stood to attention, awaiting his reprimand. He was now clean-shaven, bathed and in a fresh uniform, but his expression didn't bode well for her. Needing to break the silence she said, 'There are six messages for you on your desk, sir.'

He didn't reply as he studied her intently. *He has startling pale eyes*, she thought, *and they don't miss a thing*. Also, there was an air of intelligence that shone through those all-seeing eyes. You didn't mess with this man, and with that realisation she knew she wanted to stay with him. He would get things done and she needed to be a part of that, even if it meant just assisting him as his secretary.

He took a step towards her and began to speak softly. 'I went through dozens of records until I had a shortlist of women recruits, then I began to interview people who knew them. In the end I settled on you. I understood what you had been through and was impressed when I heard the way you had dealt with it. When Commander Jackson assured me you had your feelings under control, I thought you were just the kind of person I needed.'

Kathy's heart thudded as she waited for the axe to fall, so to speak. She had already noticed that when he spoke softly, then it meant trouble for someone – in this case, it was her!

'Did I make a mistake, Hammond?'

'No, sir,' she replied firmly. 'I was taken by surprise when I realised who the civilian was. It won't happen again, sir.'

'No, it won't. If I see that expression of sheer hatred on your face again you will be back in civilian life quicker than you can blink. The only reason I am considering keeping you is the speed and manner of your recovery. When you returned with the food you were efficient and gracious.'

She drew in a silent breath, praying this meant he was going to give her another chance.

Turning away, he went to his desk and sat down. 'You could be faced with many unusual situations like this. It is what I do. I need someone by my side that will obey orders without question and face any situation we find ourselves in with calm composure. Often having a female present can ease a tense and difficult situation just by being there. That is what I need, not someone who will erupt in fury, as you just did.' His penetrating gaze swept over her. 'Are you with me, or shall we end this now?'

She stepped up to his desk, stood to attention and said, 'I am the one you need, sir. I won't let you down.'

The nod he gave her was slight, but it was enough for Kathy.

'No second chances, Hammond.'

'Understood, sir.'

Indicating the chair in front of his desk, he said, 'Sit down. It is only fair you know what Otto was doing here. He was dropped in two days ago to work as a German spy, but he came to us straight away. He is a naval expert and willing to help us.'

'Why would he do that, sir?'

'He was educated here and spent most of his youth in this country. Not everyone agrees with what is happening in Nazi Europe. He is going to work as a double agent, and through him we will be able to send misinformation to the enemy.'

'Do you trust him, sir?'

He pursed his lips. 'Only time will tell, but he will be watched all the time. We have recruited others like him and they could prove very useful.'

She nodded. 'I can see that, and I have a lot to learn about the kind of work you do.'

'We work behind the scenes, and hopefully unnoticed, but that doesn't make the intelligence section unimportant. What we do might not always appear right, but it could be vital in saving lives.'

'That's the most important thing,' she declared.

'No, the most important thing is that we defeat the enemy; saving lives comes close behind that.' His gaze drilled into her. 'You could be asked to do things that you find unpleasant and disagree with, but I need your absolute loyalty and obedience. Can you handle that, Hammond? Can you face another German without wanting to lash out at him?'

He was still offering her a way out if she wanted it, and a short time ago she would have taken it. Not now, though. 'I'm with you, sir. Can I learn Morse code?'

That clearly surprised him. 'Why would you want to do that?'

'The more skills I have, the more use I can be.'

'Or perhaps you are considering gaining more skills while here and then asking for a new posting?'

'That is not my intention, sir.'

'Very well. I will take the word of the daughter of a captain and trust she is as honourable as her father.'

'I am, sir.'

'In that case I will arrange instruction for you.'

'Thank you, sir.' Kathy was elated. Perhaps she was going to be able to do something useful after all.

Chapter Six

Commander Evans had been as good as his word, and a week later Kathy was sent to learn Morse. He had arranged for the instructor at Abbot's Cliff station in Dover to give her an intensive course as he could only spare her for two weeks. She picked it up quite quickly and even spent a few days at the listening post actually working to intercept wireless transmissions. She wasn't as skilled as the other girls but enjoyed the challenge.

There was warmth in the sun now and she stared out to sea on her last day. It had been a cold March night when that raid had torn her life apart, and now it was May. How her life had changed in that short time, and so had she. Now there was only one purpose in her mind, and that was to be as useful as possible. She really didn't have much idea what she was letting herself in for with David Evans – the man was a mystery – but he was also a man with a mission, and she wanted to be a part of that, no matter how small her role would be.

There was a sense of pleasure and anticipation as she walked the tunnel to their Dover office. For some reason she had become fond of this strange underground place. It was almost like home to her, and the only one she had now. There wasn't a sign of her boss when she reported back for duty, so she asked the base commander where he was. She was simply told he was away, and where or when he was expected back no one would say. For the next three days the telephone rang continuously, and she took messages, stating that he was unavailable and would be informed of their call the moment he arrived back.

Kathy made use of the spare time by practising her Morse on a training key she had brought back with her, trying to increase her speed and proficiency. She had been impressed by the girls' concentration and speed at the station.

Towards the end of the third day the office door swung open and David Evans strode in. Kathy leapt to her feet.

'Ah, you're back,' he said, removing his hat and jacket before sitting at his desk.

'There is a pile of messages for you in the folder, sir.' When he nodded and closed his eyes for a moment she studied him closely. He looked bone-weary, and she immediately put the kettle on to make a strong pot of tea.

It was soon ready, and she placed a mug in front of him, and then asked gently, 'Are you hungry, sir?'

He emptied the mug before speaking. 'I'm starving.'

Kathy refilled his mug. 'I'll get you something. What would you like, sir?'

'Anything.'

The cook smiled when she walked in. 'I know. He's back from one of his little trips and is starving.'

'That's right. Does he do this often?'

'Now and again. I'll make a pile of sandwiches and give him a couple of bottles of beer.'

'I'm sure he would appreciate that.'

'It's good he's got you to look after him now,' the cook said, then turned to give orders for the food to be prepared double-quick. 'He needed someone to take on the office work because he has little time for it himself.'

That was obvious, Kathy thought as she made her way back to the office with a loaded tray. The pile of sandwiches was huge, and she was sure he wouldn't be able to eat all of them.

Putting the tray in front of him, she watched in astonishment as he cleared the lot and drank the beers. How long had it been since he'd had anything to eat?

'Would you like some more, sir?'

Evans shook his head and gave a wry smile. 'That was just what I needed. Have you ever been seasick, Hammond?'

'No, sir. I've only ever been in small boats.' Kathy looked at him curiously.

'It's something I struggle with every time I go to sea.'

'Sailors don't get seasick.'

He laughed then. 'Don't you believe it. There are many who throw up every time they set sail, but eventually get over it in a couple of days.'

'My father never told me that, and I assumed all sailors didn't suffer in that way. Have you been to sea, sir?' she asked.

'I had to take a trip in a submarine.' He actually shuddered. 'Ye gods, that isn't a fun way to travel!'

'What were you doing in a submarine?' She knew she shouldn't be asking but couldn't help herself.

'Going somewhere I wouldn't want to be seen.'

'I see, and did you accomplish what you set out to do?'

He nodded again but didn't say more. Reaching out, he flipped open the folder and began to look through the messages, removing only three. 'I'll deal with these. The rest I'll write replies to and you can phone them back for me.'

Evans began writing and she walked up beside him and removed the pen from his hand. 'Tomorrow will be soon enough for that. You need to get some sleep.'

He glanced up, surprised. 'Ah, you can be bossy as well.'

'Only when necessary, sir. You are exhausted and must rest. Whatever you have been up to has drained even your formidable energy. And don't you dare get on that bike. I'll get you transport, so don't disappear while I'm away.'

He grinned, rested his head back in the chair and closed his eyes.

Picking up the empty food tray she returned that to the galley, then went to the duty officer and demanded transport for her officer. A car was immediately brought round, and she returned to the office. David Evans was in the same position, but his eyes were open. Handing him his hat and coat she told him, 'There is a car waiting for you, sir.'

Evans stood up, put on the hat and tossed the coat over his shoulder. 'I'll need you to escort me out.'

Ignoring the glint of amusement in his eyes, she replied, 'I have every intention of doing so, sir. You have a habit of disappearing.'

'You are packing up for the day as well, so bring your bag with you,' he ordered. 'We'll drop you off at the Wrennery.'

When they reached the waiting transport he sat in the front and Kathy climbed in the back. She was quite pleased she had given orders to an officer – and got away with it. A secretary's job was always to look after the man she worked for and that training had surfaced when she had realised how exhausted he was.

When they arrived she got out and saluted. 'Goodnight, sir. Sleep well.'

'I will. Goodnight, Kathy.'

She was nearly at the door before she realised what he had said. For once he hadn't called her Hammond. A feeling of elation swept through her and she spun round to watch the car disappearing up the road. He had accepted her.

* * *

Their working relationship became more informal when they were alone and they used Christian names, but reverted back to the military terms when anyone was around. David began taking her to meetings so she could make notes for his future reference only, and her skill at shorthand was proving useful. In the past he had made rough notes himself and he clearly appreciated being relieved of this chore. She was finding quite a few ways to take routine jobs off his hands.

Towards the end of May she was alone in the office, but that was nothing unusual. She knew David was around in the tunnel somewhere but had hardly seen him for several days. If he did return he would need her help, so she decided to wait, even if it was all night. His hours were erratic, and she always tried to be around when he appeared again.

Deciding it was time for a fresh pot of tea, she was busy making it when the door opened, and he walked in. 'Oh, that was good timing. Would you like tea, and something to eat?'

He shook his head and sat at the desk, his expression alerting her to the fact that something momentous had happened. Placing a mug of tea in front of him anyway, she waited, knowing he would tell her when he was ready.

After drinking the tea, he sat back and sighed. 'The Royal Navy has just sunk the *Bismarck*.'

'Oh, that's terrific news!' she declared excitedly, and then noted how serious he was. 'What aren't you telling me?'

'HMS *Hood* was blown apart in the battle.'

Kathy's thoughts went immediately to her father and she sat down with a thump. 'Survivors?'

'No definite news yet, but from all accounts they didn't stand much of a chance. It's been a high price to pay, but it had to be done, and they sunk the battleship in the end.' He held out his cup for a refill. 'I know what you're thinking, but I can tell you that your father's ship wasn't involved in that battle.'

She let out a ragged sigh of relief. 'He won't tell me the name of his ship, so when I hear about one of ours being sunk I never know if it is his.'

'That's for the best.' He stood up. 'Come on, let's get some rest. I'll give you a lift.'

'On the motorbike?'

He grinned at her look of doubt. 'It's the fastest way to get around. It's a pity you can't manage one, because if you could you would be able to deliver messages for me.'

They were walking towards the exit when she saw the chance to increase her skills. 'We'll never know if I can do it unless I try. If I learnt how to ride a motorbike, then I could be of more use to you.'

He stopped walking and looked at her intently. 'Being useful is very important to you, isn't it?'

'It's what I joined up for, and I'm serious. I might not be quite so nervous if I was in charge of the bike. You drive like . . . you drive too fast,' she corrected herself quickly.

'Are you inferring that I'm a dangerous driver?'

'I wouldn't dream of it, sir.'

'Oh, I think you would, Leading Wren Hammond. Your skill as a secretary is excellent, but that clearly isn't enough for you. First you want to learn Morse, and now you want to ride a bike. Is there anything else you want to do?'

'Win this damned war, and I'll do whatever it takes to help in some way. Because I'm a woman I am not able to join a fighting force, but I'll make a contribution in any way I can. I want to see them defeated for what they did to my family, and the hundreds of other families that have been torn apart by this senseless war!'

'I understand.'

'Do you?'

He turned and faced her. 'My brother was involved in that battle to sink the *Bismarck*.'

The anger drained from her. No wonder he had looked so tired and worn when he'd returned to the office that day. She was immediately ashamed of her outburst and asked softly, 'Is he all right?'

'I don't know, but he wasn't on the *Hood*, thank heavens. It will take a while for the list of casualties to come through.'

'I apologise for my outburst. You have enough to cope with without having to deal with an angry woman.'

'Don't apologise for caring, Kathy. When you first arrived, I thought I might have made a mistake in choosing you, especially when I saw that fury come to the surface. You quickly controlled it, though, and that told me you have a strong character, which is what I need in you if we are going to work together successfully.'

'You need someone with a strong character to do your office work?'

'That's your official job, but I will probably take you with me on a trip now and again.'

That sounded more promising. 'I like to travel.'

'Good. Now, about the bike. Your instruction will begin in the morning.'

'Thank you.'

They continued walking and when they reached the bike she began to have doubts but pushed them away. Kathy had declared that she would do anything, and she damned well would.

The next morning, she was surprised to find that David was going to teach her himself, and relieved to note they had given her a machine used by the despatch riders. It was lighter than his powerful bike and would be easier to handle. The first lesson was a run through of the controls while she sat on it.

'You are going to need to maintain it as well,' he told her. 'If you break down at any time you will have to be able to carry out repairs yourself.'

Kathy nodded. 'That's sensible. Can I have a go at riding now?'

'That's enough for you today. We'll work on

steering tomorrow, and then we'll see about letting you ride it – slowly.'

She clambered off the bike and grinned. 'That was interesting.'

Back in the office he dumped a large book in front of her. 'That's the maintenance manual.'

She flicked through the pages in astonishment, and then looked up. 'Am I expected to learn all this?'

'The basics will do.'

Just then the telephone rang, and he snatched it up, listened and said only one word. 'Right.' Then he swept out of the room.

Kathy had seen concern on his face as he had reached for the phone. He must be very worried about his brother, but that wasn't going to stop him doing his job, and she fervently hoped that the news was good when it did come through. At least she had known during that night that her mother and aunt had been killed. Waiting for news must be dreadful.

Chapter Seven

Within three days of her first lesson David allowed her out on the road, riding beside her on his own machine. He was even letting her tinker with the engine and was turning out to be a very patient teacher. At first, she had been puzzled that he was doing this himself instead of handing her over to a navy instructor, but she was pleased he had decided to do so. She felt as if it was bringing them to a better understanding of each other.

He praised her progress and stated that he would soon be able to send her off on her own, and she found the prospect exciting. She had always loved learning new things, and she was certainly being given that chance now.

They were still working at ten o'clock one evening when the door opened, and an officer walked in. David glanced up and shot to his feet, nearly sending his chair flying in his eagerness to greet the visitor.

'Ben! Damn, it's good to see you.'

Kathy watched the two men so obviously delighted to see each other, and she didn't need to be told who he was. He was slightly older than David, but there was no mistaking their relationship. They were brothers.

'I was told you were all right and were on your way back. Where did you dock?'

'Portsmouth, for repairs.'

'Much damage?'

'Enough, but we got back under our own power.'

David nodded, serious now as he gripped his brother's arm. 'Well done.'

When his brother winced, David frowned and quickly removed his hand. 'You're injured.'

'A few stitches, that's all. I had a worse injury the day you pushed me out of that tree when we were children,' he joked.

'You fell. Go on, admit it after all these years.'

'Never.'

They both laughed, and David winked at Kathy. 'Let me introduce you to my big brother. Ben, this is my partner in dirty tricks, Kathy.'

She had been standing since the officer had walked in, now she stepped forward. 'I am pleased to meet you, sir.'

'It's my pleasure and forget the formalities.' He reached out and shook her hand. 'David has told me about you, and I have met your father on several occasions.'

She found herself under intense scrutiny from a pair of eyes so like his brother's. It was easy to see these were two intelligent and astute men.

He turned back to his brother. 'I can see Jack Hammond in her, but you have been rather modest in your description.'

Davis shrugged. 'I know, but it took me a while to make up my mind.'

His brother burst into laughter. 'I've never known you to be cautious before.'

'Ah, well, it's a tricky situation.'

This conversation was going right over Kathy's head. There was clearly some meaning underneath the words and what they were saying meant something to them. It was a puzzle to her, though.

'Would you like some tea, sir?' she interrupted. 'And I'm sure I could rustle up some food if you are hungry.'

'The name is Ben, and something to eat would be welcome.'

'Good idea,' David agreed. 'See what you can get, and I'll make the tea while you're away.'

Because people were on duty all the time, food was always available, and she was soon on her way back with a tray loaded with two hot pies, sandwiches and she had also managed to get two bottles of beer.

'My word,' Ben said when she put the tray on the desk. 'They certainly feed you well here, and that's just what a hungry man needs. You've even found beer. Well done, Kathy.'

She smiled at his obvious pleasure, but when she looked at David he was frowning. 'There are only two plates and two pies.'

'I thought that was enough for the two of you. Did you want more?' she asked, puzzled.

'You must be hungry as well. Why didn't you get something for yourself?'

'I can get a meal at the Wrennery. I thought you would like some time alone with your brother, so with your permission I will leave now.'

'Of course.' He sat back and smiled. 'I have kept you long enough. I will be taking a couple of days' leave, so look after everything for me.'

'I'll do that.' She turned her attention to Ben. 'It has been a pleasure to meet you. Goodnight, sirs, and enjoy your time ashore.'

Ben watched Kathy leave, and when the door closed behind her he turned to his brother. 'Tell me about her.'

David had a detailed file on Kathy and he told his brother what he knew about her.

When he'd heard all, Ben swore under his breath. 'Damn, that's quite a story. What on earth made you take her on? After what she's been through she could lose control in a fraught situation and put both of your lives at risk. I hope you are just going to keep her in the office?'

'Bill Jackson assured me she can control her anger, and I saw that for myself. One day the man with me was a German and the fury that blazed in her eyes at that moment was something to see. Her recovery from the shock was swift, though, and she then handled the situation perfectly.'

'I still don't like it. You need a man at your side.'

'Oh, come on, Ben. Women are doing all manner of jobs now. Some of them are working in enemy territory as agents. Sometimes a woman can go unnoticed in places where a man could arouse suspicion.'

'I know that.' Ben sat back and sighed. 'I worry about you. I don't know exactly what you do, of course, but I do know the last man who went somewhere with you was killed, and you came back injured. Do you have to go on some of these trips? Couldn't you send someone else?'

'You're a fine one to talk. When you were in the thick of the battle to sink the *Bismarck*, did you ask someone else to take your place?'

'Don't be ridiculous.'

The brothers grinned at each other. Not only did they look alike, but they had both been born with the same adventurous character – which had got them into a lot of trouble while growing up.

'Point taken, Dave, but for heaven's sake be careful.'

'I always am, and now I'm a senior intelligence officer I only go out when my presence is absolutely necessary, and I don't go alone. I have specially trained men with me, and if I need to take Kathy we will be well protected. Jackson has an uncanny knack of summing people up, and when he tells me she is sound, then I believe him.'

'You're right, of course.' Ben finished the last of his beer. 'Our parents will be pleased to see both of us this time, but I'll need somewhere to sleep for a few hours, and then we can be on our way. Travelling early in the morning will give us more time at home. Have you got enough petrol in that machine of yours?'

'Of course.'

'Good, that will be quicker, and save us messing about with trains.'

The brothers enjoyed the ride to their home in Berkshire. They laughed and joked all the way, shouting to each other over the noise of the engine, and enjoying the exhilaration as David pushed the bike to its full speed. Just for a short time they were boys again, and the war they were both fighting was pushed aside.

They roared up to the house and the door flew open as their parents rushed out to greet them. There were huge smiles on their faces when they saw both of their sons.

'I'd know the sound of that monster anywhere,' their father declared, hugging them both.

'This is wonderful!' Their mother kept hugging them in turn – several times. 'Can you stay? How long have you got?'

'Mum, we've only just arrived,' Ben teased. 'Give us a chance to get inside before you bombard us with questions.'

She laughed and slipped her arm through both of

theirs, and with a son on either side of her she led them in to the house.

'Have you had anything to eat?'

'Not much, Dad, and we're starving,' David replied. 'We haven't come empty-handed, though. There's some tinned food on the bike.'

'I'll get it.' Still smiling with the joy of having both boys home, Sam Evans went outside again.

'Now, tell me how long you can stay,' Jean Evans demanded.

'Two days,' David told her.

'Oh, I was hoping it would be longer, but two days of having you both here will be a treat, so we must make the most of it. Your rooms are always kept ready for you. Do you want a cup of tea before I start cooking you a meal?' she asked as she walked towards the kitchen.

'No, they don't.' Sam reappeared, carrying the bag from the bike. 'I've got something stronger than that.' He winked at his sons. 'I've got a good bottle of whisky I've been saving. I'll just put this bag in the kitchen and we can have a drink to celebrate us all being here together. You as well, Jean.'

'It's a bit early in the day for that, isn't it?'

'Not when we have both the boys home together. That's cause for a celebration, so don't look disapproving,' he told his wife, lining up the glasses and beginning to put a shot in each.

'You're right, of course.' She looked lovingly at her

two handsome sons and smiled, accepting the glass from Sam.

After enjoying the celebratory drink and their mother's cooking again, with another drink to round it off, they all settled down to catch up on the news.

'From what we've heard that was some battle to sink the *Bismarck*.'

'It was,' Ben replied.

'Of course, we would only get a sanitised version of it. No good asking for details and if you were part of it, I suppose.'

Ben shook his head. 'You know better than to ask a question like that, Dad.'

'Of course I do, but I thought I'd try.'

'What have you two been up to?' Ben asked, veering away from a subject he didn't want to talk about.

'I've joined the WVS and Dad is now in the Home Guard. It makes us feel as if we are doing something.'

Both sons looked at their father in astonishment, and said together, 'You've done what?'

'Don't look so amused. If we are invaded, we are going to need every man available to fight.'

The boys were now laughing openly, unable to contain their amusement.

'But you're a navy man, Dad. Have you told them that, and your rank?' David asked.

'Of course not. They treat me like one of them and that's what I want.'

'Let's pray we don't have to fight on our own soil.'

Jean smiled at her youngest son. 'You told us in your letters that you have a Wren working for you now. What is she like?'

'I'm not sure I know how to answer that, but I'll try. She was a secretary in civilian life and she's efficient and knows how to handle people. She's taken a load of work off my shoulders.'

'Why the deep frown? She sounds ideal.'

'She is as long as you don't put a gun in her hand.'

'What on earth do you mean by that?' his father asked. 'Explain.'

'I had been in a meeting all night and we needed food, so I sent for her. The man we were with was a spy who had turned and was willing to help us. I saw the moment she noticed what his nationality was, and I swear if she'd had a gun in her hand she would have shot him there and then. To her credit, though, her recovery was quick, and she carried out her duties perfectly. I was impressed by her self-control at that moment.'

'I advised David to get rid of her,' Ben explained. 'She's clearly troubled and could let him down, but he doesn't agree.'

'Tell us her story,' their mother urged.

David then gave them a brief outline of what had happened to Kathy during that night raid.

'Oh, the poor dear. I'm not surprised she is angry, and one can only imagine what she must have gone through searching for her mother and aunt. Still, working as your secretary will probably help her to recover.' She smiled wistfully at her eldest son. 'I wish you could get a nice safe desk job like David.'

'I'm a career sailor, Mum, David isn't. As soon as this war is over he will be out and back to his job as a lawyer. Anyway, they can't send him to sea because he gets seasick all the time,' he teased. 'He's used to cross-examining people, so intelligence is the right place for him.'

'You are right, of course.' She beamed at David. 'When you do return to your proper business you are going to need a good secretary, and your Wren might be right for you.'

'That's a long way off.'

The next day the brothers took a walk through the countryside they knew so well, and Ben gazed across the tranquil scene and sighed with pleasure. 'You wouldn't know there was a war on out here. It's lovely to see green trees and fields instead of a churning sea hiding deadly subs.'

'It must have been hell with all those guns blazing during the battle to sink that ship.'

Finding an old fallen tree, they sat down and lit cigarettes, relaxed, enjoying the June sun and the pleasure of being together again for a short time.

'If we're going to survive we have got to gain superiority of the sea, David. Our losses are too high, and we must find a way to deal with those U-boats.'

'The best minds this country has are working day and night to find the answer. We will succeed.'

'Make it soon. We are all depending on you.' Ben smiled at his brother. 'I don't know how I stopped myself laughing when Mum said she wished I had a nice safe desk job like yours.'

David chuckled.

'What are you going to do about Kathy?'

'I'd like to keep her, but I know she wants to do more than be a secretary, and if I don't give her something more challenging soon, she will put in for a transfer.'

'That might be for the best.'

David shrugged and stubbed out his cigarette. 'Maybe, but only time will tell.'

Chapter Eight

The two days seemed to drag, and Kathy was becoming disheartened. She had hoped to be assigned to something interesting, but all she had done so far was scrub floors during training, and now she was running errands and answering the phone. She was aware that David Evans' work involved more than she was being told. If she was a man it would have been easy for her to join in the fight, but she was a woman, and as such was being made to do the mundane jobs. If it hadn't been for that dreadful night she might have been content with this – but not now.

Well, there wasn't anything else she could do today, so she might as well go to the Wrennery. She began to put everything away for the night and anger flared up again. When the memories flooded in it was never far from the surface, and it was so hard to keep it under control. For much of the time now she was reasonably content with her work here, but every so often her spirit plummeted, and this was one such moment. She wished she had someone to talk to, but with her father at sea she felt alone.

'What should I do?' she demanded of an empty room. 'I'm trying to stay calm and carry on, as the slogan says, but I'm lost.' She sat down and buried her head in her hands. 'Someone help me, please.'

The door opened, and she leapt to her feet, not wanting anyone to see her in such a state. If they thought for one minute she was not up to being in the Wrens she would be out, and no matter how hard she was struggling to find her place, that was the last thing she wanted.

'Can I help . . . ?' The words tailed off as the answer to her prayer smiled at her. 'Bill! Commander Jackson.' Then she noticed the braid and saluted smartly, addressing him correctly this time. 'Captain Jackson.'

'It's lovely to see you, Kathy. I have a few hours free and wondered if you and David would join me for dinner.'

'I'm afraid he's on leave at the moment.'

He tipped his head to one side slightly and studied her intently. 'In that case would you join me? I hate to eat alone, and you look as if you could do with some company.'

Astute as ever. He hadn't missed a thing. 'Thank you, and you are right, I do need someone to talk to.'

'I'm a good listener.'

'I know that.' The heavy weight on her was already easing off a little. She didn't know what it was about this man, but he was special.

'Are you hungry?' he asked, as they walked along the tunnel.

Kathy nodded. 'Where are we going? If we need transport I could always take you on my bike,' she teased.

'You ride one of those things?'

'My boss taught me, and he let me learn Morse. I enjoyed that.'

'Your boss?'

'Sorry, that's a hangover from civilian life and I use it without thinking.'

'Well, it sounds as if you have been kept busy.'

'Not busy enough.' She sighed and looked up at the tall man beside her. 'I'll be honest, I'm still struggling.'

When they reached the outside, he guided her towards a car and helped her into the passenger seat. Then he got in and they were soon on their way.

'I must say this is more comfortable than the bike.'

He gave a deep rumbling laugh of amusement, making her smile. It had been silly to allow herself to fall apart like that, and she must be careful not to let it happen again.

'How is the new ship?'

'Good. The sea trials went well, and we are now on active service. We are in port at the moment to have a new gadget fitted. The boffins keep coming up with new ideas, for which we are very grateful.'

Ah, so that was why he had a few hours, and she was glad he had come here before setting sail again.

He drove inland until they reached a small hotel and were shown to the dining room, where they enjoyed the meal and talked about everything but the war. He was excellent company and had the same air of confident authority as her father. The similarities between the two men made her relax.

'We will take our coffee in the lounge,' he told the waiter when they had finished their meal.

'I'll bring it straight away, Captain Jackson.'

'Thank you, Charles.'

The lounge was empty, and they settled in two comfortable, easy chairs, and the coffee arrived the moment they sat down.

'They know you here,' Kathy observed.

He nodded. 'It's peaceful and I come whenever I'm in this area.'

Kathy gazed around at the elegant surroundings and guessed this was probably a busy place before the war. It must be hard now to keep it going. 'It's lovely, and thanks for bringing me here.'

'Thank you for being such charming company.'

'I feel anything but charming; however, I appreciate the compliment.'

'If you want to talk over what is troubling you, please go ahead.'

'I don't want to spoil your evening with my foolish worries.'

'You won't spoil it, Kathy. Bring your concerns out, and you'll feel better if you do. Bottling things up inside is debilitating.'

That brought a wry smile to her face. 'You sounded just like my father then, and if you don't mind I would like to talk.'

Bill sat back and waited for her to start.

'I have always been organised, sure of what I was doing and where I was going, but since that awful night I have been struggling. I want to do something that will help to win this war. I thought joining the Wrens would give me the opportunity to feel I was making a contribution, but all I have been doing is office work.'

'And you don't think that is important?'

'It is, of course, and it's what I have been trained for, but the way I'm feeling now it isn't enough. I know Commander Evans is involved in special work, but he never includes me in anything more than typing unimportant reports, answering the phone and running errands.'

'You told me you went on a course to learn Morse code, and he taught you to ride a motorbike. Did he order you to do these things?'

'No. I asked him if I could and he agreed.'

'Why do you think he did that?'

That was a question she had never asked herself and it made her frown. 'I really don't know.'

'Let me tell you something about David Evans. I have known him and his family for many years. Before the war he was a lawyer and gaining a lot of respect in the profession. He has a prodigious mind and is able to see things that others miss. He can piece together minute details and see the answer. That is why he is in the job he is. With these abilities he never does anything without a good reason, without a clear picture in his mind of what is needed, even if no one else understands why he has taken such a course. He is trusted, and no one ever questions his motives.'

'No one?' she asked in disbelief.

'Not if they've got any sense. There are many ways to fight a war and everyone is using what talents they have. Some of us sail the seas, others fly planes or drive tanks and fight on land, and there are others working quietly behind the scenes – using their minds to help us gain the upper hand against the enemy. David is one of those men, and we need them as much, if not more, than men with guns.'

'I hadn't thought of it in that way.' Kathy chewed her bottom lip thoughtfully. 'The only talent I have is to be a good secretary and look after my boss.'

'I have been told that you excel in that.'

'I know I should be happy doing that work, and most of the time I am, but I can't settle.' She sighed deeply. 'It's as if there is a little demon inside me, prodding all the time and whispering, *You can do more than this*. I can't seem to get my thoughts straight, and every now and then I flounder around feeling lost. What should I do?'

'I would say the demon is your anger you haven't been able to completely erase. It is making you discontented. What would your father say if you asked him what you should do?'

'He would say I was the master of my ship, keep a clear head, and whatever course I steer is my decision.'

'Exactly. No one can tell you what to do. The only thing I will say is that you do what makes you happy. Decide what that will be and go for it.'

She laughed then. 'Thank you for listening to me. I am no nearer to knowing what to do but discussing it has helped to ease the worry. I must admit, though, to still feeling confused.'

'I understand what you are going through, Kathy, but we can't change the past, no matter how much we long to – no matter how traumatic, we have to move on. That is clearly the problem you have.'

'I know you're right, but it is hard to accept that my mother and aunt died in such a violent way. I will have to try harder to sort my emotions out. Thank you for being so understanding. We have only met a few times, but I feel as if I've known you for ever. Are you married?'

'I was. My wife died in childbirth ten years ago. The child was stillborn.'

'Oh, I'm so sorry,' she exclaimed. 'Have you never thought about marrying again? You'd be a good catch for any woman,' she teased, wanting to take his mind off what must be a very painful memory.

'I haven't met another woman who would put up with

my long periods at sea. How did your mother cope?'

'Dad was a sailor when they first met, and she understood what she was letting herself in for. She used to laugh and say it was like another honeymoon each time he came home. It worked for them and they were very happy.'

'Then your father has many happy memories.'

'Yes, he has, and so do I. That's what I must remember, isn't it?'

'Now you've got it!' Bill smiled and stood up. 'I must take you back now. It has been a lovely evening.'

'Yes, it has. May I ask you one more question before we go?'

He nodded.

'You always seem so calm and yet you must have lost friends and colleagues when your ship sunk. Don't you hate the men who did that to you?'

'No, most of the men are like us – carrying out orders. The individual soldier, sailor or airman is not responsible for this war. Hitler and his entourage are the culprits. The crew of that U-boat were doing what was demanded of them – just as we are.'

'So much suffering,' she said sadly.

'Unfortunately, that is the result of total war, and it is a war we must win, whatever the cost.'

'How high is that cost going to be?'

'That we cannot predict, and I wouldn't even try,' he told her as they left the hotel. 'Let's take each day as it comes, shall we, and be grateful for pleasant interludes like this?'

'That is sound advice, and it's the only way. Thank you, Bill. You arrived like an angel in my time of need.'

He laughed out loud. 'That's the first time I have been likened to an angel.'

Sleep was elusive that night as Kathy ran over and over the conversation she'd had with Bill. He'd had sorrow and danger in his life, yet he could still smile and tell her to remember the happy times. That wasn't going to be easy, but she would try to keep those memories uppermost in her thoughts, and perhaps that crippling anger burning inside her would someday burn itself out. She sincerely hoped so, and Bill's sound reasoning had helped her a lot. He was such a gentle man, and yet there was an air of strength there, and she imagined once on board his ship he would be a formidable adversary. Her love went out to her father, making her smile. These naval captains were certainly a special breed, but she was prejudiced, of course.

While listening to Bill talk about David she'd realised that her assignment had been to another special man. Kathy had been so caught up in her own grief she hadn't taken the time to work out who he was and what he was doing. Her impression had been that he was a man who walked so fast she had a job to keep up with him, and who tore around the countryside on that powerful bike. She hadn't taken him seriously, and she could see now that was a serious mistake on her part.

Her attitude must change, and if she could make his

life run smoothly by looking after the small details then that was what she must do. It was a talent she had, after all, and in that way, she would be helping to fight this war. As Bill had pointed out, those working quietly in the background were as important as those in the front line, and that was something she had overlooked in her desire to fight back after what had happened.

Feeling a sense of peace and calm that had been missing from her, she settled down and drifted off in to a sound sleep.

Chapter Nine

The day David was due back, Kathy went in early to see everything was in order and was surprised to see him already at his desk and going through the folder of messages.

'Oh, good morning, sir. I didn't expect you to be here so early. Did you enjoy your leave?'

'It was very pleasant, and our parents were delighted to have us both home at the same time.'

'I'm sure they were. Have you had breakfast?'

He glanced at the clock. 'Not yet.'

'I'll go and get you something.' She stopped at the door and glanced back. 'Captain Jackson called in to invite us both to dinner. He was sorry to have missed you.'

'Captain?'

'Yes, he has command of his new ship.'

'About bloody time too. I've lost count of the times he has turned down a command and am sorry it has taken a war to make him accept promotion.'

'Why would he do that? In my opinion he is perfectly suited to the job.'

'He has never said, but he has his reasons, and I respect his desire not to say what they are. Did you go with him?'

'Yes, and it was a very enjoyable evening. It was lovely to have someone to talk to. He is so like my father and doesn't seem to mind listening to me pouring out my thoughts and troubles. My aunt was the same, and I could always go to her for a chat.' Her expression clouded with pain, and she said quietly, 'I can't do that any more, of course.'

David sat back and frowned. 'You can always come to me if something is bothering you.'

'I couldn't do that, sir. You are my boss and it wouldn't be right to burden you with my silly worries.'

'What the hell is all this "sir" business? I thought we'd agreed to use Christian names when we are not in company.'

Kathy shrugged. 'We did, but I've always called my boss "sir". It is a habit that is hard to break, sir.'

His eyes narrowed. 'Don't push me too far, Kathy. You are in the service now and I'm your commanding officer – not your boss – and I expect you to obey me without question.'

'I'll try to remember that. What would you like for breakfast, David?'

'Whatever they've got.'

She left the room and before closing the door behind her she was sure she heard him laugh, making her smile as she headed for the galley. That talk with Bill had certainly helped to straighten her out, and she was already seeing David in a different light. He was really quite nice.

Over the next month she settled in, trying to make David's life as easy as possible as far as the necessary paperwork was concerned, and fending off unwanted intrusions. Summer turned to autumn and then it was November. She had seen her father only once in that time and had been given leave to be with him for a few days. They had stayed at a small hotel in Portsmouth, and she was upset to see how weary he was, so had insisted that he rest. She had enjoyed making sure he was back to his usual self before he rejoined his ship and was once more sailing away.

She was busy typing a lengthy report and David was deep in thought over something he was reading when the door burst open and an officer swept in.

'We've just had a report that the *Ark Royal* has been sunk off Gibraltar! It's a terrible loss and you are needed in the operations room.'

David rose to his feet, and when he looked at Kathy she could see the pain in his eyes, but his outward composure was unruffled. Without saying a word, he left the office with the other man.

Every loss of a great ship was devastating and something for the enemy to gloat over. They desperately needed to turn the tide of the war in this country's favour. It would happen, of that everyone was certain, and David and men like him were trying to make that happen as soon as possible.

She could just picture the gathering of officers taking place, and wished she could be there as well, but since her talk with Bill she had settled down to the role she had been given, telling herself continually that every contribution, no matter how small, was helping. The most satisfying thing was that David was relying on her more and more to deal with the office, leaving him free to do other things.

Three hours later he returned, and she looked at him expectantly, hoping for news.

'How fluent are you in Italian?' he asked.

'I'm a bit rusty, but it will soon come back once I start to use it again.'

'Good. Go and pack your bag. We are going on a trip. Be back here in an hour. Oh, and wear trousers.'

She leapt to her feet, excited to realise he was taking her with him this time. 'If I can take the bike I will be back in half an hour.'

'Do it.'

Sensing the urgency, she ran along the tunnel, taking the steps two at a time, and jumped on the bike, racing towards the Wrennery. Once there she stuffed clothes in a kitbag, not bothering to look at what she was packing. Then she was back on the bike and kicked it into action. She knew he always kept a packed bag at the office, so speed was necessary as the picture of him continually checking his watch was clear in her mind. He was not the most patient of men at times.

Dumping the bike, she ran to the office and tumbled in out of breath.

He glanced at his watch and smiled. 'I applaud your eagerness. That only took you twenty minutes, and you don't even know where we are going.'

'I don't care. I'm just delighted to be included in whatever it is you are planning.'

'Even if it's dangerous?'

'Even then.'

'Well, it isn't.' He slung his kitbag over his shoulder. 'Come on, we have a ship to catch before she sails.'

She was burning with curiosity but didn't ask where they were going. He would tell her when it was necessary for her to know, but at the mention of a ship she remembered that he suffered from seasickness. 'Have you got some pills from the medic?'

'I can't take anything in case it dulls my senses. The need is always to keep control of your thoughts and actions. You told me you have only been on small boats, so we'll see how you handle the Bay of Biscay in November.'

There was a car waiting for them outside and to her surprise he sat in the back with her. The moment they were on their way he leant his head back and closed his eyes, leaving her to wonder what she was about to be faced with. She couldn't even guess where they were heading, but he did ask her about her Italian. Italy? Surely not – he'd said it wasn't dangerous.

She studied his calm and composed face and thought he was asleep, but he wasn't.

'Relax while you can, Kathy.'

'That's hard to do when I don't have the slightest idea what this is all about.'

'I need you to help me find out something. I speak three languages, but not Italian, and we might need that. Now, will you relax? All will become clear when we reach our destination.'

'If the U-boats will let us.'

'There is that, of course. Can you swim?'

'Yes, I used to compete in races when I was at school.'

'That's useful. You can save me then, because I can't swim.'

'You are joking?'

'Nope.' He closed his eyes again, not appearing to be at all perturbed about being chased by submarines.

How on earth did he know she would be any help in a crisis? Then it dawned on her that he had been watching and assessing her ever since she'd joined him. Bill was right, David Evans never did anything without a good reason, and he had obviously kept her doing mundane work until he was sure she could handle something more challenging. That realisation gave her huge satisfaction, and whatever their mission was she wouldn't let him down.

Taking his advice, Kathy rested her head back and closed her eyes, trying to relax while they had time.

Suddenly she sat upright. The *Ark Royal* – of course, they must be going to Gibraltar.

A deep chuckle came from the man beside her. 'It took you long enough to work that out.'

'I know it should have been obvious, but I was so surprised to be ordered to go with you that it threw me off somewhat. Are you a mind-reader as well?'

'I have many talents.'

'I'm beginning to realise that.' *I'm also beginning to see you have a dry sense of humour*, she thought.

When David sat back and pulled his hat over his eyes, it was clearly to tell her to shut up, which she did.

After a while the countryside became very familiar and she watched with excitement. They were heading for Portsmouth, she was sure.

She was right, and they were waved through and onto the dock. They stopped by a ship. 'A corvette,' she said, smiling broadly.

'You know your ships.'

'Of course I do. My father is a captain, remember.' But he wasn't listening, and she had to move quickly to keep up with him as he got out of the car and headed towards the ship.

Once on the deck they were greeted by the first officer, who clearly knew David. He saluted smartly. 'Welcome aboard, sir, and it's good to see you again. The captain will see you and Leading Wren Hammond once we are underway. Follow me, please?'

While they were making their way below deck the ship roared in to life and began to move away from the dock. Kathy longed to be topside to see them move out to sea, but her duty now was to stay close to David and help him in any way she could.

'I'm afraid we don't have proper facilities for a woman,' the officer told her as he opened a door to reveal a tiny cabin with only enough room for a bunk. 'We've rigged this up for you. The head is down the passage on the left.'

'This will be fine, thank you, sir.' Turning to David she asked, 'Where will you be sleeping, sir?'

The first officer tried hard to conceal his grin, without success.

'You can wipe that smirk off your face, Bob,' David told him. 'She is well aware I throw up every time I go to sea. What is the weather forecast?'

'Stormy.'

'Oh, great. Then you needn't bother about a bunk for me. I won't be sleeping.'

Bob had the cheek to laugh. 'You can use one of the crew's bunks if you need to. Now, if you will excuse me, I have duties. Oh, and there will be something to eat and drink in the galley if you want it, and I must ask you not to wander around the ship or go on deck.'

She looked at the officer, disappointed. 'I have to stay down here all the time?'

'Yes, until we reach our destination. We can't risk you getting in the way if we encounter a U-boat. It gets a bit hectic and very noisy when we release the depth charges.'

'I understand.'

He nodded, then turned and walked back to his duties.

'Let's get something to eat before we hit the storm,' David said.

It was all hands on deck while they got underway, so the galley was empty except for the cook. David only had tea and a few biscuits, but Kathy tucked into spam and chips. The ship was beginning to roll a little now, but he looked all right. She cleared her plate and held on to the mug of tea to stop it sliding along the table.

'We must be getting out to sea now and you look fine, so perhaps you will be all right this time.'

'Hmm,' was all he said.

'Should I change into a skirt when we meet the captain?'

'No, the trousers will be more suitable while we are at sea.'

An hour later the captain sent for them and they were escorted to his quarters.

She was prepared to salute smartly, but that wasn't required, because when they walked in the two men beamed at one another. They clearly knew each other, and formalities were dispensed with.

'David, good to see you again. What are you up to this time?'

'The usual, Henry, going anywhere there might be

some useful information. I was pleased to hear you had survived when your last ship was sunk.'

'Fortunately, she took a while to go under and we all managed to get off. They won't get this one, though. She's faster and well equipped.' Henry turned to Kathy. 'Welcome aboard.'

'Thank you, sir. When we reach port would it be possible to have a look over the ship?'

'Of course. I'll arrange it.'

'My assistant is interested in ships,' David told him, 'and knew this was a corvette the moment we arrived on the docks. Her father is the captain of a destroyer – Hammond.'

'Jack Hammond? You're his daughter?'

'Yes, sir.'

'I know your father well, and I'm delighted to meet you.'

'She's also friends with Bill Jackson, and now she works for me. I'm not sure if that's a bit of a demotion,' he said dryly.

'Two captains.' Henry smiled at Kathy. 'I hope you will add me to your list of friends?'

'I would be delighted to, Captain . . . ?'

'Tennant – Henry to my friends.'

'I shall add you to my list at once.'

He bowed gracefully. 'I am honoured, Kathy. Now, what can I get you to drink?'

It was a very pleasant hour and Kathy was included in the conversation, not feeling at all out of place with the captain of this fine ship. The atmosphere was relaxed and friendly while they talked about many things, including the war, and she found listening to their views fascinating. It was like being with her father again, and the roll of the ship felt strangely comforting. *I would have made a good sailor*, she thought rather smugly.

Chapter Ten

The moment the storm hit, David disappeared, but the rolling of the ship didn't bother Kathy at all, for which she did feel grateful, because it was a bad storm. Her thoughts went out to him, and she hoped he wasn't suffering too much. She had wanted to stay with him and help if needed, but he wouldn't allow it, stating that he would ride out the storm, and hoped it wouldn't last long. Being left on her own, she lurched her way to the galley where the cook had prepared sandwiches for anyone who wanted them.

'You all right?' he asked as she grabbed hold of a table and carefully sat down.

'Fine, thanks.' She tapped the table and grinned. 'Good job these are bolted down.'

'There won't be a hot meal tonight, only sandwiches, but I've been able to make a fresh pot of tea.'

'I wouldn't like to try and cook with the boat rolling like this. Tricky.' She laughed. 'I'll have a sandwich, please, and a mug of tea.'

Eating the cheese sandwich was easy but trying to drink the tea without spilling it all over her was difficult. Somehow she managed it, finding the whole thing highly amusing.

There wasn't anyone else around, and the cook seemed pleased to have some company, so she stayed there for a while. Now and again someone staggered in, grabbed a sandwich and disappeared again. One or two appeared to be a bit pale, but on the whole, they were like her and not bothered by the motion of the ship.

As the storm continued she began to worry about David and on her way back to her bunk she looked for someone to ask if they knew how he was. It was disappointing because there just wasn't anyone around this part of the ship. They were all occupied with their duties, she surmised.

Once back she sat on the bunk and decided she was worrying unnecessarily. He was used to this and knew how to cope with it himself. She might as well get some sleep, and she stretched out on the bunk, not bothering to get undressed. If there was an emergency of some kind she wasn't going to be found in her underclothes on a ship full of men.

* * *

The sound of one explosion after another woke her suddenly and she sat bolt upright, fully awake. The storm had passed, but the ship seemed alive with activity. Had they been torpedoed?

She caught a sailor as he hurried by. 'What's happening? What are those explosions?'

'We're hunting a sub and are dropping depth charges.'

'Oh, of course, I should have guessed. I thought we'd been hit.'

'Not yet. Stay where you are, please.'

They appeared to be circling around for ages, and she longed to go topside to see what was happening. But of course, the last thing they needed was a girl getting in their way, so she sat on the edge of her bunk and waited.

'Are you all right?' a familiar voice asked.

'David! How are you?'

'Better now we're through the storm.'

'Do you know what's going on?'

'They detected a sub and are dropping depth charges. They won't give up until they've sunk it or lost it.'

'That racket woke me up.'

He stared at her in astonishment. 'You were asleep during the storm?'

'Yes. It seems I'm all right on large ships. Do you think there's any food in the galley? I'm starving, and I've got to keep my strength up in case I have to save you.'

He smiled and guided her towards the mess. 'I was afraid I would find you cowering in fear.'

'I might be frightened, but I do not cower!'

'So I have discovered. Come on, let's see if we can find you something to eat.'

It had gone quiet topside and there was a lovely smell of frying bacon coming from the galley, and Kathy was surprised to see several sailors there tucking in to breakfast. They all moved along to make room for them.

'Did you get him?' David asked.

'Don't think so. The crafty bugger gave us the slip, but we'll get him next time.'

The rest of the voyage was uneventful, and when the first officer came and told her she could go topside now, she almost ran up the steps in her eagerness. The bright sun was almost blinding and made her close her eyes for a moment. When she opened them again she gasped in excitement. In front of them was Gibraltar.

When they had docked the captain kept his word and let Kathy have a look round the ship, which she found fascinating.

Watching her animated expression as she came topside again, Henry said, 'You can tell she's the daughter of a captain.'

'You certainly can. I expect she has been brought up on stories of ships all her life. Ready to go?' David asked her when she reached them.

'Ready, sir.' She smiled at the captain. 'Thank you so much for the tour. I love your ship.'

'It's been a pleasure having you aboard.'

They took their leave of the captain, thanking him for

getting them to their destination safely, and then went ashore. It was like another world when compared to battered London and many of its other cities, and she looked forward to exploring it if there was time.

There was a car waiting for them and they were taken to headquarters where they were greeted by two men in civilian clothes.

'What news?' David asked immediately.

'We think he's genuine, but he's very nervous and won't come over to this side. He thinks we will arrest him and hang him as a spy. His English is practically non-existent, so that presents a problem, and he also refuses to meet us again.'

David ran a hand through his thick hair. 'Right. I'll sleep on it and decide what to do in the morning. Come and see me before light tomorrow.'

The two men were studying Kathy intently, and as if remembering she was there, David made the introductions, and told her, 'We will be working with Alan and Ted while we are on the Rock.'

She shook their hands, wondering who they were. They were obviously navy if David was dealing with them, but the civilian clothes puzzled her.

'I need to keep my assistant close by, so has accommodation been arranged as I requested?'

'Yes,' Alan replied. 'A Wren first officer has been assigned to stay with her in a house two doors away from you.'

'I want a guard there as well.'

'Already arranged.'

'Good.'

She couldn't believe what she was hearing. She had expected to be sent to a Wrennery, but it seemed she was going to stay in a house – with a guard. What on earth did she need a guard for?

'If you would come with us. It's only a short walk,' Ted told them.

'Come on, Hammond, let's get you safely settled.' David held the door open for her.

The walk to the accommodation was an education to Kathy. David was one side of her, Alan the other side, and Ted walking in front of them. This tiny rock of British territory was full of military men, and the whistles and shouts at her were continuous. The fact that she was with a naval officer seemed to bring forth rude remarks, and after a rather insulting one about the officers getting all the girls, she looked at David in astonishment. 'That was a sailor who said that.'

'He did remember to salute, though,' he chuckled. 'A word of warning. You don't go anywhere in the evening without an escort. It isn't safe, and most places are for officers only. I will make sure you are protected from amorous men.'

'My goodness, how do the Wrens here manage?'

'The telegraphers here work long shifts and don't get a lot of spare time, but they do get invited out quite a lot.'

'By officers?'

'Sometimes.'

The first officer was waiting for Kathy when they arrived at the house, so she saluted smartly, then turned to David. 'What time tomorrow, sir?'

'Six o'clock, and wear civilian clothes. Sleep well.'

'Yes, sir.' She saluted him and followed the Wren in to the house, rather disappointed. She would have liked to explore the Rock later, but without a male escort that was obviously forbidden.

The officer was friendly and insisted on them using first names while they were staying in the house. Her name was Susan, and they spent the evening talking as she told Kathy about the work the Wrens were doing here. The listening station was apparently on the top of the Rock.

'You had better retire early,' Susan told her. 'I expect you have a busy time ahead of you.'

Kathy shrugged. 'I really don't know what I'm doing here.'

'Well, Commander Evans didn't bring you here to watch the ships in the harbour, and he certainly doesn't come here without a very good reason.'

'He's been here before?'

'Many times.' Susan gave a little smile. 'When he's around it usually means trouble for someone. I'll call you in plenty of time tomorrow. You mustn't be late.'

Much to Kathy's surprise she slept well, was ready early, and was just about to walk the short distance to the other house when a guard came to escort her. She wasn't even being allowed to walk to the house two doors down. The precaution seemed excessive, but that was obviously how things were here.

When she arrived the three men were deep in conversation. After a while David looked up and studied her carefully. The only civilian clothes she had consisted of a straight skirt in dark brown and a cream blouse. He was clearly not impressed.

'It's all I've got,' she said defensively. 'Everything I owned was lost when the house was destroyed.'

He nodded in a distracted way and turned his attention back to what he had been doing.

She sighed inwardly, knowing he was a man of few words, but a brief good morning would have been nice, or even an order to sit down and wait.

'You can't do that, sir,' one of the men told him. 'You are too well known, and if he sees you he will run, and we'll never see him again. If he's really got information about submarine activity in this area, then we need it.'

'You're right, of course.' David ran a hand through his hair, as he always did when he had a problem to solve. 'Can we get a message to him?'

'There's a drop zone we can leave messages for him.'

'Right.' He then walked over to Kathy, who had been listening avidly to their conversation. 'I'm going to ask you to do something, but it is not an order. You can refuse, and no one will think any the worse of you.'

'I'm listening.'

'I want you to cross into Spain and meet up with an Italian man who has information we need. You must act like his Italian girlfriend, so put on a good performance. Questions?'

'Can I cross the border without problems?'

'Yes, that will be arranged.'

'How will I know the man?'

'Alan will give you a description. The man will be waiting in a place of his choosing and we will let you know where later. Before you answer – if you do this you will be on your own. If he suspects for one moment that any of us are there, then he won't show.'

'I'll do it,' she replied at once, excited to be asked to do something like this.

Kathy was subjected to David's penetrating scrutiny for a moment before he nodded and turned back to the men. 'Send the message and say that his Italian girlfriend will meet him at a time and place of his choosing.'

'It will be delivered today,' Ted told him.

The men left the room leaving David and Kathy alone.

He smiled then. 'You will not be in any danger. The reason I'm asking you to do this is because the man is very nervous, and he thinks we look too military and might attract too much attention.'

'I understand, and I'm quite happy to do this.'

'Good. I was sure you would. Now, all we can do is wait. In the meantime, I will take you shopping for something to make you look more exotic.'

That remark made her burst into laughter. 'Not possible.'

'I disagree. Come on, I'll show you round the Rock.'

Once outside he held out his arm, and when she hesitated, he caught hold of her hand.

'You are in civilian clothes, so you have my permission to look friendly.'

Oh well, if that was the way he wanted it, she would do as asked, and it felt quite nice, really.

She was surprised to see people streaming across the border as they walked past it. 'Why are so many coming in?'

'They are Spaniards who work here, but it is also a good way for spies to enter. We have to be very watchful.'

'Have you ever caught any of them?'

'We've had some success. The shops are this way,' he said, changing the subject.

It was an eye-opener to Kathy when she saw luxury goods on sale, but the cost shocked her.

'These are pretty.' He pointed to a lovely selection of silk scarves.

'But look at the price! I can't afford one of those.'

'You are not buying it – I am.'

'I couldn't possibly accept such an expensive gift.'

He gave an exasperated sigh. 'It isn't a gift. You have agreed to do a job for me, and you need something colourful like that to make you look the part.' He turned away from the assistant and spoke so that only she could hear. 'You need to wear something distinctive, so the man will recognise you.'

Glancing down at her plain clothes she knew he was

right. 'I never got around to buying clothes after the raid that destroyed our house.'

'I know that, Kathy,' he said gently. 'It would have been the last thing on your mind, but it's time you had something pretty.'

The shop assistant spread lots of scarves on the counter for them to look at, and David took his time, finally picking out four. Then he held each one up to her face and draped them around her neck, stepping back to see how each one looked.

She stood there bemused. He appeared to be enjoying himself, and as relaxed and at ease as an attentive boyfriend – for that was clearly his intention for anyone watching.

'I think the one with reds and browns in it,' he stated. 'It suits your dark hair and eyes.'

She caressed the silky material. 'It's beautiful and the one I would have chosen.'

'Good.' He turned to the assistant. 'We'll take this one.'

They then went for a walk along the harbour and watched the huge ships that were docked there, then into a cafe for a drink.

'I'll take you to the top when our business has been taken care of. I'm sure you would like to see the listening post where the telegraphers work.'

'I would, thank you. How long will we be here?'

'I'm not sure how long. We will have to wait for our friend to get back to us. Are you eager to return home?'

'Oh no, I'm enjoying the experience. Thank you for bringing me.'

'No need for thanks. I brought you because I guessed we might have trouble with this informant and thought he might be more willing to meet a girl.'

'All I've ever wanted to be is useful. So, what would you have done if I had refused?'

'I would have had to find another way. If the man really has good information, then we need it.'

'You'll get it,' she told him with determination.

Chapter Eleven

It was two days before Ted found a message in the drop zone, and much to Kathy's relief the man had agreed to meet her the next day at four in the afternoon.

When the time came for her to cross the border the men went over and over what she had to do, making sure she had everything clear in her mind.

'If he doesn't show within ten minutes, or if anything feels wrong, you are to return immediately. Is that understood?' David asked.

'It is, but why should there be any trouble? It's a neutral country.'

'It is, but we don't know much about this man, and there could be many watching who are hostile to us. Of course, if he had wanted to betray us he would have insisted one of us met him, so we are fairly confident it will be trouble-free. If there had been any doubt I wouldn't be allowing you to meet him, but in this line of business you can never be too careful.'

'I understand.'

'Be sure you do. Now, Ted will give you a description of the man again, and directions to the meeting place.'

She listened carefully to the instructions again, and much to her surprise he gave them to her in Italian. She was then asked to repeat them in the same language, which she was able to do without hesitation. It was simple enough. Meet the man, pretend to be his girlfriend, and bring back whatever it was he gave her.

'Well?' David asked Ted the moment she stopped talking.

'Not bad. She'll pass if she speaks quietly so no one close by can hear.' Ted grinned at her. 'Your Italian is a bit rusty, but you understood very well.'

'You are very good,' she told him. 'I would have thought you were Italian.'

'My grandmother was Italian, and she made me speak the language from a young age. I'm glad she is no longer alive, because it would have broken her heart to see our two countries fighting each other.'

'I'm sure it would.'

'Time to go, Kathy.' David stood up, picked up the scarf she had left on a chair and draped it around her neck, leaving it loose and flowing. 'Don't forget this. He will recognise you by the colour of the scarf.'

'Is this how I should wear it?' she asked, feeling nervous now but trying not to show it.

'Yes, don't take it off. Here is your special pass. Our guards at the crossing have been told, and they will let you through without comment.' He smiled. 'Thanks for doing this, and good luck.'

While she walked towards the crossing her heart was thumping, but there was a smile on her face, and a determination to do a good job. At last she was being trusted to do something important.

The guard made a show of checking her pass, and then gave her a sly wink as he let her through. She grinned at him and walked into Spain.

The meeting place was only a ten-minute stroll away, and she ambled along, stopping to look in a shop now and again so she reached her destination exactly on time. Scanning the faces carefully it was clear he hadn't arrived yet. Not wanting to attract any attention Kathy walked on a little way, then made her way back and gazed out to sea as if admiring the view. The ten minutes were nearly up, and she desperately wanted to return with the information needed. *Please come*, she pleaded silently.

Glancing at her watch she turned from the view and there he was, she was sure. He was carrying a newspaper in his left hand, as Ted had said he would be. A huge smile lit her face and she walked towards him. 'Roberto! I was afraid you wouldn't be able to meet me today,' she told him in his own language.

He caught her in a hug as if they were delighted to meet up. Keeping his arm around her waist they began to stroll along the road.

When they were in a quieter part of town he said, 'I cannot stay long, or I shall be missed. Take this newspaper to your friends.'

'I'll do that. Thank you.'

'I must leave you now. Can you find your own way back?'

Kathy nodded.

'You tell them I won't do this again. It is too dangerous.'

Then he turned and hurried away, obviously glad to get the meeting over. While they had been walking she had taken note of where they were, so she made her way back without any trouble. The whole thing had taken less than an hour.

The same guard just waved her through this time, and the first person she saw was David.

'How did it go?' he asked when he reached her.

'No problems. I've brought you back an Italian newspaper.'

'Well done, Kathy.'

'He was very nervous and said he wouldn't do this again because it was very dangerous for him. He rushed away as soon as he could.'

'Ted and Alan are waiting for us back at the house, so let's see what's in the newspaper.'

The moment they entered the house, the three men

opened the newspaper and spread it on the table, turning the pages and frowning at each other.

'There's nothing here,' Ted exclaimed and turned to Kathy. 'You didn't drop anything out of the paper, did you?'

'No, I was very careful about that.' Surprised by their reaction, she couldn't control her curiosity and joined them at the table. 'There must be something here because he was very nervous, and I was sure he wasn't giving me just a newspaper.'

'I agree.' David was turning the pages slowly now.

She watched carefully, and then she saw something. 'Stop! There's a dot under some letters and numbers.'

'So there is. Well done.'

'Start at the first page again and call them out to me.' Alan had a pen and pad at the ready.

This took some time and didn't make any sense to her. It just looked like a jumble of random letters and numbers. She watched, fascinated, as David did something with what they had, and after a while he tossed the pen down and sat back, his expression unreadable.

'Isn't it any good?' she asked, concerned now.

'Promising,' Alan told her, 'but it might be misinformation.'

'I doubt that,' Ted remarked. 'I followed him once to a building he worked in. Pretending I was lost and needed directions to a certain street, I went in and began asking if they knew where the place was in rapid Italian. When a door opened I glimpsed inside the room and saw it was filled with maps plastered on the walls, and navy officers who were not speaking Spanish or Italian.'

'That's good enough.' David chuckled. 'Did you get your directions?'

Ted shook his head. 'They never understood a word I said, and quickly escorted me out of the door.'

They were all laughing now, and she realised just what dangerous and vital work these men were engaged in. She was bursting to know what she had brought back with her but knew she shouldn't ask.

'I must get this information to the right people.' David picked up his notes and disappeared – as he always did.

Kathy looked at the other two. 'I gather the news was important?'

'Could be,' Alan replied.

'Ah, well, I'm pleased about that. Would you like some tea?' She stood up knowing she wasn't going to be told anything.

'No, thanks. We have to go now.'

Kathy watched them leave and went to put the water on to boil. She hadn't been dismissed, so she might as well make herself comfortable and wait for David's return. She felt quite deflated now after her little escapade.

She busied herself sorting out some of the paperwork that had gathered in a pile on his desk. This was all everyday stuff, because anything of a secret nature he always kept locked in his case, which never left his side. Security was of the utmost importance, and she understood that, but would have liked to know what they had found in the newspaper. Still, she had done her part and they were pleased, so that was what mattered.

By ten o'clock that evening Kathy was beginning to wonder if he would be coming back, when the door opened, and David strolled in.

'Why are you still here?'

'You hadn't dismissed me, so I stayed in case you needed me for anything.'

'I would have come to your place if there was a need.' He walked over to the desk and took a bottle out of the drawer and held it up. 'We've finished for the day, so have a drink with me.'

It sounded like an order. 'That would be highly irregular, sir.'

'Everything we do in this section is irregular.' He found two glasses and poured the spirit into them. 'Sit down, relax for a moment, and then I'll walk you back to your house.'

Kathy took the glass from him and sat, as ordered. From the smell she guessed it was whisky, and that was something she had never tried before.

He sat down, stretched out his long legs, sighing with pleasure, holding up his glass in salute. 'You did well today.'

'I was happy to do it and hope the information will

be useful.' She took a cautious sip of the drink, and after the first shock decided that it wasn't too bad.

'The information might be good, but only time will tell.' He downed half of his drink in one go. 'It was details of a proposed deployment of U-boats in this area.'

Kathy sat up straight, surprised to have been told. 'That could be enormously valuable.'

'It could, if it's genuine. We are assuming it is and an operation is being planned at this moment.' David topped up his drink and held up the bottle.

She shook her head, studying him intently. He looked tired, so she stood up. 'I'll go now. You need sleep.'

'Stay for a few more minutes. I want to talk to you.'

'All right.' She sat down again, puzzled. He was in a strange mood, so perhaps he just wanted company for a while.

'I had intended this to be a quick visit, but as things have turned out we will have to stay here longer than planned.'

'How long?'

'We are almost at the end of November now, but I promise to get us home before Christmas.'

'I don't mind staying. There isn't anything for me there now, so it doesn't matter where I am, and our time here could, hopefully, be productive.'

'I'll drink to that.' After draining his glass, he stood up. 'I've kept you long enough.'

'You don't have to come with me. It's only two doors down and I'll be fine.'

'I will not allow you out there at night on your own, so don't argue with me. I was worried enough sending you across to Spain on your own.'

'Why? I'm a grown woman and quite capable of looking after myself.'

'I know you believe that, but I am responsible for you.'

This was the last thing she wanted him to feel about her. 'Permission to speak freely, sir?'

He nodded.

'I don't want to be treated like some helpless female. We are involved in a war we have to win, and I'll do whatever I can to contribute to that outcome. If I can help you at any time I will do so willingly, but if you only need a good secretary, then that's what I will be. You decide, but don't you dare worry about me just because I am a girl. There were women and children in that shelter, and the men who dropped those bombs didn't worry about them.'

'How can you be sure of that?' he asked quietly. 'You can't possibly know how those men were feeling.'

She stopped abruptly, realising what she was doing. The fury had erupted in full force, and Bill's words came clearly to her that she would be of no use to anyone if she didn't control her anger. Turning away from David, she fought for composure, unclenching her fists and taking deep breaths. He was right, of course, how did she know how those men felt? Would that horror never leave her?

The moment Kathy felt calmer she faced him again. He hadn't moved and was watching her closely.

'I apologise, sir. That was out of order and you are quite right, I don't know what they felt as they released their bombs.' Trying to make light of her outburst she pulled a face. 'I really mustn't drink strong alcohol. I cannot apologise enough, and if you put me on a charge for rudeness to an officer I will quite understand.'

'If you were working in any other section you would certainly be reprimanded, but I'm not going to do that because you are right. The fact that you are a woman was causing me concern, and I can see why that would upset you, but you must also understand my reasons. Someone who was working with me was killed. He was a man and that was hard enough, but to have something happen to you would be on my conscience for the rest of my life.'

'Why did you decide to accept me, then, if it worries you to have a woman working for you?' Kathy asked.

David raised his eyebrows. 'A moment of madness?'

Panic swept through her. 'Don't have me reassigned, sir. You won't regret your choice, I promise.'

'I have considered doing that many times. Perhaps you would be happier working somewhere else, like the telegraphers, perhaps?'

'No, sir. I want to stay with you.'

'In that case we both need to amend our ways. I will stop worrying that you are a woman, and you must heal that anger you are still carrying around with you.'

'I give you my word that I will try,' she told him, feeling ashamed of her loss of control.

A slight smile appeared, and amusement shone in his eyes. 'Do you think we will succeed?'

'I'm sure we will both try very hard, and I don't think we can do more than that.'

'True. Now we've cleared the air between us I will walk you to the house, so you can get some sleep. We don't want you looking worn out when your father arrives here, do we?'

Kathy stopped suddenly as they left the house and David bumped into her. 'Dad's coming here?'

He nodded. 'I don't know exactly when, but it should be within the next few days. That piece of information is just between us.'

'I'll guard it safely.' She smiled, thrilled at the prospect of seeing her father again. 'Thank you for telling me, sir.'

'When he arrives, you can take time off to spend with him. And when we are alone the name is David, remember, Kathy?'

'I didn't like to use your name when I had been so outspoken. I thought I was in enough trouble without making it worse.'

He chuckled. 'Yes, you were, but it's a good job I'm a kind and understanding man.'

'Indeed. I am very lucky to be working for you, David.'

They were both laughing when he said goodnight and returned to his own billet, and Kathy sighed with relief. They were back to normal, thank goodness.

Chapter Twelve

For the next few days Kathy was kept busy and David took her everywhere with him, even when he had meetings where sensitive matters were discussed. She was learning quite a lot about the intelligence work that was going on in an effort to gain the upper hand on the sea. She stayed quietly by his side, making notes when needed, and only speaking when spoken to.

One day they had a few hours to spare and he took her to the listening station at the top of the Rock, and she spent a couple of interesting hours listening for messages with the girls there. They had come up on a motorbike he had borrowed from somewhere, and it had been a hair-raising ride as he sped to the top.

David had been busy talking to one of the officers, and

glancing at his watch he called her over. 'Time to go.'

'Yes, sir.' Kathy said goodbye to the girls and walked outside with him, stopping suddenly and bursting into laughter. There was a Barbary ape sitting on the bike and another inspecting a tyre to see if it was eatable.

David glared at them, and as if sensing his authority, they edged away from the very interesting item.

'Do you think they took anything?' Kathy asked, highly amused as she watched him inspecting the bike.

'No, it looks all right. Jump on.'

'Could you go a little slower on the way down, please?'

'If you don't like the view, then close your eyes.'

'I might do just that.' She climbed on behind him and held on tight, praying he didn't take any of the sharp bends too fast.

They were back in no time at all, and when he parked the bike he grinned at her. 'You told me to treat you the same as I would a man, and that's what I'm doing.'

'I'm glad you are taking our agreement so seriously,' she replied sweetly. 'Thank you for an exhilarating ride.'

'My pleasure. You are also controlling your anger, so I think we both deserve a drink. There's still some whisky left.'

'Oh no, I'm not drinking that stuff again. I'll make a pot of tea.'

'All right.' He opened the door for her. 'Have we got any biscuits?'

'Custard creams?'

'Lovely. What a treat.'

She was smiling as she made the tea. He was fun when he was in this relaxed mood.

'Do you know when my father is arriving?' she asked, putting a cup in front of him and the plate of biscuits.

'I don't know exactly, but the latest news I have is that he should be here within the next few days. When he does arrive, I will only be able to spare you for two days at the most. Once our work here is finished we must get back to Dover.'

'Two days will be lovely. Thank you. Would you like more tea?'

He held out his cup. 'Have you got any more of those biscuits? They are my favourites.'

She glanced at the plate where there was one lonely biscuit. 'I'm afraid not – I'll try and cadge some more for tomorrow, but I don't know if I'll be able to get the same ones. They are hard to come by, even here. You might as well finish them off.'

He gave her an amused look. 'Where did you get them?'

'Ah, that would be telling, but I can smile sweetly and beg when necessary.'

'I can imagine,' he told her, laughing.

The next four days were hectic as he went from meeting to meeting. She took notes, typed reports and tried to keep up with him. He was in full flow now as they decided what to do about the information they had received. Alan and Ted were back in uniform and they were both lieutenant commanders.

She saluted when they walked in. 'You do look smart, sirs. We haven't been properly introduced, so what do I call you? I can't continue to address you by your Christian names when we are in company.'

'"Sir" is all right, just the same as you do for David.'

She was about to question this when the door opened, and David walked in.

'Come on, Kathy. You've got to see this.'

David took her to the dock and handed her a pair of binoculars. With a little adjustment she focused the glasses and gazed out to sea, and then she gasped in pleasure. A destroyer was heading towards the Rock. 'Is that my father?'

'It is, and I thought you would like to see him arrive.'

'Oh yes, thank you so much. Mum and I always went to Portsmouth when he returned from a voyage.' Her voice wavered a little at the memory, but she resolutely pushed the sadness aside. *Don't look back*, she told herself, remembering Bill's words. This was no time for sadness, and her father would want to see her happy, smiling face, not one streaked with tears.

The majestic ship was closer now and she put the glasses to her eyes again, and then she frowned. 'She's damaged.'

'They've been in a scrap with a U-boat, but they are all right.' David grinned. 'They caught the sub on the surface and sunk it. So that's one less to worry about.'

'Good for them. Is that why they are later than expected?'

'Yes, they picked up the crew and took them to Malta before coming here.'

Lowering the glasses, she turned to study the tall man beside her. 'You know an awful lot about what's going on, don't you?'

'It's my job to be aware of what is happening at sea.' He took the binoculars from her. 'You are now officially on leave. Enjoy yourself.'

'I will and thank you.'

David nodded, turned and strode away.

It was another hour before her father had docked and left the ship, but Kathy didn't mind waiting. The moment she saw his familiar figure she hurried towards him.

His face lit up with a huge smile when he saw her, and she saluted him first, and then hugged him, laughing with pleasure.

'Ah, it's good to see you looking so well, my dear.'

'And you, but what did you do to your lovely ship?' she teased.

'A sub got in my way.'

'You rammed it?'

'Just a little nudge to stop him diving. I hope you are on leave now,' he said, changing the subject.

'David has given me two days, but what about you? Can you leave the ship while repairs are carried out?'

He nodded. 'My first officer will send for me if I'm needed. Let's get something to eat.'

Kathy walked proudly by her father's side, overjoyed to be spending time with him. These occasions were few and far between, especially now there was a war on, so she was determined they should enjoy this unexpected time together.

The hotel he took her to was small but comfortable, and they were greeted warmly.

'You've been here before?' she asked as they sat down.

'A few times. How are you getting on with David?'

'All right. We've had a few rocky moments, and at one time I was afraid he was going to have me reassigned, but we worked it out. He's a difficult man to fathom. He can be distant, and at rare times he is relaxed, considerate and amusing, but whatever his mood he is always fair. I do believe he is good at what he does, though.'

'That is my understanding as well, and it is men like him we need in the background. Those in the front line get all the attention, but the information gatherers are vital. What have you been doing while you are here, apart from running around after David, of course?'

'I had a little errand to run, but you know I can't give you any details.' She smiled apologetically at her father, and he nodded, understanding the need for secrecy. 'I went up to the top of the Rock to the listening station, and saw the girls searching the airwaves for messages. David sent me to learn Morse, but I don't think I could sit there for hours like those girls do.'

'It takes good concentration. So, do you like working for David?' he asked, returning to the subject that clearly interested him.

'Yes, I do. He doesn't involve me in everything he does – he's very secretive – but if I can take care of the routine things to make his life easier, then I'll settle for that.'

'Good. Now, let us forget the war for a while, relax and act like tourists.'

She laughed. 'There isn't much to see on this small piece of rock.'

'I wouldn't say that. The place is full of military and apes.'

She then told her father about the episode with the apes and the motorbike and had him roaring with laughter.

They decided to treat the short leave as a holiday and booked rooms in the hotel. After a good night's sleep, they had breakfast and spent the day walking and talking. Later in the day they were enjoying a cup of tea in the hotel when she saw her father looking round and frowning.

'What's the matter?' she asked.

He was on his feet. 'Something has happened. People are rushing around and talking animatedly about something.'

'So they are. We had better find out what is going on.'

They had reached the door when David appeared, slightly out of breath from running. 'The Japanese have bombed Pearl Harbor and sunk the American fleet,' he told them. 'The news is just coming through, and indications at this point are that every ship in the harbour has been sunk or damaged.'

Kathy was shocked by the news. 'How could they do such a thing? America isn't at war with the Japanese.'

'They are now.' Jack shook his head in dismay, his expression grim. 'They must have been caught unawares, and to have their fleet attacked in this appalling way is a declaration of war. This is going to change things, you know that, David.'

'Undoubtedly, and I'm sorry but I will have to ask Kathy to return to duty. We must get back to England as soon as possible.'

'Of course, and I have to see that my ship is seaworthy as quickly as possible.' He hugged his daughter. 'Our holiday must be cut short, my dear.'

'We have had a few hours together and they have been lovely.'

'Yes, they have.' He held her tightly for a few moments and then strode away towards his ship in the harbour.

'What do you think will happen now?' she asked David as they made their way to the headquarters building.

'America will certainly declare war on Japan. This has changed the face of our war completely, but exactly what will happen now, only time will tell.'

They didn't have to wait long to find out. The next day, 8th December: Britain declared war on Japan; 10th December: HMS *Prince of Wales* and *Repulse* were sunk by the Japanese; 11th December: America declared war on Germany and Italy.

It seemed to Kathy that the world had gone crazy and her mood was gloomy when David swept in.

'Get packed, we're going home.'

'You've managed to find a ship to take us?'

He nodded. 'We are leaving in three hours.'

'May I have permission to see my father before we leave?'

'He sailed an hour ago, and I'm sorry I didn't know in time to tell you. It was a hurried departure.'

'I didn't think they had finished the repairs.' The news was disappointing.

'They must have done. Your father wouldn't have left unless the ship was in good order, no matter how urgent. You know that's true.'

'Of course.'

'Oh, and we'll have company on this trip. Alan and Ted are coming with us.'

'That's nice. I'll go and get my things.'

'Don't be depressed,' he told her. 'Look on the bright side.'

'There's a bright side?'

'Since this war began we have been alone and fighting for our lives to hold off invasion. We have succeeded against all the odds. Now we are not alone any more, Kathy.'

'I never thought about it like that, but this is a terrible way for it to happen.'

'Agreed. However, this is the situation we find ourselves in now, and we fight on.' He smiled at her. 'How do you feel about learning how to intercept Japanese messages?'

'My goodness, of course, the girls will be trying to pick up their messages as well from now on. I don't envy them that task.'

'You're not interested in learning, then?'

'Not really, but I will if you order me to. I only asked to go on that course when I couldn't make up my mind if I would stay with you.'

'You appear to have settled down, so I assume you made up your mind.'

'I did some time ago. You need someone to look after you, and I've decided that's my job.'

He chuckled. 'That's the first time anyone felt I needed looking after, apart from my mother, of course, and she gave up when I was quite young.'

Just then, Alan and Ted arrived and dumped their bags down.

Alan felt the teapot. 'It's cold. I need tea and something to eat before we sail.' He grimaced. 'I'm not a good sailor.'

'Not another one,' Kathy declared as she put the water on to boil. 'What about you, Ted?'

'I'm fine. I quite like being tossed around in bad weather.'

'Don't.' Alan groaned. 'I'm feeling bad already.'

David was laughing. 'Now you've got someone else to look after.'

'Ah.' Alan's eyes lit up with devilment. 'Are you going to look after me?'

'Not likely. You and David can disappear to the crews' quarters while Ted and I enjoy a cruise.'

'That's cruel,' Alan complained.

The laughter and joking had lifted her spirits and the gloomy mood drifted away. They would get through this and come out as victors, no matter how long it took. They had to remain positive and believe that.

They sat drinking tea and eating the sandwiches Kathy had hastily made, until it was time for them to join the ship. She was looking forward to getting back to Dover and walking along that tunnel again.

'I hope your motorbike has been well looked after while we've been away,' she told David.

'I'll have to take it for a good run when we get back. I'll see if I can take you somewhere interesting.'

'As long as it isn't up a mountain with sharp bends,' she joked.

'Or Barbary apes.'

'I told my father about that and he thought it was hilarious.'

'I'm sorry you had such a short time with him.'

'Well, we never expected anything like this to happen, and we had a few hours together. We didn't stop talking the whole time.'

'I expect you had a lot to catch up on.' He stopped walking. 'That's our ship.'

'A frigate this time.' She smiled with pleasure, straightened her hat and took a step back to allow the men to go up the gangplank first.

Alan grimaced. 'I never look forward to the first couple of days at sea.'

'You won't be seasick this time,' she declared. 'I've ordered the sea to be like a millpond, so we will all be able to enjoy the journey.'

'Have you ordered the subs to avoid us as well?' Ted joked.

'Of course. They've all gone home for a rest.'

David was laughing quietly. 'Then we haven't got a thing to worry about.'

'Nothing at all. Now, sirs, there's a reception waiting for you on the ship,' Kathy told them respectfully. Any form of familiarity would now have to be dropped. They were officers and had to be respected as such while they were on the frigate.

Chapter Thirteen

Walking along the tunnel at Dover made Kathy smile gently. The trip to Gibraltar had been exciting, and she had seen her father for a short time. That had been unexpected, and she did wonder if David had delayed leaving the Rock when he knew her father's ship was due to arrive. She was beginning to suspect that under that tough exterior there lurked a kind, caring man.

Alan and Ted were still with them as they made their way to the office. It was just as they had left it, except for a pile of paperwork on David's desk. He grimaced, picked it up without a word and dumped it on her desk. It would take a while to sort through that lot, she thought, but first she must look after the three men.

When she looked up they were all staring at her in a strange way. 'Sirs?'

'How did you do that?' Alan asked.

'Do what?'

'I've never seen the sea that calm all the way over, and not a sign of U-boats. That's the first sea journey I've had without being sick. The same goes for David.'

'True,' he replied. 'I almost enjoyed it.'

Ted was laughing. 'No one was more surprised than me, so how did you do it?'

'I told you before we left that it would be a smooth trip. You just need to believe.'

'As simple as that, is it?' There was a teasing glint in Ted's eyes. 'In that case could you order the war to end? I'd rather like to get back to my proper job as a teacher.'

'A teacher?' Kathy looked at him suspiciously to see if he was joking, but he looked perfectly serious. 'What do you teach?'

'Mathematics and languages.'

'What about you Alan?' she asked.

'I'm in the same business as David, only my speciality is shipping.'

'My goodness. I assumed you were both career navy.'

Ted shook his head. 'We have all been conscripted. So, what about it? Can you work your magic and put an end to this madness?'

'That would be beyond me, I'm afraid.'

'Damn!' Alan turned to Ted. 'That means we are

going to have to learn to jump out of a plane, after all.'

'A daunting prospect, I agree. Perhaps David would like to join us.'

'No need. I've already done it and found it quite exhilarating.'

Kathy was perplexed. 'What are sailors doing jumping out of planes?'

'Don't ask us.' Ted shrugged. 'We only do as we are told.'

She studied them suspiciously. 'I think you're spinning me a tale.'

'Never!' they both declared together.

'I still don't believe you. Now, are you staying, and if so, do you want food and drink?'

'Yes, please.'

'I'll see what I can rustle up.' Kathy left the office and walked along the passage with a smile on her face. Those men were incorrigible. The journey back had been hilarious, and because they hadn't gone down with seasickness, they had taken every opportunity to tease her, and they were still doing it – except for their peacetime professions: that was true, she was sure. She was going to miss them when they went off to do whatever it was they did. One thing she did believe, though, was that they weren't going to jump out of planes.

When she returned they were in deep conversation, and stopped talking the moment she walked in. The joking was clearly over, and it was back to the serious business.

'Would you like me to leave?' she asked David after she had given them the food and a pot of tea.

'I won't need you any more today, but before you leave would you check that our bikes have been looked after while we've been away?'

'Of course.' She smiled at Ted and Alan. 'It has been a pleasure to meet you, sirs, and I wish you luck and safety.'

'The pleasure has been all ours,' Ted replied. 'But you haven't seen the last of us yet.'

Kathy walked out of the tunnel wondering if she would ever find out their full names. That was clearly another game they were playing with her, but they were fine men and she liked them very much.

A quick check showed her that the bikes were all right, and she ordered David's to be filled with petrol in case he needed it tonight.

Feeling quite tired, she was glad to get to bed early and slept soundly. The next morning she was relieved to realise that the nightmares that had plagued her were becoming less frequent, and she hoped she was at last recovering from the horror of that night. It would probably never leave her completely, but the passage of time would help her to live with it.

The next couple of weeks, David was so busy that Kathy was working long hours with very little sleep. The bike was proving very useful, enabling her to run errands for him and ease some of the pressure from his shoulders. The Winchester listening post was the most often visited destination and she got to know a few of the girls quite well. She missed Alice, though, and was sorry she had lost touch with her. Her bright smile and no-nonsense attitude to life had been appealing, and wherever she was, Kathy hoped she was happy and doing well.

When she arrived back after a trip one day, David was in the office. 'Anything?' he asked.

She handed him a leather satchel. 'The airwaves were busy, and all the despatch riders were out, so the commander asked if you could get these to their destination for him. He didn't tell me where, but just said that you would know.'

David was already on his feet, slung the bag over his shoulder and headed for the door. He stopped and looked back. 'I'm sorry we've been too busy for you to take the leave due to you. Do you mind?'

'Not at all. I haven't anywhere to go.'

'Nevertheless, I'll put that right as soon as I can,' he said, and disappeared.

She settled down to work and deal with the constantly ringing telephone, even though it was Christmas Day. It was ten o'clock at night when he arrived back, and instead of sitting down he began to pace the room. Kathy watched for a while, and then said gently, 'David, please sit down.'

He spun round to face her. 'What?'

'I suggested you sit down. You are wound up tighter than a clock. I can feel the tension coming from you.'

'I'm thinking. I always pace when I'm thinking.'

'I can see that, but can't you do it at your desk? I've made a fresh pot of tea.'

Still distracted, he sat in the chair and took the mug from her. 'Is there anything I can do for you?'

'Hong Kong has surrendered to the Japanese!'

Her heart lurched. 'That's terrible. All we seem to be getting lately is bad news.'

'I agree, but don't get disheartened. We've got a long fight on our hands, but we are making progress.'

'Are we?'

He nodded and said quietly, 'We have a group of the finest minds working on deciphering messages being picked up by our listening stations, and soon the U-boats will find the sea a very dangerous place.'

'Is that where you've been?' she asked, interested in this piece of news.

'Yes.' He glanced at his watch. 'It's late and we at last find ourselves with some unexpected free time. I'll take you to the Wrennery and you can pack your party frock. We need to take advantage of this lull in our work and forget the war for a few days.'

'Er . . . I haven't got a party frock. You know I haven't bothered to replace anything since our house was destroyed. The only pretty thing I have is the scarf you bought me in Gibraltar.'

'And you haven't bought anything since we arrived back?'

Kathy shook her head.

'Never mind. Your uniform will have to do, but you

must do some shopping. There are some good shops where we're going.'

'Where are we going?' But she was speaking to an empty office; David was already on his way along the tunnel. She hurried to catch him up. He could be the most exasperating man at times, leaving her wondering what the devil was going on.

She fell into step beside him. 'You can't be seen socialising with a Wren of lowly rank. You are an officer, sir.'

He cast a sideways glance. 'I can do what I bloody well like, and if you're angling for another promotion, you can forget it.'

'I was not!' When they arrived outside she kept walking, angry now.

'Hammond!'

She stopped and turned smartly. 'Sir?'

'Where the hell do you think you are going?'

'To the Wrennery, where there will be some agreeable company, sir.'

'Get on the bike . . . and that's an order. If you think I am going to leave you alone and homeless at this time of the year, then you are very much mistaken.'

'The navy is my home now.' She was well aware of her situation and didn't need to be reminded.

'Are you going to disobey an order from an officer?' David asked firmly.

'You know I can't.' She returned and sat behind him on the bike, hoping he hadn't noticed how upset she was.

'I apologise, Kathy. I didn't mean to remind you of a distressing time, but I've got a lot on my mind and we both need to get away for a few days. Forgive me.'

'Nothing to forgive, sir.'

He sighed and started the bike with a roar as they headed up the road.

'Go and collect your things,' he told her when they stopped. 'You've got ten minutes.'

Much to his obvious surprise she was back in five minutes, and he stubbed out his half-finished cigarette. 'That was quick.'

'I keep a bag already packed.'

'Right. Hop on and let's get going.'

She was beginning to get uneasy. This journey they were going to make was clearly not work-related, and she wasn't naive. 'I'm not going anywhere with you unless you tell me where we are heading and why.'

'You don't trust me?'

'I've been brought up to be cautious, and if this was to do with our work, then I wouldn't question it. Therefore, I feel I have the right to know your plans.'

He lit another cigarette and leant against the bike. 'I wouldn't dare try to take advantage of you. Your father has already warned me off in no uncertain terms.'

'He has?'

David nodded, a slight smile touching the corners of his mouth. 'I told him I would resist the temptation while the war was on. Then all promises are off. So you see you can trust me, because I never break a promise.'

Kathy burst into laughter. 'What did he say to that?'

'I couldn't possibly repeat it.'

Knowing her father, she could just imagine how he would react – if such a conversation ever took place, which she doubted. 'I still want to know where we are going.'

'We are off to spend a few days with my parents, and you'll be quite safe there.'

'I can't do that. I haven't received official permission to take my leave right now, and anyway, your parents might object to having a stranger dumped on them.'

'Regarding your leave, you are under my command . . .'

She held up her hand to stop him. 'I know, you can do what you like.'

'That's right, and as for my parents, they are looking forward to meeting Captain Hammond's daughter. There is also another thing you ought to know. My folks love a full house.' He ground out the cigarette. 'So, if you're coming I would like to get going. We've missed Christmas Day, but we can still enjoy the rest of the holiday.'

'How could your parents know we are coming? You only decided a short time ago.'

'Messages are part of my business and I sent them one by Morse.'

'Oh, and they replied the same way, I suppose.' She shook her head in disbelief.

'Of course. Father is a retired admiral. Now, will you get on the bike, or are we going to discuss this all night?'

She was still laughing as she settled behind him. 'No

wonder you are in intelligence. You can spin a tale to confuse anyone.'

David chuckled and then the bike roared into life and they were off. It was quite a way and they arrived in the early hours of the morning at a large house set in the beautiful Berkshire countryside. Kathy couldn't wait for the dawn, so she could see the view.

The door of the house swung open and a tall, upright man strode towards them. 'Glad you were able to make it, son. Your mother has started cooking breakfast because she knows how hungry you must be.'

Kathy got off the bike, windswept, tired and feeling uneasy. She shouldn't be here. Why had he insisted she come to his home?

'And you must be Katherine.' The man smiled warmly and shook her hand. 'Welcome to our home. We are so pleased you could come.'

'Thank you, sir.' She glanced at David, who was busy retrieving their bags from the bike. 'It is very kind of you, but I wasn't given much choice,' she admitted honestly.

'Ah, ordered, were you?'

'Yes, sir.'

David stood beside her. 'It was the only way I could get her to come. She doubted my motives.'

'Very wise of you,' the father told her with a huge grin on his face. 'Come in and let's get out of the cold. We've a good log fire going, and breakfast must be ready by now.'

The house was warm and welcoming, just like David's

parents, making Kathy relax and enjoy the breakfast of eggs, bacon and fried bread. It was a wonderful luxury and she was well into clearing her plate when the thought struck her. 'Oh, Mrs Evans, are we eating your rations?'

'No, my dear, we have a large farm, so you eat up and enjoy it.'

'Ah, I thought I could smell food cooking. Hello, Kathy.'

She stared in amazement at the man who had just walked in and made himself at home beside her. 'Alan! How lovely to see you. Is Ted here as well?'

He shook his head, dismissing the subject, and turned to David. 'So you managed to wangle some leave after all. How long can you stay?'

'Three days; longer if I'm not recalled.'

'Same here unless Ted gets into trouble and I have to go and get him.'

Kathy wasn't given the chance to question this strange remark before the back door opened and a tall man walked in, and when she saw him she leapt to her feet. 'Bill. How wonderful to see you.'

'You're looking well.' He bent to kiss her on the cheek, much to her surprise. 'Have you heard from your father?'

'Much better than that, we were able to spend a few hours together when we were in—' She stopped suddenly and glanced at David.

'You can tell Bill,' he told her.

'We were in Gibraltar and he came in for repairs after he'd sunk a submarine.'

'Ah, yes, I heard about that.'

'Do you want some breakfast, Bill?' Mrs Evans asked.

'I came for two things: to see Kathy and enjoy one of your famous breakfasts.'

She laughed. 'Sit down, then.'

'How did you know I was coming?' Kathy asked him.

'This is a small village and word gets around,' was all he said.

'When are you due back?' Mr Evans asked.

'Today, Admiral.'

Kathy was surprised. She had assumed David was joking when he'd told her his father was a retired admiral. Bill had addressed him with respect, so it was obviously true.

When they had finished eating it was daylight and they were all sitting around the large kitchen table talking.

After a while Bill glanced at the clock and stood up. 'Thank you for the breakfast, Jean, and it's been lovely to see you again, Kathy.'

'You take care now,' she told him, giving him a hug.

'Always.' He said goodbye to everyone and Mr Evans walked out with him.

When Kathy sat down again, David was studying her with narrowed eyes.

'Something wrong?' she asked.

'I didn't know you were on kissing terms with Bill.'

'He's special to me,' she stated. 'He helped me when I was at my lowest, and I don't mean useless sympathy.

What I needed at that time was a firm mental shake, and that's what he did. I'll always be grateful to him for straightening me out.'

David's father, who had just returned, was nodding. 'Bill's a fine man, and he's not having an easy time, but no matter how tough things get, he remains calm and steadfast.'

The statement about Bill having a tough time alarmed her. 'He hasn't lost another ship, has he?'

'No, he's home because his father died two weeks ago. Fortunately, he was close enough to these shores to be able to get home. He's been on compassionate leave.'

'Oh, I'm so sorry to hear that.'

'Did you let him know his mother will be welcome here anytime?' Jean asked her husband.

'I did, and I also promised we would keep an eye on her for him. She's got a friend with her at the moment and they are going to have a quiet couple of weeks.'

'Good.' She smiled at her son and Kathy. 'Now, what do you two youngsters want to do?'

'Sleep for a couple of hours, and then I must fill the bike with petrol in case we have to leave in a hurry,' David told her.

'Have you got enough petrol coupons, son?'

'Yes, thanks, Dad.' David stood up. 'Mum will show you to your room, Kathy, and tomorrow we will go shopping.'

Jean watched her son leave the kitchen before asking Kathy, 'Shopping?'

'He thinks I should buy clothes because I lost everything when our house was bombed. I haven't got much in the way of civilian clothes.'

'Then you must certainly have something pretty. I'll show you to your room, so you can get some rest. I don't suppose you get much working with our son.'

'Not a great deal,' Kathy admitted, as she followed his mother up the stairs.

Chapter Fourteen

Over the next few days Kathy enjoyed the warmth of the Evans' home. They seemed to have an ever-open door with people coming and going all the time. After a determined tussle she had managed to persuade David that new clothes were not necessary for her at this time, and he left her free to explore the farm and run around with the pet dogs. She was almost happy. The only problem was that being in a home with a family who clearly loved each other highlighted the loss she had suffered. The awful anger bubbled under the surface at times and when that happened she clung on to Bill's words until it faded in to the background once again.

A party had been arranged to see in the new year and Kathy hoped they would be able to stay until then. David appeared relaxed and not concerned about anything, but she knew his moods by now. Every time the telephone rang he was the one who reached it first.

'Will we be able to stay for New Year?' she asked him when they were in the field choosing a cabbage for his mother.

'I hope so.' He sliced off a large cabbage. 'I still think we should see about buying you something nice to wear.'

'I thought we had settled this? I don't want to buy anything,' she told him firmly.

He frowned. 'Do you have any money?'

'Not much. Almost every penny I had was used to pay for the two funerals.'

'In that case, I'll pay for it.'

'You will not!' She swept her hand around to indicate the acres of farmland, coming to rest on the impressive house. 'It's obvious you come from a wealthy family and buying anything is probably easy for you, but I will get through this hard time by my own efforts, and in my own way. My father sends money, but I'm saving that. One day we will need to buy a home again, and that's the most important thing to me. Having pretty clothes is low on my list of importance. Can you understand that?'

'I can, and I apologise if you felt insulted by my offer. I was trying to help, that's all.'

'I wasn't insulted, and it was kind of you to want to help, and I'm sorry to be so stubborn, but I have a driving need to climb out of this by myself. I know I haven't fully recovered from that terrible night, but I will, eventually, and no one else can do it for me.' Then a thought struck her. 'Do you keep insisting on this because you will be ashamed of me at your parents' party wearing the simple clothes I have?'

'Certainly not! That never entered my head. I just thought you might feel more relaxed in something dressy.'

'What I wear is the last thing on my mind. No doubt the time will come when I will again enjoy dressing in nice clothes, but that means nothing to me at this time. There are thousands trying to cope with grief and loss, and everyone deals with it in their own way. It may seem silly to you, but this is my way, and the thought of trying to replace the things I lost in that raid are completely unimportant. Bill told me not to look back, and if I start buying clothes I feel as if I will be doing that.' She grimaced. 'I know it doesn't make sense, but that's how it is.'

'I can see what you mean, but I don't agree with your reasoning. Nevertheless, I do understand that you have to work your way through this, and don't need anyone interfering – however good their intentions. You have my permission to tell me to mind my own business.'

'Mind your own business, sir.'

Two of the dogs came bounding up to her then and she patted their heads as they milled excitedly around them. 'Want to go for a run?'

They barked and jumped up at her, then began running away and looking back to see if she was following. 'Come on, then.'

'Where's Kathy going?'

David looked away from the retreating figures and sighed deeply before speaking to his mother. 'I've just been put in my place and told to mind my own business.'

'She's a beautiful girl, but she's hurting, and you need to be careful. I know you mean well and you brought her here because she hasn't got a home or family to spend the holiday with, but I'm not sure it was the right thing to do.'

When her son opened his mouth to protest she stopped him. 'I'm sure she understands that you are only trying to help, but you must back away and let her work through whatever demons she's fighting with. I know the lawyer in you wants to step in and take control, but she isn't one of your cases, David, and you must remember that. From what I've seen she is a strong, sensible girl and she will come to terms with what she has lost in her own way and in her own time.'

'Her father is at sea and she hasn't got anyone she can turn to. I'm only trying to help.'

'I know, but you are going about it in the wrong way. The only way you can help is to keep her busy and give her work she feels is worthwhile. However, if having her work for you is proving difficult, then you must have her transferred to another posting.'

'She's the best damned assistant I've ever had. She never complains about long hours, is a master at handling people and manages to take a lot of the everyday tasks off my hands, leaving me free for the more important work. I'd be a fool to send her away.'

'The decision is yours, but don't get distracted, son. We've never believed your assurance that you have a safe desk job – that isn't your way.' She took the cabbage from his hands. 'So, you be wise and careful, because when this war is over we would like both of our sons to come home.'

'We'll do our best.'

'Remember you are an officer and she is a Wren assigned to you. Keep it that way, at least for the duration of the war. After that you can go back to being a lawyer and help as many people as you like.'

David smiled then. His mother was always full of good advice he didn't often agree with, but she was right about one thing, he must step back and let Kathy sort things out for herself. He'd be watching carefully, though.

She squeezed her son's arm, and then walked back to the house, having said all she'd wanted to.

With a thoughtful expression on his face he turned and strode off in the direction Kathy had taken. When he approached a small copse of trees he heard the barking and her laughter first, then she appeared running and laughing with the dogs. He had never seen her like that and knew at that moment that his mother had been wrong. It had been right to bring her here, because at this moment she was happy.

One of the dogs saw him and bounded over, begging him to come and join in the fun, which he did.

They ran all the way back to the house and skidded to a halt by the back door, doubled over and gasping for breath. Even the dogs flopped down, tongues out and sides heaving.

'Oh, that was fun,' Kathy gasped, straightening up and grinning at David's father, who had come out to see what all the commotion was about. 'You have a beautiful place here, Mr Evans. How wonderful to have all this space around you. Perhaps I'll buy a home in the country for me and Dad when the war is over.'

'I'm sure he'd like that,' he replied. 'You two look as if you could do with a drink.'

'All of us could.' David motioned to the dogs and they jumped to their feet to follow them into the kitchen.

The phone remained silent, much to everyone's relief, and they were all still there on New Year's Eve.

Kathy put on her skirt and blouse and draped the silk scarf David had given her around her shoulders. When she came downstairs he nodded approval to see she was wearing his gift. It was lovely to find that Ted had made it to the party as well, and his two friends were clearly pleased to see him. Where he had been was not mentioned, but that was not unusual when there was such a need for secrecy. *Need to know* was the phrase always used, and if that didn't include you, then there was no way you would be told.

The house was full of friends and neighbours, and regardless of the grave situation, everyone was determined to welcome in 1942 with a smile.

* * *

The plotters were tracking a convoy, and David studied it carefully, knowing his brother was out there. The relaxing few days seemed a long time ago now, although it was only the middle of February.

The admiral was listening on the telephone and looking grim. He put the phone down and called for attention. 'I have some grave news. Singapore has fallen to the Japanese.'

This news was greeted with mostly silence, except for one soft murmur of 'Oh hell!'

Suddenly movement on the table caught David's attention. 'What's happening?' he demanded.

'Information is coming through that they are under attack. Two merchant ships and an escort have been sunk.'

'Which escort?'

'We don't know yet, sir,' one of the plotters told him.

'Are they close enough for air support?'

'Just about.' The base commander, Peter Douglas, reached for the phone.

The conversation was brief, and David heaved a silent, deep breath when told that planes were being scrambled to help them.

It was two hours before they began to receive details and Peter came over to him. 'The name of the Wren working with you is Hammond, and I understand her father is a captain, is that right?'

David nodded, feeling a sense of unease at this question. 'Jack Hammond.'

'It is his ship that has been sunk. We haven't details

of survivors yet, but would you like me to go and break the news to her?'

'No, I'll do it.' He left the room dreading what he had to do, but it was his place to tell her. How much more heartbreak was she going to have to endure, and how would she handle this?

Kathy was busy typing when he walked in, and she looked up and smiled. 'Would you like me to get you something to eat? You've been a long time and I don't suppose you have bothered with food.'

'I couldn't eat.' He perched on the edge of her desk. 'I have something to tell you.'

She looked concerned then. 'Bad news?'

There wasn't any easy way to do this, so he told her bluntly. 'I'm so sorry, but your father's ship has been torpedoed and she's sunk. We don't have news of any survivors yet.'

He watched the colour drain from her face, but she didn't move or make any sound of distress. His instinct was to reach out and comfort her, but he knew it would be the wrong thing to do – she had wrapped herself in a shell of protection.

'There are plenty of other ships nearby and he could have survived,' was all he could think of to say.

'The captain is always the last to leave the ship – and the water is so cold this time of year.'

Her words were so softly spoken he could hardly hear them, and for the first time in his life he didn't know how to handle this crisis. Tea. His mother was a great believer in the soothing properties of a good strong cup of tea, so he began to make a pot for both of them.

When he'd poured two mugs, he stooped down in front of her. 'Drink that and tell me what I can do to help you through this.'

She picked up the mug with shaking hands and sipped the tea, then she looked straight at him and the pain in her eyes tore at him.

'Can you take me to ops? I want to be there as the news comes in.'

He nodded. 'Drink your tea first.'

When Kathy had obediently drained the cup, David walked with her along the passage. 'It will be up to the admiral whether you are allowed to stay or not.'

'Understood.'

'Wait by the door while I talk to him,' he told her once they were inside the room. Then he went to use all of his skill to get permission for Kathy to remain in the room.

'I'm not sure that is a good idea. The last thing we need is the distraction of a grieving woman.'

'You won't even know she's here.'

The admiral studied the silent girl for some moments, and then nodded. 'Very well, but give her something to do. We have a long night ahead of us, so tell her to keep us supplied with refreshments.'

When David told Kathy she nodded agreement, and without a word set about her task.

The hours passed and as dawn approached they still

did not have clear details of survivors, and David's hope that Jack Hammond had survived began to fade. The same worry was going on everywhere, as he knew only too well with his own brother out there, but she had already lost so much. If her father was dead, then he didn't know what would happen to her.

Kathy was busy handing round another tray of refreshments, relieved to have been given something to occupy her, when the commander called her. 'Sir?' she answered.

'It may be some time before we receive news, so you might as well get some sleep. We will send someone when there is anything definite.'

'With your permission I'll stay, sir. I'm not tired.'

'As you wish.' He turned to David and shook his head. 'She's as white as a sheet and can hardly stand upright. What's holding her together?'

'Anger,' David told him. 'She's keeping grief at bay by replacing it with anger. If a U-boat captain came in here now I wouldn't rate his chances of survival.'

'Really? How do you know that?'

'I've seen it erupt and been on the receiving end of her fury, which is a great shame because she is really a very gentle person. It was how she dealt with the previous disaster she had to face, and she will do the same now.'

'This bloody war is changing everyone, and none of us are going to be the same by the time it's over.'

'That's true.'

Peter Douglas sighed wearily. 'Can you at least get her to sit down?'

'I'll try.' David went over and guided Kathy to a chair. 'You've done enough, so rest now.'

She was just about to sit down when one of the operators called out, making everyone turn expectantly in her direction.

'Sir! News is coming through.'

Kathy went to move forward, but David caught her arm and shook his head. He could feel her trembling, so he stayed by her side. If the news was bad, then she was going to need someone with her.

The wireless operator was writing quickly, and they all waited anxiously. When he removed the headphones and handed the list to the admiral, everyone moved closer to hear what he had to say.

'We now have a partial list of casualties, and unfortunately, with the loss of three ships the final tally will possibly be long.' He looked straight at Kathy. 'Leading Wren Hammond, your father and most of his crew have survived. That is all the information I have on them at the moment.'

For a moment she bowed her head as the news sunk in, and then looked up. 'Thank you, sir.' Without another word she turned and left the room.

David glanced quickly at Peter, and when he indicated he could leave, he moved hurriedly to catch her up. 'I'll take you to the Wrennery.' It was only then he saw the tears of relief on her face and as she swayed a little he took hold of her arm. 'I'll find out where and when he docks and take you to him.'

'Thank you.' Her voice was husky with emotion. 'Could you also find out if he is injured?'

'Of course. Try to get some sleep and I'll come for you the moment we have more details.'

They were outside by now and without speaking she climbed onto the back of the bike and settled behind him.

When they reached the Wrennery he watched her walk in, wishing he could stay with her, but he knew she wouldn't allow that. She would deal with this crisis in the same way she had for the other one – on her own. That girl had courage. His admiration for her increased.

Chapter Fifteen

It was only when Kathy crawled into her bunk that she allowed the exhaustion to finally take over. Waiting for news had been a nightmare, and it was a blessing she'd had something to do. There hadn't been any details about her father's condition, but the news that he had survived was enough for now. Tomorrow they would have a fuller picture, and she would be there to meet him when they docked.

Her gratitude went out to the man she worked for. He had been so good. Commander Douglas hadn't wanted her there, and that was understandable, but David had somehow persuaded him to let her stay. Determined not to let him or herself down in front of the officers, she had managed to hold her emotions in check.

Releasing a ragged sigh, she settled down and willed herself to relax, knowing sleep was essential. 'Thank you, David,' she murmured as she drifted off from sheer emotional exhaustion.

Waking up suddenly, Kathy looked at her watch and tumbled out of bed. She had slept for six hours! Had David come with messages, and if so, why hadn't he woken her?

Washing and dressing hastily she rushed to reception. 'Has Commander Evans sent any messages for me?'

'No,' the girl on duty told her.

'I need to get back there. Is there a ferry due soon?'

'One has just arrived. If you run, you might catch it.'

'Thanks.' Kathy shot out of the door and was relieved to see the ferry with its engine running, so she waved to alert the driver she needed a lift.

He waited. 'You're just in time. I was about to cast off again.'

She jumped in the back, remembering the first time she had been told to catch the ferry, and found out it was road transport. It hadn't taken long, though, to get used to using navy terms for everything, even when on dry land.

There was no sign of David when she reached the office, and as much as she wanted to rush to the operations room, she knew she couldn't do that without permission, so she busied herself with the routine work. Perhaps he had gone to get some rest as well.

An hour later he walked in. 'Ah, you look better. Did you manage to get some sleep?'

'Yes, much to my surprise.' Kathy studied his face and noted the dark circles under his eyes. 'You've been up all night, though, haven't you?'

'Too busy. I have news about your father. He's aboard one of the merchant ships and they will be docking in Liverpool in a few days' time.'

'Oh, thank you, that is a relief. Is he all right?'

'He has been injured, but not seriously, as far as I can discover.'

The worry flooded back. 'You don't have details?'

'Sorry, that's all there is at the moment. When they've docked I will take you to Liverpool, so you can see him.'

'You're busy here. I can go on the train.'

'I'll take you,' David stated firmly. 'One of the escorts is with them and I need to discuss something with the captain. You can then take seven days' leave to spend with your father, and you will have to make your own way back.'

'Thank you. I'll be grateful for the lift.' She gave a slight smile. 'If we are going on that bike of yours, it will be a quick journey.'

'How else would we travel?' He stifled a yawn.

'Why don't you snatch some sleep? I'll take care of everything here.'

'I'll use one of the bunks here. Send someone for me if I'm needed.'

She watched him leave and gave a sad sigh. Men like him were working themselves to a standstill in an effort to gain the upper hand over the U-boats, and she had seen how every loss tore at them. They would do it, though – they had to, and that was a heavy responsibility to carry.

Three days later she was on the back of the bike as they sped towards Liverpool. Spring was still a way off and it was bitterly cold, but that didn't worry her. The way David drove meant they would get there much faster than going by train, which would probably be just as cold and very crowded. They stopped once to have something to eat and get petrol.

'Do you have enough petrol coupons to get to Liverpool and back?' she asked.

He replaced the petrol cap and nodded. 'This bike is more economical than a car, and as I have to get around on navy business I am allocated what I need. Hop on, I want to get there before the ships dock.'

Kathy was cold and stiff by the time they reached the docks and jumped up and down to get the circulation going again. Looking at the scene before her she was only too aware that she wouldn't be allowed here without David's influence.

The dock was frantically busy with ships being unloaded, and others waiting to come in. 'My word,' she said in wonder as she watched the dockworkers go about their task, 'I've never seen anything like this.'

'The convoy was huge, and some ships have gone to other ports as well. It's good to see so many have made it this time. Sadly, that isn't always the case.'

'Do you know which one my father is on?'

'Yes, let's find it.' He showed his pass and they were allowed on to the dock. 'Do you know if the *Dorian* has docked yet?' he asked the guard.

The man consulted a list. 'She's just come in, sir. You'll find her way down the dock. The sergeant here will show you the way.'

'Thank you.'

They followed the man for quite a way until he pointed to a merchant ship just tying up. 'That's her, sir.'

Kathy was immediately alarmed. There were ambulances lined up waiting for casualties. The moment the gangplank was in place the medical staff boarded the ship carrying stretchers. She could hardly breathe.

Her whole attention was on the ship as the injured were brought out. 'I can't see their faces,' she whispered, 'we're too far away.'

A slight touch on her arm moved her forward until they had a clearer view. David never said a word, but she could feel him standing close and giving support.

One by one the ambulances were driven away, and when the last one left she was frantic. 'I didn't see him. You did say he had survived, didn't you? Perhaps he's on another ship. Where is he?'

Sensing her fear, David gripped her arm to steady her. 'Look at the sailors waiting to disembark and the man by the rail at the top of the ramp.' He handed her the binoculars he had been using.

After focusing them she scanned the men and stifled a

cry of relief. 'He's walking! Oh, he's being supported by another officer.'

More ambulances began to arrive, and Kathy watched as the walking wounded were helped into them. Her father was among the last to disembark, and she wanted to rush up and see how he was, but David still had hold of her arm.

'You can see him at the hospital,' he told her gently. 'We mustn't interfere or get in the way.'

'No, of course not.' She handed back the binoculars. 'Thank you very much for doing this for me, and I am grateful to have had you by my side.' Taking a deep breath, she smiled at him. 'I know I once told you to mind your own business, but it was comforting not to be alone this time.'

'There's no shame in turning to someone for help and support in a crisis, and I am pleased you are beginning to see that. We have to help each other.' He smiled down at her and released her arm. 'I'm glad your father has returned safely. The guard at the gate will know where they have been taken.'

They were walking along the dock when she looked out to sea. 'There's a destroyer coming in. Is that the one you want to see?'

'That's her. Hell, she's badly damaged. I was told it was only slight.'

Ambulances were arriving at the dock again, and she fought away the tears that threatened to spill over. Being here and seeing all this made her even more aware of the struggle going on, and its high cost. 'They've got casualties as well. Oh, David, we must put an end to this barbaric war.'

'We will, never doubt that, but it isn't going to be quick or easy, and everyone knows that. I have high hopes, though, that the tide will soon turn for us at sea. It is absolutely vital that it does.' Seeing the concern on her face, he frowned. 'Perhaps I shouldn't have brought you here to see all this.'

'Yes, you should,' she told him firmly. 'I am shocked, of course, but I can handle it.'

He studied her face intently for a few moments, and then nodded as if satisfied that he hadn't done the wrong thing.

They stood there as the battered ship eased into the dock. 'If you want to go aboard her now, I can find out where my father has been taken and go there at once. I'll be all right.'

'I know you will. Take seven days' compassionate leave and then I'll see you back in Dover.'

'Yes, and thank you again, sir.' She saluted smartly for appearance's sake and made her way to the gate. Their working relationship had become quite relaxed and informal, but when outside the office she still gave him the respect and recognition due to an officer.

The guard on the gate gave her directions to the hospital, and Kathy went there straight away, eager to find out how her father was. When she arrived, it wasn't easy to find him because the place was crowded and everyone was busy dealing with the influx of casualties.

It was impossible to get near the front desk, so she didn't try, and started searching the corridors to see where the casualties were being taken.

'Excuse me.' She stepped in front of a nurse who was clearly in a hurry. 'Can you tell me where Captain Hammond is, please?'

'Ask at the front desk.' The nurse stepped around her and was gone.

Having no choice, Kathy returned to the front desk and to her relief found the crowd had cleared a lot. There wasn't much help there, though, because not all the casualties had been allocated wards or even listed yet. 'How do I find him?' she asked. 'He's my father.'

'Oh, in that case I suggest you walk round the hospital and see if you can spot him, but please keep out of everyone's way. I believe they are taking the wounded up to the top two floors, so try there first.'

'Won't I be stopped if I go looking in the wards?'

'You might get away with it as you are in uniform.'

That proved to be true, and Kathy was able to search the wards without challenge. There were beds everywhere as the staff struggled to cope with the large amount of casualties. She was about to give up until the chaos had been dealt with and some sort of order was in place, when she saw him. He was in a ward on the top floor and her heart lurched when she saw him. He was propped up in bed with his head resting back and his eyes closed. There was a bandage around his head and a cradle over his legs to keep any pressure off them. He had walked off that ship with help, but she guessed it hadn't been an easy thing for him to do.

Walking quietly over to his bed she took hold of his hand. 'Dad?'

His eyes opened, and he smiled when he saw her. 'Hello, my dear. How did you get here so quickly?'

'David found out where you would be docking and brought me here on the bike.'

'That was good of him, and it's a lovely surprise. Can you stay a while?'

'He said I can have seven days.'

'Good, I'll be out of here in a day or so.'

She wasn't sure about that but said nothing and nodded in agreement.

A ward sister bustled up. 'Only close relatives are allowed.'

'This is my daughter, Sister, and I'd like her to stay.'

'Very well, but only for another half-hour.' She smiled at Kathy then. 'You can come back tomorrow, but your father needs rest now.'

'I understand and thank you for allowing me a little longer.'

When the sister left them, he took hold of her hand. 'We must buy a house somewhere, darling. Both of us need a home again – a base to call our own.'

'That would be lovely. I have been saving the money from you and it might be enough for a deposit.'

Her father frowned. 'I sent you money so you could spend it on yourself. You were left with only the clothes you stood up in after that raid. Haven't you bought yourself anything?'

'I'm in uniform all the time and don't need anything. I considered having a home again was more important, so I've been saving as much as I could.'

'You didn't need to deny yourself some pretty clothes, my darling. I can afford to buy us a house.'

'In that case we can use the money I have to furnish it.' She smiled happily. 'Where do you want to live?'

'I fancy a small village somewhere in Hampshire, within a reasonable distance from Portsmouth. Will you mind if we leave London?'

'Not at all. I would be relieved after what happened, and I had already decided that it would be nice to live in the country.'

'Splendid. That's settled, then, and as soon as I'm out of here we will start hunting for somewhere pleasant.' He squeezed her hand. 'Now you had better go, or the sister will be after you again.'

Kathy stood up and bent over to kiss his cheek. 'Sleep well.'

'Don't look so worried,' he told her. 'My injuries are not serious, and I expect to be up and out of here in a day or so.'

After leaving the hospital, Kathy found a cheap bed and breakfast place and booked in for a couple of nights. She knew her father's determination, and if he said he would soon be out of hospital, then they would have a job to keep him there.

The next day she was concerned to see his bed empty. 'Sister, where is my father?'

'He's visiting his men. They are all here and we couldn't keep him in bed.'

'Could you tell me exactly what injuries he sustained?' she asked. 'He just dismissed them as minor and nothing to be concerned about.'

'He has a gash on his head and one leg. We had to keep an eye on him because he had been unconscious when some of his crew got him out of the water and onto the merchant ship.'

'Oh, bless them,' Kathy murmured.

'Indeed. They undoubtedly saved his life. His leg isn't broken and the medic on the ship stitched the wound, but he had lost a lot of blood. He is a strong man, though, and will heal quickly.'

'Thank you, Sister, that's a relief to know. May I go and find him?'

'Of course. He'll be in one of the wards along the corridor.'

It didn't take Kathy long to find her father. Not only was he up and walking with a cane, he was also in uniform. The hospital laundry had obviously cleaned, repaired and pressed it overnight.

When she entered the ward, he turned and smiled at her. 'Gentlemen, I would like you to meet my daughter, Katherine.'

She spent the next hour doing the rounds with her father. He insisted on seeing and talking to each one of his men, although she could sense that it was hard for him, but like any seasoned captain he never once showed a hint of tiredness or distress.

They finally got back to the ward and he eased himself into the chair beside the bed and sighed. She knew he was feeling the loss of every one of his crew who hadn't made it, and for those badly injured.

'The majority of them survived,' she told him gently.

'And I'm grateful for every one that did.' When he looked up, pain flashed through his eyes. 'But the ones that died will always be with me.'

'Yes, I expect they will, just as the people who were in that shelter are always with me. Bill Jackson gave me some advice and I have tried to remember that. He told me not to look back – focus on what has to be done to win this war.'

'That's sound advice and Bill knows what he's talking about, but it isn't easy.'

'No, it isn't, and I hope that one day my anger will fade, but only time will tell.'

'That is very true. They do say that time is a healer.' He smiled at her. 'So we will try to look forward to a peaceful and happy future in a place we can call home. I'll be out of here tomorrow.'

'Are you sure?'

'Positive.'

Chapter Sixteen

'This looks promising.' Jack leant on the cane and gazed at the surrounding area, then smiled at his daughter. 'What do you think, is this far enough into the country for you?'

'Definitely. It's a pretty village, there are green fields and trees all around, and it's only ten miles from Portsmouth. I'd say it was just what we are looking for.'

'I agree, so let's see what it's like inside.'

They waited while the agent unlocked the door and followed him in. It was a two-bedroom cottage, but surprisingly spacious inside.

'The place has been empty for some time, sir,' the man told Jack, 'but it's a sound property and ready for immediate occupation.'

'Do you think this would suit us?' he asked his daughter, who was gazing out at the back garden.

'It feels homely, and just look at that view, Dad.'

Standing beside her, he rested his arm around her shoulder. 'I've been desperately worried about you,' he admitted, 'and I want to give you a home we can both come to when on leave. With me at sea most of the time you need something in your life to give you a sense of stability, and a place you can call your own would help, I'm sure.'

She reached up to grasp his hand, knowing just what was on his mind. He had been lucky this time, but from what she had seen at the docks only a fool would think the sea was a safe place to be. Pushing the fear aside, she smiled up at him. 'You mustn't worry about me, but I do agree with what you've said. I have felt rather like a ship without an anchor. It would give me a sense of belonging again to have a place of our own, and I do admit that it has been hard not to have a home to come back to. This is lovely, but can we afford it?'

He kissed the top of her head and winked. 'I'll have a word with the agent while you go and explore the garden. It looks as if there are a couple of fruit trees over to the left.'

'If there are, they should be coming into bloom over the next few weeks. I'll go and check.'

The negotiations didn't take long, and Jack walked out to join his daughter in the garden. 'All done,' he told her. 'This charming little property is now ours.'

'That's wonderful! How soon can we move in?' she asked excitedly.

'I told the agent that I will be returning to sea soon and that you only have another four days' leave, so we would like everything settled very quickly. He assured me there won't be any delay because the owners are eager to sell. He also told me there's a good pub in the village with rooms, and if we stay there tonight he will get their permission to give us the keys tomorrow.'

'That would be marvellous!'

For the next few days Kathy scrubbed every inch of their new home and joked about the amount of scrubbing she had done during training. They went shopping for carpets and curtains and bought furniture from second-hand shops and anywhere else they could find what they wanted.

By the end of her leave they had a comfortable home they could relax in on the rare occasions they were there.

Jack was pleased to see the change in his daughter. She was laughing and joking, so like the girl he had always known. It was a relief to see her so happy and enthusiastic, and he knew he had done the right thing – for both of them. They were both carrying burdens of horror and grief – nightmares that would be with them for a long time.

'I wish I could stay longer,' she said on the night before her return to Dover.

'I know, darling, but we have accomplished a lot in a few days, and I now have a comfortable home to enjoy until I am passed fit to return to sea.'

'Do you know how long that will be?'

'I'm seeing the medical officer in a few days.'

'He might not pass you as fit enough to return to active duty,' she pointed out, secretly hoping they would keep him onshore for a while.

'I will be by then.'

'You mean you won't show you are in any discomfort.'

'I have to get back to sea. You understand that, don't you?'

'I know exactly how you feel.' Her smile was a little forced. 'You be more careful this time.'

'Don't worry, the boffins are working hard, and we will soon gain the upper hand now.'

'That's what David keeps telling me, but although I work for him I really don't know exactly what he does. Anything of a secret nature he deals with himself.'

Jack laughed. 'Oh, he's up to all sorts of skulduggery.'

'I don't doubt that. He has the habit of disappearing for days sometimes, leaving me to deal with the continually ringing telephone and the routine work.'

'That's important too,' he pointed out.

'I know, and I'm not complaining. I've accepted my role now.'

'We all have to do what we can, and you are a very good secretary.'

'Good? I'm the best,' she declared, pretending to be offended, making them both laugh.

* * *

After Kathy had left the next day, Jack pottered around the garden, and then walked to the local pub to see if he could get a meal there.

'Good day, sir.' The owner greeted him with a huge smile. 'You've just moved in to number 28, I believe. What can we do for you?'

'I was looking for lunch and a pint of beer.' He held out his hand. 'I'm Jack.'

'Pleased to meet you, Jack. My name is Stan, and we can certainly get you a meal.'

'Much appreciated. My daughter has gone back now, and I don't feel like cooking for myself.'

'We've seen you around and you're both navy.' Stan glanced at the cane Jack was leaning on but said nothing. 'Take a seat and I'll bring your drink over to you.'

The woman who served him was in her early thirties, he guessed. She had dark-blonde hair, blue eyes and a trim figure. She greeted him with a ready smile. 'It's only vegetable pie, sir, but Stan's wife is a good cook and you'll find it filling and tasty.'

'It looks and smells delicious. Thank you.'

She smiled and introduced herself as Pat.

While he was eating, several customers came in and they all smiled at him, making him feel welcome. He finished his meal and took his half-finished pint with him up to the bar where he spent time chatting to the locals, including the owner and Pat, who joined them when she had finished serving customers. This was a pleasant place and he knew he would spend time here whenever he was on leave. Pat was a charming woman and he enjoyed talking with her. He missed his wife and female company when he was on shore leave. It was a shame Kathy had had to return to duty so soon, but he would bring her here next time they were together.

As he walked back to the house he thought, with sadness, about the circumstances that had given him this unexpected shore leave, but it had been put to good use. When he did return to sea this time he would know that whatever happened, his daughter now had a home. At least that worry was off his mind, now all he had to do was convince them that he was fit enough to return to sea and take command of another ship.

There wasn't a sign of David when Kathy reported back – as usual. When he walked in two days later, she was pleased to see him. At least he didn't look worn out this time.

'How is your father?' he asked as he settled at his desk and began to read the messages.

'Recovering well, but anxious to get back to sea. The phone has been ringing constantly and some of those messages are urgent. A Commander Saunders demanded to know where you were, and I don't think he believed me when I told him I didn't know. Couldn't you tell me when you are going to disappear and where you can be contacted in an emergency?'

'No.'

Silly question, she admitted to herself.

He closed the folder and held it out to her. 'Deal with those in the usual way.'

A quick glance told her he hadn't written on any of the messages. 'What do I tell them?'

'Anything you like. I'm sure you can be inventive enough to stop them troubling me.'

'I was used to doing that in my job before the war, but this is different. They are officers and I could be in trouble if they discover I am being economical with the truth.'

David laughed softly. 'Lying, you mean. If that happens, you tell them that you were following my orders.'

'Then you could be in trouble,' Kathy pointed out.

'No, I won't.'

'How can you be so sure?'

'Because they know that the intelligence section has its own way of working. Information is vital, and we go anywhere, at any time in an effort to track down something that could be useful. Many times, we get nothing of note, but occasionally we are successful.'

'From your expression I would guess that this time you were successful.'

He shrugged. 'It's promising, but only time will tell. What did you and your father do?' he asked, changing the subject.

'We bought a cottage in a country village about ten miles from Portsmouth. My father is still there.' She smiled happily at the thought. 'We managed to make it comfortable and homely, but it was a rush. I'll be able to make it nicer when I have the time, but it will do for now.'

'That's terrific. You and your father have a home base again.'

'Yes, and it's a good feeling.' David seemed genuinely happy for them and that pleased her. 'Are you hungry?'

'Always.' He stood up. 'We'll go out to eat to celebrate your new home, and your father's speedy recovery. We'll go in a car for a change. Come on, let's play truant.'

'That's something you frequently do,' Kathy teased. 'I'd say you are an expert at it.'

He winked at her as they made their way along the tunnel. 'I'm an expert at many things.'

The weeks passed, and Kathy settled quite happily into the routine of dealing with David's unconventional way of working.

He had been missing for two days again, when the door burst open and he erupted into the office.

'They've done it!' He caught hold of her and lifted her off her feet, swinging her round and round.

'Who has done what?' she asked breathlessly.

He placed her back on the ground and whispered in her ear, 'They've broken the new German naval code, and we will be able to read their communications again. We haven't been able to do that for a while, but now we can direct our convoys away from the wolf packs.'

'That's wonderful!' Kathy caught his excitement. 'Does that mean our ships will be safer now?'

'The danger will still be there, of course, but it should

help to cut our losses. This could help to turn the battle of the Atlantic in our favour. Have we got any whisky in this place?'

Kicking the cabinet to open it, she removed a small bottle. Holding it up, she asked, 'Will this do?'

'It certainly will. Where did you get it?'

'I told the supply officer that I needed it for medicinal purposes when you returned from one of your trips.'

David laughed. 'Did you get glasses from him as well?'

'Of course.' She produced one out of the drawer and began pouring him a shot of whisky.

'You must have one. I don't like to drink alone.'

'Oh no. The last time I drank strong spirit it had a strange effect on me. In Gibraltar – remember?'

'I do.' He reached into the drawer for another glass, poured a very small amount in it and drowned it with water, then handed it to her. 'It's a crime to do that to it, but you might find it more palatable.'

'Thanks.' She took it from him and they clinked glasses, before drinking to celebrate the good news.

'This doesn't go beyond these walls, Kathy.'

'I know that, but thank you for telling me. Will my father and the other captains be told?'

'Those hunting the subs will know, of course, but it will be a closely guarded secret. The enemy must not know we have done this.'

'I know that's absolutely vital, so the fewer people who know, the safer it will be.'

'Exactly. The next few months will show what

difference this knowledge makes. The Atlantic could soon become a very uncomfortable place for the U-boats.'

'Let's hope so. Those merchant ships have had a bad time, haven't they, and not forgetting the naval losses as well.'

David poured himself another small drink. 'I think Hitler believed he could destroy our air defences, bomb and starve us, and then just storm his way in here, but that didn't work. He underestimated us.'

Kathy nodded. 'We were alone, and I expect he thought it would be easy to defeat us, but we are not alone any more, are we?'

'No, we are not, and he has made too many mistakes. That was a huge blunder when he invaded Russia.'

'We're going to come through this, aren't we, David?' she asked.

'Never doubt that, and I do believe things are now turning in our favour.'

'I feel like that as well.'

'Put the rest of that whisky back for another time. We are going to be busy over the next few months. Is that bike of yours in good working order?'

'It is. I took it out for a run yesterday.'

'Good, I will probably need you to run errands for me. I won't be able to be everywhere myself.'

Over the next few months, Kathy was out on the road visiting various listening stations and delivering messages to London and other places.

On returning from one trip with an urgent message for David, she found him in ops. When she walked in it seemed as if everyone there was smiling. She went straight up to David and saluted smartly. 'I have an urgent message for you, sir.'

He took it from her, read it and then tucked it into his pocket.

'Was there anything else, sir?'

'Come and look at this.' He led her over to the large board on the wall listing all the ships in a huge convoy.

Kathy studied it for a while and then gave him a questioning look.

'Every one of those ships got through.'

'No losses?'

'Not one.'

'That's absolutely wonderful.' Her smile was as wide as all the others in the room. She knew what a relief this was to everyone, so she moved closer to him and whispered, 'I've managed to get another bottle of whisky.'

'Excellent. I'll see you back in the office. I'm expecting a visitor so rustle up another glass.'

Still smiling, she left the room.

It was another hour before he returned to the office, and when she saw the man with him she leapt to her feet. 'Captain Jackson! How lovely to see you again.'

'It's lovely to see you looking so well.' He kissed her cheek. 'Your father told me you have bought a cottage in the country.'

'Yes, we wanted to have a home again.'

'So you should. And the name is Bill – remember? Now, where's that whisky you promised me, David?'

'Kathy's in charge of that.'

She kicked the cabinet and the drawers shot open, then she took out the glasses and bottle.

They sat around talking and laughing for an hour, and she couldn't remember when she had been so happy.

When their little party broke up and she was in her bunk at the Wrennery she fell asleep the moment her head touched the pillow. The dreams that night were peaceful.

Chapter Seventeen

1942 had flown by and David's parents had invited her to join them for Christmas again, but she had politely refused. With ten days' leave due to her she wanted to spend it at the cottage. They had been so busy she had only been able to make fleeting visits to their new home, and there was a lot she wanted to do to it before her father came home again.

On Christmas Eve she decided to visit the pub and get to know some of the locals. Her father had told her in his letters how friendly everyone was, and although she never went in a pub on her own, she decided to make an exception this time.

When Kathy walked into the crowded pub all eyes turned towards her, and then she was surrounded by smiling people.

Stan, the owner, came straight up to her. 'Welcome. You must be Captain Hammond's daughter. We heard you had arrived in the village. Is your father here as well?'

'No, but I thought this might be a good time to come and meet everyone.'

'So glad you did.' Stan went back behind the bar. 'What would you like? The first drink is on the house.'

After a while a woman called Pat brought over another drink and sat down with her. 'I met your father when he was here. He's a charming man and you must be proud of him.'

'Yes, I am, and he told me all about his visits here. He was right, everyone is very friendly. Is your husband here?' she asked, noting the wedding ring.

Pat shook her head sadly. 'No, he was a pilot and was killed some time ago.'

'Oh, I'm so sorry. I shouldn't have asked.'

'Not at all, Kathy. I may call you Kathy?'

'Of course.'

More people joined them, and the evening went very pleasantly. Walking back to the cottage, Kathy was pleased she had gone to the pub and met some of the locals. They had insisted that she join them for a New Year's Eve party, and she would certainly do that. She could tell her father and he would be pleased she was making herself at home here.

By the time she returned to Dover the house was comfortable and more to her liking. Her father would enjoy his time onshore there.

She had a feeling of optimism about 1943, but this was dented somewhat when London was bombed again in the middle of January. However, the U-boats were not having it all their own way now, although the sea was still a dangerous place to be.

David had rarely been in the office since her return, but Kathy was used to that now, and able to take care of anything that came up.

Early one morning the office door opened, and a sailor looked in. 'You're to come with me, please, and you are to bring plenty of your shorthand notebooks. I've been told it's urgent.'

She was on her feet at once, quickly filling her bag with the necessary items. 'Where are we going?'

'I am to drive you to London.' He was almost running along the tunnel.

'Can you tell me what has happened?' She was quite alarmed by now. 'Is Commander Evans all right?'

'As far as I know. He's the one who sent for you.'

That was a relief. She was beginning to fear he had had an accident – or something.

The car sped along, and it seemed no time at all before they were pulling up by a building on the docks. Sitting magnificently in the dock was a destroyer, but being anxious to find out what this was all about, she didn't stop to admire it. Instantly she could see that the building in front of her was well guarded.

'Something interesting going on here,' the driver remarked as he held the door open for her.

Kathy hurried in, wondering what on earth she was going to find inside.

A military MP greeted her. 'Leading Wren Hammond?'

'Yes.' She showed her identification and after studying it he nodded. 'This way, please.'

They walked along a corridor and he unlocked a heavy door, holding it open for her. As soon as she walked in the door clanged shut and she heard the lock turning. She found herself in a large room and it was full of sailors. Then she went cold – German sailors!

Another guard escorted her to a smaller room containing only a table, four chairs and a sink in the corner with all the necessary items for making tea. That was always a requisite wherever they went. This country was keeping going on cups of tea.

David turned from gazing out of the window to face her. 'Good, you got here quickly.'

She saluted smartly. 'What is happening, sir?'

'I need you to take down every word while I interrogate the prisoners. They are a U-boat crew captured by the destroyer in the dock. I'm starting with crew members first, the officers last.' He gave a wry smile. 'It's going to take some time.'

'Understand, sir. One question, though, before we start. Do they speak English?'

'Some do, and if not, I will translate for you. Bring the first one in,' he told the MP standing just inside the door.

They sat on one side of the table and she got her notepad and pencils ready, praying she was going to be able to keep the anger at bay. She was well aware that it was still simmering under the surface.

The young boy who was brought in was clearly distraught, and the moment he saw the naval officer there he stood to attention. David said something to him and he sat down.

They were about to start when David was called away and Kathy was left with the young sailor and a guard by the door. Concerned by the obvious distress of the boy, she quickly made a pot of strong tea and put a mug in front of him.

'Drink that,' she told him. 'It will make you feel better.'

He looked at her with terrified eyes and when she pointed to the mug again he picked it up. His hands were shaking as he gulped the hot liquid, never taking his eyes off her.

She knew he didn't understand her, but she talked anyway, hoping a smile and a soft voice would help to calm him. 'It's all right. Nothing bad is going to happen to you here.'

When he drained the mug he cautiously reached across the table and touched her notebook and pencil, his eyes pleading.

'Do you speak any English?'

'Little.'

'What are you asking me for?'

'Brother!' His eyes filled with tears. 'Not here.'

Grasping what he meant she asked, 'Your brother was on the ship as well?'

'Not here. Brother.'

She pushed the notebook towards him. 'Write his name.' When he looked puzzled she mimed writing and said, 'Brother – name.'

He did this and pushed it towards her, his eyes now holding a glimmer of hope in them.

Desperately sorry for this young boy – for that was all he was – she gave him another mug of tea and two biscuits, then picked up the pad and said slowly, 'I will see if I can find your brother.'

The first person she saw when she left the room was Ted. 'Oh, thank goodness you are here. I need your help. You speak German, don't you?'

He greeted her with a wide smile. 'That's why I'm here.'

'Come with me.' She caught his sleeve and pulled him back to the room she had just left. 'This young sailor is very distressed and has been trying to tell me something. I think he had a brother on the ship with him and he keeps saying "not here".'

Ted sat down and began to talk to the young boy who broke into a torrent of words. 'He's worried about his brother and fears he is dead. He's given you his name.'

'Tell him I will try to find out why he isn't here.'

Ted did so, and the young boy stood up and bowed to her, saying something she didn't understand. 'He thanks you for being such a kind lady.'

If he only knew what unpleasant thoughts she had been battling with since that awful raid, she thought silently. Leaving Ted talking to the boy, Kathy hurried out to track down someone who might know what happened. There was no sign of David – he had disappeared again.

As luck would have it there was a navy captain just walking in, and guessing he was from the destroyer, she went up to him and saluted. 'Sir, I am looking for information about a sailor from the U-boat. This is his name and he is not among the prisoners here.'

The captain looked at the pad. 'You need to see my first officer, he has the full list.'

'Where would I find him, sir?'

'He's somewhere around, probably in the room at the end of this corridor. They've set up a communications room there.'

'Thank you, sir.'

There was a guard on the door who wouldn't let her in. 'I must see the first officer of the destroyer. His captain sent me here.'

'I've been told not to admit anyone, but if you will wait here I'll tell him.'

He disappeared, and Kathy waited impatiently, hoping David didn't reappear and start looking for her. When the guard came out again he had the officer with him and she quickly told him what she needed.

'I can't give out that information to you,' he told her.

'Sir!' she told him sharply, exasperated now. 'I am Senior Intelligence Officer Evans' assistant and have the highest security clearance. Do you think I would be here otherwise? I need this information – now, sir.'

'Ah, that's different.' He gave an apologetic smile, stepped back in the room and immediately came back with a folder. 'What's his name?'

She handed him the pad. 'Gerhard Keller.'

He ran his finger down the list. 'Here he is. He was one of the injured and has been taken to Saint Bart's Hospital.'

'Do you know how badly injured he is?'

'I can't say exactly. We caught them on the surface, and after a fierce exchange of fire they were too damaged to dive so they surrendered. There were some injuries but nothing life-threatening.'

'That is very helpful. Thank you, sir.'

'What's your name?' he asked when she began to walk away.

'Leading Wren Katherine Hammond, sir.'

'Well, Katherine Hammond, I hope you will forgive my earlier rudeness. It's been quite a day.'

'Nothing to forgive, sir. We are all under some stress.'

Ted was no longer there when she returned, and the boy was looking in an even worse state of distress. She sat down and smiled at him, wondering how on earth she was going to communicate with him, when David walked in. She quickly explained the situation and asked him to tell the sailor about his brother.

He began to tell him, and she watched as the boy listened. He was shaking badly and almost in tears. 'Sir,' she said softly to catch David's attention. 'This boy needs medical attention, and he must see his brother. We can't leave him like this, it isn't right.'

'I agree. Wait here with him.'

After he left, Kathy sat beside the boy and took hold of his hands in an effort to calm him down, and although she knew he couldn't understand her, she smiled and talked gently to him. 'Everything is going to be all right. The commander will see to that. No one here is going to hurt you.'

David was back in about fifteen minutes. 'I've spoken to the hospital and he can go there now. There is a car waiting outside with a guard, but I want you to go with him. He trusts you. Once he is with his brother you are to come straight back here. The car will wait for you.'

'Yes, sir. Will you explain that to him, please?'

The boy listened to what he was being told, and turned to Kathy, still trembling badly, but she could see he was trying very hard to control it.

'I couldn't tell him what condition his brother is in,' David explained. 'You will only find that out when you get there because they wouldn't give me any details. I think this boy – Erik is his name – is suffering from a combination of fear and battle fatigue, which has probably been building up for some time.'

'And now he finds himself a prisoner in another country. Poor devil!' Kathy said with feeling.

The young sailor hadn't taken his eyes off her and she smiled at him again, hoping to assure him that everything was going to be all right. 'Come on, Erik, I'll take you to your brother.'

After being told what she had said Erik stood up, a little unsteady on his legs and bowed to David, then they left the room with the guard.

David watched them leave and took a deep breath. For the first time since Kathy had come into his life he felt as if he was seeing the real person behind the walls she had put up to protect herself. Bringing her here had been chancy, because he really didn't know how she would react when finding herself facing an entire U-boat crew, but he needed her skill at shorthand if he was going to have an accurate record of the day. It was unlikely that any of them would say much, of course, but they had to try and gather any snippet of information they could. There was always a chance that it might prove useful at some time.

Ted poked his head through the open door. 'Ah, there you are. When are we going to start the interrogations?'

'Not until Kathy returns from the hospital.'

'In that case, would you like something to eat? We've had food sent in to feed everyone. That crew out there are very hungry.'

'We might as well take a break and eat now, because this is going to take some time. We must get through as quickly as possible and get these men settled in a camp.'

'Transport is already on its way for them. Do you want to talk to every one of them?'

'We must vet them all, because if we find any who might be difficult, then they must be sent to a different camp. I haven't had time yet to get amongst them. In fact, the only one I've seen so far is that young sailor Kathy has whisked off to the hospital.'

'I've been chatting to them and I think I can put your mind at rest on that score. They appear to be an ordinary lot of sailors who have just been carrying out orders.'

'Your judgement is sound, Ted, but we must make sure.'

'Agreed. What about the one Kathy has taken to the hospital – will he be coming back?'

David shook his head. 'No, he should have been taken to the hospital straight away.'

'I must say, knowing her background I was surprised to see her with the young boy. She was even holding his hands trying to comfort him.'

'She saw a boy in great distress, and I believe at that moment his nationality didn't mean a thing to her. I always felt there was a kind, compassionate girl under that anger, and we have just seen it come to the surface. She's healing at last, and I couldn't be more pleased about that.' He smiled at his friend. 'Now, where's that food?'

The hospital was expecting them, and they were immediately shown to a ward on the top floor with guards on duty in the corridor.

A sister swept up to them. 'Ah, this is the young man. The doctor will see him now.'

Erik grabbed Kathy's hand, very agitated. 'Brother?'

'Sister, he needs to see his brother first, if you don't mind?'

'Of course. We've told Gerhard he is coming.'

'Gerhard! Gerhard . . .'

'Yes, young man.' She actually smiled. 'Come with me.'

They followed her to the ward and Erik scanned each bed anxiously until he saw someone waving at him. With a cry of relief, he ran to his brother and held on to him tightly.

'I'll put him in a bed next to his brother,' the sister told Kathy. 'That young man is traumatised.'

'Yes, he is.' She watched Gerhard comforting his young brother and was moved by the scene. This terrible war was causing grief to everyone involved in it, no matter what side they were fighting for. It was hard to understand the sheer stupidity of it all.

Erik rushed over and caught hold of her arm, tugging her towards his brother, telling her something she couldn't understand.

When she reached the bed, Gerhard held out his hand and bowed his head while they shook hands. 'My brother has told me of your kindness, and I thank you for bringing him to me. I have been worrying about him.'

She smiled, pleased he could speak English. 'He needs medical help and Sister has arranged for him to be in a bed next to you. I hope you will both recover quickly.'

'That is gracious of you.'

'Doctor is waiting to examine your brother.' The sister appeared beside them. 'Will you explain to him, please, so we can get him settled? He needs rest.'

Erik listened to his brother and then nodded before turning to Kathy and saying something.

'He is asking if we will see you again,' Gerhard explained. 'He is still very frightened, and he trusts you.'

'Tell him that I will try to come and see you again, and will you also tell him that he doesn't need to be afraid.'

After hearing that, Erik reached for her hand and kissed it gently. It wasn't a kiss of a man flirting with a woman, it was a kiss of sheer gratitude, and at that moment something happened to Kathy. It was as if the clenched fist inside her uncurled and she almost cried out, so great was the feeling. Somehow, she managed to hold on to her control, and she smiled at the boy, grasping his hands for just a moment before releasing them and stepping back.

He began to speak rapidly, and she turned her attention to the brother. He was a good-looking man and clearly the stronger of the two.

'My brother says that he is a prisoner in your country and he is overwhelmed to have found such kindness. He will always keep you in his heart.'

She was touched by such a display of gratitude, and a little embarrassed. She had only done what anyone would have done when finding someone in such distress and needing help. 'I was pleased to be of help,' she said simply, not knowing what else to say.

The sister then ushered him along to see the doctor, and his brother said quietly, 'I would also like to express my gratitude. My brother is an artist and very sensitive. The brutality of war has upset him very much.'

'I can see that, but his war is over for him now. Is he a good artist?'

'He shows great promise.'

'What medium does he work in?'

'Oils are his favourite, but he is always drawing and will use anything to hand.'

'I will see if I can get him some drawing materials. Now I must go. My officer is waiting for me.'

'Of course. It was good of him to allow you to come.'

'He's a good man.'

'Thank him for us.'

'I will.' Kathy hurried out of the ward back to the waiting car, hoping she hadn't spent too much time at the hospital.

'Is everything all right?' David asked when she arrived back.

'Yes, they are going to put Erik next to his brother and that should help to calm him down.' She then gave him the brother's thanks and told him what she had learnt about the young boy. 'The sister said he is traumatised.'

David nodded. 'I expect she sees that a lot. I'm glad you recognised it in him and dealt with it so quickly.'

'I don't know about quickly. It has taken some time and I hope I haven't held you up too long.'

'They shouldn't put brothers in the same submarine. The connection is too close and could cause trouble – as it clearly has in this instance.'

'I can see that,' she agreed. 'You wouldn't want to

be on the same ship as your brother, would you?'

'Good heavens, no. Now, before we get down to work, go and get something to eat. Then we'll work our way quickly through the crew and leave the captain to last.'

Chapter Eighteen

It was a long afternoon and Kathy was on her third notebook by the time they had seen everyone but the captain. Quite a few of them spoke a bit of English and when necessary David or Ted had translated for her. She admired the way they changed from one language to another but guessed they must be feeling the strain by now.

David stood up, stretched and walked over to look out of the window. 'All right, Ted, bring in the captain.'

The man who walked in was about the same age as David, she noted, as he sat opposite her, and he was almost as good-looking. 'It's been a long day so would you like a cup of tea?' she asked.

'No, thank you. I would like to thank you for looking after one of my crew.'

David spun round and stared at the man in disbelief. 'Max! What the hell are you doing in one of those U-boats?'

'Much the same as you pretending to be an intelligence officer – following orders.'

'You've been sinking our bloody ships! How could you do that?'

'I was faced with a choice to become a spy or a submarine commander.'

'You could have chosen spy and then come over to us. We have others who have done that.'

'I could not risk my family and put that shame on them if it had been discovered that I was a traitor to my country. You have met my parents, David.'

'Yes, I spent pleasant term holidays with them.' He sighed, sat down and stared at the man in front of him with a mixture of disbelief and sadness. 'I understand your choice, but the life expectancy in a submarine is not good.'

'That was a risk I was prepared to take.'

'Were you a part of those wretched wolf packs?'

'Ah, I see you haven't forgotten your job, and throw in a pertinent question when your prisoner is relaxed. I won't answer questions on submarine strategy.'

Kathy was so astonished by this turn of events that she forgot to write anything down. They were talking as if they knew each other well, and although the captain's English was excellent there was still a slight trace of a German accent.

'I only have to tell you my name and rank.'

'I already know that!'

The captain sat back, a slight smile on his face. 'So, are you going to torture me for information?'

'Would you like me to?'

'Not particularly.'

'Damn, I was looking forward to that.'

They looked at each other and burst out laughing.

'This is ridiculous,' David declared. 'What a ludicrous situation to find ourselves in.'

Realising she wasn't doing her job, Kathy began to hastily write until a hand came across and stopped her.

'Don't record this. Kathy, Ted, meet Maximilian Fischer. We were friends at Eton and kept in touch until the war started, when all communications had to stop.'

Ted pulled up a chair and sat down. 'You obviously know each other well.'

'We do.' Max grimaced. 'Now we are on opposing sides, and that is a sad state of affairs.'

'Agreed, but the fact is that you are our prisoner and we have to get information out of you if we can.'

'Not a chance. Name and rank are all I need to give you.'

'Don't waste your time, Ted. I know Max very well and if he says he won't give us any information, you can believe it. He's as stubborn as hell.' David ran a hand through his hair and said to his friend, 'Will you tell me one thing? Do you have any crew members who could cause trouble in a camp?'

'No, I made sure of that. I discovered one and managed to get rid of him. I can vouch for the entire crew.'

'I'm pleased to hear that.'

'Now I would like to ask a favour of you, David. I would like to go to the same camp as my crew.'

'You could go to an officers' camp.'

'No, I want to stay with my crew.'

'Very well, I will arrange it.'

'Oh, and one more request.'

'Just a minute, Max, I'm supposed to be the one asking questions, not granting favours.'

'Really? I thought we were two old friends meeting after quite a while.'

'You haven't changed at all, have you?' David grinned. 'All right, what's the other request?'

'I would like to visit my injured crew members to see they are being taken care of.'

'They are receiving the best treatment.' David narrowed his eyes. 'Surely you know us well enough to be sure of that?'

'I do, but some of the crew might not be aware of this. If I could tell them that I have seen our injured friends, it will put their minds at rest.'

Kathy gasped and couldn't keep silent any longer. 'Do they believe they will be mistreated by us? Is that why the young boy was so frightened?'

Max turned his head to look at her. 'No, Erik is suffering from battle fatigue, and I had intended to have him hospitalised once we returned to port. As for what my men believe, during a war many things are said that are not necessarily true. Truth can become an early casualty. I want to make sure my crew understand the situation they are in. There will be concern, because we have been sinking your ships, and they don't know how you will react when faced with a U-boat crew.'

'In that case you do need to talk to them. I'll take you to the hospital tomorrow.'

'Thank you. I ask this for my men.'

'I understand.' David studied his friend carefully. 'We are going to win this war, you know. Your regime thought they could demoralise us into surrendering, but it was never going to happen, Max.'

Max gave a wry smile. 'Living amongst you all those years I knew they were underestimating you. They were sure you would crumble under the assault. I knew it wouldn't be that easy.'

'They made us bloody angry, though, and that was a big mistake. One of many, but now your fighting is over, my friend.'

'Do you still consider me a friend?'

'I do, but that doesn't mean I don't want to sink every blasted U-boat. Ben is out there and so is Kathy's father. We will drive you out of the Atlantic, and that day may not be far away.'

'To use one of your favourite sayings, David – only time will tell. Now, if this interrogation is over I would like to see my crew settled. They need rest.'

'Now he's giving the orders!' David turned to Ted.

'Take him away while we decide what to do with him until tomorrow.'

Max stood up and bowed, then said softly, 'It is good to see you again. I could only wish it were under better circumstances.'

They watched the tall, elegant man leave the room, and then David walked over to the windows and stared out, lost in thought.

Kathy didn't speak, knowing he needed a few quiet moments to clear his mind and come to terms with what had just happened. It must have been a great shock to him. She saw his shoulders heave as he took a deep breath, and when he turned round, he was his usual composed self.

Ted soon returned. 'As it is so late in the day they have taken over a small hotel to put them in for the night. It will be well guarded.'

'Can you find rooms for the three of us, in a different hotel if possible? Our work in London isn't finished yet. We need to talk to the men in the hospital before returning to Dover.'

'No problem, I know just the place. Wait here while I arrange it.'

Kathy was pleased about this, because it meant she could keep her promise and visit the brothers again. 'Do you know where I can buy some art materials?' she asked.

'What do you want those for?' David asked, clearly puzzled.

'The young sailor is an artist and I thought it might help with his recovery if he had something he could draw on.'

'Really? That's interesting. The shops are all closed now, but we'll have a look round in the morning.'

The hotel Ted found them was modest but comfortable and Kathy was glad to finally get to bed. It had been an unusual, emotional and tiring day. She tossed and turned for a while, her mind buzzing with all that had happened. Uppermost in her thoughts, though, was the feeling that had swept through her when the young boy had shown his gratitude by kissing her hand gently. Something had happened to her at that moment and she tried to analyse it. There was a sense of peace where there had only been anger before. It was as if that touch from an enemy had healed her.

She sat up and hugged her knees, deep in thought. Then there had been that bizarre meeting when the U-boat captain turned out to be a friend of David's. He had even spent his holidays with Max's family, so it was no wonder David's German was so good. The meeting had affected him, she knew that, but he was expert at hiding his feelings.

What an extraordinary day! Since that night of the raid the lines of this war had been clear – there were them and us, and they were the enemy. Suddenly the lines were blurred. The regime who started all this suffering was the real enemy, but how could she think of the ordinary people like that young sailor as the enemy? Yet he had been part of a crew who had been sinking their ships.

Sighing deeply, she settled down to try and get some much-needed sleep. It was all too confusing. She'd think about it some other time.

She had overslept! Kathy tumbled out of bed, annoyed with herself. Last night she had spent far too much time thinking when she should have been resting. And what had all that soul-searching achieved? Nothing. She had helped a young sailor who needed someone to look after him. Anyone would have done the same, and that was all there was to it.

It didn't take her long to get ready and she hurried downstairs, stopping suddenly when she saw three men walking in the front door. One of them was causing quite a stir as other people looked in disbelief. It was the U-boat captain, Max.

She saluted smartly to David. 'Sorry if I'm late, sir, I overslept.'

'That's all right. You are just in time for breakfast.'

As they walked to the dining room, she whispered to Ted, 'Shouldn't there be a guard with him?'

'We're his guards.' He grinned. 'Do you doubt our ability to stop him escaping?'

'No, of course not.'

'Don't be concerned. We told the management we would be bringing him here for breakfast.' He handed her a paper bag. 'This is for your young sailor.'

Now that Max was rested, shaved and his uniform spruced up a bit, he was a most impressive man. Not conventionally handsome like David, but there was an air of strength about him that was quite compelling. His manners were impeccable, and Kathy could hardly take her eyes off him, along with just about everyone else in the room, and she had to keep reminding herself that he was a U-boat captain who was now their prisoner.

While they were waiting for their breakfast to be served she glanced in the bag Ted had given her, and gasped. 'Where did you get all this?'

'It was too early for the shops, but David seems to have contacts everywhere.'

David had been talking quietly to Max, and at the mention of his name he turned his attention to her. 'Will that be all right?'

'I'm sure it will, and you've even managed to get some watercolours and brushes. You must let me give you the money for these. How much do I owe you, sir?'

'Nothing.'

'I insist, sir,' she told him firmly. 'I was the one who promised the young boy I would try to get him some drawing materials, so I should pay for them.'

'How much did I pay for those materials, Ted?'

'I don't recall money changing hands. I understood the man owed you a favour.'

He raised his eyebrows and looked at Kathy. 'Does that satisfy you? They were given to me as a gift for the young sailor.'

'That was very kind of whoever did that, sir, and I'm sure Erik will be delighted.' Kathy saw the devilment in his eyes and wondered what kind of a debt he had collected.

Their breakfast arrived then, and she realised she was starving hungry.

As soon as they had finished eating, David stood up. 'Come on, Max, let's go and see the rest of your crew.'

All eyes watched as the unusual and impressive group of officers walked out to the waiting car.

On arrival at the hospital they were shown up to the top-floor ward, and when Max walked in everyone smiled with relief at seeing their captain. They greeted him with respect and enthusiasm, obviously holding him in high regard.

David was allowing him private time with his crew, and while he went from bed to bed, Kathy waited, pad in hand.

'You can put that away,' he informed her. 'We will keep this informal.'

'Yes, sir.' She tucked the pad back in her bag and watched. Those who could get out of bed were now crowded around their captain, bombarding him with questions, including the brothers. Erik had waved and smiled across at her when they had entered, and already looked more rested and less troubled. She was pleased to see that.

Eventually Max came back to them. 'Thank you for allowing me to talk to them, David. Fortunately, there are no serious injuries, and I have assured them that we will all be sent to the same camp in Kent.' He smiled wryly. 'I was also able to tell them that it is a lovely part of the country.'

'We would like to talk to them now, and you will accompany us.'

Max bowed his head, every inch the U-boat captain now. 'Of course, and that will make them feel easier. They will tell you nothing, you know that, don't you?'

'I do, but we have to see each one. Ted and I will not put any pressure on them. You have my word on that.' David glanced at Kathy. 'I think one of the prisoners is eager to see you, so you can go and give him the gift.'

'Thank you, sir.'

Erik was smiling as she walked over to him. He was sitting on his brother's bed and she could hardly believe it was the same boy she had brought here the day before. Gerhard was also much improved and now sitting in a chair. They both shook her hand when she reached them.

'I've brought something for you.' She handed him the bag of art materials.

Erik frowned, but the moment he looked inside he began to speak rapidly with excitement. He tipped the contents of the bag onto the bed, exclaiming with delight as he examined each item.

'My brother is overwhelmed with your kindness,' Gerhard told her, smiling with amusement at Erik's reaction to the gift.

'My officer has an artist friend and he got them from him. Please tell your brother that.'

Erik listened, and his eyes fixed on David, watching him talking to the other crew members in their own language.

'Your captain and Commander Evans went to school together and are good friends,' she explained. 'That's why he speaks your language so well.'

Gerhard nodded. 'Our captain told us, and it is sad they now find themselves on opposing sides.'

Erik stood up, walked over to David, saluted smartly and talked to him for a few moments, then came back, smiling even more. He told his brother something and indicated that Kathy should know.

'He said your officer is very kind, and he can see that the two men are still friends, regardless of the war. That is good, even though the situation must be difficult for both of them.'

'Yes, it is.'

The sister came over and told Kathy she was needed. 'Please excuse me. I will try to come and see you before we leave.'

'I need you to make a record of all the men here and when they will be fit enough to be transferred to the camp. Sister will come round with us and give you the information,' David informed her.

'Yes, sir.' Retrieving the pad from her bag she followed the sister round and recorded the necessary details.

This took time because David talked at some length to

each man again. While they were doing this the captain was with a group of his men, but when Kathy glanced across at Erik he was propped up on the bed, completely lost in sketching something.

The moment she was free she rushed over to say goodbye to the brothers. Erik handed her a drawing and she gasped in pleasure. It was a superb drawing of David. 'This is beautiful,' she exclaimed, and went to hand it back to him, but he shook his head and indicated that she should keep it. Then he shyly showed her another one. It was of her and equally as expertly drawn. This one he didn't let go of.

'Erik said he keeps this one to remind him of the kindness of a beautiful girl to an enemy.'

That brought a lump to her throat. 'Tell him I am pleased he is recovering well, and I will treasure his beautiful drawing.'

They both bowed in respect, and she left the ward with their captain and the two British naval officers.

Chapter Nineteen

'What have you got there?' David asked when they were in the car.

Kathy handed him the drawing and Max leant across to look as well. 'He has caught your likeness well.'

David pursed his lips. 'The boy is good.'

Ted was in the front seat and turned round, took the drawing from David, nodded and then handed it back to him. 'That is superb.'

When David went to put it in his case, she touched his arm. 'That is mine, sir.'

'Why do you want a drawing of me? I was thinking my mother would like this.'

'I expect she would, and perhaps one day I will give it to her, but for now I want to keep it.'

'Why?'

'Because it was given to me with gratitude from an enemy,' she said softly. 'And in the midst of war that is something special. Do you understand what I'm saying?'

'Yes, I do.' He handed the drawing back and smiled. 'We both find ourselves in a strange situation, don't we?'

She nodded agreement. That was certainly true, she thought, and looked at Max who was with them on the back seat. He was staring out of the window and appeared to be lost in thought. It was only then Kathy realised they were heading out of London. 'Where are we going?'

'We are taking Max to the camp in Kent where his men are. I want to see the camp for myself as well.'

The rest of the journey was made in silence as each person in the car had their own thoughts to deal with.

They pulled up at the entrance of the camp and all got out of the car. She studied the wire perimeter fence and felt a surge of sadness for Max and his crew. They would spend the rest of the war here – freedom denied them. The look of dejection on Max's face told her he was well aware of that, and she watched him straighten up as some of the men on the other side came to attention when they saw him.

'Stay here,' David told her.

'I hope we shall meet again under pleasanter circumstances,' Max said to her.

'I hope so too,' Kathy replied, not knowing what else to say. Then she watched him walk to the camp entrance, flanked by David and Ted.

They were gone for almost an hour, and when they returned both men looked grim, especially David, who must have found it painful to see his friend put in the camp for the duration of the war.

Conversation was sparse all the way back to Dover, and she knew that not one of them was going to sleep well for a while.

They received news two days later that the hospital had discharged the injured men, and all were now in the camp with their fellow crew members.

Over the next few weeks Kathy began collecting paper and pencils for Erik, not wanting him to run out of drawing materials. David never mentioned the crew or his friend again. It had clearly disturbed him more than he was willing to say.

Spring turned to summer and on 25th July Mussolini resigned and was arrested. David was preoccupied and had been missing most of the day, so Kathy waited, as she always did, in case he needed anything when he returned.

Late in the evening he walked in and began clearing his desk. 'I'll be away for a while. If anyone asks where I am, tell them I am on leave and cannot be reached.'

'How long will you be away?'

'No idea.' He looked up and smiled. 'But I know I can leave everything in your capable hands.'

'Can I come with you?' she asked, guessing he was off on one of his trips.

'Not this time.' He dumped papers on her desk. 'Destroy those.'

'I'll do it tonight.'

'Thanks.' He picked up his hat and headed for the door, then he stopped and walked back to her, kissing her gently on the cheek, and then he was gone.

She was stunned and very worried. It was as if he had just said goodbye for ever. 'Be safe,' she murmured quietly, 'and come back soon.'

The weeks passed and there was no sign of him. Not even one tiny bit of news had reached her regarding his whereabouts, and the longer that went on, the harder it became to keep hopeful.

Then Commander Peter Douglas called her to his office. 'I am informed that you know Morse.'

'Yes, sir.'

'You are being transferred to the Y station in Winchester, with immediate effect.'

'But why, sir? I am not qualified. I only had a very brief session of instruction. What about my work here?'

'You can complete your training at Winchester. The intelligence office here is being closed.'

It felt as if the floor had dropped away from her. 'Where is Commander Evans, sir?'

Noting her distress his mouth thinned in a grim line. 'We have lost contact with him, and he has been declared missing, presumed dead.'

The pain that shot through her was agonising, and

her thoughts went out to his lovely family. 'What about his parents, sir?'

'They have been informed. I am sorry to have to give you this news. He is my friend as well. You are to report to Winchester tomorrow.'

'Sir.' Turning smartly, Kathy left his office and made her way back along the tunnel, fighting to keep the tears at bay. His family had been informed, but there was another person who must be told, and it had to be done face-to-face, not by letter. However, there was a huge problem to that – would they let her see him?

No one knew yet that she was no longer attached to the intelligence section, so that could be used to her advantage. Not wanting to linger in the office that held so many memories, she hastily gathered her things together and hurried out. The bike she used was there, sitting next to David's powerful machine, and the sight of it was nearly her undoing. Kathy had faced distressing situations before and she could do it again. Instead of anger, this time she felt grief – grief at the loss of a man she had become much too fond of, which was a foolish thing to do in such perilous times.

Starting up the bike she went first to the Wrennery, collected the parcel of art materials she had collected and headed away from Dover. It wasn't very dignified riding in a skirt, but she didn't give a damn, nor for the fact that she shouldn't have taken the bike. Hopefully she could return it before it was missed.

The days were long at this time of the year and

it was still light when she reached the camp. Making sure her skirt was smoothed down and her hat straight, she put on her best air of authority and walked to the main entrance.

'I have a message for one of your prisoners – Captain Maximilian Fischer – from Senior Intelligence Officer Evans.'

'Wait here,' the guard told her.

He was soon back with the camp commander. 'Give me the message and I'll see he gets it.'

'My orders are to give it to him personally.' She didn't even blink as she lied.

'I see.' He studied her face for a few moments. 'You were with him when they brought the captain here.'

'Yes, sir. I am his assistant.'

'What have you got in that bag?'

'Art materials for another one of your prisoners – Erik Keller.'

'Ah, yes, I've seen some of his drawings. He's very good.' He took the parcel from her and handed it to the guard and told him to check its contents, and then he turned back to Kathy. 'This is highly irregular, but I will allow it. Come with me.'

Stifling a sigh of relief, she followed him to a small room and waited for the guard to bring the prisoner. She wasn't looking forward to this and her insides were churning.

Max arrived and smiled, but that soon faded when he saw the pain in her eyes. 'What has happened?'

'I thought you ought to know that David went on a trip somewhere and they have lost contact with him. He has been declared missing, presumed dead.'

The colour drained from his face, and he muttered something in his own language. 'Thank you for coming to tell me. Will you let me know if there is any definite news?'

'Of course.' She held out the bag. 'Would you give that to Erik for me, please? How are you all coping with being behind barbed-wire fences?'

'We are well, and Erik will be grateful for the materials. He often talks about you. It is a shame you cannot see the brothers, but this is not the right time.'

'No, it isn't, but give them my best wishes.'

'I will, and thank you again for coming.'

Kathy nodded and left the camp, relieved that difficult task was over.

Fortunately, no one had missed the bike and she put it back in its place.

That night she allowed the silent tears to flow unchecked. Was there no end to the sadness this war was bringing to so many people? And when it was finally over the memories and feelings of loss would still be there.

The next day she reported to Winchester, and because she was not officially qualified, she worked under instruction. The complete concentration required to pick up signals was a help as it took her mind off David for a while.

At the finish of the shift she removed the headphones with a sigh of relief. It had been a tough day, not only because she was doing a job she wasn't used to, but she was also struggling with resentment at being moved when they didn't have any definite news about David. In her opinion, closing their office had been premature.

One of the other girls introduced herself. 'My name is Joan.'

'Kathy.'

'We are pleased to have you aboard, and you'll soon get used to it. We can get something to eat now.'

'Thanks. I'm gasping for a cup of tea.'

'Where are you from?' Joan asked when they were settled with a plate of food in front of them.

'Dover. I was an officer's secretary.'

'Did you ask for a transfer?'

Kathy shook her head; she really didn't want to talk about this. 'They didn't need me any more, and as I had some knowledge of Morse they sent me here.'

'You don't look very happy about it, if you don't mind me saying.'

'I've just lost someone I was close to,' she admitted.

'Ah, I'm sorry. Do you want to talk about it?'

'No.' Kathy dredged up a smile and changed the subject. 'Tell me about yourself and how long you've been doing this work.'

It was an effort, but she managed to make polite conversation with Joan, and some of the other girls later that day.

Over the next couple of weeks, Kathy threw herself into the new assignment, but in her free time she fretted, desperate for information about David. All she had been told was that he was missing, presumed dead, which meant they didn't have any idea what had happened to him. He could still be alive, but who could she ask as to whether there was any news? Alan and Ted might know something, but there was no way she could trace them. They were shadowy figures and she only knew them by their Christian names – even in Gibraltar their full names had not been mentioned. With David missing they might know something – unless they were with him, of course, and that was worse, because it meant all three were missing. She had sent a letter to David's parents, trying to sound optimistic that he was probably all right, but didn't feel it was right to approach them again to ask if they had received any further news. They must be suffering enough without her pestering them.

Feeling helpless and praying that someone would have the kindness to contact her if they heard anything, Kathy settled in to the work. During her free time, she scoured the shops for art materials. They were considered non-essentials and hard to find, but after two weeks she had a nice collection for Erik. When she had some leave, she would take a trip to the camp, but didn't want to go until she had something definite to tell Max.

The weeks dragged by and in early September the station was alive with excitement as messages began to fill the airwaves. On 3rd September the Allies landed in Italy and the country surrendered unconditionally a few days later, on the 8th.

Kathy celebrated with everyone else, and there was certainly reason to raise a glass. 1943 was turning out to be a hopeful year. The U-boats were not having it all their own way as Allied technology improved, and they now often found themselves the hunted instead of the hunter. Now Italy had surrendered, giving hope for the future.

Yes, there was hope, she acknowledged, but for her and many like her the cost had been high. And it wasn't anywhere near over yet.

She had just settled down for another session on the wireless when she heard the commander asking irritably, 'Where are those blasted despatch riders?'

'They are all out, sir,' someone told him.

Turning round quickly she said, 'If you have a spare bike, sir, I can deliver the messages.'

He frowned. 'It doesn't say on your record that you can ride one of those things.'

'An oversight, sir. I used to deliver messages for the intelligence officer I worked under when I was at Dover. I came here quite a few times.'

'I want this message delivered to the control room there. Someone find her a bike, and get a replacement for her station,' he ordered.

A bike was soon found, and he handed her a sealed envelope. 'Take that to the operations room at Dover and hand it, personally, to Commander Douglas.'

'Yes, sir.'

He glanced at the clock and frowned. 'You will not

be able to get back in daylight, so stay there overnight. I will expect you back in time for your afternoon shift tomorrow.'

'Thank you, sir.'

Grabbing a few essentials for the overnight stay, Kathy then changed into a pair of trousers, eager to get on her way. It was terrific to be on the motorbike again. How she had missed it, and Dover. She had become attached to the place and it had hurt when they had made her leave. Of course, it had all been due to the dynamic man she had been working for. She missed him the most of all, but clung to the happy times they had shared together.

She drove up to the entrance of the tunnel, got off the bike and stood looking at it, smiling as she remembered her first day here. Entering the tunnel, she went up to the desk.

'Hello, are you back?' the man on duty asked.

'Sadly no. I have a message for Commander Douglas and my orders are to hand it to him personally.'

'He's in the operations room. You know where it is.'

As she began walking, the memories came flooding back. 'Oh, David,' she whispered to herself, 'why did you have to go and put yourself in danger? And where are you? Are you still alive somewhere, and will we ever know what has really happened to you?'

After knocking on the door, she opened it and walked in. It was the usual busy scene – and she froze. The group of officers were deep in conversation, as they had been the very first time she had come here. When one of them turned his head and studied her intently, as he had before, it was as if she was back in time. The only difference was that the man staring at her was thinner, but it was unmistakably David! He was alive, and no one had bothered to let her know. Even he hadn't sent a message to say he was all right. How could he not do that? Didn't he know she would be upset? There was tremendous relief that he was alive, but also a deep hurt she had been left to find out like this.

A Wren first officer came over to her, and somehow Kathy managed to salute. 'I have a message for Commander Douglas.'

'I'll give it to him.'

She handed it over, ignoring her orders to give it to him personally, and then turned swiftly to leave the room, almost running down the tunnel, only wanting to get away. He hadn't even bothered to come and speak to her; he had just stared as if he didn't know her, and then turned away to continue his conversation. Not even a nod or smile of acknowledgement.

'Hammond!'

The command from the first officer halted her flight, and she turned.

'You are in a hurry.'

'I have been ordered to stay overnight and return to Winchester in the morning. I am going to see if I can get a cabin for the night at the Wrennery.'

'You can have a bunk here for the night. I will see that

is arranged for you, but in the meantime, you can wait in the SOI office.'

She made her way to the office, knowing she couldn't disobey an order, but after the shock of seeing David, and the way he had ignored her, to walk into that room again was going to be painful.

Chapter Twenty

Taking a deep breath to steady herself, Kathy opened the door and stepped inside, stopping in surprise. She had expected the room to be empty, but there were two officers in there.

One of them looked up from examining the tea caddy and smiled. 'Ah, there you are. You seem to be out of tea and milk.'

With her gaze shooting from one man to the other she placed her hand over her racing heart. 'I don't work here any more,' was all she managed to say.

'Why not?'

'When David went missing they transferred me. Where the hell have you been?' she exploded. 'You look terrible.'

Alan pursed his lips and turned to Ted. 'Hell is a good description, don't you think?'

'Pretty accurate.' Ted held out the caddy. 'We are gasping for a decent cup of tea.'

'And we are starving,' Alan added.

'I can see that. You both look like matchsticks with the wood scraped off.'

'That bad, eh?' Alan grinned. 'I've never heard that saying before.'

'It was a favourite of my mother's. Will you two sit down before you fall down? You should be in the hospital, not sitting around here asking for tea.'

'We haven't had a chance to see or do anything. The moment our feet touched this country again we were whisked here.'

'Didn't they want you in the operations room as well?'

'Oh, they did ask us some questions, but David is the one with all the facts, so they sent us here to wait.' Ted raised his eyebrows. 'Tea – food?'

'I'll go and get you something in a moment.'

'Thanks, you are an angel, and get enough for David as well. They should finish the debriefing soon.'

'I assume you have all been together, so when did you get back?'

Ted glanced at his watch. 'Two hours ago.'

Ah, that explained why she hadn't been told; there hadn't been time. 'Didn't you let anyone know you were alive and on your way back?'

'Couldn't.' Alan shook his head. 'We lost our wireless set.'

'But they would have had a wireless in the ship you were on, surely?'

'There was one, but it didn't work.' Ted smirked as Alan shuddered. 'I don't know how it kept afloat, really. It wasn't much of a boat, but we couldn't be choosy. There were some rather nasty men after us.'

Kathy ran a hand over her eyes. 'I don't think I want to know the details. I let the three of you out of my sight for a moment and you get yourselves into a mess,' she teased.

'Food, Kathy,' Ted prompted.

'I'm going, and for goodness' sake behave while I'm away.'

They grinned at her as she left the office.

'Hello,' the cook greeted her with a smile. 'Good to see you again. I hear they are back.'

'Yes, all three of them and they are starving – quite literally. I'll also need tea and milk, please.'

'Coming up.'

With the help of two of the kitchen staff she was soon back, and the two men dived into the food while she made a pot of strong tea. There was no sign of David, and if he was in the same condition as Alan and Ted, then she was worried about him. She had been so shocked to see him there that she hadn't taken a good look at him.

She was just passing round the mugs when he walked in. He shut the door, leant against it and closed his eyes.

'That was a long grilling they gave you.' Alan got to his feet and led David to a chair.

The sigh he gave was ragged, and once he was seated he fixed his gaze on Kathy but said nothing.

'Eat something,' she told him gently and handed him a mug of tea.

'Thanks, this is just what we need, and if that damned phone rings, we are not available.'

'I don't work here now, or for you.'

'Of course you do.'

'They told me you wouldn't be coming back and transferred me to Winchester.'

'Huh!' Ted snorted. 'They didn't have much faith in our ability to survive, did they?'

David swore under his breath. 'They didn't tell me that. I'll sort it out. Any more tea in that pot?'

Watching them eat and drink umpteen mugs of tea, Kathy waited until they had cleared the plates of every morsel of food. 'You will all need rest for a few days. I'll get the doctor to check you over.'

'We don't need a doctor,' all three said in unison.

'Have any of you looked in a mirror since you got back? You need medical attention, and a lot of sleep.' She gathered up the crockery. 'Don't you move while I'm away.'

'You can't give me orders,' David told her. 'I'm the one in charge here.'

'In charge of what? Not me, because I don't work for you any more. All I'm doing is showing concern for three men who haven't the sense to look after themselves.'

'You sound just like my mother,' Ted remarked. 'She's bossy as well.'

'And you do as she says?'

'No.'

'That doesn't surprise me.' Kathy picked up the trays, headed for the galley, and then on to the hospital annexe.

'Can I speak to a doctor, please?' she asked a military nurse.

'I'll find you one. Please wait here.'

She soon returned with a doctor and Kathy explained the situation.

'I wasn't informed they were back. I'll come at once. Nurse, you come with us.'

The three men hadn't moved and looked nearly asleep. The doctor took one look at them and ordered the nurse to go and prepare three beds.

'Yes, sir.'

That stirred the men and they sat up straight. 'We're all right, Doc,' David said. 'We're just a bit tired, that's all.'

'How long have you been back?' he demanded.

'Not long. We had to go straight in for debriefing.'

The doctor made an exasperated sound. 'You should have been brought straight to the hospital. On your feet – that's if you can stand. If not, I'll get stretchers.'

'That won't be necessary.' Alan heaved himself out of the chair.

The other two did the same and the doctor reached

out to steady Ted. 'What the blazes have you three been up to? You are a mess. Help me get them to the hospital,' he told Kathy.

Once they were settled she made her way to the accommodation section, relieved she could stay near the men for a while. She settled down for the night and marvelled at the good fortune that had sent her to Dover at just the right moment. They had not been in any condition to make sensible decisions, and if she hadn't been here they would never have bothered with medical attention.

It was a restless night as her mind kept going over and over what had happened. David was back – he was all right, so what would happen to her now? Would she go straight back to working for him or would she have to stay where she was? The officer had told her to stay overnight when she really could have driven back to the station. She had made journeys in the dark before.

After very little sleep she was up early the next morning, anxious to see if the men looked better after a rest. She was lucky they didn't have her up on an insubordination charge the way she had bossed them around, but they hadn't been in any fit state to bother with something like that.

On her way to check on the men she met the first officer and asked what her orders were for that day.

'You are to return to Winchester this morning,' she told her.

Disappointed she couldn't stay longer, she made her way to the hospital annexe and into the ward. There were three empty beds! 'Where are they?' she asked a nurse.

'I have no idea.' She sighed. 'Doctor said they were to stay there for at least three days, but they discharged themselves. I suppose they have gone back to work.'

The doctor she had seen the day before came over and smiled wryly. 'They said they had a war to win and couldn't spend their time lolling about in bed.'

Kathy rolled her eyes in exasperation. 'That sounds like them. Are they all right?'

'A few days' rest would have been sensible, but they are strong men and will recover quickly. However, try and persuade them to come and see me during the day.'

'I'll try.' The corners of her mouth twitched. 'Couldn't you chain them to the bed?'

'That wouldn't work. They can pick locks like skilled burglars.'

Kathy burst out laughing. 'You're joking?'

'Don't you know the three of them are trained for undercover work? There isn't much they can't do in the dirty tricks department. Ask them.'

'I think you are making all this up, Doctor. What they do is gather information that could help to keep our shipping safe.'

He shrugged. 'When they come back in need of medical help, it is clear they go about gathering that information in a dangerous way.'

'You're right.' She glanced at the empty beds and

sighed. 'Now I need to see if I can find the truants.'

They were all in the office and smiled when she walked in.

'You're just in time.' Ted shook the tea caddy at her. 'We've run out again.'

'Good heavens, how much tea have you been drinking? And what are you all doing here? You are supposed to be in the hospital for a rest.'

'Too much to sort out.' David held out a sheaf of papers. 'Deal with that lot for me.'

'I can't. My shift starts at two o'clock and I have to get back. I only came to see how you are.'

'We're fine,' Alan told her.

'You can stay. I'll sort this mess out,' David told her confidently.

'You know that isn't possible. I will need an official transfer before I can come back here. I'll be in real trouble if I stay. I have to obey orders as well, you know.'

He dropped the papers on his desk with a thud, clearly exasperated by the situation, and then asked softly, 'Are you happy at Winchester?'

That didn't take any thought. 'No. This is where I want to be – and this is where I belong.'

He nodded. 'I'll get on to your transfer right away.'

The tea caddy was placed in her hands and Ted pleaded, 'Before you go, get that filled up. We also want milk and sugar.'

Glancing at her watch she hurried out to get the required items, returned to the office and put them on the table. 'You must make your own tea, and I know you are experts at that. Oh, and the doctor would like to see you sometime today.'

They ignored that request.

'By the way, the doctor said you can pick locks. Can you?'

That caught their attention, and David replied with an innocent look on his face, 'Why, has the doc lost some keys?'

'Not that I know of. I suggested he chain you to the beds, and he told me it would be useless because you can pick locks like experts.'

Their expressions gave nothing away, but Ted told her, 'Tell the doc I've got my lock-picking tools with me if he ever gets locked in the operating room.'

She watched the amusement cross their faces, and decided it was a waste of time trying to get any sense out of them. 'I think you've also been trained in the art of how to avoid answering questions.'

Glancing at the clock, she gasped. 'I must go.'

She made it in time for her shift and sat down ready to work. Searching for messages took total concentration and it was only later in the day she was able to mull over what the doctor had said that morning. It had been obvious, of course, that David's work was far from routine, and that realisation had only deepened when she had met Alan and Ted in Gibraltar. The sooner she was back at Dover, the better. Those three needed looking after, and that was what she was good at doing.

Intercepting messages was vital work, but her heart wasn't in it. She didn't belong here. Her place was at Dover with David.

A week passed, and she didn't hear anything about a transfer, so perhaps he wasn't having any success in getting her assigned to him again.

Deep in concentration one afternoon, she felt a hand on her shoulder and looked up. It was the station commander, and he motioned that she should remove her headphones. The moment she did so and stood up, another girl took her place. 'Sir?'

'Someone is here for you.'

Kathy glanced over to the door and saw David standing there. He looked better, but still far too thin.

He came over and handed the officer some papers, then told her, 'Collect your things. Your transfer has come through.'

'I was hoping you wouldn't be able to do this,' the commander told David. 'We need all the telegraphers we can get.'

'I know, but I also need her help as well.'

'Sorry to lose you, but good luck.'

'Thank you, sir.'

Their first stop was to pick up her belongings and accept a hastily found little gift from some of the girls she had come to know and like. Then they were speeding back to Dover on his powerful motorbike.

It looked as if Alan and Ted had moved in as well. Another desk had been crammed in and they sat either side of it with a map covering the surface, which they were studying.

They looked up and smiled when she walked in with David.

'Ah, good, you got her back at last. Put the kettle on, Kathy,' Ted told her.

'I've never seen anyone drink as much tea as you.' She glanced around the office. It was chaotic, and she glared at David. 'There isn't room for all of us in here. And am I taking orders from three officers now?'

'I know it's cramped, but it is only for a while.' He looked pointedly at his friends. 'And let us all remember that I'm the boss here – I give the orders.'

The two men raised their hands in surrender, huge smiles on their faces.

'I'm glad that's understood. Make us some tea, Kathy.'

'Any biscuits?' Ted asked.

As she looked at the three happy faces she started to laugh. 'Whatever you have been up to hasn't changed you.'

The tea was soon made, and she took a tin of biscuits out of her bag and placed it in the middle of the map.

'Where did you get that?' Ted asked, diving in to see if he could find his favourite custard creams.

'From the Wrennery.'

'You pinched it?'

'No, Alan, I was given it as a gift because I was leaving suddenly.' Kathy reached over, took a biscuit and squeezed herself past them to reach her own desk.

David sat back, a mug of tea in one hand and a

biscuit in the other and sighed contentedly. 'Ah, but it's good to be alive.'

The other two raised their mugs in salute. She knew they wouldn't talk about what they had been through but hoped that one day she would find out.

Refilling the mugs, she told David about her visit to Max. 'Since then I have sent a message to let him know you are all right. I hope I did the right thing?'

'Yes, you did. I'll go and see him as soon as I can.'

'Can I come with you? I've managed to collect some more paper for Erik.'

'Of course. I'll arrange for us to see the three of them.'

'Thanks. Max will be relieved to see you, and I'll look forward to finding out how they are.'

Chapter Twenty-One

One week passed and another without a mention of going to see the prisoners, and Kathy was beginning to think she would have to go on her own. If she did, though, there was a chance she wouldn't be allowed in. She had been lucky last time, but with David back she really did have to wait for him. The three men were busy, clearly involved in something important, and it was frustrating not to be told, but she was well aware they gathered information in any way they could, and because of the need for secrecy never talked about it in the presence of anyone not directly involved.

One afternoon they were all in the office when the admiral himself opened the door and looked in. They immediately sprang to attention.

'At ease. I thought you would like to know that today, 13th October, Italy has declared war on Germany.'

Slow smiles spread across their faces, and David said, 'Thank you, sir.'

He returned the smile. 'Well done, all of you. Your information was helpful to our ships.'

The admiral left, and Kathy took a silent breath. Now she knew where they had been – Italy, prior to the landings. 'My goodness, the admiral comes himself to give you that news. What an honour,' she teased.

Ted's eyes were glinting with amusement. 'Got any whisky tucked away?'

She laughed and went over to the cabinet, kicked it, and when the drawers shot open she took out a small bottle.

'Oh, well done that girl!' Alan took it from her and the glasses she also produced, and then grinned at David. 'I can see why you keep her. She's good, isn't she?'

'Very talented,' he replied while he poured generous amounts in each glass. He held the bottle up and when she shook her head he raised his glass to his friends and they drank a silent toast.

'Do you think they'll give us a medal?' Ted wanted to know.

David burst into laughter. 'Not after the mess we got into.'

'Guess you're right.' Alan held out his glass for a refill. 'The next one will be the big one, so let's drink to that.'

Kathy watched them clink glasses and her heart lurched. The feeling she'd had for a while that something was happening had just been confirmed. 'The big one' could only mean the invasion of Europe. Of course, the planning of such an undertaking would take some time, but perhaps some time next year . . .

'You look thoughtful, Kathy.'

David's voice cut through her thoughts, and she asked softly, 'Have we turned the corner at last?'

He nodded. 'There's a long way to go yet, but there is light at the end of the tunnel.'

'That's an appropriate saying considering where we work. With Italy turning against Hitler, he's in a precarious situation now, isn't he?'

'We think so, only he doesn't know it yet, but don't get your hopes up too soon,' he warned. 'We are still in for a tough time, and the victory won't come quickly or without great cost.'

'I know.' Her expression clouded. 'This must be a hard time for Max and the other prisoners. Do you think they know what's happening?'

'I don't suppose so, but I agree it must be worrying not to know what is going on. We'll go and see them tomorrow without fail.'

'That would be lovely. I've managed to get some good drawing paper for Erik.'

The next day the weather was bright and surprisingly warm for October. Kathy settled on the back of the bike, looking forward to the ride and seeing Max and the brothers again. It was difficult to think of them as enemies, and she marvelled at the difference that meeting had made to her. Helping a troubled and frightened boy had healed her rage. Forgiving the regime that had unleashed such suffering was another matter, though, and she doubted that would ever happen.

David opened up the power on his bike and they sped along, making her smile. None of that mattered now. David was alive when there had been a chance he was lost; they were spending the day together and she was happy. At that moment she couldn't ask for more.

They didn't stop once and were soon pulling up outside the camp. Kathy got off and waited while David parked the bike, then they went into the camp.

The guard on duty knew them, but still insisted on checking their papers, which was only right. 'We had received instructions that you were coming, sir. The prisoners you want to see are on work duty at a farm a couple of miles from here. You'll find them there. Turn left when you leave here and then it's a straight road to the farm.'

Thanking the guard, they returned to the bike, and Kathy asked, 'What did he mean by work duty?'

'I expect they have been helping the farmer with the harvest, and anything else he needs doing.'

'I didn't realise they let them out to do something like that.'

'Some prisoners are allowed out to work on farms. It helps the farmers and also eases the boredom of being behind barbed wire all the time.' He started the bike. 'Hop on.'

They roared into the farm, making two dogs race up to them, barking excitedly. A woman came out of the house and scolded the dogs. 'What can I do for you?' she asked after the bike had been turned off.

'Good morning, madam.' David smiled and introduced both of them. 'I believe you have some prisoners working here today. There are three we would like to talk to, if that would be all right with you?'

'Go round the barn and head for the orchard. You'll find them near there.' She frowned and studied the officer in front of her. 'Not in any trouble, are they?'

'Not at all. As a matter of fact, I went to school with Captain Fischer, and my assistant helped the Keller brothers when they were brought ashore.'

'Really? My goodness, fancy that. They will be pleased to see you, then. There is a break coming up, so I'll send food out for you as well.'

'That's very kind of you,' Kathy told her.

She retrieved the package of paper from the bike and they began to walk in the direction pointed out by the farmer's wife. The dogs bounded along with them, not wanting to leave these new arrivals.

Erik saw them first and waved frantically, shouting to the others to let them know. Max spun round and smiled when he saw David.

There was only one guard standing with the farmer and the three men said something to them, then hurried over to meet their visitors.

The difference in Erik was remarkable. Hurrying

towards them was a young, good-looking boy, obviously happy to see them and fully recovered from his ordeal.

Max shook Kathy's hand, and slapped his friend on the back. 'You gave us a fright and thank you for sending the message to say you were all right.'

'Sorry we couldn't get here sooner.'

Kathy greeted the brothers and handed Erik the bag. 'There's some more drawing paper for you, and I managed to find a few coloured pencils.'

He looked in the bag, exclaimed with delight and then beamed at her. 'Thank you. So kind and I happy to have more paper.'

'Oh, you're learning English.'

He nodded. 'People like my drawings and I make many pictures. I speak to them.'

'That's very good. Well done!'

'You give paper and I make many pictures. You want to see?'

'Yes, please. Have you got them here?'

Gerhard laughed. 'He never goes anywhere without them.'

Kathy watched Erik rush off to find his bag, and said softly to his brother, 'He's a prisoner, and yet he's happy.'

'He is, and he wants to stay here.'

Erik was back and had heard what his brother said. 'Stay here. You help me, please, when war over?'

'Of course. If you need someone to sponsor you, I'll be more than happy to do that.'

The boy turned to his brother, not understanding all she had said. He listened while Gerhard explained, then he turned back to Kathy and grasped her hands. 'Thank you. I lucky to find such kindness.'

She smiled at the brother. 'What about you, do you want to stay in this country?'

'I will go back to see that our parents are all right, and then I would like to return to be with my brother.'

'If you want to come back we will help you,' David said as he came up to them with Max.

'Thank you. I would be grateful.'

'What about you, Max?'

His expression clouded as he looked at his friend. 'It all depends what happens when this war comes to a close, but once I know my family are safe I would like to return and spend some time with you and your family, David. Then I will make a decision about my future.'

'I understand. You know where I am, and if I can help in any way, you call on me.'

'I'll do that and thank you. I have seen troops and tanks rumbling past the farm. You are strong now, and I feel you are going to be the victors in this war.'

'It was never in doubt,' David told him gently.

Just then a van arrived with lunch for everyone, and they all settled down to enjoy the fresh farm food. There were eight of the U-boat crew at the farm, and Kathy recognised them from the interrogation. They were all talking in their own language, including David, so she concentrated on helping Erik with his

English while they looked through his pile of drawings.

'Who is this?' she asked, holding up a pencil sketch of a young girl.

'Jenny. She live here.'

'She's very pretty.'

He smiled. 'Nice. I like.'

The farmer came over. 'You boys had enough to eat? If not, there's more in the van.'

Max translated for his men and several of them went to help themselves to another plateful.

'Mr George,' Erik called. 'This my friend, Kathy.'

The farmer smiled and came over. 'I thought it might be. Erik and Gerhard have told me about you. It's a pleasure to meet you, miss.'

Kathy stood up and shook hands with him. 'I have just been looking at the lovely drawing of Jenny.'

'That's my daughter, and the lad has given us a larger drawing of her. He's very good, isn't he?'

'Yes, he is.'

'Well, you and your officer take as long as you like with them. The harvest is in, so we can ease up a bit now.'

'That is kind of you, sir.' She settled down again with the brothers, and they proceeded to help Erik with his English.

Max touched David's arm. 'Walk with me.'

After letting the guard know, they left the group and wandered through the orchard.

'That's a nice girl you have there.'

'I was getting snowed under with paperwork and needed someone who could cope with it for me. I picked her from several suggested candidates, but I wasn't sure I had the right one because she came carrying a burning rage. She's a strong-willed girl and had it under control most of the time, but one day something happened and it erupted to the surface. However, she was quickly back in control and carried out her duties perfectly. I was impressed by her strength of character.'

'You surprise me. There's no sign of that in her now. May I ask why she was so angry?'

David thought for a moment, and then gave his friend a brief outline of what had happened to her.

Max listened in grim silence, and then said, 'No wonder she was furious. How can she even bear to look at us, let alone help us like she has?'

'Because she saw a young boy who was traumatised and desperately worried about someone he loved – his brother. I believe she saw in him the same desperation she had faced, and regardless of his nationality he had to be helped. Then seeing the happiness of the brothers as they were reunited healed her. The girl you see now is the real Katherine Hammond, and it does my heart good to see the change in her.'

'She came herself to tell me you were missing, and she was very upset. You are fond of each other?'

'We are friends now,' David replied. 'When I was missing they transferred her to another posting and I had the devil of a job to get her back.'

'Does she know you had that difficulty?'

'Probably,' was his reply.

Max bent down and picked up a few fallen apples, wiping one clean and handing it to David. 'Farmer George allows us to take any windfalls, so eat up. I don't know what you were up to while you were away, but you are much too thin.'

He laughed. 'I know, but Kathy is making sure I eat well. I'll soon put the weight back on.'

'I like her, but after what she has been through . . .' Max shrugged.

'I know what you're thinking, and you can forget it,' David warned.

His friend smiled. 'You had better stake your claim or you could lose her, especially with all the Americans around.'

'This is no time to form serious attachments, and with the losses she has already suffered, she hasn't shown the slightest inclination of getting too close to anyone – whatever their nationality,' David told him pointedly.

'That's understandable, I suppose. Now, help me collect some apples to take back to the men.'

While they were doing this, David asked, 'Have you had many letters from your parents?'

'A couple. They have been informed that I am a prisoner here, and quite frankly they are relieved. Life expectancy in the subs can be short, as you well know.' Max bit into an apple, looking thoughtful. 'I can't say much in letters, of course, because they are censored, so I haven't mentioned meeting you.'

'That would raise a few questions, wouldn't it?'

Max grimaced. 'More than a few, especially with you attached to naval intelligence. Knowing each other so well has placed us both in a difficult situation, hasn't it?'

'I agree it's damned awkward to find ourselves on opposing sides, but I won't allow our years of friendship to be destroyed, and I hope you won't either.'

'Not a chance, and I'm relieved you feel like that. Nevertheless, we find ourselves in this tricky situation and we owe our loyalty to our own countries. I can't tell you anything, and the same goes for you, but we are worried about our families at home.'

'I understand that.'

'I'm not a fool. You have the men and armaments now, and I am sure plans will be drawn up to launch an attack. After Dunkirk it was widely believed that you were beaten and would surrender, but I was certain they were underestimating you.'

David gave an amused smile. 'You should have told them we would never surrender.'

'So Churchill said,' Max quipped. 'I don't suppose you even knew you were in desperate trouble, did you?'

'Oh, we knew, and there was only one way left for us, and that was to get back up as fast as we could.'

'And you did.' Max placed a hand on his friend's shoulder. 'It's been good to be able to talk with you like this. I know you are busy, but could you come and see us now and again? Bring that lovely girl with you as well. The brothers adore her.'

'We will come when we can.'

'Thanks. Now let us get back. It will be time to return to the camp soon.'

David and Kathy watched as the lorry drove out of the farm with Erik waving at them.

When they were out of sight, she smiled. 'I can't believe that is the same boy, and I'm still amazed I am helping one of the enemy.'

'It is hard to think of them in that way, I know. They are just like us, and the real culprits for this mess are the regime who wanted to rule the world regardless of the cost to human life.'

'I can see that now. They drop bombs on us, and now we are doing the same to them. It is madness, isn't it?'

He nodded and reached up to straighten her hat. 'We've had our day out and now it's time to get back to our tunnel. Are you ready, Leading Wren Hammond?'

'Yes, sir.' Kathy laughed, and walked contentedly with him back to the motorbike.

Chapter Twenty-Two

David watched Kathy pounding away expertly on the typewriter, totally focused on what she was doing. He knew she was worried because it showed in the dark circles under her lovely eyes. A month ago, when they had visited the camp, she had been relaxed and happy, and he had been so pleased to see her like that, but now she was fretting. She hadn't received a letter from her father for many weeks, and that was most unusual. She was a strong girl, mentally and physically, but her father was all she had and if she lost him as well, David didn't dare imagine what it would do to her. Then he had an idea that might help her. It was worth a try.

'You've got some leave due to you, so why don't you

go to that cottage you bought a while ago. It must be feeling neglected,' he joked.

'Pardon?' Kathy looked up, distracted.

'I said take the leave due to you and visit your new home. It might be your only chance for quite a while. We will have a lot to do over the next few months and probably won't even get a break over Christmas. Hitler must suspect that we are going to invade next year, but we have to turn his attention away from our chosen beaches.'

'By feeding them misinformation?'

He nodded. 'It is vital we succeed in fooling them. So, take a break while you can.'

'Thank you. I would like to go and see everything is all right.' She hesitated. 'But will you manage while I'm away? I know there's a lot to do.'

'I'll be fine. I did before you came.'

'Oh, yes, I remember, you were knee-deep in paper.' She gave a tired smile.

'I can't do much damage in a few days.' He signed the necessary authorisation and held it out to her. 'Go now, and I don't want to see you for seven days.'

'Thank you.' Pausing at the door she turned. 'If you hear anything you will let me know, won't you?'

'Of course, but I expect you will get a bunch of letters all at the same time. You know how unpredictable the mail can be, especially for those at sea.'

'You're right, of course.' She gave a hint of her teasing smile. 'Don't get into any trouble while I'm away.'

'Trouble? Me? Where did you ever get that idea?'

They both grinned at the joke, and then she was gone.

David stared at the closed door for a while and then sighed. To be honest he was also concerned, not only for Jack, but for Bill too. He knew they were on a Russian convoy and hadn't been heard from for too long. They should have been back by now. The weather could have held them up, of course, because November on that run could be brutal and the temperature of the sea could kill in minutes if they were torpedoed.

He breathed in deeply to try and ease the tension in his body. Bill was a good friend, and the fact that Kathy's father was also out there was causing his imagination to run riot, not to mention the constant concern for his own brother.

Surging to his feet he strode to the operations room. Perhaps they knew what was going on.

'Hello, David,' Peter greeted him when he walked in. 'Thank heaven those damned U-boats have stopped hunting in large packs. They've had to change tactics because they were beginning to suffer too many losses. What's on your mind?'

'That Russian convoy is overdue. Any news?'

'You must be a mind-reader because a message has just come through. It's been rough with atrocious weather and they have lost ships, but they are now in better conditions and are on their way back.'

'Do you know which ships were sunk?'

'Not yet. They can't transmit for any length of time until they are in safer waters, as you know.'

David grimaced. 'I'm not sure there are any safer waters. The subs are still out there.'

'True, but with the advances we have made in detection, they are no longer safe. What's your interest in this particular convoy?'

'Personal. Kathy's father is captain of one of the escorts, and so is a family friend.'

'Ah, I understand your concern. That nice Wren of yours is worried, then?'

'She doesn't know what convoy he is on, but she hasn't heard from him for some time and that is fretting her. I've sent her off on seven days' leave.'

'We'll have a clearer picture by then. I'll let you know the moment anything comes through.'

David glanced around. 'You seem to be rather short-handed.'

'We are. One of the girls got married and another one was pregnant. We have a replacement coming tomorrow and I've been assured she is very observant, so we'll put her to checking aerial photos. It's a shame your girl is on leave because I was going to ask if we could borrow her. She seems intelligent.'

'She is.' David laughed softly. 'I've never been so organised. If you are still short when she comes back, you can have her for a while. Only temporary, remember. I had enough trouble getting her away from Winchester. They fought hard to keep her.'

'I can imagine, and thanks. I might take you up on that offer once we find out how good this new girl is.

We are going to need all the help we can get because it's going to be our job to get the troops on the beaches as safely as possible.'

David nodded. 'And they mustn't know where the landings will be.'

'I'm praying they don't even believe we are coming. Though with the country beginning to fill up with troops and equipment, that isn't going to be easy.'

'Only when the landings take place will we know if we have succeeded in fooling them.' He gave a wry smile. 'Let's hope good fortune is smiling on us. Now back to the convoy. Send someone to find me the moment news comes through.'

'I'll do that.'

'Thanks.' David turned to leave, and then glanced back. 'I'll give you a hand tomorrow, if you like?'

'That would be appreciated if you can spare the time?'

'I'll make time. See you in the morning.'

'Thanks, David.'

The operations room was a hive of activity when David arrived. The admiral was studying maps with two other officers, and the commander was busy writing on the blackboards. He went up to him. 'Any news, Peter?'

'Nothing new.' He smiled, understanding his concern. 'Can you spare us a few hours today?'

'Yes, what would you like me to do?'

'The new girl is at the table over there, so would you help her go through the photographs that have just come through? If there are gun emplacements we don't know about, we've got to find them. We mustn't miss anything. It will be up to our ships to bombard the landing areas to destroy them before the troops go in.'

'Right.' David walked over to the table and pulled up a chair. The girl glanced up but didn't say anything. 'I've come to give you a hand,' he told her.

'Thank you. There are rather a lot of pictures to check.'

'There certainly are,' he remarked, looking at the large pile of prints. 'Have you found anything?'

'I've been going through the older shots first, so I can see if anything is different in the latest ones.'

He saw the large stack of prints she had already checked and doubted it would be possible to remember what she had seen. There were far too many of them. 'Wouldn't it be better to check the old and the new of each area together?' he suggested.

She looked up and smiled. 'You can do it that way if you prefer, but I'll remember what I've seen.'

Cheeky little devil, he thought with amusement. And she hadn't once addressed him as 'sir'. 'How can you be so sure?'

'I've got a photographic memory.'

He was astonished and watched as she fixed her gaze to the magnifying glass again. Where on earth did they find this girl? Not only did she tell him how he could do the job, but she then stated, quite simply, that she had a photographic memory. Well, he doubted that, but he would soon find out by working beside her.

Totally absorbed in the important work he suddenly became aware that the girl beside him was urgently searching through a pile of prints. 'What are you looking for?'

'Something I saw earlier. Ah, here it is.' Pulling out one photo, she placed it beside a similar one and began examining both of them. 'Got you!' she exclaimed.

'What have you found?'

'Have a look.' She pushed the prints over to him.

After studying them for a while he shook his head. 'I can't see anything. They look the same to me.'

She stood up and leant over his shoulder, pointing to a spot on the photo. 'Just there.'

He stared at the place, and then he saw it. Sitting back, he ran a hand through his hair. 'It looks as if there's a new gun emplacement there, but it's very well hidden. Well done on spotting that.'

She grinned and turned to beckon Peter over.

'Found something?'

'They've put a blooming great gun here, and the crafty devils have hidden it well – but not quite well enough.'

Peter sat in the chair to study the prints. It took some time and the girl was leaning across him to guide him to the new feature.

David watched in amazement. She had never once addressed either of them in the correct naval manner, but she was good. He would have missed that. But who the devil was she?

'Yes, I see it,' he said at last. He got up and made for

the table where they had a mock-up of the landing sites.

The girl trotted along with him, and after looking briefly at the model, told Peter where to mark the new gun.

'Now let's see if there is anything else they've done,' she declared, and marched back to her table.

David raised his eyebrows at Peter and said quietly, 'What a strange girl. Where did you find her?'

'When I put in a request for replacements I explained what I wanted them for, and I was told they had someone who might be useful. She's certainly got a sharp eye for detail.'

'I won't argue with that.'

David only had another hour working with the intriguing girl when he was called away. He left, letting Peter know that he would come back if possible.

For the next two days he was in London, and on his return to Dover he went straight to ops.

'Ah, there you are,' Peter said the moment he walked in. 'I've been trying to contact you, but you'd disappeared – again.'

'I was in London. Do you have any news?'

'That Russian convoy was on the way back when Hammond had engine trouble and had to stop to make repairs.'

David drew in a deep breath. 'Dangerous.'

'Very. He was a sitting target. The convoy had to keep going with reduced protection because Jackson stayed with him and circled the destroyer until they could start the engines again. We've heard they have now caught up with the convoy and should be docking in Liverpool in about a week – providing they don't run into trouble.'

'Let's hope they don't. Thanks, that's a relief.'

'You'd better let your girl know her father is all right.'

'I will.' David glanced around the room and saw two girls studying photographs. 'You've managed to get both replacements, I see.'

'Yes, thank goodness. It's going to be a hectic time in the build-up to the invasion.'

'I never did ask the name of the strange girl I worked with. How is she doing?'

'Her name is Turnbull, and she's bloody marvellous. Once she sees something she remembers it in detail.' He chuckled. 'She's not good at remembering naval protocol, though, and even talks to the admiral as if he's just one of the boys. I haven't heard her say "sir" once.'

'I noticed that. Has the oversight been pointed out to her?'

Peter shook his head. 'She's so good no one cares. That memory of hers is phenomenal and proving invaluable.'

'Glad to hear it. I might want to borrow her myself sometime,' David said with a perfectly straight face.

'You can forget that. You've already got one Wren and that little genius is ours.'

At that moment there was an exclamation from the table, making everyone look in her direction. 'That isn't right. What the heck is it?'

He followed Peter over to the girl who was studying a photo intently, and then she sat back and shook her head.

'What have you found?' The admiral also joined them.

'I don't know, but it shouldn't be there.' She stood up to let the admiral sit in her chair and pointed to the spot on the print. 'I haven't seen that before. See, just there.'

'I can't make it out.' He stood up and said to David. 'You have a look.'

'Yes, sir.' He sat down, put his eyes to the magnifying lenses and concentrated on where her finger was pointing. At first, he didn't see anything unusual, and then it came into focus. 'Would you say it's a ramp of some kind?'

She slapped him on the shoulder and broke into a broad grin. 'That's it! It's a ramp. What would they want that for?'

'I can only guess. It might be to launch a weapon of some kind,' David told them, looking concerned.

'Oh, hell!' Peter picked up the photo. 'Someone get me several copies of this at once. As large as they can make them.'

The room burst into activity. The admiral was already on the phone to air command asking for more photos of the area.

Turnbull watched for a moment and then turned her attention to David. 'You've got a good eye. What do you do here?'

'I'm Commander Evans – intelligence.'

'Ah, that figures.' She sat down again. 'Wonder if I can find any more of those things?'

'Have to go,' David told Peter. 'Will you let me know when any news comes through?'

'Of course.'

He returned to the office and found Alan and Ted there. 'Are you moving in here again?'

'No, they've given us our own office,' Alan told him. 'Where's Kathy?'

'On leave. Why?'

'We thought we'd take her out. We don't suppose she gets much relaxation and fun working for you.'

'Fun?' David glared at Ted. 'We are trying to win a war here. There will be time for fun when it's over. And anyway, what makes you think I would allow you to take her out without me?'

'There you are.' Alan nudged Ted. 'I told you, didn't I?'

'You were right.'

'What on earth are you talking about?' David demanded.

Alan smirked. 'If you don't know, then I'm not going to tell you. It's something you will find out for yourself – eventually.'

'You two are impossible.'

'We know.' Ted grinned. 'As Kathy isn't here, do you know of any other lovely Wrens who might like to come out with two lonely sailors?'

'There are a couple of new ones in ops. One of them is bit odd, but she's very pretty.'

'Really? What's her name?' Alan asked.

'Turnbull. I don't know her first name.'

Alan stood up. 'I think it's time we visited the operations room. Ted?'

David watched them leave and couldn't help laughing to himself. They were a terrible double act on the surface, but underneath that facade were two very dangerous men where the enemy was concerned. Still, they were right about one thing: Kathy wasn't having much fun, and neither was he.

He walked out with a smile of amusement on his face. He would love to be a fly on the wall and see how they got on with that extraordinary girl. Come to think of it, they might be well suited.

His motorbike was always ready for him and he was soon on his way to give Kathy the good news about her father.

The cottage was quite small but in a lovely setting, and he imagined it would be a nice cosy home. He knocked on the door and waited. It opened after a few moments and her face paled when she saw him.

'It's all right,' he told her. 'I bring good news.'

Kathy smiled then and held the door open for him. 'Come in, you must be frozen.'

The front room had a lovely log fire burning in the grate and he warmed his hands before turning to face her. Hope was etched on her face and without further delay he told her what had happened to her father's ship. 'They have caught up with the convoy and will dock at Liverpool in about a week.'

'That's such a relief, and I bless Bill for staying with him. I must give that man a big grateful hug when I see him again.'

'Don't I get a hug for coming to give you the good news?'

She gave him a startled look and then burst into laughter, the worry wiped from her face. 'Certainly not. You are my boss, and it wouldn't be proper to be too familiar with my senior officer. Will my thanks do?'

'If you feel like that I suppose it will have to.'

'I'll feed you as well. It's only vegetable pie, but it's my mother's recipe and she was a marvellous cook.'

'Sounds like an offer I can't refuse.'

It was the tastiest meal he'd had for some time, and he helped her wash the dishes before taking the tea into the front room.

'This is a charming cottage,' David told her, feeling relaxed and happy to see her smiling again.

'Yes, we liked it the moment we walked in. The village also has a friendly pub within walking distance, which my father approved of.'

'An absolute essential, I would say.' He put his cup down on the small table and stood up. 'Let's go dancing.'

'Pardon?'

'I said let's go dancing. You can dance, I take it?'

'Of course, but I can't go dancing with you.'

'Why not? And don't you dare say it wouldn't be proper.' When she hesitated he pulled her out of the chair. 'Surely we have known each other long enough to become friends. Ted and Alan told me we don't have enough fun. So let's go out tonight as friends and have some fun.'

'Well, if you put it like that, but I don't have a pretty frock to wear.'

'Everyone will be in uniform. Come on, Kathy,' he urged. 'Wouldn't it be good to relax for a while, raise a glass in thanks for the safety of two fine men, and dance the night away?'

'You're right, and those two brave captains would approve. It would be a relief to forget the damned war for a few hours. I'll get ready. It won't take me long.'

He watched her leave the room and said softly, 'That's my girl.'

Chapter Twenty-Three

There were dances going on everywhere. It was a popular activity, because it gave people a few hours' respite from the war when they could relax and enjoy the music. Saturday night was a busy time and David took her to a hotel where a dance was in full swing. The place was crowded with military from all the services and many civilians, especially girls.

They found somewhere to sit and had drinks in front of them when the band began to play a foxtrot. David led Kathy to the dance floor. It was some time since she had danced, but he was excellent, and she soon began to move smoothly, enjoying the happy atmosphere.

'You dance well,' she told him.

He looked down at her and smiled. 'Does that surprise you?'

'Not really. I suspect that anything you put your mind to, you do skilfully.'

'Max and I were always a hit at the school dances.' He chuckled quietly at the memory. 'I could never match him. He had a charm and grace the girls found irresistible.'

'He still has.'

'You like him, don't you?'

Kathy thought about it for a moment before answering. 'He's impressive, but I can't forget that he has been sinking our ships. I know he's your friend, but I'm not sure about him. He doesn't seem like the kind of man who would do something he disagreed with.'

'They were conscripted into the services, just like us, and told they must fight for their country and loved ones. Do we question that?'

'Of course not. Our survival depends on us winning this war.'

'That's what every country believes – so we fight, and in the case of Max and myself it is friend against friend. That we know each other well doesn't change the facts. We are on different sides of the conflict, and if I could get any information out of him that would be to our advantage, then I would. But I know him well enough to be certain that he wouldn't be disloyal to his country.'

'You could have someone else to interrogate him.'

'I have. Ted is very good but failed to get him to talk.'

'It must be hard for you.'

'It is for both of us.' He gave her a playful shake. 'I thought we came here to have fun, not talk about the war.'

'Sorry, not another word, I promise.'

The dance ended, and they returned to their seats.

'Excuse me, sir.' A young sailor was standing in front of them. 'Would you mind if I asked your young lady for a dance?'

'You have my permission to ask.'

'Thank you, sir.' The sailor smiled at Kathy. 'Would you like to dance?'

'I'd love to,' she replied, and allowed him to lead her to the dance floor.

'Can you jive?' he wanted to know.

'I've never tried.'

'I'll show you. It's what the Americans do and it's great fun.'

He was right. The next few minutes were hilarious and had her laughing in a way she had almost forgotten how to do.

When the dance ended the sailor looked across at David, who was standing at the edge of the dance floor, laughing at their antics. The young sailor guided Kathy back to him. 'She soon picked it up. Would you like to learn, sir? It's good fun.'

'Well, fun is what we came for.'

'Hey, boys!' the sailor called over to his mates. 'The officer wants us to teach him how to jive.'

For the next hour, fun is what they had, and she watched the young boys showing David how to do the American dance. They were obviously enjoying themselves. He picked it up quickly, and at the end bought them all a round of drinks as a thank you.

The young sailors took their drinks back to their own table and Kathy smiled at David. 'Those boys thought that was marvellous. It was kind of you to join in like that, and it has made their evening. The story that they taught an officer to jive will go round their ship like wildfire.'

He laughed and urged her to the dance floor. 'Let's have a go.'

They did quite well, considering they were beginners, and when they were near the young sailors they clapped and shouted, 'Well done, sir.'

David grinned, turned briefly to thank them again, and then continued with the dance.

The rest of the evening flew by and Kathy danced with the sailors while David found a couple of young girls to dance with.

'That officer of yours is not a bad bloke,' one of them said while they were dancing. 'Are you his girlfriend?'

'No, I work for him as his assistant.'

'Ah, he's onshore, then?'

'Part of the time.' She thought that was near enough the truth. 'Are you on leave?' she asked, changing the subject.

'Yes, only a couple of days left. What about you?'

'I'm back on duty tomorrow.'

'That's a shame. We won't see you again, then.'

'I'm afraid not, but thank you and your friends for making this an enjoyable evening.'

'It was a pleasure.' He grinned. 'Fancy us teaching an officer to jive. The lads will never believe us.'

The last dance was a slow waltz she shared with David, and when they went outside the sailors were all gathered around the motorbike, admiring it.

'Crumbs, is this yours, sir?' one of them asked.

'Yes, do you like it?'

They all nodded.

David started up the bike and Kathy climbed on the back, waving to the boys as they roared away.

Back at the house he stayed on the step, and she asked, 'Do you want to come in for a cup of tea?'

'Better not. I'll pick you up in the morning and we'll go back to Dover together.'

That surprised her. 'I thought you would be returning tonight.'

'I booked a room at that hotel for the night. I thought I might as well stay and save you a train journey in the morning.'

'Thank you. A lift back will be quicker. And thank you also for the evening. It was fun.'

'Yes, it was.' He leant forward and kissed her briefly on the lips, then stepped back. 'Sleep well.'

The bike started up and then he was gone, leaving her

astonished. He had kissed her! She didn't think he'd had that much to drink.

The next morning, Kathy made sure the cottage was clean and tidy in case her father was able to come here when he arrived back. It was a shame she had used up all her allotted leave, but she hoped she would be able to talk to him on the phone. She locked the door and was waiting outside when David arrived. 'How was the hotel?' she asked, while she stowed her bag on the bike.

'Fine,' he told her. 'I was tired after all that jiving.'

She didn't believe that for one moment. It would take more than a few dances to tire this man out. Settling on the back of the bike they set off for Dover.

When it came in sight she smiled. It was hard to believe she had become so attached to this place. It would be quite upsetting if they moved her to a new posting now.

They were both cold when they reached the office, and the first thing she did was make a pot of tea.

'Lovely,' he said, curling his hands around the mug to warm them.

Sitting quietly for a while they enjoyed the tea, and then he said, 'By the way, there are two new Wrens in ops. They are going through aerial photos and I worked with one for a couple of hours.' He started to laugh quietly.

'What's funny?'

'She isn't up on naval protocol. I never once heard her say "sir", not even to the admiral.'

'And she gets away with it?'

David nodded. 'She's extraordinary and so observant they allow her a lot of leeway. There was a huge pile of photos and when I suggested it would be better to compare the ones taken on different days together, she just looked at me and said, "I don't need to do that. I'll remember each because I have a photographic memory."'

Kathy leapt to her feet. 'Alice! Is her name Alice?'

'I only know her surname and that is Turnbull.'

'It *is* Alice,' she exclaimed excitedly.

'You know her?'

'We trained together. I tried to keep in touch, but lost track of her.'

'Has she really got a memory like she said?'

'I believe so. She told me that was the only reason the Wrens took her on. Do you think I could go and see her?'

David stood up. 'Come with me.'

They were approaching operations when the door opened and a girl with dark-red hair came out. Her face lit up when she saw who was walking towards her.

'Kathy!' Giving a squeal of delight she rushed up and hugged her friend.

Laughing, Kathy disentangled herself. 'Where have you been? I lost track of you.'

'I've been moving around a lot, but I'm working here now.' Alice pulled a face. 'Until they shift me again. To be honest I don't think they know what to do with me.'

'The admiral won't let them take you away from here,'

David told her as he watched the scene with amusement.

At the sound of his voice, Alice turned her attention to him. 'Ah, there you are. I thought you were going to work with me, but you disappeared.'

'He has a habit of doing that,' Kathy told her.

'Do you work for him?'

She nodded. 'I've been here right from training, apart from another brief posting.'

Alice smirked at her friend. 'He's good.'

It was difficult not to dissolve into helpless laughter, but Kathy managed to say, 'I know he is.'

Alice hadn't taken her eyes off David and she caught hold of his arm to tow him towards the door. 'I was going to take a break, but that can wait. Come with me, I want to show you something. You come too, Kathy. We can catch up in a minute.'

The room was buzzing with activity as usual, and she watched as David was made to sit at a table littered with photographs.

'Have a look at that and tell me what you see.'

'Where?'

Alice leant over him and pointed. 'There.'

After a while David sat back and pursed his lips thoughtfully. 'It could be a gun, but if it is they have hidden it well.'

She grinned and slapped him on the shoulder. 'That's what I think, and it's pointing right out to sea. It wasn't there in the photos taken some months ago, because I checked back.'

He studied the print again, and when he sat back this time he nodded. 'You're right.'

She spun round and called, 'Admiral, I was right, it is a big gun. You had better do something about it or it's going to sink your ships.'

'Are you sure?' the admiral replied. 'No one else can see it.'

Pulling David out of the chair, Alice guided him over to the group of officers studying a large map. 'I'm positive, and Intelligence here has just confirmed it. He's got sharp eyes.'

'Show us exactly where you think it might be.'

Alice stretched her arm over the map. 'Just here, don't you agree?' She turned her head to look at David.

'That's the spot.' He ran a hand through his hair, and then turning to the admiral he said, 'Would it be possible to send in commandos to take a look, just to make sure, or perhaps the Resistance could help?'

'Risky. The last thing we want to do is alert the enemy to the fact that we are interested in that beach.'

'I could go with two of my men,' he offered.

'If I come with you I could get a good look at it for you.'

All eyes turned towards the girl standing with them.

'It's all right. I've been before when they needed an identification of someone. I remember faces as well as things. Even if changed or disguised I can still spot them.'

Kathy listened to them with mounting alarm. What they were discussing was highly dangerous.

The admiral and Commander Douglas stepped aside to talk in private, and then came back to them. 'We can't risk drawing attention to that area, but I'll get the RAF on this and get more photos. It will be our job to bombard the beaches, so we can target any suspicious areas.'

'Of course, sir.' David nodded in agreement.

Alice sighed. 'That's a shame. I would have loved to get a look at that thing and one of those ramps.'

'We wouldn't put you in such danger,' Peter told her, giving a slight smile. 'You are far too valuable to us here.'

She beamed at him. 'That's nice to know. Can I take a long break to catch up with Kathy? We haven't seen each other for a long time.'

'Take an hour,' Peter told her.

'Thanks.' She grabbed hold of Kathy's arm and pulled her out of the room. 'Let's go to the mess. I'm gasping for a cup of tea, and then I want to hear all about that gorgeous man you're working for.'

'You didn't give me a chance to ask if I could have an hour as well.'

'Oh, that nice man wouldn't mind.'

I sincerely hope so, Kathy thought as they found a quiet table where they could talk without being overheard. She started to laugh.

'What's so funny?'

'I couldn't believe what I saw in ops. How do you get away with it?'

'Get away with what?' Alice asked with a completely innocent expression on her face.

'You don't call anyone "sir", not even the admiral, and he really is a sir.'

'I know. Those men in there are planning an invasion, and it will be the navy's responsibility to get thousands of fighting troops onto the beaches as safely as possible. If they fail, then the consequences for this country and Europe will be unthinkable. They think I'm clever but a bit potty and I make them laugh. They need some light relief, and that's what I provide.'

Her friend was completely serious now. 'But I don't understand why they don't reprimand you.'

'They don't because I'm good at finding things others miss. And as for calling them "sir" all the time, it isn't in my nature to bow down to anyone. I was brought up in a rough area, and I found out at a very early age that I was different. That didn't go down well, and I had to stick up for myself or they would have made my life hell. I am what I am, Kathy, and people just have to accept that. I treat everyone the same, even a peer of the realm.' She grinned. 'Anyway, that's enough of my life history. What do you call that man you work for?'

'Sir, when anyone is around, but David when we are on our own.'

'There you are, then. You be sure you make him smile because intelligence sections have got to convince Hitler we are going to invade at the shortest route, and that isn't going to be easy.'

'I'll do my best.' Kathy studied her friend with interest. 'I think that scatty person you present to the world is just a front in an effort to hide just how intelligent you are.'

Alice shrugged, and just beamed her bright smile.

'All right, I know you're not going to talk about it any more, so tell me what you have been up to.'

Chapter Twenty-Four

David stared at the closed door for a few moments, deep in thought, and then he walked over to Peter. 'I can't believe the admiral lets that girl get away with it.'

'He likes her and she's very good. Her memory is extraordinary – once seen, never forgotten. Would you have taken her with you if the admiral had sanctioned you going in to have a look around?'

'Fortunately, I don't have to make that decision. The thing that would concern me the most is whether she would take orders – if not she would be a danger to everyone. I have a nagging feeling that she's not as potty as she makes out, though.'

'She isn't.'

He looked at Peter with interest. 'How do you know?'

'I've seen her record. It's very detailed and goes right back to her childhood. She's had a tough upbringing, and this was discovered when they did a security check. That girl was born in the slums and has had to fight her way to a better life. She played down her memory because it caused trouble while she was growing up. You know how kids can react to someone who is different from them. However, the war has changed all that, and her talent is needed by us. Don't be fooled by the outward appearance; she's tough, David.'

'You all like her, don't you?'

'We do and feel protective towards her.'

'Ah.' His smile was wry. 'So I take it that if I did want to take her with me anytime, there would be opposition?'

'Without a doubt.'

'Would you mind if I ask two of my men to have a look at those photos?'

'Not at all. We would appreciate any opinions.'

When he returned to the office, only Ted was there. 'Where's Alan?'

'Just popped out for a minute. He'll be right back.'

'I'll wait. There's something I want you both to have a look at.'

The moment Alan returned David took them to ops and set out the photos. 'Tell me what you see.'

Ted took his time, then sat back and shook his head. 'Damned if I can see anything. They look the same to me.'

Alan then took his place at the table. 'They look the

same . . . Oh, wait a minute, there is something there, I think. But what on earth is it?'

'We think it could be a new gun facing out to sea,' David told them.

Alan was still studying the photos. 'I doubt that very much.'

'Alice is sure,' Peter came across and stood beside them.

Sitting back, Alan said, 'There is a slight change in the area, but it could be anything.'

'Someone could go in and have a look,' Ted suggested.

'No, the admiral has already vetoed that idea. We don't want to alert them that we might be interested in that beach.'

Alan nodded. 'If it was desperate to know for sure what is there, then someone would have to go in by sub and swim to shore.'

David grimaced. 'Well that would rule me out. I can't swim.'

'I can,' Alice told them, all smiles as she joined them. 'If I come with you I could tow you ashore. You ought to be able to swim and I'll teach you if you like, Intelligence.'

They all laughed, and Alan asked, 'Why do you call him Intelligence?'

'That's what he is.'

'No, he's called "sir".'

Alice frowned. 'Really? I don't think I know that word.'

'Wren Turnbull, stop teasing my men and come over here,' the admiral ordered.

'Oops! The boss calls.' Alice turned quickly and walked over to him, the smile still on her face.

'How long has she been in the Wrens?' Ted asked.

'Since 1941,' Peter said.

'Good heavens,' Alan exclaimed. 'How has she lasted that long?'

'She's got a talent that is proving useful.' Peter gave the men an amused look. 'I wouldn't say any of you are what one would call conventional, but we make allowances because you are good at what you do.'

'In what way are we not conventional?' David asked, trying to hide a smile.

'You come and go – mostly go, without a word to anyone. Some of the time we don't even know where you are or what you're doing. Also, David roars around on that powerful motorbike instead of taking a car like any respectable naval officer.'

'Ah, there is that, of course.' Ted shrugged. 'But we don't pretend to be respectable officers, sir.'

Peter laughed. 'Go back to whatever it is you do, and for heaven's sake don't disappear for a while. We might need you.'

'Wouldn't dream of it, sir,' Alan replied. 'We are busy trying to find ways to confuse the enemy.'

'That should be easy. You sure as hell confuse me.'

As they left ops, Ted said dryly, 'He trusts us, really.'

David strode into the office with the other two right behind him. He turned his head. 'Did you want something?'

'Tea and biscuits?' Ted replied, looking hopefully at Kathy.

As soon as the two men had followed them into the office, Kathy knew what they were going to want, and was already making a large pot of tea.

'If you are staying, sit down; you are making the place look untidy,' David told them.

'I can't believe they allow that potty girl to practically order them around,' Ted said, stretching out his legs and keeping his eyes on what Kathy was doing.

'Watch what you are saying,' she told him. 'She isn't potty, and she's my friend.'

'I agree with that.' Alan took a biscuit. 'I believe there is a sharp mind behind that ready smile.'

'You could be right,' Ted admitted. 'But for a moment there my heart stopped beating at the thought that we might be ordered to take her on a mission. It would have been crazy for several reasons. One – it would be damned dangerous. Two – taking a girl who was unlikely to obey orders would put everyone at risk. Three – it would be a waste of time because there's nothing there.'

'But suppose there is,' David pointed out.

'Let the ships pound it before the troops go in.'

'Fortunately, that's what has been agreed. This isn't our job.' Alan took a mug from Kathy, smiling his thanks. 'Our task is to distract attention away from that area.'

David nodded. 'I agree, though I'd dearly love to know for sure what is there.'

The door of the office swung open and Alice came in. 'Ah, good, I'm just in time for tea.' She perched on the end of Kathy's desk. 'Pity we can't go and have a look, but never mind. What about those swimming lessons, Intelligence?'

'No, thanks.'

She gave him a saucy look. 'That's a shame, because I was looking forward to seeing you in swimming trunks.'

Trying very hard not to laugh he said in his best military voice, 'Wren Turnbull, the admiral might tolerate your cheek, which is close to insubordination, but I will not. You address me as "Commander" or "sir".'

'Kathy calls you David.'

He lowered his head until he was level with her face. 'Don't you dare.'

She grinned at Alan and Ted. 'He's lovely when he's trying to be stern, isn't he? I was hoping he'd give me a ride on his motorbike. Kathy told me he drives ever so fast.'

David gave an exaggerated sigh. 'I can see I'm wasting my time trying to get you to behave in the proper manner. What are you doing here, anyway?'

'I came to see Kathy.'

'I didn't say you could.'

'Do I need to ask you?'

'Yes, you do. You ask, politely, "May I see your assistant for a moment, *sir*?"'

'Well, I don't need to do that now because she's standing right here and making tea.' She looked hopefully at him. 'I'm gasping for a cuppa.'

Kathy had kept her face turned away from the men all the time this was going on in case she burst out laughing. She knew exactly what David was doing – he was playing with her.

'The admiral will be looking for you.'

'No, he won't. I've finished my shift and I'm free for the rest of the day, so I thought I'd come and have a nice chat with my friend, and all of you.'

David raised his eyes to the ceiling as if in prayer, and then told her, 'You are the most exasperating girl I have ever met. How did you even get into the Wrens?'

'They took me because I'm clever. I don't usually tell anyone that, but my education wasn't up to their standard, so I used what talent I had to convince them to take me.' She found a chair and sat down, clearly intending to stay.

Alan and Ted were struggling not to dissolve into helpless laughter as they watched David trying to cope with Alice.

'Oh, for heaven's sake!' he finally said, allowing his amusement to show. 'Give her a cup of tea, Kathy, or we'll never get rid of her.'

'Fancy going to the pictures or dancing tonight?' she asked, as Kathy handed her a mug of tea.

'Dancing, I think.'

'Good idea.' Alice look pointedly at David, and then back to her friend. 'Can you come now?'

'No, she can't,' David told her firmly. 'I need her for about another hour.'

'I'll wait, then, and we can go back to our digs together.'

'It's called the Wrennery,' Alan reminded her.

'That's a daft thing to call it, and I never did get the hang of all that naval terminology.' She finished her tea and sat back comfortably in her chair.

Seeing she had every intention of staying, David sighed. 'Goodnight, Alice.'

'Are you going somewhere?'

'No, but you are. You can't wait for Kathy in here. She will join you later.'

'Oh, right.' She stood up. 'I expect you want to discuss secret things. See you soon, Kathy, and we'll have a great time tonight.' Giving a little wave to everyone and her usual grin, Alice left the office.

'I don't think I've ever met anyone like her before,' Ted remarked the moment the door closed. 'She wasn't in control when we went to inspect the new arrivals, or we would certainly have tried to persuade her to come out with us, wouldn't we, Alan?'

He nodded, looking thoughtful. 'She must be exceptional to be tolerated. You can bet she has been thoroughly assessed.'

'She has,' Kathy told him. 'Towards the end of our training they took her away somewhere for two days. When she came back she wouldn't say anything except they had just wanted to see how good her memory was. She always joked and played down her talent, just as she is still doing.'

'In my work as a lawyer I have only come across one person with that kind of memory. It's a rare thing.'

Alan stood up. 'I'd like to get to know her. I'll see if I can catch up with her.'

'And I'm also packing up for the day.' Ted winked at Kathy. 'I've got a date.'

After they had left, David dumped a pile of paperwork on her desk. 'Perhaps we can get some work done now. That lot needs filing, and once you've done that and finished typing the report, you can call it a day. Tomorrow we will go to the camp. I have parcels for the boys. Christmas is only three weeks away and that's a difficult time for them.'

'Yes, I expect they are worried about their families knowing they can't do anything to help them. I have some things for Erik and will find a small gift for Max and Gerhard as well.'

'I doubt there will be any work for them at the farm this time of year, so we will probably have to see them in the camp.'

'Will they let me in?'

'I'll see they do.' David smiled at her. 'Erik will be disappointed if not. I wonder how his English is coming along?'

'Quite well, I expect. He's eager to learn and he has good teachers in his brother and Max.'

He glanced at his watch. 'On second thoughts, you had better get going or I will have your friend storming in here accusing me of working you too hard.'

'She's only testing you to see how much she can get away with.'

'I know that and enjoyed our little battle.'

Kathy tipped her head to one side and smiled at him. 'She likes you, I could tell.'

'That's a relief. I wouldn't like to be her enemy,' he joked. 'That could be seriously dangerous. Enjoy your evening and don't let her get you into any trouble.'

When she arrived at the Wrennery, Alice was waiting with four of the other girls.

'Ah, there you are at last,' she exclaimed the moment she walked in. 'Hurry up and get ready because we are all going dancing. The men won't know what's hit them when six smart Wrens walk in. Wonder if there will be any officers there?'

'Why, are you going to salute and call them sir?' Kathy teased.

'Don't be daft.'

They all laughed, and Kathy hurried to her cabin to get ready for what could prove to be a hilarious evening. She was so pleased Alice had been assigned to Dover because they had got on well during training, and she had missed her.

Alice came and sat on her bed while she changed, chatting away just as she had always done. 'That man you work for is quite something. I like him.'

'He likes you too.'

'Does he?' Her friend beamed. 'Do you mind?'

She stopped lacing her shoes and looked up in surprise. 'Why would I mind?'

'Well, I saw the way you look at each other.'

'What do you mean by that?'

'There's something special between you. Any fool can see that.'

Kathy shook her head. 'You've got it wrong. We've been together quite a while now and have become friends.'

'If you say so. Ready? Let's go and find some handsome men to dance with. I fancy an airman. How about you?'

'What about an American?' she joked.

'Hey, that might be interesting. Can you jive?'

'As a matter of fact, I can. I went to a dance with David and some sailors taught us how to do it.'

Alice smirked. 'Aha!'

Chapter Twenty-Five

'Did you enjoy your evening?' David asked the next morning.

'It was fun. Six of us went to the dance.'

'Did Alice behave herself?'

'Good as gold, and she was very popular, never lacking a partner.' Kathy chuckled at the memory. 'I was so pleased to see her again. When the letters stopped coming I thought she had forgotten me.'

'Did she say why she didn't answer your letters?'

'No, all she would say was that they moved her around a lot. She thought I had forgotten her as well.'

'Things can get snarled up at times.' He looked at the packages she had put on her desk. 'Presents for the boys?'

'I had to find something in a hurry, so I hope they will be all right.'

'They will be pleased to receive anything, and the fact we have remembered them in this way will be a present in itself. We are limited in what we can give them. Everything will be checked before they are handed over.'

Kathy nodded. 'Are we going on the bike?'

'It's the quickest way, and I'm afraid this will have to be a short visit. If we go now we can be back before lunchtime.'

The early morning frost was almost gone by the time they were on their way. David was clearly in a hurry, and she leant into his back to shelter from the wind whizzing past her face.

On arrival she was struck by how bleak the camp looked on a cold winter's day, and she shivered as she followed David in.

He paused at the gate. 'Be careful what you say. Max is a long-time friend, and you have helped the brothers, but we must both remember we are at war with their country and they are our prisoners. They will be hungry for information and Max in particular might try to catch us off guard.'

'I'll be careful,' Kathy assured him.

The guard saluted when they entered, and as usual inspected their papers, although he knew them by now. 'The prisoners you want to see have been informed you are coming, sir. They will be here shortly.'

'Thank you. We have parcels for them.'

'Put them on the table and we will go through them

first.' He smiled at Kathy. 'I can't promise they will be as expertly packed when we've finished with them.'

'I'm sure you will do your best,' she told him, smiling warmly to let him know it didn't matter.

'Come with me, please.' The guard took them to a small room containing only a table and several chairs, but at least it was warm.

'Any chance of a pot of tea?' David asked. 'It's perishing out there.'

'Of course. You must have had a cold ride on that motorbike, sir.'

'We did, but we are pushed for time, and it is the quickest way to travel.'

Another guard arrived with the parcels after checking them, and then went to collect the prisoners.

The faces of the three men lit up with pleasure when they came into the room. Erik's English had improved a lot and his attention was focused mostly on Kathy. Clearly the way she had helped him had made a great impression on the boy.

She handed out the gifts they had brought with them, and then said to Erik, 'There are more pencils and paper for you, and a small gift as Christmas is nearly here.'

'Thank you. I know not how I can repay you for your kindness. Gerhard feels the same.'

'You don't owe me anything, because you have already given me a gift beyond price,' she told both the brothers.

They looked puzzled and Gerhard asked, 'How can that be?'

She chose her words carefully. 'Something had happened to me and I was consumed with anger. When I met you, that debilitating fury drained away from me. So you see, we helped each other.'

Erik was frowning and had to ask his brother what she had said. He listened and said something in his own language.

It was her turn to ask for a translation.

Gerhard smiled gently. 'My brother is concerned that you have been hurt, and wonders what could have made such a gentle girl so angry.'

'What caused it is in the past, and what matters is that the feeling no longer troubles me.'

Erik understood what she had said that time and reached across the table to squeeze her hand for a moment.

Kathy smiled at him and changed the subject. 'I see you have your folder with you. May we have a look at your drawings?'

He pushed it across to her and she began turning the sheets one by one, taking her time to study the drawings. They were all of life in the camp and of the men doing various things. They were exquisite. 'Look at these,' she said to David.

He stopped talking to Max and leant across, and after a brief glance took the drawings from her and studied them carefully. 'My word, Erik, these are wonderful.'

The boy was clearly pleased with the praise. 'You think they good?'

'Better than good. Please keep them very safe because when the war is over we could probably have an exhibition. They will be of tremendous interest.'

That needed a translation and David repeated it again in German.

That prospect excited both the brothers, but Max was subdued. He asked softly, 'And will the war soon be over, my friend?'

David turned his attention back to Max, taking his time before speaking. 'That is something no one can answer. Only time will tell how and when the fighting will stop.'

'You still use your favourite saying – only time will tell.' Max smiled then. 'But, of course, you are right. Forget I asked.'

The conversation then turned to more ordinary subjects, and they spent an hour laughing and joking, avoiding all serious topics.

When they left the camp and walked over to the bike, David lit a cigarette and drew in deeply, blowing the smoke up to the sky. Kathy could see his tension. 'You found that hard, but it was worth coming. They were so pleased to see us.'

'I know, but seeing Max behind barbed wire like that and knowing what is being planned is very hard. I know him and his family well and it's difficult to keep in mind that he is the enemy, and yet that is what he is.'

'That is bound to change once the war is over and time will heal the wounds.'

'Let us hope so.' He stubbed out his cigarette and smiled at her. 'You handled the brothers well by showing them they had helped you without going into details.'

'I didn't want them to feel indebted to me, and I wanted to show that meeting them had been to our mutual benefit.'

'Knowing that brought them some comfort because I saw it in their eyes.'

'Thank you, that's a relief.'

David got on the bike and she settled behind him. When the machine roared into life, Kathy glanced across at the camp and saw three men waving. She waved back as they moved off, pleased the visit had gone so well.

There wasn't much time off for any of them over Christmas, but on New Year's Eve Alice breezed into the office.

David glanced up from what he was doing. 'Hello, Alice, we haven't seen you for a while. Are you still bossing the admiral around?'

Her bright grin appeared. 'I have persuaded him to let us all have the night off, so we can go to the dance.'

'What's this about a dance?' Alan walked in with Ted.

'There's a big dance in the town,' Alice told him. 'Want to come?'

He glanced at Ted who nodded. 'You can count us in. Who else is going?'

'Kathy, six more of the girls, and Intelligence, of course.'

'I haven't agreed to come,' David told her.

'Oh, come on, Intelligence, we can't go without you.' She gave him a saucy grin. 'I've been told you can jive, and that I've got to see.'

David thought for a moment, then put some papers in the drawer of his desk and locked it. 'All right. What time?'

Alice did a little jig of delight. 'We'll meet at the castle at eight o'clock, and then we can all go into town together.'

'We'll be there,' Ted told her.

'Don't be late and wear your best uniforms. I always wanted to go out with gold braid ever since I saw Kathy with her dad when we were training.'

Kathy laughed. 'Don't try and kid us that you haven't had a date or two with an officer.'

'That would be telling.' Alice smiled sweetly at David. 'I'm off duty now so can Kathy come with me? There's something we have to do before tonight.'

'Is there?' Kathy gave her friend a questioning look, wondering what she was up to now.

Alice nodded. 'And it might take some time. So, what about it, Intelligence?'

'I'll agree just to get you out of my office. And whatever you do, don't call me Intelligence at the dance.'

The breezy, cheeky girl became serious. 'I'm not daft, Commander. What happens in this tunnel doesn't come out with me.'

'I believe you, and I'm well aware you are not daft, as you put it.'

The bright smile was back. 'We'll have a lovely time tonight, and we must make the most of it, because 1944 is going to be a busy and special year. Come on, Kathy, we have things to do.'

'See you later, girls,' Alan called as they left the office.

'Have you got any clothing coupons?' Alice asked, as soon as they were outside.

'Yes. Why, do you want some?'

'No, but you do. Run, there's the bus we need.'

'Why are we catching this bus?' Kathy asked the moment they had successfully jumped on.

'We're going shopping, because all of us girls are discarding uniforms and dressing like proper women. I've seen your meagre wardrobe and you haven't got a party frock.'

'I keep meaning to buy some civilian clothes, but it just doesn't seem necessary,' she admitted.

'It is, and I bet that man of yours has never seen you in anything pretty.'

Kathy sighed. 'He isn't mine. I just work for him.'

'So you keep saying. Ah, this is our stop. I know a shop that might have something suitable. Oh, I forgot, have you got any money on you?'

'Some.'

'That's all right, then. I've got a bit as well, so we might manage between us.'

Knowing it was useless to protest, Kathy followed her friend to the shop. She was right, anyway, because if all the girls were wearing frocks, then she couldn't be the odd one out in uniform.

Being wartime there wasn't much available in the way of smart frocks and Kathy doubted they would find anything to suit her.

'How about this?' Alice held up a brightly coloured garment.

She grimaced and shook her head.

'Perhaps something like this would be more to your taste.' The shop assistant appeared from the back of the shop holding a plain, deep-red frock. 'This has only just arrived, and I think it is your size. Try it on.'

Kathy took it from her and went into the changing room. The moment she slipped it over her head she knew it was for her. It had a fairly high slashed neckline, long sleeves, fitted snugly around the waist and the skirt had a slight flare that came to just below her knees. She liked it a lot.

Stepping out of the changing room she did a twirl for Alice to show how the skirt moved.

Her friend clapped in approval. 'It's plain but elegant, and the colour is stunning on you. It just needs a little something to liven it up for the dance.'

'I think I have the very thing.' When Kathy asked the price, that made her hesitate. It was expensive, but she did have enough money to buy it, and it was worth it because she liked it very much. It seemed like a lifetime since she had indulged in buying pretty things for herself.

'How many coupons have you got left?' Alice wanted to know, taking them from her hand and counting them. 'Good, you've just got enough for a pair of shoes.'

'If I buy shoes as well I won't have enough money left to buy a round of drinks tonight,' she protested.

'We won't have to do that. We'll be with three highly paid naval officers.'

'I don't think they would agree that they are highly paid,' Kathy said dryly.

'Perhaps not, but they're certainly paid more than us. They are also gentlemen, and gentlemen don't let their dates buy the drinks.'

'We are not their dates. You invited them, not the other way round.'

'Minor details.' Alice ushered her out of the shop to the next one.

The only thing they had remotely suitable was a pair of black patent court shoes with a small heel. They weren't too expensive, and more importantly they were comfortable.

'Can we go now?' Kathy asked after paying for the shoes. 'I've used nearly all my coupons and most of my money.'

'It will be worth it. Come on, let's get back.'

There was a lot of laughter and excitement as they all got ready. They had to work out a rota system for the bathroom, and then their hair had to be washed and brushed into a non-military style. Make-up was scarce, but they managed to find enough lipstick for everyone. One of the girls even had a small bottle of perfume and everyone had a dab of that.

Finally, they were all ready and gathered to inspect each other.

Kathy had tied the silk scarf round her waist, and she was pleased with the effect. It emphasised her slim waist and the colours matched the dress perfectly.

'Oh my, that looks lovely,' Alice exclaimed, reaching out to touch the scarf. 'Is that real silk?'

'Yes, it was given to me. I like your dress. Green really suits you.'

'It's my favourite colour. I have to be careful what I wear with my pale skin and red hair.' She sighed when she looked at her friend. 'Not like you with your exotic dark looks. I'll bet you can wear any colour.'

'Exotic?' Kathy laughed. 'What on earth makes you say that?'

'Because that's what you are. Take a good look in the mirror sometime.' Alice clapped her hands to gain attention and stop the chatter. 'Time to go and meet our officers, my beauties, and they are not going to recognise us.'

That brought forth more laughter, and after putting on their coats they left for this night of celebration.

The dance hall was already crowded when they arrived, and the men went straight to the bar to order drinks and reserve a table while the girls left their coats.

When they walked up to the men they stood up and stared in amazement, and David's eyes fixed on Kathy.

'My goodness!' Ted exclaimed. 'Who are these lovely ladies? Do we know them?'

'I think we've seen them somewhere.' Alan bowed and held out a chair for Alice. 'I remember now, they live underground and rarely come to the surface.'

'Hey, this isn't fair.' Two more officers from the tunnel came over. 'You can't keep all these beauties to yourself.'

'You'd better come and join us, then,' David told them. 'And the next round of drinks is on you. Now, that's fair,' he teased.

It turned out to be a riotous evening with the party getting larger all the time with a mix of nationalities.

David had admired Kathy's frock and whisked her to the dance floor for the first dance, and from then on, they had only passed each other briefly as they moved from partner to partner. As midnight approached they all gathered round their table with drinks at the ready.

'Where's Alice?' Alan was scanning the room. 'That girl is hard to keep track of.'

'I'm here.' She squeezed herself in beside him. 'You didn't think I was going to let you toast the new year without me, did you?'

He laughed and placed an arm around her shoulder,

making Kathy take a good look at the two of them. Was there something between them? It certainly looked as if there was.

The countdown of the last few seconds began, and on the stroke of twelve the dance hall erupted with ear-splitting cheers. Everyone was kissing and hugging, whether they knew each other or not, then they all linked hands and sang at the top of their voices.

Kathy was enjoying the sheer exuberance of the crowd when she felt hands slip around her waist. She turned to face David, who had come up behind her.

'Happy New Year, Kathy.'

'And to you. Just look at this. There is such a feeling of hope here tonight. It's a shame Dad and your brother, Ben, can't be here as well. Is this the year we are finally going to see the end of the war in Europe?'

'That's impossible to predict. The preparation has got to be right, and the task of keeping the plans secret is enormous. There won't be any turning back this time. We have got to succeed.'

'We will,' she said confidently.

'You said that with such certainty, but—'

Kathy held up her hand to his lips to stop him. 'I know, only time will tell.'

He laughed and was about to kiss her again when they were dragged onto the floor by Alice to join in the boisterous revelling.

'No serious talking tonight,' she told them.

'All right, Alice.' David lifted her off the ground and

swung her round and round, making her squeal in delight as she was passed from one man to another.

It was a good night and wonderful to see everyone in such a buoyant, hopeful mood.

Chapter Twenty-Six

January passed into February and then March as the tension built for those closely associated with plans for the invasion of Europe. There were long hours of planning meetings and many messages to be delivered by hand. The admiral was away a lot of the time, somewhere secret with the generals and officers of all the services. Everyone was keenly aware that the plans had to be flawless for such a huge undertaking, and the navy was busy finalising details of its role. Every tiny detail had to be gone over time and time again, and it was an immense task.

The intelligence sections of all the services had one vital job and that was to fool the enemy into believing the landings would be in the Calais area. All manner of tricks were being employed, such as dummy tanks, vehicles and even landing barges, making it appear as if the build-up was for the shortest route across. Fortunately, the German code had been broken, and the Allies could read their wireless transmissions, and this was a tremendous advantage, but keeping details secret was the concern of everyone. The success of the invasion depended upon it.

One day towards the end of March, Ted and Alan arrived in the office.

'What news?' David demanded.

'We've got him, but he won't talk. The problem is, if he doesn't check-in within the next two hours they will know he's been caught,' Alan told him.

'He obviously didn't know we had tracked him down, because we found his code book.' Ted handed it over to David. 'And he's carefully written his call sign in the back. We also got his wireless set.' He put the case on the desk.

David let out a pent-up breath. 'Careless of him, but good for us. We might be able to put this to good use.'

'It's worth trying, but the slightest mistake and they will know it isn't him.'

'When you were tracking his messages what was he like? Fast, slow, any peculiarities?'

Alan pursed his lips in thought. 'He sounded rather hesitant.'

David stood and picked up the wireless set. 'Come with us, Kathy.'

He led the way along the tunnel until they reached a small, secure room, containing only one desk and a chair. They crowded in and he put the wireless set on the desk, and held the chair, indicating she should sit there.

Burning with curiosity she waited patiently while he wrote something on a pad.

He handed it over for the other two to look at and perched on the edge of the desk while they read. When they nodded he put it in front of her. 'We don't know if this will work but we have to try, because it could be of immense help in our campaign of misinformation. We have been aware for a while that someone has been using a wireless to send messages, but he kept moving and was difficult to find. It was Ted who tracked him down in the end. He was in Portsmouth and very interested in our shipping movements. We are keeping his arrest secret in the hope we can use this to send false information through.'

Kathy read the brief message, and her heart was thumping, guessing what they were going to ask her to do.

Alan came to the other side of the table. 'What we'd like you to do is send that message and see if an acknowledgement comes through. If it does, we will be in business. You will have a lighter touch than any of us and are more likely to fool them. He was quite slow, so don't rattle it off. Imagine how you felt when you were learning. Take a moment to look through the code book and let us know if you think you can do this. If not, we will have a try.'

She studied the book for a while, and then nodded. 'I'll try, but I might make a mistake or two.'

'That's all right,' Ted told her. 'He wasn't always accurate either. I think he must have been a hasty recruit and dumped here without much experience.'

She switched on the wireless and concentrated on sending each letter carefully. It was only three short words, and she sat back when finished, her hands trembling a little.

David squeezed her shoulder gently and smiled down at her. 'Well done.'

Almost immediately an acknowledgement came through and she wrote it down. The men were jubilant when they read it. Kathy looked up at the smiling faces. 'Does this mean it worked?'

'So far so good. From now on you are going to feed them false information, mixed in with a few true facts to make it believable,' David told her. 'That reply means they accepted the check-in as coming from their man. Come on, we've got work to do in preparing you to send a longer message.'

They left the small room and Ted locked it, putting the key in his pocket.

Back in the office she went to put on the water to boil when the kettle was taken out of her hands.

'I'll do that,' Alan told her. 'You see if you can get us something nice to eat as a treat. It's going to be a long day.'

Ted sighed. 'A lovely big doughnut oozing with jam and cream.'

'That's a distant memory.' She laughed, feeling relaxed now. 'But I'll see what I can do.'

She walked to the mess feeling exhilarated. They had trusted her to do an important job and were clearly delighted with the success. She couldn't ask more than to see the smiling faces of the three men she had become very fond of.

Cook smiled when he saw her. 'I know, they are hungry. What do they want?'

'Huge doughnuts oozing with jam and real cream.'

He tipped his head back and roared with laughter. 'They haven't lost their sense of humour, have they?'

'They want a treat,' she told him.

'Ah, they've been up to mischief again and are obviously pleased with the outcome. Those three parade themselves as naval intelligence, but we are damned sure they are more than that, because they often disappear and come back in a mess.' He winked at her. 'I'll see if I can find them a treat.'

'Thanks.' Kathy waited while he disappeared, mulling over what he had just said. He was right, of course. They did have a bad habit of getting into trouble.

He was soon back carrying a tray covered with a tea towel. 'Tell them I wouldn't do this for anyone else.'

'I will.' She took the tray, wondering what was on it.

'Here's a little treat for you.'

'A bar of chocolate!' she exclaimed. 'Where did you get that?'

'Made friends with some Yanks. They've got loads of the stuff, so you enjoy it. You are the one in need of a treat for looking after those officers.'

'Thank you so much.' She hurried back with a smile on her face.

The tea was already made, and she put the tray on David's desk.

'What have you got there?' he asked.

'I haven't the faintest idea.' The chocolate was on the edge of the tray and she quickly picked it up when she saw Alan begin to reach out for it. 'That was given to me as a treat.'

Three curious faces turned in her direction. 'By whom?' Alan asked.

'Cook.'

'Oh, we can't have him giving our girl gifts, can we, David?' Ted asked. 'We'll have to have a word with him. Where did he get it, anyway?'

'From some Americans. He said I was to keep it for myself, but I might share it with you.'

'Lovely.' Ted turned his attention to the tray. 'Let's see what we've got.'

David whipped away the cloth and they all stared at the tray.

'A whole sponge cake! Only the admiral gets things like that.' Alan rested his hands on Kathy's shoulder.

'That cook must really like you. Do you think you could ask him for some large, juicy steaks?'

'Don't push your luck,' she told him as she picked up the knife to cut the cake.

At that moment the door opened, and Alice swept in. 'Where did you get that?'

'Kathy wheedled it out of the cook,' Alan told her.

'Oh, well done.' She pulled a chair up to the desk. 'I'm on a tea break.'

David sighed and shook his head. 'Give her a mug of tea and a slice of cake, or we'll never hear the last of it.'

Laughing quietly to herself, Kathy served her friend first and then the men, cutting only a thin slice for herself.

'Thanks. I came just in time.' She winked at Kathy and nodded towards the man behind the desk. 'He likes me, really.'

The cake disappeared in a very short time and was enjoyed by all. She collected up the crockery. 'That was lovely. I must thank Cook.'

'Didn't you say you might share the chocolate?' David reminded her.

'Chocolate!' Alice spun round to look at her. 'You've got chocolate as well?'

'Yes, a whole bar.'

'Wow! This is like a party. Are you celebrating something?'

'Mind your own business.'

'Now don't be like that, Intelligence. Tell.'

'There's nothing to tell, and what the blazes are you doing just walking in here uninvited?'

'I don't need an invite because I work in this rabbit warren, and I came in here to tell you something.'

'What would that be?'

'I'll tell you when we've finished our tea.'

Everyone was laughing now, and Kathy set about breaking the chocolate into equal pieces and handed them round.

Alice rolled her eyes with pleasure as she popped a piece in her mouth and after a moment said, 'We've got photos of the dummy landing craft, and I thought you might like to see them. They look good from the air.'

'Dummy landing craft?'

Alice glanced from her friend to David. 'Don't you tell her anything, Intelligence?'

'We are dealing with something else at this time.'

Her eyes lit up with curiosity. 'And what would that be?'

'As I've said before, mind your own business.' He stood up. 'Show me these photos.'

'Kathy will tell me.'

'No, she won't. She knows enough to keep a secret, which is more than I can say for you.'

'Alan! Tell him he can't talk to me like that. He knows I only talk freely in here. We are all on the same side, aren't we?'

'I can't do that. He outranks me.'

Kathy watched the scene being played out in front of her, and saw that David was having great difficulty keeping a serious expression. Ted on the other hand was laughing openly, while Alan was clearly enjoying teasing Alice. Again, she wondered if there was a romance developing between them.

Popping another piece of chocolate in her mouth, Alice's bright smile was back. 'You boys are little devils, aren't you? How do you put up with them?' she asked Kathy.

'It took me a while, but I finally figured out that the only thing they are serious about is their job. This is just their way of relaxing.'

'Ah, right. What exactly do they do?' Alice whispered.

'I really don't know,' Kathy whispered back.

'Top secret, eh?' She grinned at the men. 'Come on, boys, and have a look at some pretty pictures.'

'Boys,' David muttered as they all made their way to ops. 'I swear I'll have her up on a charge before long.'

There wasn't anything wrong with her hearing and Alice turned her head to look at him. 'No, you won't, Intelligence. The admiral wouldn't allow it.'

That was too much for Ted, who roared with laughter, and David glared at him. 'Don't encourage her.'

'Sorry, sir,' Ted spluttered.

Alice fell into step beside Kathy, her usual devilish grin in place. 'He's too good-looking to dislike, isn't he?'

'Far too handsome,' she agreed.

All joking was put aside as they studied the prints.

Peter came over. 'They look convincing, don't they?'

David nodded. 'That should give them something to think about. How are the army doing with their stage setting?'

'Their rubber tanks and other vehicles are excellent and it's a damned clever idea. How is the misinformation going?'

He led Peter over to where they could talk without being overheard by the sharp ears of a certain Wren, and Ted and Alan joined them.

'He's up to something,' Alice stated.

'He's always up to something. That's his job. And that includes the other two as well.'

'Well, you tell them not to do anything dangerous. This blasted war could end this year.'

'That's optimistic, Alice.' She studied her friend. 'Are you going out with Alan?'

'When he's around, but he has a habit of disappearing.' Alice was serious for a moment. 'I know it is daft getting attached to someone while the war is on, but it crept up on me.'

'He's a good man.'

'I know, and so is your David, but I worry about them. How you manage to stay so calm when your father is out there dodging U-boats, I really don't know.'

'It was bad when the wolf packs had all the power, but things have changed, and the U-boats are the hunted now. Their losses are high.'

'Alice.' Peter came over. 'The admiral has just

returned from a strategy meeting with the other services, and he wants you to bring him those latest prints.'

'Right. See you later, Kathy.' Alice quickly gathered up the required photos and hurried out of the room.

'How does the admiral put up with her?' David wanted to know.

'He told me she reminds him of his daughter; she's evidently a bit of a rebel as well. He likes her, but he wouldn't have her here unless she was damned good at what she does. She addresses him by rank and is always polite.'

'That's more than she is with me.' David laughed softly. 'She calls me "Intelligence".'

'You're lucky, she doesn't call me anything and I keep expecting to hear her call – "Hey, mister!"'

They all laughed, including Kathy, who was always meticulous about giving the officers the respect they were entitled to.

When they were back in the office, Alan checked the time. 'We'll have to send another message in half an hour. What are we going to say?' he asked David.

'We'll mention that landing barges are being assembled and slip in a couple of unimportant things they probably already know.'

'If we keep this up too long they might twig that it isn't their man sending,' Ted pointed out.

'We'll see if we can get away with it for a week, and then say that he can't send for a while because he has been tracked down and is on the run.'

'That's a good idea, and then when they don't hear from him again they will assume he can't transmit or has been caught. We could feed them quite a bit of misinformation in a week.'

All the while Alan was talking, David was writing and handed it over for them to read.

The two men nodded in approval and Ted stood up. 'That should do nicely. Come on, Kathy.'

Over the next week, Kathy sent short messages each day, and as far as they could tell, they had got away with the deception.

'This will be the last one,' David told her. 'We are pushing our luck. I want you to appear to be in a hurry because you are in fear of being caught. They must believe this, or they might question the messages they have been receiving over the last few days.'

'Make it faster than usual, and don't worry if you make mistakes,' Ted told her. 'It will seem as if you've got to stop sending and run to avoid getting caught.'

Taking a deep breath, she did as instructed. It was easy to appear agitated – she was.

'Disconnect now!' David ordered before the complete message was sent. 'Well done, Kathy. Let's hope they bought that and all the other messages we sent.'

Now it was over she felt relieved and prayed that what they had done would help to confuse the enemy. It was absolutely vital that the campaign of misinformation was successful. So much depended upon it, and she was proud they had trusted her to do this for them.

Instead of going back to the office they guided her to the mess, found a table and sat down.

The cook saw them and came straight over. 'I can see from the look on your faces that you've been up to no good again, sirs. What can I do for you?'

'Why does he always think we've been up to mischief?' Ted complained.

'Because we usually are,' David replied.

'Ah, that's true enough.' Alan smiled at the cook. 'That was a lovely cake you gave us last time. Any chance of something like that again?'

'The chocolate was lovely too.' Ted smiled at him hopefully.

'You didn't give that to them as well, did you?' he asked Kathy.

'We shared it between five of us. I couldn't keep it all for myself.'

'Five?'

'Alice Turnbull invited herself to my office just in time for tea and cake,' David told him.

'Now there's a smashing little girl. Why isn't she with you now?'

'I expect she's with the admiral,' Alan explained. 'He likes her.'

'Everyone likes her.'

'I don't,' David told him, trying to keep a straight face.

'Of course you do, Intelligence.'

David groaned. 'Blast, here she is again.'

Undeterred by this, Alice pulled up another chair and looked at the cook. 'What are we having?'

'I'll see what I can find.' He walked away, laughing loudly.

Chapter Twenty-Seven

Bad weather held up the invasion and everyone involved waited anxiously. Ships were full of soldiers from many countries, and the huge armada of boats was ready to sail, but still conditions were not considered good enough.

Kathy could see the tension on the faces of the men in ops, and the plotters remained quiet – waiting . . .

Alan ran a hand over his tired eyes and murmured to David, 'Dear Lord, this is dangerous. We've done everything we could to see this was kept a secret, but if their planes fly over now, then they will know we are ready to invade.'

'Delay is the last thing we wanted.' Ted rolled his shoulders in an effort to ease the tension. 'I wish I could go over on the first navy ships. Waiting here is purgatory.'

'I know,' David agreed, 'but for the moment our work is done. Let's hope Hitler believes the weather is too bad for us to invade and doesn't bother to check what we are doing.'

Alice joined them, serious for a change and looking just as tense as everyone else. No one had even attempted to sleep.

Alan placed a hand on her shoulder and gave a tight smile. 'You all right?'

She nodded. 'I can't help thinking about those poor soldiers crammed into the boats, not knowing if they are going or not.'

'They will be going,' David told her. 'The moment there is a gap in the weather they will sail. We have to. There's no turning back this time.'

Suddenly the telephone rang, making them all jump, and the plotters moved towards the table. The admiral was somewhere with the heads of the other services, and Commander Douglas picked up the phone.

All eyes were on Peter when he finished listening to the call.

'The weathermen have predicted a window of better weather. Today, 6th June, is D-Day and the fleet is on its way.'

The sighs of relief were audible as the operations room sprang into action once more.

David smiled at Kathy. 'Now we have time to get something to eat. I'm starving, how about you?'

'Now you mention it, I am hungry.'

Alan turned to Alice. 'Can you join us?'

'I've got to stay here in case the admiral comes back and needs me, but I'll see you later.'

The three men and Kathy made their way to the mess, and the moment they walked in they were besieged with anxious men all wanting news.

'If you've surfaced it must mean something is happening,' the cook said. 'Is it on?'

'The invasion fleet is on its way,' David told them.

Everyone sagged with relief and one lad asked, 'Do you think they know we're coming?'

'They must know an invasion is being planned, but we are pretty sure they don't know where or when,' Alan explained.

'Let's hope you are right.' Cook studied the group of tired people in front of him. 'I suppose it's some time since you bothered to eat.'

Ted grimaced. 'I've almost forgotten what it's like to eat and sleep.'

'I don't doubt it. You all look exhausted. What would you like?'

'Anything,' they all said together.

Much to everyone's relief the enemy had been taken by surprise by the Normandy landings. The campaign of misinformation had worked and hopefully saved some lives. Within a week the Allies were moving inland, but Hitler hadn't given up. London was facing a new threat from unmanned flying bombs, nicknamed doodlebugs.

Kathy was outside looking out to sea and watching what was going on in the sky when David joined her. 'Look at that. The RAF is trying to shoot them down before they reach London.'

'Those boys can certainly fly, and that must be damned dangerous. Now we know what that ramp was for that Alice spotted in a photo.' Without removing his gaze from the sky, he said, 'One of the despatch riders told me he was riding along in London yesterday and something made him look up. There was a doodlebug coasting along with its engine cut, and it was low and right above him. He spun round and tore off in the other direction as fast as he could. He said that when it hit the ground the blast nearly knocked him off the bike. Fortunately, it landed on an old bomb site and no one was hurt.'

'That was a blessing and he had a lucky escape, then.'

'The man didn't quite see it that way. He was furious, saying that they weren't supposed to do that. They should cut their engines and dive, not glide silently along. His language was more colourful than that.'

Kathy couldn't help it and began to shake with laughter. 'I imagine it was.'

David also had a wide smile on his face. 'I told him they were machines, and as such, liable to do all sorts of strange things.'

'What did he say to that?'

'I couldn't possibly tell you.'

That made her burst into helpless laughter. 'I'm sorry, it really isn't a laughing matter, but I can just picture him looking up and seeing this thing following him.'

'Don't apologise. We must never lose our sense of humour. It's healing to laugh and relieves the tension.'

'Yes, I agree, and that's something I've learnt during this war.'

'It has taught us many lessons and made us all do things we would never have believed possible.'

'We won't be the same people we were before, will we?'

'No, we will be stronger, more resilient – and grateful for a peaceful night's sleep,' he joked.

'Sleep? What's that?'

The sky was clear now and he touched her arm. 'Come back to the office. I want to talk to you.'

When they got back he shut the door and leant against it. She waited, expecting to hear of some special job he wanted her to do.

'We've been together since early 1941,' he began. 'We have shared difficult times and some laughter. We've also had rocky moments together, but I believe they helped us to understand each other.'

Kathy straightened up in alarm. Was he going to send her away after all this time?

'I've watched you cope with grief, tragedy and anger, and I've seen you overcome those emotions with determination and courage.'

'David! Where is this going? You are frightening me.'

'I'm just stating my case so there is no

misunderstanding. You have always fiercely rejected any attempt of mine to give you a gift. The only thing you have ever accepted was the silk scarf, and that only because it was needed for a job you had to do.' He pushed away from the door and took something out of his pocket. 'I want you to allow me to give you something now and accept it without question or argument.'

Relief swept through her. He wasn't sending her away. He just wanted to give her a gift in appreciation of the time they had spent together.

He stepped forward and opened the box for her to see what was in it. It was the most beautiful gold locket she had ever seen. 'Oh, that's exquisite.'

'I'm glad you like it. The locket was my grandmother's, and I want you to have it. Will you accept it as a token of my gratitude for what we have shared together?'

'You have stated your case expertly, and I would be honoured to accept such a beautiful gift.'

Removing it from the box he held it up for her to examine closely.

'It doesn't open,' she said with surprise.

'There is a secret catch, but I'm not going to show you because I don't want you to open it until I tell you to.'

Kathy looked at him curiously. 'That is all very intriguing, but I will not attempt to open it, if that is what you want.'

'That is an order,' David told her with a smile, and

fastened it round her neck. 'I know you can't wear jewellery while in uniform, but if you tuck it under your shirt no one will know it's there.'

She looked down and touched it gently before tucking it out of sight. 'It's the most beautiful gift I have ever been given. Thank you so much. Do I have permission to hug you, sir?'

'Highly irregular, but I will allow it,' he teased.

Laughing she stepped forward, wrapped her arms around him and hugged as hard as she could, then stepped back. 'I will treasure your gift.'

His smile told her he was pleased she had accepted it.

'You have come a long way since you first arrived here.'

'That is kind of you to say so. It is largely due to two navy officers. The understanding and support I have received from you and Bill helped me through the worst times, but the healing finally came when I met Erik and his brother. I saw a frightened, worried boy who needed help, and after what I had been through I could empathise with him. His nationality didn't matter. He was just another person caught up in a war not of his choosing. We ought to go and see them sometime. They must be worried.'

'We'll go when I get back.'

'Are you going somewhere?'

David nodded and glanced at his watch. 'I'm leaving in an hour with Alan and Ted.'

'Can you tell me where you are going and how long you will be away?'

'The Allies have captured a lot of prisoners and have someone they think the navy might be interested in. We are going over to check that out.'

'All three of you?'

'We might have to bring him back with us.'

Kathy nodded. 'When does your ship sail?'

'We are flying over.'

The door opened, and Ted walked in. 'Time we were moving. Alan is already at the airfield.' He smiled at Kathy. 'We've got a nice quick plane ride this time, so could you tell the Luftwaffe to take the day off?'

'Already done,' she teased.

'That's our girl.'

David slung his bag over his shoulder and nodded to her. 'I don't know how long this is going to take. It might be a waste of time, and if so we will soon be back.'

'Take care,' she told them as they walked out of the door.

Kathy sat down, pulled the locket up and studied it. What a strange episode. Why hadn't he just given her the gift without the long explanation first? And why had he given her something that was obviously a family heirloom? It was hard to fathom.

The door opened, and Alice looked in. 'Have they gone?'

'Just a minute ago. Come in. Are you on a break?' When her friend nodded she put the kettle on to make tea. 'Did you know they were going?'

'Alan told me last night. Where did you get that?' she exclaimed when she spotted the locket Kathy hadn't slipped back under her shirt after looking at it. 'That's lovely. What's inside?'

'David gave it to me, and I don't know what's inside. It doesn't open.'

'Why? It's a locket and should open,' Alice said, examining it closely, her fingers running over it. 'There doesn't seem to be any way of opening it. Why did he give it to you? It looks old and valuable.'

'He said it had been his grandmother's, and he wanted me to have it in appreciation of the years we have worked together.'

Alice gave her friend a disbelieving look. 'And you believed that?'

'Of course. What other reason could he have?' Kathy slipped it back under her shirt. 'He said he'd show me how to open it sometime.'

'Oh, that man is devious. Wouldn't you like to know what Intelligence is playing at? You know those three; they are always up to something. From what you've told me he softened you up before giving you such an expensive present. And I've no doubt he's expert at that from his time in courtrooms. That man could convince anyone that black was white, but why use that skill on you?'

Kathy laughed. 'You are letting your imagination run away with you. We've become friends while working together, and I believe he just wanted me to have something nice. He's always been concerned that I never bothered to replace some of the things I lost when our house was destroyed by the bombs. For some reason it worried him, and we've had a couple of disagreements over it. I think he just wanted to make sure I accepted this time.'

'I suppose that might be so.' Alice still didn't look convinced. 'It seems an odd way to go about it, though.'

'It was his way, and he never does anything without a very good reason. Now, how are you getting on with Alan?' she asked, changing the subject.

'Great. He's looking forward to getting back to his proper job, as he calls it, and hinted he might have a job for me.'

'That's wonderful. Would you take it if offered?'

Alice nodded, her expression serious. 'All my life I've kept quiet about my ability to remember things once I've seen them, but joining the Wrens is the best thing I ever did. No one has made fun of me or called me names like they did when I was growing up. I've been able to use that talent to help, and it's been appreciated.'

'You should be proud to have such a talent.'

'I know that now.' Her bright smile was back. 'I'll be going up in the world if I work for Alan. What are you going to do?'

'Go back to being a secretary.'

'David might take you with him. He'll need a good secretary.'

'No doubt about that, but we'll have to see.'

'Ah, yes, only time will tell.' Alice used David's favourite saying.

'That's right. The war isn't over yet, Alice, and you never know, he might decide to stay in the navy after all.'

'No, he won't. He and Alan are both lawyers, and from what I can gather they are planning to set up in business together.'

'Really? I didn't know that.'

Alice sighed. 'For a man good with words, as he must be, he doesn't say much.'

Kathy laughed. 'That's right. When I first arrived, I found him most frustrating, but have got used to his ways over the years. My father knows him quite well and told me that David Evans never does anything without a very good reason.'

Alice looked thoughtful. 'Hmm . . . then I wonder what his reason is for giving you that locket?'

'I'm just as puzzled as you, but I'll find out when he's ready to tell me.'

'Gee, I'd like to be a fly on the wall when that day comes.'

Chapter Twenty-Eight

'Good flight, Commander?'

'Yes, thank you. What have you got for us, Colonel?'

'We've gathered up quite a lot of prisoners and they are all army, except one. He's navy and it was thought you might be interested in talking to him.'

'And why was that?' David asked.

'It seemed strange he was in this area alone.'

'Have you spoken to him?' Alan wanted to know.

'He insists he doesn't speak English, and I don't have anyone fluent enough in German to interrogate him. I'll send the sergeant for him.'

'Let's have a look at him first. Take us into the camp.'

The colonel nodded, and they followed him to an area that had been hastily fenced off to hold the prisoners.

'This is only temporary. We didn't expect to have so many prisoners to accommodate.'

The guard on duty saluted and watched the three naval officers with interest as they strode in amongst the prisoners and began talking to them in their own language.

They took their time walking through the camp, stopping every so often to talk, looking friendly and casual. When one complimented David on his German, he told them about the friend he'd had at school, causing interested questions, which he answered. There was quite a crowd around them as they listened to David talking about his friend – the U-boat captain.

The sailor they had come for was standing away from the crowd and watching them with suspicion.

As they moved away from the group David murmured quietly to his companions, 'Did you notice those two?'

Ted nodded. 'We clocked them. They don't look as if they belong here.'

'You go over to our sailor while I have a quick word with the colonel.' David had almost reached the colonel when he overheard their conversation.

'Who are they?' the sergeant was asking, giving his colonel a questioning glance.

'Navy intelligence.'

'Ah. Tell you what, Colonel, I wouldn't want to mess with those three. Looks like they know what they are about. Look at them walking around and talking to everyone in German as if they are old friends. They might appear to be navy gents, but they ain't. Clever bastards, I'd say.'

'Watch your language, Sergeant.' David appeared in front of them.

The soldier spun round. 'Sorry, sir. No disrespect intended, sir.'

David nodded and turned back to the colonel. 'It would be wise to check those two standing by the fence in deep conversation. Don't look over there, Sergeant. They are not what they appear to be. Our guess is SS masquerading as ordinary soldiers. They could make trouble for you.'

The colonel frowned. 'I'll take your word for it and get them moved.'

'Do it quickly,' David advised. 'They don't like us being here. We'll take the sailor out of here, and once we have gone, deal with those two.'

He called a guard over. 'Go and get the military police and look sharp about it.'

'Yes, sir.'

'Thank you, Commander. Will you be bringing the sailor back when you've interrogated him?'

'No. He's the only sailor in the group and is clearly uneasy. We will probably take him back with us.'

'Very well. You can use the house I've commandeered as headquarters until you can arrange a flight back. It is well guarded, and your prisoner will be secure there.'

'That will be helpful.'

The colonel gave a wry smile. 'If you are around for a while I might ask you to take another look at the prisoners for me.'

'Glad to help.' When he turned to walk over to where Alan and Ted were talking to the young sailor, he heard the sergeant mutter, 'That man moves like a bloody panther, and I almost feel sorry for their prisoner. You sure they are navy and not special forces?'

'What's so amusing?' Ted asked when he reached them.

'That sergeant doesn't know what to make of us.' He nodded to the prisoner who was watching them warily, clearly uneasy. 'Come with us.'

'I'm not going anywhere with you,' he declared. 'Once you get me out of this camp you will torture me and then shoot me.'

David sighed. 'Where do they get these ideas from? I give you my word we will not harm you in any way. We thought it would be better if we took you away from the other prisoners. You don't belong here, and that is obvious by the way you are keeping away from them.'

Although not sure he could believe them, the sailor went quietly with them in the end.

'What's your name?' David asked as they walked to the house.

'Hans Kline.'

'And what are you doing in this area of France?'

'I am recuperating from an appendix operation and came here for a rest. I chose the wrong place.'

'That's hard luck.' Alan opened the door of the house

and they went into the kitchen-cum-office, where they had first met the colonel.

'Wonder if they've got any tea here?' Ted was busy going through the cupboards.

A soldier had followed them in. 'The colonel said I was to look after you. Would you like me to make you some tea?'

'Please,' they all said together.

David smiled at the prisoner. 'Do you like tea, Hans?' He nodded.

'Good, that will be tea for all of us, Corporal.'

'Anything to eat?' Alan asked. 'I'm starving.'

'I have bread and could make you spam sandwiches.'

'That will do nicely.' Alan turned to Hans. 'Did you come here on your own?'

'Yes, sir.'

They talked casually for a while, not putting Hans under any pressure and getting him to relax in their company.

'Ah, thank you, Corporal.' Ted smiled when a plate of sandwiches and a pot of tea appeared on the table. 'Dive in everyone. Do you take sugar, Hans?'

'No sugar.' He was looking from one man to the other, clearly confused by the three British naval officers who spoke good German, and even more bewildered by their friendly attitude.

'Are you completely well now?' David asked. 'If you are not, there is a good medical team here.'

'I am fully recovered, sir, and came here just for a rest as my ship had sailed. I had time for a short holiday, but unfortunately found myself in the middle of an invasion. I hid for a while but was caught trying to get away from here.'

David held out the plate of sandwiches for him, and when he took one, asked, 'More tea?'

'Yes, please.'

The food and tea disappeared at a fast rate and Alan sighed. 'That's better. Thank you, Corporal.'

'My pleasure, sir.'

'When were you due back from your holiday?' Ted asked casually.

'Several days ago.'

'Ah, then your shipmates will wonder where you've got to.' David shook his head in sympathy. 'What's your ship?'

'*Tirpitz*—' The moment he said it he stopped suddenly, dismayed.

'I've seen photos of her,' David continued as if he hadn't noticed the sailor's mistake. 'She's a fine ship.'

'The best.' Hans looked at them defiantly. 'You will not be able to sink her.'

'No vessel is unsinkable, Hans. What is your rank?'

'I'm the wireless officer.'

'That's an important job and they must miss you. Where were you going to rejoin her?'

'I will say no more. I know what you are doing. You are trying to make me careless with your friendly manner.' Hans folded his arms and glared at David, lips firmly pressed together.

'Well, we had to try.' David stood up, stretched and said to his companions, 'What say we go and have a look round the place? I could do with a walk.'

'Good idea,' Ted agreed.

'I wouldn't recommend that, sirs,' the corporal told them. 'We haven't cleared the area completely yet. There are still a few pockets of resistance.'

'We'll be careful.' Alan went over to the bags they had left in a cupboard and removed a leather belt containing a gun, then strapped it on, waiting while the others did the same.

When they were ready David asked the corporal if he would guard the prisoner while they were away. 'We won't be long.'

'Yes, sir.' He still looked doubtful. 'Would you like a military escort, sirs?'

'That won't be necessary.'

'Then may I suggest you keep within our perimeter. That is the only area we have cleared for sure.'

'Understood.' David nodded agreement as they walked out of the house.

'I assume our afternoon stroll is to give our prisoner time to stew,' Alan remarked, and then smiled. 'A wireless operator from the *Tirpitz*, now that is very interesting.'

'It is,' David agreed, 'and we must take him back with us. We need to get him on our turf and see if we can prise more out of him.'

'Might not—' Ted stopped abruptly when a voice shouted from some bushes.

'Halt!'

They watched two very young men emerge from their hiding place pointing guns at them.

'So much for this area being cleared,' Ted muttered softly.

'Damn,' Alan swore, 'they are only kids.'

'Speak only in German,' David told his friends.

The tallest of the boys waved his gun and told them to put their weapons on the ground.

David laughed as if it was a joke and said to Alan, 'We must recommend these brave soldiers for a medal.'

The other two joined in, nodding agreement and talking expertly while they watched the confusion appear on the youngsters' faces.

'You British?' the other boy asked.

Ted grinned and shook his head, taking a step forward. 'We are pretending to be in order to avoid capture.' He edged forward a little more, appearing relaxed.

The moment the boys dropped their guard they found themselves without weapons and now the prisoners.

'You fooled us!' one of the boys said, clearly frightened by this sudden turnaround. 'Now you will shoot us.'

'Don't be silly,' David told them. 'We don't kill young boys. We are going to take you back to the camp.'

When they arrived, the colonel smirked with amusement. 'What have you got there, gentlemen?'

'We found these two hiding in bushes.' Alan handed over the rifles to the sergeant. 'I would say they are not very experienced, and we confused them quite easily.'

The colonel raised his eyebrows. 'From what my corporal tells me you are very good at that.'

'That's kind of him to say so,' Ted joked. 'We do our best.'

'I suppose you were involved in convincing the enemy we would land in the Calais area?'

'We were part of that, of course,' David told him. 'They were certain we would need to secure a large harbour to bring in supplies, but the boffins had invented the Mulberry Harbour, which we towed over.'

'And what a damned clever idea that was.' The colonel beckoned to the sergeant. 'Take the prisoners' details and search them for weapons before putting them in the camp.'

'We've already done that,' Alan told him.

'I'm sure you have, but we'll do it again.'

'May we use your wireless to arrange a flight back?'

'Of course, Commander. What about the sailor?'

'He's coming with us.'

They landed at Biggin Hill where there was a car waiting for them.

'I've been instructed to take you and your prisoner straight to the camp, sir. They are expecting us.'

David sat in the back with Ted, and Hans between them, and Alan got in the front with the driver.

As they drove through the Kent countryside their prisoner leant forward to get a better view. It was a lovely day and showed the scenery at its best.

'Beautiful, isn't it?' David said quietly.

Hans nodded, looking rather apprehensive and still confused.

They hadn't questioned him again, knowing he wouldn't tell them any more at that time. Once he was settled in the camp there was always the chance he would be more talkative later. It was late afternoon when they reached the camp and still warm, so the prisoners were all outside enjoying the sun.

Erik saw them first and after alerting the others he ran towards the fence and began waving, a big smile on his face. Gerhard and Max immediately joined him.

When David waved to them Hans stared in astonishment.

'Let's get you settled,' he told him. 'They are all navy here, so you will be all right with them.'

The camp commander was waiting for them and Ted asked, 'Is there any chance of a meal? We are starving.'

The army officer grinned. 'Now why doesn't that surprise me? Corporal!' he called. 'Ask the cookhouse to feed these men.'

'Yes, sir.'

'While we are waiting, can we see Max and the brothers? They saw us arrive.'

'Of course. Make yourselves comfortable. I'll send for them.'

When he'd left, Alan said, 'Sit down, Hans. You must be hungry as well.'

The door burst open and Erik erupted into the

room, quickly followed by his brother and Max.

Hans shot to his feet when he saw Max and saluted smartly.

Alan and Ted had only seen them once before, but they smiled and shook hands. Max greeted David like the old friend he was and slapped him on the shoulder.

'Where's Kathy?' Erik wanted to know.

'She isn't with us, but I'll bring her next time,' David told him. 'We have just come to deliver another guest for you. This is Hans Kline, and he will be joining you.'

With the introductions made, Hans looked as if he couldn't believe what he was seeing. 'But, Captain, you talk to these men as if they are friends.'

'They are. I went to school here with David and we spent many happy times with both of our families. When we were captured, David's assistant, Kathy, helped Erik and Gerhard, and continues to do so. We are all very grateful and fond of her.'

'How can that be? We are enemies.'

'We may be on different sides of this conflict,' David explained, 'but we must not allow that to destroy kindness and friendship.'

Hans turned again to Max, shaking his head in bewilderment. 'They try to get information out of us.'

'That's their job and they do it well, but they do not use force to make us talk to them. These three men are clever, and we don't forget that, but we must remain loyal to our own country. That is the nature of war,

Hans. Friend or enemy, we do not tell them anything that could be used against us.'

'This is all very strange.'

The men laughed and nodded.

'We would agree with that,' David remarked dryly. 'Ah, here comes the food. Have you had your meal?'

'Yes,' Max told him.

'In that case you can watch us eat. We haven't had anything for ages.'

Everyone sat around the large table talking in German, so Hans could understand. Gerhard sat next to the new prisoner, trying to put him at his ease, for it was clear he still didn't believe they could be this friendly.

'Do you need more drawing materials?' David asked Erik.

He laughed. 'I always need more. Farmer George kindly gave me a pad to draw in.'

'Good, and we will see what we can get you. I hope you are keeping your drawings safe.'

Erik nodded, serious now. 'Will the war be over soon? By Christmas, perhaps?'

'The hope is that it will be, for everyone's sake,' David told him gently, 'but it is impossible to predict when that will happen.'

'We are worried about our families,' Gerhard told him. 'Would you be able to come now and again to talk to us? There is little need for secrecy now.'

'We will come and tell you what we can, I promise.' He

turned to Erik. 'Could I borrow one of your drawings of the camp? I have an artist friend I would like to show it to.'

His face lit up with pleasure and he jumped to his feet. 'I will get them, and you can choose.'

'This friend of yours would be interested?' Gerhard asked when his brother had left the room.

'I'm sure of it. He has a gallery and is very keen on supporting up-and-coming artists.'

Erik must have run all the way because he came back with a pile of drawings and was slightly out of breath.

Ted cleared a space on the table and they spread out the drawings to be examined. He whistled softly. 'My word, they are good.'

While David studied each one carefully, Erik never took his eyes off him. 'I was so frightened of you the first time we met, and I never believed to find such kindness.'

David looked up and smiled. 'After Kathy saw you I would not have been allowed to be unkind to you,' he joked.

'Ah, beautiful girl.' Erik turned to Hans and began to tell him what had happened when they had been captured.

Continuing to look through the drawings, David shook his head. 'I don't know which to choose, they are all so good. What do you think, Alan?'

'Why not take several?' Erik suggested.

'Would you mind? If my friend likes your work, he might want to put some in his gallery. Would that be all right?'

'I would be honoured.' He was clearly excited and looked at his brother. 'That is good, yes?'

'That is very good and so kind of David to take such an interest.'

'Not at all. I think these should be seen.' David held up one of the drawings. 'This is beautiful. I will buy it from you. Name your price.'

The boy looked shocked and shook his head in denial. 'I will not take money from you. Please, it is yours.'

'Thank you. I will bring you lots of drawing materials next time I come.'

'That I will accept,' Erik said.

Alan took the drawing from David and showed it to Ted. 'That is an exquisite drawing of Kathy.'

'Quite stunning.' David then removed three drawings from the pile. 'With your permission, Erik, I will take these to my friend. They will be taken good care of.'

With Erik's agreement they made ready to leave, and Max came to stand next to his friend, speaking softly in English. 'The *Tirpitz* battleship is still out there, and I will not let Hans talk to you. You will not try to trick him into revealing vital information.'

'As if I would.'

'Oh yes you would, my friend, and I suspect you have brought him here to confuse him even more.'

David just grinned, and with Alan and Ted, they left the camp.

Chapter Twenty-Nine

The office door swung open and when the three men walked in David stopped so suddenly the others nearly bumped into him. 'What the blazes are you still doing here, Kathy?' he demanded.

'I always stay late when you are away in case you need me when you get back.' She smiled at Alan and Ted. 'Though I must admit, I didn't expect you back so quickly. You have a habit of getting lost.'

'If you didn't think we would be back yet, then why are you still here?' David persisted.

'Where else would I be?' she asked, puzzled by his questions.

'You could have gone out with Alice, or one of the other girls, to the pictures, or something.'

'Alice isn't here and—'

'What do you mean Alice isn't here? Where is she?' Alan wanted to know.

'I don't know. She just told me she would be away for a while.'

Alan didn't look pleased. 'She didn't tell me.'

'Do you tell her where you are going?'

'Not all the time,' he admitted.

'There you are, then. I expect she's off doing something secret the way you do.' Kathy studied the three men with interest. 'You are all a bit ratty tonight. Are you hungry?'

Ted shook his head. 'We had a meal at the camp, but a cup of tea would be welcome. The stuff they make there is an insult to tea.'

'You've been to the camp?' she spun round to confront David.

'We brought a prisoner back with us and took him there.'

Alan began to laugh, his earlier bad humour completely gone. 'We left him in the care of Max and the brothers.'

While checking to see if there was enough water in the kettle, Ted was also laughing. 'I almost felt sorry for Hans. He didn't know what to make of it. He was so confused.'

'Why was he confused?'

'First he was questioned by David – and that's enough to confuse anyone because they are never sure if they are being interrogated or just having a friendly chat. Then we bring him here and take him to a camp where we are greeted as old friends by the prisoners. He didn't know what to make of it.' Still chuckling, Ted opened the biscuit tin, found it empty and held it out to Kathy. 'Biscuits?'

She sighed. They were all in a strange mood and she guessed they were in for a very long night – if they got any sleep at all. Giving the filing cabinet a kick in the appropriate place to make the drawers shoot open, she took out a bag of biscuits, put them in the tin and then made a large pot of strong tea. Once this was done and they were all sitting down with mugs in their hands, she noticed the amused expressions on all of their faces. 'So you brought a prisoner back with you, but what else have you been up to? And don't try to tell me you haven't been up to some kind of mischief, because I wouldn't believe you.'

That set them off again and she eyed them suspiciously.

'We went for a little walk while we were over there,' David told her.

'And two young boy soldiers jumped out of some bushes and demanded that we put our hands up.' Alan was shaking with laughter at the memory.

Kathy wasn't amused. 'What on earth is so funny? They could have shot you!'

'They could have, but they were young and inexperienced – and David confused them so much we were able to take their guns away from them.'

Still grinning, Ted held out his mug for a refill.

'Dear Lord,' she muttered as she refilled all the mugs. 'You three shouldn't be allowed out together. If they put you on a ship in the middle of the ocean you would still get into mischief.'

'Never!' David declared. 'We are perfectly behaved naval officers.'

'Some might believe that, I suppose,' she told them, beginning to see the funny side of this episode. They were incorrigible, but they knew what they were doing, of that she was certain. 'So, how are our friends at the camp?'

'Fine, but Erik was disappointed you weren't with us.'

'Could you take me there? I have paper and pencils for him.'

'We'll go soon, but first there is something we have to do.' David carefully took Erik's drawings out of a satchel he had been carrying, except the one of Kathy. 'Have a look at these.'

'Oh, they are good. I'm sure that boy is improving all the time. I love that one of the men in the orchard. Did he give you these?'

'I asked him for them because I want to take them to my artist friend. I'll go and see Robert tomorrow, and might be able to get more materials from him. The boy is so prolific it's hard to keep him supplied.'

'When you go to the camp again would you like us to come with you?' Alan asked.

'Might be a good idea. Max has warned me off Hans,

but the sailor might be more open with you and Ted. I don't think he trusts me,' David said wryly.

'I don't think he trusts any of us,' Ted remarked. 'Why not get Kathy to talk to him?'

'I would, but she doesn't speak German, and he only knows a few words of English.' David looked at Kathy. 'Want to learn German?'

'No,' she replied firmly. 'It's too late for that because the war could soon be over. Some are predicting it will be by Christmas.'

The men all shook their heads, and Alan said, 'Once winter arrives it will slow up the advance, but next year will see the end, for sure.'

'No use speculating about it.' David stood up. 'The war will end when it ends, and until then we have a job to do, but what we all need now is sleep.'

The next morning all three men were in the office when Kathy arrived, and empty plates were stacked up on the desk. The tea caddy was empty, as it always was with Ted around. She surveyed the debris and sighed. 'Don't tell me you have been here all night. I thought you were going to get some sleep?'

'We did,' David told her. 'We stayed in the sleeping quarters here.'

'From the look of the mess you couldn't have slept for long.'

'We had a couple of hours.' Ted was holding out the tea caddy. 'It's empty.'

'I can see that. It's always empty when you are around.' It was then she caught sight of the full waste bin and her typewriter with paper in it. 'What have you been doing?'

'Is she always this grumpy in the mornings?' Alan asked David.

'Perhaps she didn't sleep well,' he replied, his eyes glinting with amusement.

Ignoring the remark, she fished a crumpled sheet out of the waste bin, smoothed it out, and studied it in disbelief. 'What were you trying to do?'

'The admiral was on night shift, and when he knew we were back he sent word that he wanted a typed report before he went off duty,' David explained.

'That's why we didn't get much sleep. The duty officer came and woke us up, and we've been trying to type.' Ted pulled a face. 'Not very successfully.'

'Why on earth didn't you send for me?'

'No need to disturb you. He accepted a written report in the end.'

'I wouldn't have minded, David. This is the navy in wartime, not a nine-to-five job. You can call me anytime, night or day. Surely you know that by now.'

'I do, but we managed. However, now you are here to man the bridge we will catch up on our disturbed sleep. You know where we are if anyone needs us.'

'Only if that someone is very important.' Alan rose wearily to his feet.

As soon as they left she began to clear up the mess,

determined not to disturb them even if Churchill himself called.

An hour later Kathy was working her way through a pile of reports and letters waiting to be typed when the door opened.

Commander Peter Douglas looked in. 'Where are they?'

'Sleeping, sir.'

'What, at this time of day?'

'They've had very little sleep in days, sir. Is there something I can help you with?'

He thought for a moment, and then said almost to himself, 'I suppose it might work. Bring your shorthand notebook and come with me.'

She picked up a couple of pads and followed him to the operations room.

'Gentlemen,' Peter said to the three officers waiting there. 'It seems the intelligence section have gone to bed exhausted.'

That raised a few smiles.

'So Leading Wren Hammond will sit in and take notes for them to read later. However, she will not speak or offer an opinion,' he stated, looking pointedly at her.

Damn, she thought with amusement. *I get to sit in with the big boys and I've got to keep my mouth shut.*

'Do we have to speak slowly?' one of the men asked.

'You may speak quite normally and as quickly as you like, sir. My shorthand speed is fast. Just forget that I am here.'

They all settled down and the strategy meeting commenced. The task of getting supplies to the advancing troops was vital, and she listened with interest as she worked. By the time the meeting closed she had pages of detailed notes.

Peter glanced across at her notebook and shook his head. 'I don't know how you girls can read all that. It just looks like a load of squiggles to me.'

'It makes perfect sense to those of us who have studied it, sir. Would you like a copy when I've typed it?' She felt like adding that he could then check that it was correct, but she liked the commander and didn't want to insult him.

'Yes, please, that would be helpful. Could you manage copies for all of us?' He gave a slight smile. 'We didn't bother with keeping minutes of the meeting as you were here.'

'I will see you all have a copy, sir.' She took her leave and returned to the office.

Her fingers flew over the keys until she had the report finished and checked for any mistakes. When satisfied, she returned and handed out the copies.

Peter stared at her in surprise, glancing at the clock. He read through the beautifully typed report, turning the pages slowly.

Kathy waited.

'Excellent,' he finally said, 'and you've done it so quickly. No wonder David won't let you go. We must invite you to more of our meetings.'

'I would be happy to help anytime, sir.'

'When the admiral hears about your efficiency he might try to take you away from David.'

'That would be an honour, sir, but I like it where I am and have no wish to move. I have been with Commander Evans since I joined in 1941 and want to see the war out working for him.'

'Understood, and I've no doubt there would be a hell of a row if we tried to reassign you.'

Pleased she had stated her case so there would be no misunderstanding, she returned to the office.

The three men wandered in two hours later, washed, shaved and looking more rested.

'Anything important happen?' David asked her.

'Commander Douglas wanted you to attend a meeting, but I went instead.' She handed each of them a copy of the meeting notes, and while they were being read she made a pot of tea, knowing they would ask the moment they had finished.

David looked up first. 'Has Peter seen this?'

'I gave them all a copy.' Kathy handed round the mugs of tea. 'He was pleased with it.'

'I'll bet he was. Did he, by any chance, say that you might help them in the future?'

'He did mention that, and I told him I would be happy to attend meetings if needed.'

'Oh, I'd better go and have a word with him before he tries to reassign you.'

'I've already made it clear that I would not want to be

moved. I told him quite plainly that I wanted to see the war out working for you. I would have to follow orders, of course, but he said he understood.'

David had been half out of his seat, and then sat down again. 'I thought I was going to have another fight on my hands. I've lost count of the times they have tried to move you.'

'Really? I didn't know that. How many times?'

'Never you mind. Once word got round that you were efficient and dedicated, it has been pointed out to me that I don't need a secretary.'

'And what did you say to that?'

Alan burst out laughing. 'Believe me, Kathy, you don't want to know.'

'Perhaps you're right.' From the amused look on David's face she knew he wasn't going to tell her. It was interesting, though, to discover he had fought several times to keep her with him. That pleased her. She touched the locket she always wore under her shirt, and saw that he noticed – but then, he never missed a thing.

The office door opened, and Peter looked in. 'Ah, I see you are all awake. Can I borrow your secretary, David?'

'No.'

He walked in. 'Come on, it will only be for an hour. My man is on leave.'

'She's had a long day and should be off duty by now.'

'So should we all, but we'll rest when the war is over. Isn't that right?' he asked, turning to Kathy.

'Yes, sir.' She glanced across at David. 'I've finished all my work here.'

'All right, you can help him. But only for an hour, and you can't damned well keep her, Peter.'

'I wouldn't dare try.' He smiled at her. 'Bring your book with you.'

Kathy walked with him to his office, and once there he got down to work immediately, dictating letters and reports to her. Then using the typewriter there, she worked steadily.

When everything was finished and signed he sat back and studied her. 'You are very good. I knew from your record that you had the skills, of course, but if I'd known how efficient you are I would have asked for your transfer to me.'

'I think Commander Evans would have had something to say about that, sir.'

'That's for sure, and I don't doubt that I would have lost. Before the war I saw him in action in a courtroom, and he's impressive. It was clear he was going to go far in his profession, but he put his career on hold when the war started. I expect he will return to it as soon as he can.'

'Most likely.' She glanced at the clock. 'Is there anything else, sir?'

'No, and thank you very much.'

'My pleasure, sir.'

Walking back to her office she pondered the things she had heard. The most surprising thing was that David had fought to keep her with him, and yet in the beginning she had been certain he would have her reassigned to another post. He really was a most confusing man. Even after working for him all this time she still didn't have any idea what went on behind those sharp, all-seeing eyes.

Chapter Thirty

The weeks flew by and Kathy could hardly believe they were now well into August. The navy had the enormous task of seeing the troops were kept supplied and her father hadn't been onshore long enough for them to meet up. It was the same for David's brother, Ben, and his family must be missing him as well.

When David had returned from France with their prisoner he had said they would go to the camp, but since then he had been so busy it hadn't been mentioned again. He was never in the office for long, only appearing to give her work and then disappearing again, sometimes for days. He could have gone to the camp with Alan and Ted to question the sailor again, of course. If he had, she wished he had told her because he could have taken the materials she had collected for Erik.

She hadn't slept well last night and was ready early so decided to go to the office. The seven o'clock ferry would be arriving any minute, so she went outside to wait for it.

When she arrived, the three men were there and didn't notice her come in through the door they had left slightly open. She closed it and they still didn't look up. Their complete attention was on a map spread out over the desk.

'They are about here,' Ted murmured, pointing to a place on the map.

She was about to ask what he meant when the door opened, and Alice breezed in, the usual smile on her face.

'Good morning, everyone.'

The men looked up and Alan demanded, 'Where the devil have you been, Alice? No one would bloody well tell me.'

'Language. I've been helping out somewhere highly secret.'

'Where?'

'I said it was a secret, and I've been told not to talk about it – ever.'

Kathy could almost hear their minds working, and then they looked at each other and nodded, without saying a word.

'Did you enjoy yourself there?' David asked.

'It was interesting.' She grinned. 'I saw you come in one day.'

'Why didn't you come and say hello, then?'

She shook her head. 'I was told not to.'

Alan was frowning. 'I hope you didn't flirt with any of the boffins there.'

'Mind your own business.' She laughed. 'Aren't you pleased to see me?'

'Of course I am,' Alan told her. 'Pictures tonight?'

'Love to.'

'What did you think of the machine they've built?'

Alice stared at David. 'You mustn't talk about it!'

'We all know that place and have been there on numerous occasions.'

'Excuse me, but I haven't,' Kathy interrupted. 'What are you talking about?'

'You know about it, though,' David pointed out. 'It has been mentioned in reports you've typed for me.'

It only took a moment to recall the name. 'Bletchley Park.'

Alice raised her hands in the air. 'Some secret.'

'We know about it because we are a naval intelligence section and in need of their skills. We only mention it amongst ourselves, being very careful we can't be overheard. We are safe to discuss anything in this tunnel.'

She sidled up to David. 'I know that, Intelligence. What do you think of that machine?'

'A work of genius.'

She nodded. 'What minds those people have got, and yet no one will ever know what they have done. They must have saved countless lives by cracking the German codes. It doesn't seem fair, does it?'

'Maybe not, but although they have worked in the background, they can be proud of what they have achieved.'

'You are right, as always.' Alice glanced at the clock. 'I'd better get back. Just thought I'd let you know I'm around again.'

'Are we supposed to be pleased about that?' David kept a perfectly straight expression.

'Of course you are, Intelligence.' She grinned at Kathy. 'He likes me really. I'll catch you later.' Then she was gone.

David shook his head. 'I hope you know what you're doing, Alan. You'll never be sure what that bundle of energy is going to do next.'

'True, but I'll take that chance, and one thing is for sure, life with her will never be dull.'

'It's serious, then?'

'Very.'

'In that case I will wish you luck.'

'Thanks, I—'

He never finished what he had been about to say because the door burst open and Alice erupted back in to the office.

'News!' she said, almost bouncing with excitement. 'Paris has been liberated!' Then she turned and ran out of the room with Alan and Ted on her heels.

'Don't you want to go with them?' Kathy asked David when she saw he was still there.

'I'll hear all about it later, but we must go and see the men at the camp.'

'I thought you'd forgotten about that.'

'I've been there a couple of times to talk to Hans.'

'Were you able to see the others while you were there?'

He nodded. 'Briefly. This is a difficult time for them, and now Paris has been liberated they know the war is only going to end one way now – the defeat of their country. That is upsetting for them.'

'I'm sure it is. When can we go?'

'Today, but first I must see Robert. I gave him Erik's drawings some time ago and haven't had time to follow-up on it, so we'll see him first and then go on to the camp.'

Kathy opened her desk drawer and took out a large packet. 'I've been collecting materials for Erik. Do you know that after the raid that killed my mother and aunt, and destroyed my home, I never imagined I would feel concern for anyone who came from the country who did that terrible thing? The day I met the captured U-boat crew changed all that. Now I feel for all the decent people caught up in this mess, whatever their nationality.'

'I was so proud of you that day.'

She looked up quickly. 'Were you?'

He smiled. 'That surprises you?'

'It does rather, but thank you for telling me. Your opinion means a lot to me.' She was shocked to hear herself say that, but it was true. Over the years she had come to respect him, and perhaps like him a little too much, she admitted to herself.

'We've worked well together,' David said, as if reading her mind.

'Yes, we have.' Kathy laughed softly. 'I thought I would soon be out the door on my way to another posting. I thought you took an instant dislike to me.'

'I must admit that the moment I saw you I thought I must be crazy – I still do.'

'What does that mean?'

'I'll tell you when the war is over. Come on, we've got people to see.'

I ought to be used to him evading questions, she thought, amused, as they walked out. The list was growing of things he was going to tell her when the war ended.

Their first stop was the art gallery in Chelsea, and when they walked in there were several people admiring the pictures.

A man of around sixty came to meet them, all smiles. 'Ah, David, I wondered when you were going to find the time to return. Who is this lovely lady?'

'This is Kathy, my assistant.' He made the introductions and gazed round.

Robert studied her intently for a moment and then smiled. 'Ah, yes, of course it is. That special picture you gave me has been framed and is ready for you.'

'Thank you. I'll collect it later. You look busy.'

'No one is buying pictures at the moment, but I keep the gallery open and invite people to come in and see the paintings. They can spend a relaxing hour looking at beauty and forget the ugliness of war for a while. It's my way of helping.'

'I'm sure the people who come are grateful,' Kathy told him. He was a distinguished man with dark hair greying at the temples, pale-blue eyes, and she had the impression of a kind, gentle man. She liked him on sight.

'I'm glad you came,' he said to David. 'I want to talk to you about that young man. His drawings have been much admired. In fact, one elderly man is showing great interest in his skill. Do I have permission to sell them if an offer is made at any time?'

'I'm sure Erik would be delighted. We are on our way to see him now, so I'll ask him.'

The pale eyes lit up with interest. 'I would very much like to meet him. If I came with you, would it be permitted?'

'I expect I could arrange it, but we are on the motorbike, and there's only room for two,' David remarked.

Robert laughed. 'You wouldn't get me on one of those things. We can use my car. John, my driver, has little to do these days but polish it. Now, tell me, does Erik work in oils?'

'I was told that was his favourite medium,' Kathy explained, 'but he doesn't have anything like that at the camp. I try to keep him supplied with paper but haven't been able to find oil paints anywhere.'

'We can remedy that. Give me a moment to call John, clear the gallery and gather together the necessary materials for our young artist. Oh, and don't leave your bike in the road. Bring it round the back.'

While David was doing that, Kathy wandered round looking at the pictures, stopping in front of Erik's drawings.

'They look good expertly framed, don't they?' David came and stood beside her.

'The car is outside.' Robert appeared carrying a large amount of art materials. 'Give me a hand with this.'

'What have you got there? Is that an easel?' David began taking the heavy items from him.

'Of course. The boy can't paint properly without one.' Suddenly Robert looked uncertain. 'Will they let him have it?'

'We'll have to ask,' David told him.

When they stepped outside Kathy stopped in amazement and said under her breath, 'A Rolls-Royce?'

'He's a very wealthy man.'

'I guessed that the moment I saw him by the quality of his clothes. What I'm wondering is how he's going to have enough petrol to run this monster.'

'He doesn't use it very often, so I suppose he has been saving his ration.'

The chauffeur had finished packing the items to Robert's satisfaction, and then asked, 'Where to, sir?'

'We are going to Kent. Have we got enough petrol to get us there and back?'

'We should manage that, sir.'

'Good, good. Get in everyone.'

Kathy couldn't help smiling as they drove along. One thing she could say about working with David – she never knew what was going to happen. The men were busy discussing the pictures, so she settled back to enjoy the ride.

When they reached the camp, David told them to wait in the car while he went to see if he could get permission for Robert to enter. He was soon back. 'It's all right, you can come in with us, Robert, but you will have to let them see what you want to give to Erik.'

'Understood.' He got out of the car and gazed at the camp, a look of sadness on his face, but he said nothing.

Once inside, two guards went through the packages carefully, then handed them back. 'The prisoner can have those things. We'll send for the ones you want to see, sir,' they told David.

The moment they were escorted into the room Erik's face lit up and he made straight for Kathy. 'You come! Not see you for long time.'

'I'm sorry. I have to wait for David, because if I come on my own they might not let me in. We've brought you lots of materials.'

'Where's Hans?' David wanted to know. 'I asked to see him as well.'

'He's coming – reluctantly.' Max laughed. 'He still doesn't trust you.'

At that moment the tardy prisoner came in and looked relieved to see such a crowd. He was obviously afraid he would be seeing David on his own.

David said something to him, making all the others laugh, and Kathy wondered what had been said. Perhaps she should have learnt German after all.

'Erik, I want you to meet Robert. He's the artist friend I told you about, and he is eager to meet you.'

Robert stepped forward and shook Erik's hand. 'I'm delighted to meet you, son. Your drawings are hanging in my gallery and are causing a lot of interest. I want you to do something in oils for me.'

'But I don't have any, sir.'

'Yes, you do.' Robert indicated to the heap of packages leaning against the wall. 'I've brought you everything you will need. Have a look and tell me if there is anything else you want, and I'll see you get it.'

Erik couldn't get the wrapping off quick enough, exclaiming in delight as he held up each item. In his excitement he reverted to his own language as he showed everything to his brother and Max.

Gerhard turned to David. 'Is he allowed to keep this?'

'Yes, I have gained special permission for him to have the materials. However, they must be kept in this room, and Erik can work on them here when he likes. If he wants to take them outside, all he has to do is ask permission. I am assured it will be granted.'

'It is good of you to arrange this for him, and we are both grateful. Our captain thinks highly of you, and it is obvious why.'

'Max and I were constant companions for many years, and our families also visited each other. My parents are sad that the war, not the making of any of us, has torn us apart. But even war cannot end true friendship, Gerhard.' David smiled then as he glanced over at Erik. 'Your brother is so excited he has forgotten English and is telling Robert something he can't understand.'

Gerhard laughed. 'I had better go and help that kind man.'

At that moment Robert towed Erik over to them, a wide smile on his face. 'I need an interpreter.'

'Once he calms down he will revert to English again, sir. We both thank you for your generous gift,' Gerhard told him. 'My brother will be so happy to be able to paint in oils again.'

'My pleasure. I have always tried to encourage anyone with talent, and I am particularly impressed with Erik's work. I would like to talk to both of you, if I may?'

Erik was still gazing with longing at the easel and no doubt imagining what he was going to paint. Robert touched his arm to gain his attention. 'Come and sit down, please. We have things to discuss, son.'

Erik nodded, and while Robert was talking to his brother he leant close to Kathy and whispered, 'Why he call me son? I not his son.'

'It's a figure of speech. It shows he likes you.'

'Erik,' his brother called. 'We are waiting.'

The boy grinned at Kathy and went to join them at the table.

'What a difference in him,' she said to Max. 'You wouldn't think it was the same boy.'

'And it is all due to you. You came to him when he was lost and helped him find his way. He will never forget that. He calls you his "*Engel*". He considers you his guardian angel.'

'No one has ever called me that before, and I'm honoured to be thought of in that way. All I did, though, was help a young boy when he needed it.'

'And for that you not only have his gratitude, but ours as well.'

David brought Hans over to them with an exasperated look on his face. 'Max, will you tell Hans that I am not going to put him on a rack to get information out of him. We've tried, and he won't tell us about his ship, and I understand that. Hell, you and your crew won't tell us anything of use, and we haven't resorted to violence, have we?'

The next few minutes were hilarious, and although Kathy couldn't understand what was being said, their expressions spoke volumes. In the end the prisoner nodded and even smiled at David.

'Does he believe you now?' she asked.

'I hope so. I told him you have never been afraid of me, although I was tough on you at first.'

'Ah, yes.' She grinned at Hans. 'I thought you were going to throw me out in less than an hour after I arrived.'

Max translated for Hans and he actually laughed.

'Kathy!' Erik rushed over and took hold of her arm. 'You come.'

She sat at the table and looked at Robert, wondering what this was about.

'We have come to an agreement,' Robert explained. 'Any paintings Erik does he is going to let me have for the gallery, and I have his permission to sell them. I have explained that people are not buying at the moment, but that could change soon. He wants to ask a favour of you.'

'Of course, anything I can do. How can I help you, Erik?'

'If Mr Robert sell pictures will you keep money for me until I am out of the camp?'

Kathy looked at Gerhard. 'Is that all right with you?'

'Yes, we think that is the best thing to do, and we trust you.'

'Very well, I will be happy to do that for you.' She thought for a moment. 'If Robert does sell anything I will give you a proper payment advice note for you to keep. In that way you will know exactly how much money I am keeping for you.'

Erik beamed at her. 'Thank you. Mr Robert said he look after me. He likes my work.'

'That's wonderful, and I am so pleased for you.'

The camp commander came into the room. 'I must ask you to leave now. Their meal is about to be served.'

'Thank you for allowing us all to have this meeting,' David told him. 'We appreciate it.'

'I like to encourage the prisoners to take up some kind of hobby. It helps to relieve the boredom, and Erik is particularly helpful by arranging art lessons twice a week. He has about twenty enthusiastic pupils now.'

They took their leave, and in the car on the way back to the gallery, Robert was delighted to have met Erik, and enthusiastic about the plans he had to promote his work.

Enjoying the ride in the luxurious car, Kathy sat back and relaxed. That had been a good visit, and only time would tell what the outcome would be for Erik.

Chapter Thirty-One

Winter was beginning to show its teeth now it was November, and Kathy was quite pleased to be in the cosy underground office. Over the months she had been following the progress of the invading forces, hoping for an end to the war this year, but it was now obvious that wasn't going to happen.

'Looks like another wartime Christmas,' she said, handing David letters to sign. 'That man is beaten, so why doesn't he surrender and save thousands of lives?'

'Max reckons there's no chance of that. He will hold to the very end.'

'Have you been to the camp lately?'

He nodded. 'I've called in, briefly, a couple of times. They are all right, and Erik has given Robert two paintings. He is delighted with them and very excited about the boy's talent.'

'Any sales yet?'

'No, but they've been attracting quite a bit of interest and Robert is hopeful. I'll get permission for all of us to see them before Christmas.'

'That would be good.'

The door opened, and Peter walked in, smiling. 'Thought you'd like to know that the RAF has sunk the *Tirpitz*. That's the last of Hitler's big battleships. He's lost in the air and at sea, leaving the land battle. The end is in sight now. What are your plans, David? Are you going to stay in the navy?'

'That's good news. Regarding plans, I'll be going back to my job as a lawyer as soon as I can. I've already started making arrangements, and I'm looking forward to picking up a career again.'

'I'm sure you'll do it very successfully, but I'm sorry you won't be staying in the navy. We'll miss you, and a lot of people will now be thinking about their future. So many lives have been put on hold. Anyway, it's good news about that battleship.'

'It is, and thanks for letting me know.'

The door closed behind Peter and Kathy stared at it for some moments. That conversation had made her face something she had been pushing away. David would be going back to his life as a lawyer – and walking out of her life. That was going to hurt. Without her noticing it he had become a big part of her life, and she badly wanted that to continue. He was clearly already making plans to leave the navy.

'Will you miss the excitement of the job you've been doing?' she asked.

'There's plenty of excitement in the law courts. You must sit in on a trial sometime and see for yourself.'

'I'll do that. Have you decided where you'll set up your business?'

'In London. Alan and I are considering working together. He can handle the shipping cases and I'll concentrate on criminal and business trials.'

'You'll need an efficient secretary, and as I'm going to need to find work I would like to apply for the job.'

He sat back and shook his head. 'You can't be my secretary.'

'Why not? You won't get a better secretary than me,' she told him confidently, hiding the hurt his refusal had caused her.

'I know that, but it wouldn't be right for us to work together.'

She frowned. 'I don't understand. Will you explain, please?'

'I'll tell you when the war is finally over.'

'And how long will that be?' she asked, mentally adding something else to her list of things he was going to tell her.

'Who knows?' He was laughing quietly now. 'Have you managed to open the locket yet?'

'I haven't tried. You told me not to and I always obey

orders from an officer.' Her hand rested on the locket under her shirt. 'Don't you think this silly game has gone on long enough? Will you show me now?'

'Not yet.'

Kathy was hurt by David's outright refusal to consider her as a possible secretary for when he left the navy but wasn't going to let him see that. 'I bet that when I do open it I will find it empty. I really don't understand why you gave it to me. If it really is in appreciation of the time we have worked together, then the end of the war would have been more appropriate, surely?'

'Maybe that is only part of the reason and there is another much more important one.'

'Maybe, maybe, maybe. It is so difficult to get a straight answer out of you. Are you sure you are a lawyer and not a politician?'

David tipped his head back and laughed, changing the subject. 'We ought to celebrate the sinking of the last big battleship, but it's too early for whisky.'

'Hans will be upset to hear his ship has been sunk. Will you go and see him?'

'The last person he will want to see at this moment is me. I'll give him time to get over his grief of knowing that a lot of his friends will have died in the attack. You've got some leave due, so when do you want to take it?'

'I've been saving it in the hope my father would be home soon, but I have no idea when that will be. I haven't seen him for some time and his letters give no indication when he might be on leave.'

'It's tough not knowing where our family and friends are, but it is something we have to live with, I'm afraid. We haven't seen Ben for some time, either.' He gave her a sympathetic smile. 'I'm going home for Christmas and my parents have asked me to bring you along as well. They would be pleased to see you again.'

'That is kind of them, but as you are going to be away then, I would like to go to the cottage. I've hardly been there, and I have some changes to make before Dad comes home again. Please thank them for me.'

'I will, but they will be disappointed.'

The door opened, and Peter peered in. 'Can I borrow Kathy, David? Just for an hour.'

He sighed. 'This is becoming a habit, Peter. Make sure it's only an hour.'

When they had gone a slight smile crossed his face. He'd guessed she would offer to work as his secretary, but she had taken his refusal quite well. It was encouraging she wanted to stay with him, though. They were all thinking about the future now and he had it all planned.

Alan strode in and sat down. 'Have you heard about the sinking?'

'I have. Are you going to marry Alice?' David asked, abruptly changing the subject.

'Of course. You know I adore the girl. Why do you ask?'

'Have you told her?'

'I was going to wait until the end of the war, but I was

afraid if I didn't, then she would find someone else, and I wasn't prepared to risk that happening. What about you? Any romantic plans on the horizon?'

David shrugged. 'I vowed I wouldn't get involved in a serious relationship while the war was on.'

'It's nearly over and our part in it almost at an end. We will soon be changing uniforms for three-piece suits, and to go with that I want a wife and children. I'm sure you do as well. This war has robbed us of a few years, and we're not getting any younger.'

'That's true, but it is going to be strange after all we've seen and done. I'm still eager to get back to it again, though.'

'Me too. I wonder what Kathy is going to do?' Alan asked innocently. 'A beautiful girl like that won't stay single for long. From what I've seen, Max is more than a little interested in her, and being a prisoner is the only thing holding him back.'

'That entire crew is in love with her, but they are all wasting their time.'

'Oh, and why would that be?'

'You know her history.'

'She's put that all behind her. Look how she's helped those prisoners, and she seems genuinely concerned about them.'

'She's got a kind heart,' David said, switching to another subject as he had a habit of doing. 'Have you managed to persuade Ted to come and join us as an investigator?'

'He's thinking about it. We are going to need a good secretary, so how about Kathy? We won't get better.'

'She has already asked, and I've said no.'

Alan stared at his friend in astonishment. 'Why on earth would you do that? She would be a real asset.'

'She would, but I don't want her working with us.'

'I thought you liked her, or was I mistaken?'

'I do like her, but I have other plans for her,' David told him.

'Have you told her, and can I ask what those plans are?'

'No and no.'

Alan was silent for a moment and then shook his head. 'Be careful what you're doing. Kathy has a strong character, and if she doesn't agree with what you're planning she will walk away, and you'll never see her again. I can't believe that's what you want. You've been together a long time, and I've always felt there was more than friendship between you. I would swear you have real affection for each other.'

'Of course we have, otherwise how would we have survived being cooped up in this underground bunker?' David joked. 'Don't worry. I know what I'm doing and intend to see she is all right.'

'You're a risk-taker, my friend,' Alan told him, shaking his head.

'So are you, and that's why we have been doing this job. Now, about the future. We need Ted, and his skill as an investigator, so we'll have to corner him and convince him somehow to join us.'

'I've had my go and will leave the next interrogation to you,' Alan told him.

The letters were typed and signed. 'Is there anything else, sir?' Kathy asked Peter.

'That's all, thank you.' He glanced at the clock. 'You work so fast that my allotted hour is not yet up. Sit down, I would like to talk to you.'

She waited, wondering what he wanted to discuss.

'Do you have any plans for the future?'

'I haven't given it much thought yet.'

'Why don't you stay in the Wrens? You are well thought of and could have a good career with the navy.'

'That is an option, I suppose, but Commander Evans is already making plans to leave, so I would be given another post. I don't know what that would be or where I would be sent.'

'If you signed on for a longer period I would put in a request that you work with me.'

That surprised her, and she turned it over in her mind before answering. 'That is appealing, sir, but I'm not sure I want a career in the navy. I would need time to give it serious thought.'

'Of course, and that's sensible. I wanted to mention it in case you were wondering whether to stay in the Wrens or return to civilian life. Let me know what you decide.'

'I will, and thank you for the offer, sir.' She returned to the office deep in thought.

'Hello, Kathy,' Alan greeted her with a smile. 'Why the pensive look?'

'I was thinking about something. Nice to see you, Alan.'

The phone rang, and she picked it up, delighted when she heard the familiar voice. 'Dad, where are you?'

'I'm at home. My ship is in for an overhaul and I have seven days' leave. Any chance of you getting away?'

'I've got some leave due to me. Hold on a minute.' When she turned to David he was already holding out a signed chitty to her.

'Your leave begins as of now. Will five days be enough?'

'That is perfect. Thank you so much.'

'Remember me to your father.'

'I will.' Kathy turned back to the phone. 'I'm on my way, Dad.'

'Splendid. We'll have a little celebration at the pub this evening.'

Still smiling she cleared her desk, said goodbye and almost ran out of the door. This was unexpected and just what she needed. A few days relaxing with her father would help to clear her mind. Working with David and Alan was clearly out, and she really ought to be deciding what to do once the war ended.

She had to wait a while for a train, and it was around eight o'clock when she walked into the cottage. 'Dad!' she called, but there was no reply. Instead she found a note on the kitchen table letting her know he was in the pub.

After dropping off her bag she went straight to the village pub, and found her father sitting at a table with several of their neighbours, including Pat.

He got up the moment he saw her and held out his arms for a hug. 'It's so good to see you, darling. I must thank David for letting you go so quickly.'

Kathy hugged him. 'He had the authorisation ready before I'd finished talking to you.'

He held her away from him, so he could have a good look at her. 'He's still a man of action, then. What would you like to drink?'

'A small beer, please.'

One of the locals she had already met stood up. 'You sit down, Kathy. This round is on me.'

'Thank you.' She smiled at Pat. 'How are you?'

'I'm fine. It's lovely you have been able to come home at the same time as your father.'

'Yes, it's a rare treat.'

They stayed until closing time, enjoying a pleasant evening, and then walked back to the cottage. Kathy made a pot of tea and they sat at the kitchen table to catch up on all the news. 'Pat's nice,' she said.

Her father nodded. 'I'm glad you like her. We've been writing to each other. Do you mind?'

'Of course not, Dad. You have the right to live your life as you want, and goodness knows you have earned that. I like her.'

'I'm pleased. I did wonder if you would be upset if I became interested in another woman.'

'Quite the reverse. I am delighted.' Kathy reached across the table and grasped his hand. 'Mum has been gone a long time now, and she would want both of us to move on with our lives.'

'Yes, she would.' He squeezed her hand. 'You are like her in many ways, you know. So sensible.'

'I don't know about that.' She laughed. 'All through the war I've had a father out there dodging U-boats, and what do I do? I become friends with a U-boat captain and two of his crew.'

'Tell me the whole story.'

Starting from the time she walked in to where the crew were being held, she explained what had happened and how the meeting with Erik and his brother had helped to heal the anger she had been burdened with since the raid. 'I suddenly saw both sides of the conflict and the suffering this war was causing, no matter what side you were on. In a strange way we helped each other. Crazy, isn't it?'

'I don't think so. When we see sailors struggling in the water we haul them out, giving no thought for what nationality they are. When the war is over you must take me to meet them. The boy must be a very good artist for David's friend to be interested in him.'

'He is, and he's a gentle soul who should never have been put in a submarine. His brother told me that the brutality of war upset and disturbed him greatly.'

'It's sad that so many are being made to do things they find unpleasant. Being captured has probably been a blessing to the lad by ending that part of the war for him.'

'Max told me he was going to send him for medical treatment when they returned to base, but of course that never happened. Still, he made a quick recovery once he was reunited with his brother.'

'Talking of brothers, I saw David's brother a while back.'

'Did you? How is Ben? I only met him once and liked him. David never talks about him very much, but I know he worries at times.'

'He's fine. Now, I want to know what plans you have for when the war comes to an end, which won't be too long now.'

'I honestly don't know. Commander Douglas has suggested I could make a good career in the Wrens, but I'm not sure that's what I want. David is going to leave the navy as soon as he can.' Her smile was tinged with sadness. 'We have been together a long time now and it's hard to imagine we will be going our separate ways. I did ask if I could apply to be his secretary, but he refused, saying we couldn't work together again.'

Jack frowned. 'That doesn't make sense. I thought he would have snapped you up. I don't understand.'

'Neither do I, but you know David, he never explains why he does certain things.'

'Never mind, darling, with your skills you won't have any trouble finding a good job if you decide to leave the Wrens.'

'You're right.' She brightened up, relaxing in the warmth of the kitchen and opening the top button of her shirt. 'If you want to spend time alone with Pat you don't have to worry about me. I can find plenty to do around the cottage.'

'We will see her, of course, but this is our time together, and she understands that.' He tipped his head to one side. 'What's that you're wearing round your neck?'

'David gave it to me.' Kathy unfastened it and passed it across to her father. 'Pretty, isn't it?'

He frowned as he examined it carefully. 'This is old, and I would say very valuable. Why did he give it to you?'

'I'm not sure. He's always seemed concerned that I didn't have much after our house was bombed, but he said it was in appreciation of the time we have worked together.'

'Why give it to you now? Surely when he leaves the navy would have been a more appropriate time?'

Kathy shrugged. 'You never know what David is going to do, or why.'

Her father handed it back and studied her intently. 'Are you in love with him?'

'Yes,' she replied honestly, and when she saw the concern on his face she said quickly, 'There's no need to worry. He doesn't know, and he's never given any indication that he feels anything but friendship for me. I can deal with it, Dad.' She gave a bright smile. 'I'm going to start looking for a good job I can go to the moment I'm out of the Wrens.'

He squeezed her hand. 'That's a wise thing to do, darling. However, try to find out why he gave you such an expensive gift. Men don't give girls things like that just because they have worked together.'

'I will, I promise.' She fastened it round her neck again, feeling troubled by what her father had said.

'Good.' He stood up and smiled down at her. 'It's time we got some sleep.'

Although it was late, and she was tired, the events of the day kept running through her mind. The fact that her father thought the locket was a valuable heirloom was cause for concern, but she couldn't do anything about it at this moment. There were decisions to make. Staying in the Wrens didn't appeal and working for David was out of the question. There was also the prospect of her father's relationship with Pat. If they were to marry, then they should have the cottage to themselves, so she would need to find somewhere to live. The best place to look for a good job would be the business part of London, and she would start looking to see what was available. It would be time enough to find lodgings when she knew where she would be working.

She let out a ragged sigh. This was not what she had hoped for. She had known for some time that she was in love with David, which was a damned stupid situation to be in. However, that was her problem and she would get over it. The only person to think about now was her father – his happiness was paramount – and it was up to her to make a good life for herself. How that turned out, only time would tell.

Chapter Thirty-Two

'How's your father?' David asked when she arrived back.

'Very well. He told me he had seen Ben and he was fine. I thought you'd like to know he was safe.'

'That is good to know. Thank your father for me when you next write.'

'I will.' Kathy began sorting through her in-tray. 'Dad's got a girlfriend and it looks as if they are happy together.'

'Really? Do you mind?'

'Of course not. I'm pleased for them. Her name is Pat and her pilot husband was killed some time ago. If they can find happiness together, then that's good, and I like her. Oh, and he said he would like to meet Max and the brothers after the war. Would that be possible?'

'I'm sure that would be all right. I saw them while you were away, and Hans had heard about his ship being sunk. He was distressed by the news.'

'I expect he was. How were the others?'

'They are all worried, and there wasn't much I could say to ease their concerns. Unconditional surrender is the only term acceptable to the Allies, and they all believe that the regime won't surrender, so that means the armies will fight their way through their country.'

'And they are prisoners a long way from loved ones who could need help. It's terrible to see the suffering this war has caused for everyone caught up in it.'

He came and stood beside her, looking very serious. 'We mustn't lose sight of the fact that if we hadn't held out, Europe would be a very different place now. It had to be faced, Kathy, no matter what the cost.'

'I know, but it's a blessing it will soon be over. Rebuilding cities and lives will be quite a task.'

'A monumental one, but let's look towards the future with relief that we have one.' He grinned then. 'It will be exciting. I know you've used up all your leave now, but I can probably wangle you some extra days over Christmas. I've got five days due to me so if I can get you the same why don't you come home with me?'

'If you could manage that I would be grateful, but if you don't mind, I want to spend some time with Pat. I believe my father is serious about her, and I want us to get to know each other. It would be lovely if we could see in the new year together.'

'Yes, of course. Leave it with me and I'll see what I can do.'

'Thanks, that would be lovely. I can't believe it's nearly the end of another year – and what a year it's been.'

David nodded. 'Next year will see us back in Civvy Street.'

'Oh, that reminds me, I've got to see Commander Douglas. I promised to let him know when I'd made a decision.'

His eyes narrowed suspiciously. 'About what?'

'It's personal, David, and does not concern my work here.' Kathy left the office without giving him a chance to question her further, and found Peter coming out of ops.

'Hello. Did you enjoy your leave? David told me your father was in port.'

'Yes, thank you, sir. We had a lovely time, and it gave me time to think. I've decided to leave the Wrens as soon as I can. I thank you for your offer, but that isn't the kind of life I want for myself.'

'I understand but am disappointed. Thank you for letting me know.' Peter smiled. 'Come and see me if anything happens to change your mind.'

'I will, sir.'

David glanced up when she returned. 'That didn't take long.'

Kathy smiled brightly, saying nothing and sat down to get on with her work. He had refused her request to work for him, so what she planned was really none of his business. It was going to hurt to walk away, but it had to be done. The time to move on and make a life for herself was coming, and she would do it without any fuss. David could get on with his life and she would get on with hers. What this war had taught her was that things didn't always work out as you wanted, and she was sure it had made her stronger to cope with whatever life threw at her.

Kathy reached up and unfastened the chain holding the locket and took it off, holding it out to him. 'My father saw this and told me it looked old and very expensive.'

'It is. I told you it was my grandmother's.'

'David, I've loved wearing it, but I can't keep such a valuable piece of jewellery. I didn't realise just how valuable it was until my father mentioned it.'

'I want you to have it.'

'Why? If it's a goodbye gift, then I don't want such a reminder.' With determination she managed to keep her voice steady.

'Is that what you think?'

'It's obvious now. You are making plans and refused my request to work as your secretary. So what else could it be but a parting gift?'

'I also told you there was something else for you to do.' He was standing by her desk, making no attempt to take the locket.

'You did but refused to tell me what that was. I have to earn a living, and like you, I need to start making plans. With the possibility of Father marrying again it also means I have to find somewhere to live as well. When I leave the Wrens, I must have a job to go to and somewhere to live. I can't waste my time. I have to start sorting everything out now before I leave.'

David perched on the edge of the desk and reached out to curl her fingers around the gift. 'That is yours, and I won't let you insult me by giving it back. I am making plans, but they can't be finalised until the war is over and we are free to rebuild our lives. My objective is the happiness of all of us, and that includes our friends in the camp.'

'Now I'm really confused. You keep saying "we", so does that include me?'

'Of course it does. Did you think I was just going to walk away after all we've been through together?'

Kathy bowed her head for a moment when she guessed what his words meant, and the pain in her eyes was obvious when she looked up. 'You are not responsible for me, David, and I thought I had made that clear when we were in Gibraltar. I am quite capable of sorting out my own life. Talk to me. Tell me what is on your mind.'

'The time isn't right.'

'I think it is, but if you are not prepared to tell me now, then you can cross me off your list of people to help. I can't hang around until you decide the time is right.'

He swore under his breath. 'You have completely misunderstood. I'm only trying to do the right thing here. Dammit, Kathy, I made a decision at the beginning of this war and I must keep to it. It isn't over yet and we don't really know what is going to happen. We could still be facing heaven knows what! Don't you trust me?'

'Yes, I do. I know you are a good man who cares about people. When I came to you I was consumed with shock and anger, but that is no longer the case, and it is due largely to you. You showed me patience and kindness, being tough when you needed to be, and I will always treasure the time we have spent together.'

Clearly exasperated now, he leant down until his face was level with hers. 'I know I'm expert at hiding my thoughts and feelings, but I have obviously been far too successful where you are concerned.'

There was a sharp knock on the door and it opened. A young sailor looked in. 'You're wanted in ops, sir.'

Straightening up, David swore again. 'This conversation isn't over. Don't do anything hasty like making some commitment to Peter, or anyone else. And that's an order!' He swept out of the office, closing the door with a thud.

That was the most muddled and confusing conversation she had ever had with him, and there had been many. Kathy was sure his motives were good, but she loved him too much to allow him to feel responsible for her. That wasn't right for him, and certainly not right for her. Whatever he was planning for all of them, she couldn't live on the outskirts of his life. That would tear her to bits. It would be far better to cut the ties when the time came.

* * *

David was furious with himself. Some lawyer he was when he couldn't state his case better than that. If she only knew how hard it had been for him to keep his distance and merely treat her as a friend, but he didn't dare let her know how he felt yet. They still had to work together, and possibly for a while after the war ended. If he changed their relationship before then things could become difficult.

The first person he saw when he entered operations was Peter. 'What's up?'

'The admiral wants you to sit in on a meeting. We've got to be prepared for every eventuality as the war draws to a close, and your opinions are valued.'

For the next hour they discussed what the German navy might do, and although it was only speculation, they had to cover every possibility.

'The U-boats concern me the most,' the admiral said, looking at David. 'Any chance your submarine captain could tell us?'

'Unlikely, sir. He's been in the camp for some time now and completely out of touch with their strategy. If he was given any orders about such an outcome they would have been changed by now. We will have to rely on our listening stations for this information.'

'You are right, of course, but just thought I'd ask.'

The meeting wound up and David stayed to talk to Peter. He steered the conversation round to Kathy, hoping to find out why she had needed to see him.

'Fine girl you've got there,' he told David. 'I tried to

persuade her to stay in the Wrens. She could have a good career in the navy if she remained. She's damned good and someone that efficient is hard to find.'

'And what did she say?' David asked, taking a silent, deep breath.

'She told me it wasn't what she wanted and she will be leaving at the end of hostilities. Pity, because she's just the kind of girl we are going to need.'

'A lot of us will soon be faced with making decisions about what to do. She has clearly made hers.'

'As have you.'

'I'm not a career sailor like my brother and only signed up for the duration. Do you need me for anything else?'

'No, thanks. All we can do now is watch and wait.'

Instead of going back to the office, David headed for his bike, put on the coat and goggles he kept in the panniers, got on and roared up the road. He needed to get away and clear his mind. Not caring where he went, he ended up in London and pulled up outside Robert's gallery.

Hearing the bike arrive, his friend came out to meet him. 'That's good timing. You are just the man I want to see. Come inside, it's perishing out here.'

'You look pleased with yourself,' David told him once inside the warm gallery.

'I've just sold one of Erik's paintings.' He handed over an envelope. 'Give that to Kathy to keep for the boy, as he asked.'

He tucked it in his pocket. 'What did you get for it?'

'Ten pounds!'

'What? Who would pay that much for an unknown artist?'

'Someone with a discerning eye. The lad is good – very good. He's working on another one for me, and the same buyer has expressed an interest in seeing it when it arrives.'

'That is good news. Erik and Kathy will be pleased.'

'Ah, how is that lovely girl?'

'Not very pleased with me at the moment.'

'What have you done to upset her, David?'

'It isn't so much what I've done, but what I haven't done.'

'Well, you had better do it, whatever it is.'

'It isn't that simple.'

'Do you want to tell me about it? I might be able to help.'

David grimaced. 'No, this is something I've got to sort out for myself.'

'Then do it. Don't let misunderstandings of any kind come between you. Can you stay for dinner?'

'Tempting, but I must get back.'

By the time David reached Dover he had made up his mind. Robert's words kept running through his head, and he was quite right. If he delayed any longer he could lose her. That was even if she felt the same about him, of course. He wasn't completely sure of that.

When he strode in to the office, Alice was there talking

to her friend. He held open the door and ordered, 'Out!'

'Dear me, what's upset you, Intelligence?'

'Mind your own bloody business.' He waggled the open door.

'All right, I'm going.' She winked at Kathy. 'See you later – and good luck.'

The moment she left he locked the door and leant against it. 'You push the clasp at the top of the locket and turn it to the left. Open it.'

Kathy stared at him in astonishment. 'Why now?'

'Don't ask questions. Open the damned thing, Kathy!' He took a step towards her. 'I'm risking my future happiness here, so let's get this over with. Open it.'

'You are in such a strange mood I don't think I want to know what's in it.'

Muttering under his breath he closed the distance between them, hauled her out of the chair and kissed her long and passionately.

When he broke off the embrace, she took a deep breath. 'David?'

'Now will you open the locket? If you don't like what you see, then you can put in a complaint about my behaviour.'

Removing the pendant from around her neck she fumbled with the opening. *Calm down*, she told herself silently. It snapped open at last and inside was a small gold heart surrounded with diamonds and three words engraved on it. She bowed her head, trying to keep her emotions in check. This was the last thing she had expected.

'Well? Am I wrong to hope your feelings are the same for me?'

Kathy looked up and nodded. 'I love you too.'

David drew in a deep, shuddering breath of relief and gathered her into his arms, just holding her. 'I wasn't sure.'

'I certainly didn't know you felt that way about me, and I didn't dare give any indication I had fallen in love with you in case you sent me away.'

'Not a chance.' He kissed her gently and then stepped back. 'I want us to have a future together. Once this war is over we can act like a normal couple in love, but until then we must keep our relationship as it was. We still have work to do, and that must come first for the moment. Will you trust me now?'

'Of course, and I understand that this must be kept between us. We must continue to act as commander and secretary who have worked together through difficult years and become friends.'

'Do you think we'll be able to manage that?' he asked with a wry smile.

'It won't be easy, but we can certainly try, sir.'

David laughed, rolling his shoulders to ease the tension he had been feeling.

Kathy fastened the locket around her neck and tucked it out of sight. 'Just one thing. When we are alone will you now and again show me you still love me?'

'Deal, and we'll try to grab a little time alone together when possible.'

'That would be lovely, and necessary. We have come to know each other well, but not on a personal level. I don't know anything about your work as a lawyer or what you hope for the future. We both have likes and things we don't like, so it would be good to go somewhere and just talk to each other without the war and work getting in the way.'

'Agreed, and to do that we need the sky above us. We have spent most of our time together in this tunnel like moles.'

She laughed. 'I quite like the place.'

'Really? Well that's one of your likes I have found out already.'

'I have lots more.'

'Me too. It's going to be fun finding out.'

'I'm curious. Why did you use the locket to tell me how you felt?'

'My grandfather had that made and used it to win over my grandmother, and I thought I would do the same. It worked for him, so I hoped it would for me as well.'

'You're a romantic!' Kathy exclaimed, surprised by the revelation.

David chuckled. 'That's something you would never have guessed, would you?'

They were both startled when someone rattled the doorknob and then pounded on the door. David shot over and carefully turned the key, then opened it, pretending to examine the lock as Peter walked in.

'Sorry, it must have got stuck,' he said with a perfectly innocent expression on his face. 'What can I do for you – or is that a stupid question?'

Peter grinned. 'Can I borrow Kathy sometime tomorrow?'

'Why don't you get yourself a regular secretary?'

'I've tried, but no one corrects my letters like Kathy. Just an hour again, please.'

David looked across at her and winked. 'All right, I can spare her for an hour at nine o'clock in the morning.'

'Perfect. Thanks.' Peter slapped him on the back and left.

'Oh, I almost forgot. I saw Robert today and he's sold one of Erik's paintings. He got ten pounds for it.' David took the envelope out of his pocket and handed it over to Kathy.

'That's marvellous. He will be so excited about that.' She put the money in her bag. 'If Robert sells any more I might have to open a bank account for Erik.'

'I expect we could arrange that, if it's what he wants. We'll go and see them before Christmas. Is there any chance you can change your mind and come home with me?'

'I wish I could, but it will be some time before I'm due leave again, and it's most important I see Pat.'

'I'm disappointed you can't come home with me, but quite understand. I'll miss you, but we will have many a Christmas and New Year together, hopefully with a family of our own.'

'Er . . . you haven't actually asked me to marry you.'

'Do I need to?'

'Yes, please.'

He turned, locked the door again and got down on one knee. 'Will you marry me when this blasted war is over, Leading Wren Hammond?'

'I'd love to, Commander Evans.'

Chapter Thirty-Three

The night was a restless one for Kathy as the picture of what had happened kept running through her mind. She had been bracing herself for the painful moment when she would have to leave him, and suddenly all that had changed. David had clearly wanted them out of the navy before making a commitment to her, but concerned she might not wait for him, he had been forced to speak before he was ready. She could understand why he had avoided a serious relationship, because his job was to seek out information, putting him in danger at times. He didn't need to worry, though, because she was no stranger to coping with difficult situations.

Opening the locket to read the words, she smiled, turned out the light and settled down to get some sleep.

The next morning there was no sign of him in the office, and the phone was already ringing. In the next hour she took several messages and was just getting ready to go and help Commander Douglas when he looked in.

'David not around?'

'I haven't seen him yet, sir. I'll take your dictation now, if you are ready?'

'Fine.'

They were leaving the office when David walked in. 'I'm just going to help Commander Douglas, sir. There are messages on your desk,' she told him politely.

David glanced at his watch. 'Only an hour, Peter. We have to go out soon.'

'Promise, and thanks, I owe you.'

'You certainly do, and don't think for a moment that I won't collect sometime.'

Peter was chuckling quietly to himself as they walked to his office. 'I'm going to miss him when he leaves. When you first arrived, I didn't think you would last a week with him.'

'I didn't believe I would last the day,' Kathy admitted. 'We didn't exactly get on well together at first.'

'That was back in 1941, wasn't it?'

She nodded. It seemed like a lifetime away now.

'And here we are at the end of 1944 and you are still working with him.'

'Quite a miracle after a rocky start,' she said, laughing. 'We gradually adjusted to each other, and I soon came to respect and admire him.' They reached the office and she sat down, pen poised ready to start.

The letters and reports were finished right on the hour, and she hurried back to the office.

David smiled when she walked in. 'Let's have a cup of tea first, and then we can go to the camp.'

'Oh, good. Are we going on the bike?'

'Not this time. It's too cold and I wouldn't be surprised if it snowed. I've ordered a car. Oh, and I could only get you two extra days' leave, and it is Christmas not New Year as you wanted. Even that was hard to get because everyone is trying to get extra leave at this time of the year.'

'I'm grateful even for that. Thank you so much. It's such a shame that we will all be scattered around the place. It would have been wonderful if my father, Pat, Bill and your brother, Ben, could all be together for once.'

'Yes, it would, but that's impossible. Still, we could be together for the Christmas after this.'

Kathy poured two mugs of tea and handed him one. 'Hopefully a peacetime celebration.'

'It will be.'

She sat down and cradled the mug in her hands. 'How long do you think it will be now, David?'

'Everyone is speculating about that, but the final push will probably come in the spring.'

'It's hard to imagine, isn't it? We have been at war for such a long time.'

'Too long, and there will be many challenges to face at the end.' He drained his mug and stood up. 'Let's get on our way to see the boys. What have you got for Erik?'

'Quite a lot of paper and pencils. He needs a never-ending supply for his art classes, but I believe Robert is keeping him well supplied with everything else he needs.'

'He is really enthusiastic about Erik's work, and if he does stay here, Robert will take good care of him.'

It was lovely to travel in a car for a change, instead of freezing on the back of the bike. David talked about the plans he had been making with Alan, and how they had been trying to persuade Ted to join them. However, he still seemed determined to go back to teaching, but they hadn't given up the hope of changing his mind.

When they arrived at the camp they were so well known they were allowed to walk straight into the room they always used. A guard didn't even need to ask who they wanted to see.

Max strode in, clearly delighted to see his friend again, and as they greeted each other Kathy could see the bond between them hadn't been broken, even though they had been fighting on different sides.

Erik erupted into the room, quickly followed by Gerhard, and they greeted each other with enthusiasm.

They all sat round the table to talk, and David asked, 'How's Hans?'

'He's all right,' Gerhard told him, 'but worried about his family, as we all are. We are very anxious for reliable news.'

'I understand that, but I can't tell you anything you don't already know.'

'But you must know more than is reported on the news,' Max said.

'I am only involved in the sea operations, and don't have inside knowledge about the land forces, Max, you must realise that.'

'Of course.' He smiled at his friend. 'I have always considered you a fount of knowledge and expected you to be privy to every detail of the invasion.'

'I understand your worries, and am sorry I can't help at this time, but I will make you a promise. If you give me your home addresses when the fighting is over, I will check to see that your families are safe. I can't do more than that.'

'That is good of you,' Max told him, 'but it might not be easy in the aftermath of the fighting.'

'Agreed, and if I have to go out there to find them for myself, then I'll do that.'

Erik wiped a tear from his eyes. 'That is a comfort. You are a good man, sir.'

'Don't you think it's time you called me David?'

'If you would permit, I would be pleased to.'

Max was sitting back in his chair and watching his friend closely. 'You must have a lot of influence if you can promise to go over yourself. You are not just an intelligence officer, are you?'

'Senior Intelligence Officer is my title, so I must be.'

'I don't care what they call you. From the number of situations you have been in I would say you are the equivalent to the army SAS.'

David laughed. 'The navy doesn't have anything like that.'

'If you say so.' Max held up his hands. 'Have it your way, but one day I will find out exactly what you have really been doing. How are your two partners in crime?'

'Ted and Alan? They are fine, and looking forward to getting out of the navy, as I am.' He then put a stop to this conversation by smiling at Erik. 'Has Kathy told you the good news?'

He had been sorting through the parcel she had given him, and he looked up expectantly. 'Good news?'

Kathy took an envelope out of her bag and handed it to him. 'Have a look at that.'

Erik removed the sheet of paper and immediately handed it to his brother. 'I don't read English too good. What that say?'

Gerhard's smile widened as he read the payment advice note she had typed. 'It says that one of your paintings has been sold, and the sum of ten pounds is being held for you by Katherine Hammond.'

The boy was so excited he could hardly sit still. 'That a lot of money!'

'And there could be more,' David told him. 'Robert said your work is being admired, and the person who bought it is interested in seeing anything else you do.'

'You must keep that payment advice note so you know exactly how much money I am keeping for you. I will give you one each time a sale is made.'

'If there are more sales we could try to open a bank account for you here,' David explained. 'That's if you want to, of course.'

Gerhard immediately answered for his brother. 'If Erik is allowed to stay it might be a good thing. It would show that he has prospects here, but we will wait and see if there are any more sales. In the meantime, we are happy for Kathy to keep the money until Erik needs it.'

Erik was nodding in agreement, holding the paper to him as if it was precious. He reached across the table and held her hands for a moment, looking quite overcome. 'Thank you, and thank you, David. You tell Mr Robert I am grateful, please.'

'I will. He told me that if you decide to stay in this country he will be happy to do all he can to promote you and your work.'

'I stay if allowed.'

'I will see to that for you, Erik,' David told him. 'What about you, Gerhard, have you given the idea any more thought?'

'I will have to return home to check that all is well, and then I would like to come back if I can. Farmer George has kindly said we can live in a cottage on his farm.' He smiled at his brother. 'We can work on it together and make a home for ourselves.'

David nodded. 'In civilian life I am a lawyer, so I will deal with the legal necessities for you. With so many people willing to sponsor you there shouldn't be any trouble. You and Erik can be my first clients,' he joked.

'That is kind of you, but I do not think we could afford your professional services.'

'Free of charge,' David told him seriously. 'We are all going to need to help each other when this mess is over. Your cases will help to get me back into the swing of things again.'

'There will be one hell of a mess to sort out when the fighting is finally over. We will need your help, David,' Max said, 'because they won't release us straight away, will they?'

'No, it will take time, I'm afraid. I will try to get you released the moment the war ends, but I doubt that will be possible.'

'You have done more than we could ever have expected,' Gerhard told him. 'You befriended us when we were devastated by the sinking of our U-boat and have continued to give us any aid you could. It has been the making of my brother, and his talent has blossomed since we have been here.'

David stood up. 'There is still a way to go yet, but as soon as we can we will set about sorting everything out for you.'

Max gave his friend a slap on the back. 'We can't ask more than that. I bless the day when I walked into that interrogation room and saw my old friend was the intelligence officer.'

'And what a shock that was.' David laughed. 'You ended up giving me the orders instead of the other way round.'

Everyone was laughing as they left the camp.

On their way back, Kathy asked, 'Will you really be able to find out if their families are all right?'

'I should be able to recruit someone to check for me, if not I'll go over myself.'

'Permission might be hard to obtain,' she reminded him, and when he just gave a slight smile, she said, 'For you I guess not. You are a very kind man and it's no wonder I fell in love with you.'

David reached out and squeezed her hand. 'You haven't seen me in court yet. You might change your mind.'

'Not a chance.'

'I'm glad to hear it. I wouldn't want my wife to disapprove of what I do.'

'You haven't said when you think we might be able to marry.'

When he just shrugged, she laughed and said, 'I know – only time will tell.'

'All I can say is that it will be as soon as we are back in civilian clothes and can get all our families home at the same time.'

'That will take some sorting out.'

'I'll leave all that to you. It's what you are expert at.'

It had been hard to see David go to his parents' and Kathy wished so much she could have gone with him, but two days' leave was not long enough to go with him, anyway. From the letters she was receiving from her father, it was clear he intended to marry Pat as soon as possible. He had also hinted that he might be retiring from the navy after the war. She was grateful David had managed to get her a little time to spend with Pat, so they could get to know each other. She had thought it would be nice to see in the new year with her, but the days allotted her didn't cover that. However, Christmas Day would be just as good, and she was happy for the opportunity to spend this time with Pat because it might be some time before she could get home again. As far as they could see, next year was going to be a busy one for all of them, and leave would not be available. He had assured her that they would visit his parents later and have a party to celebrate their engagement.

Kathy caught an early train on Christmas Eve, and when she walked into the cottage, she went from room to room deciding the place needed a good clean while she was here. It was a comfortable home now, but Pat would no doubt want to make changes when she moved in.

It was nearly time for lunch, so Kathy decided to go to the pub for a meal as there wasn't much in the cupboards. Rationing was strict, but she'd go to the local shops later and see what she could get. She had brought a few tinned items with her to leave for her father when he came home the next time.

The pub was warm and welcoming with a huge log fire burning in the grate. A few people she'd met before greeted her as if she were an old friend.

Pat must have heard, because she came rushing out from the other bar. 'How lovely to see you.'

Stan came over and shook her hand. 'We're having a big party tomorrow night. You'll join us, won't you?'

'I'd love to. Can I get something to eat here now?'

'Sit yourself down. We'll find you a good meal,' he told her. 'What would you like?'

'Anything.'

'Right. We like a customer who is easy to please. You stay and talk to Kathy,' he told Pat, 'we can manage.'

'Let me buy you a drink while we wait,' Kathy told Pat before sitting down.

They both had a beer and settled in front of the fire.

'Your father told me you are quite happy about us, but are you really?'

Kathy could see Pat's concern and was pleased she had come. 'I am very happy. You seem to get along well together, and my father's happiness is all that matters to me. He deserves to be happy, and so do you. I feel he has made a good choice.'

Pat visibly relaxed. 'I've been worried you would object.'

She reached out and clasped Pat's hand. 'You didn't need to feel like that. I will be relieved to know my father is not alone here.'

'Alone? Are you staying in the Wrens, then?'

'No, but I will be in London. That's where my life will be.'

'Oh, I thought you would be coming to live here with us.'

'I have other plans.' Kathy smiled. 'I can't tell you about them until my father knows. I've written to tell him, but you know how unpredictable the delivery of letters can be, especially for those at sea.'

'Well, whatever you are doing, I hope you will be very happy.'

'I'm sure I will be – we all will be.'

'Thank you for talking to me like this. It has certainly put my mind at rest. Your father will be pleased to know you have used your precious leave to come and see me.' Pat smiled and there was a hint of tears in her eyes. 'I am so happy now.'

'That's why I came, and now we can relax and enjoy getting to know each other.'

Chapter Thirty-Four

The first few months of 1945 were momentous. On 15th February the Allies reached the Rhine, and during March and April they watched as the Allies broke through into Germany.

Kathy's thoughts often turned to the prisoners they had befriended and knew they must be desperately worried about the safety of their loved ones as the armies fought their way through the country. They had been to see them several times, and Robert had sold two more of Erik's paintings. Kathy was now holding the sum of thirty pounds for him, and David was already looking into the legal aspects of allowing Erik to stay in this country. He was also checking to see what was needed to gain permission for Max and Gerhard to return here too. At this point it was all they could do.

* * *

Alice came into the office one day, slightly subdued, which was unusual.

'Are you all right?'

'I had to get out of the ops room for a while.' She sat down, and her grin reappeared. 'I swear everyone in there is holding their breath.'

'Do they think it is that close, then?'

Alice nodded. 'You had better have a bottle of the hard stuff ready because our men are going to need it.'

'I've got one tucked away. Are Alan and Ted in there as well?'

'Of course. Those three have to be together at the end.'

'I can't believe it will soon be over,' Kathy said. 'There will be so much to do because Europe is in a mess, and it will take this country a long time to recover. We are in debt and have given our all.'

'That's true, but at least we weren't invaded.'

'That was a blessing and nothing short of a miracle,' Kathy agreed.

Alice took a biscuit out of the tin. 'I'm out as soon as I can because Alan wants us to get married this year. What are you going to do?'

'I have plans, and like you, will be leaving.'

Alice cocked her head on one side and smiled broadly. 'You needn't be secretive now. I know how you and David feel about each other.'

'We can't hide anything from you, can we?' Kathy laughed.

'Nope. One good thing to come out of this war is

that we've found a couple of good men. They are going to work together so we will see a lot of each other. We'll need friends too, because starting over again is going to be strange.'

'I guess you're right, but we do have a future and it will be up to us what we make of it.'

'Together we'll make a huge success of it,' Alice said with bright confidence.

At that moment the door crashed open and three men erupted into the room and celebrations could be heard going on all along the tunnel.

'It's over!' Alan caught hold of Alice and swung her round and round. 'They have surrendered unconditionally.'

Kathy was hugged by Ted and Alan and when she looked up to find David, he was leaning against the door, and smiling, he held out his arms. She rushed over to him and was immediately caught up in a bear hug. Neither of them said anything because it was hard to believe the long years of heartache and struggle were finally over. Her thoughts went to her mother and aunt who would never see this day, like so many thousands of others, but she was sure they would be smiling with relief, just like everyone else.

Peter looked in. 'We've got champagne, so come and join us.'

It was bedlam in ops with everyone talking and laughing at once. Glasses were thrust into their hands, and when they all had one the admiral called for order.

'Gentlemen and ladies, raise your glasses to toast

this momentous day – a day everyone has fought and sacrificed so much for.' He held up his glass. 'To 7th May, a day that will go down in history.'

The date was repeated by everyone as they drank to victory in Europe.

'Let's go outside,' David shouted in her ear.

Even outside there were people milling about everywhere and he led her over to the bike. As they roared off she didn't know where they were going and didn't care. The war was over!

Everywhere they went the streets were full of people celebrating the news, and it took David a while to find a quiet place in the middle of a field. The bike fell silent and she got off. When he had propped the bike up he draped an arm around her shoulders, staring across the field. He clearly wanted to be quiet, so she didn't speak.

'We've still got work to do, my darling,' he finally said.

'I know.' This had also been on her mind. 'The prisoners. We need to go and see them.'

'We'll go tomorrow. I know where Max's family live, but I need to check they are still there, and get an address for Erik and Gerhard's parents. It will take quite a while to repatriate all the prisoners we have in this country, and I won't be able to do anything for them until things calm down.' He kissed her gently and smiled down at her. 'We must help them before we can think about our own future. You know that, don't you?'

'Of course I do.'

'I would like them to come to our wedding and

have Max as my best man. Would you object to that?'

'I think that's a lovely idea, and I would be delighted. You must ask them when we see them. It might help to cheer them up a little. I would also like Bill to be there, and there's my father, Pat and your brother to somehow get together. It's going to take some organising.'

'Oh, that reminds me. I had better write and ask your father for permission to marry his daughter.'

'I am over twenty-one, but I am sure he will appreciate the gesture. He could be planning his own wedding as well.' Kathy smiled happily. 'I do hope so.'

'That would be good. Now, it's going to be one hell of a party tonight. Where do you want to go – London?'

'An absolute must, I would say.'

'Let's get back and see if the others will come with us. The bigger the crowd, the better.'

The moment they walked in Ted said, 'Ah, there you are. We are all going to London tonight to join in the fun. Coming with us?'

'We were going to suggest the same,' David replied.

That evening Ted had invited one of the Wrens he had been dating for a while, so six of them commandeered two cars and headed for a London ablaze with lights for the first time in five years. It was a sight that brought smiles to everyone's faces.

They mingled with the boisterous crowds and it was a party none of them would ever forget. They danced, sang and laughed a lot. The crowds were delirious and determined to celebrate the end of the war – an end everyone had worked and prayed for.

It was the early hours of the morning before they made it back to Dover and the girls managed to catch a couple of hours' sleep only. That didn't bother them, though, because over the years they had got used to very little sleep at times.

When Kathy walked into the office the next day, she stopped and burst out laughing. The three men were there, and although they were shaved and in fresh uniforms it was obvious they had been up all night and were showing signs of the celebrations in London.

'Is there any chance of a strong coffee?' Ted asked.

'My goodness, you must be feeling bad if you're not asking for tea,' she joked. 'I've only got the liquid Camp coffee, no proper stuff. Won't tea do?'

They all nodded.

'Make it extra strong, then,' David told her.

By the time they had worked their way through several mugs they looked more awake.

'That was some night.' David straightened up and hauled himself out of the chair. 'Come on, Kathy, we have a job to do, and one I am not looking forward to.'

'Are you going to the camp?' Ted asked.

'We must.'

'Well you can't go on that bike after the amount we drank last night.'

'I've ordered a car and driver. I just hope he's sober.'

The drive there was tense, and when they arrived

David asked the guard how the prisoners were.

'Quiet,' he told them. 'I think they are relieved the fighting is over, though. You want to see your three?'

'Please.'

When they came into the room, Erik came straight over to Kathy and grasped her hands, his expression sombre. 'It over.'

'Yes, it is,' she replied softly, knowing they must be worried to have armies of different nations occupying their country.

'Sit down everyone,' David told them, pulling a notepad out of his pocket. 'I promised I would check to see if your families were all right. If you give me your home addresses and any other places you think they might be, I will do my best to trace them.'

Relief swept over their faces and they quickly wrote down the information he had asked for.

'Thank you, we are grateful,' Max told him.

'Everyone in the camp is worried,' Gerhard said.

'I know they must be.' David ran a hand through his hair. 'I can't help the entire camp, but I'll get in touch with the Red Cross and see if they can do anything for them.'

'Can I tell them that?' Max wanted to know.

'Of course. Europe is full of refugees, and it is going to take time to sort out, but organisations like the Red Cross will help all they can.'

'Understood. We will be grateful for any information.' Max tipped his head to one side and gave a slight smile. 'I would say you had quite a party last night. You look a little rough today, my friend.'

'We had a lot to celebrate. Not only the end of the war in Europe, but as soon as we can get out of the navy, Kathy and I are getting married. I would like you to be my best man, Max, and Erik and Gerhard, you are also invited.'

This news brought the smiles back.

'I would be honoured to be your best man, David.'

'When the wedding?' Erik wanted to know.

'We haven't got a date yet. There is a lot to do and arrange first,' Kathy told them. 'My father is still at sea, so is David's brother, Ben, and we would also like a very good friend of ours to be there. He is also still at sea. We will give you a proper invitation when it has all been arranged.'

Erik glanced at his brother and then at his shabby clothes. 'What we wear?'

That made them all laugh, and David said, 'Don't worry. I'll see you have decent suits.'

'I have money.' Erik smiled brightly at Kathy. 'How much I have now?'

His brother slapped him on the back. 'You have thirty pounds. Kathy has given you the papers to prove it, remember?'

'It's yours when you want it,' she told him.

'You keep longer. I not need it yet.'

Their meeting ended on a lighter note and they promised to come back the moment they had any news.

On their way back to Dover, David said, 'Don't put in

for demob yet, darling. I'm going to need your help for a while longer.'

'Of course. We'll try and arrange our release at the same time, if possible. How are you going to find out if their families are all right?'

'I'll need to elicit the help of someone who is already out there. We'll have to find out if there is someone there I know. If I was army I could possibly wangle a trip for myself, but as navy . . .' He shrugged, and then smiled at her. 'I think we eased their minds a little.'

'I'm sure we did.'

For the next few days they searched the regiments who were part of the occupying force for anyone David, Alan or Ted knew.

They were beginning to think they weren't going to find anyone when Ted declared, 'Major Andrew Porter!'

'Andy?' David was shaking his head. 'He isn't out there.'

'He's due to be shipped out tomorrow.'

'How did you find that out?' David wanted to know.

'I have my ways, you know that.' Ted was putting on his hat. 'Come on. I know where he is, so let's get going.'

David and Alan shot to their feet, and David said, 'Damn it, Ted, you have got to work with us as an investigator. We need you.'

'All right. We are a team and I'll work with you. Now for heaven's sake move or we might miss him.'

All three men left at a run, leaving the door open, and

Kathy could hear the sound of their feet as they hurtled along the tunnel.

She closed the door, silently urging them to get there in time, and then settled down to wait.

Five hours crawled by before they walked in and Ted immediately said, 'Put the kettle on, Kathy.'

'Were you able to see him?' she asked before doing anything.

David nodded. 'It wasn't easy, but we eventually gained permission to speak to him, and he's going to see what he can do.'

'Tea?' Ted urged. 'I need it to steady my nerves after that mad dash to Hampshire on the back of that beast of a motorbike.'

'You haven't got nerves.' Kathy laughed.

'Don't you believe it. I should have commandeered another bike like Alan did.'

Still amused, she set about the much-needed tea and watched them empty the pot.

'That's all we can do for today, so I suggest we get some rest.' David stood up and held out his hand to Kathy. 'Come on, I'll give you a lift.'

Back at the Wrennery there were two letters waiting for her. One from her father and another from Pat. When she read them, she let out a whoop of delight. Her father had already put in for retirement, and as soon as that came through, he and Pat were going to get married. Pat's letter showed how happy she was. Even though she was tired, Kathy answered the two letters immediately to let them both know just how delighted she was with the news. Her father also sent his congratulations to her and David, saying that he had received a letter from David asking for permission to marry her. With all this good news she just had to write to Bill asking if he knew when he would be onshore, because he had to be at both weddings.

That night she fell asleep with a smile on her face.

They were getting anxious after two weeks when they hadn't heard from Andy. David had tried all means to get through to the major but without success.

'It must be chaos out there,' Kathy told him gently.

'I know, but I was hoping to hear something by now.'

The door opened, and a sailor came in. 'I have a package for you, sir.'

'Thanks.' He took it, glanced at the front and began to tear it open eagerly. 'It's from Germany, Kathy!'

Inside were a lengthy letter and several photographs. 'Look at this: that's Max's parents and this must be Erik and Gerhard's family.' David began reading and when he looked up he was smiling with relief. 'They are all, fortunately, in the British zone and Andy was able to go and see them. They are all right and delighted their sons will be informed. Come on, we must go to the camp.'

The prisoners came into the room with worry etched on their faces, but when they saw their visitors had big smiles on their faces, they began eagerly clamouring for news. The relief on their faces as they read the major's letter and gazed at the photos was something Kathy knew she would remember all her life.

'Thank you, my friend.' Max caught David in a bear hug, and then the brothers did the same, so great was their gratitude.

Not to be left out, Kathy received the same hugs.

'I am now going to put on my lawyer's hat and try to get you out of here as soon as possible,' David told them. 'My parents would be happy to have you all billeted with them until repatriation begins.'

Gerhard gasped. 'They would do this for us?'

'My friends are always welcome at their house.'

Kathy saw Erik wipe a tear from his eye, and Gerhard was close to shedding tears as well. She felt a little tearful herself. She was marrying a very caring man who had obviously been working hard to help these men as much as he could.

Max bowed his head. 'I would love to see your family again. Please thank them for us. Oh, and the Red Cross have been here and talked to everyone. They are going to help check on the safety of the families.'

'Good.' David looked thoughtful. 'I don't know how long this is all going to take, so be patient, and I'll let you know how things proceed.'

'If I remember the admiral correctly, he can throw his weight and authority around when he wants something done,' Max chuckled.

'He's still the same, but as I said, even with his

determination the wheels of bureaucracy turn slowly, so you might have to wait for a while.'

'We are used to waiting,' Gerhard told him, smiling and placing an arm around his brother's shoulder. 'We consider ourselves fortunate that the interrogating officer turned out to be a lifelong friend of our captain, and his assistant a lovely girl with a kind heart.'

Erik nodded, and looking rather puzzled, frowned at Max. 'Why you call David's father "admiral"?'

'Because he is. Retired now, of course, but I'm sure he is still a force to be reckoned with.' Max smirked at his friend. 'And his son is just as devious, but we are in good hands. If anyone can get things done it will be father and son working together.'

A week later Kathy was alone in the office when the door opened, and she looked up, gasping with surprise. She shot to her feet. 'Mr and Mrs Evans!'

'Hello, my dear.' Mrs Evans kissed her cheek, and David's father did the same.

'It's lovely to see you . . . Er, how did you get in here?'

'We snuck past the guard.' Sam winked at her, and when he saw her astonishment burst out laughing. 'Sorry, dear, just my little joke.'

The door was still open, and Peter glanced in, then smiled broadly. 'Admiral and Mrs Evans, how lovely to see you.'

'Hello, Commander. We've come to see David. Do you know where he is?'

'In the operations room. I'll take you there.'

Kathy watched the two men leave, and turned back to David's mother, who had a look of resigned amusement on her face.

'When David told me his father was a retired admiral I thought he was joking, but he wasn't.'

Jean nodded. 'He only uses his rank when necessary.'

'Like gaining entrance to somewhere like this? I'm not sure if I should address him as sir,' she said, laughing.

'And he would scold you if you did. We are Jean and Sam, especially to our future daughter-in-law.'

Chapter Thirty-Five

David saw his father make an entrance and stifled a laugh, watching as everyone greeted him. He was up to something because he was flaunting his rank, and that only happened when he could use it to his advantage.

'Hello, Dad,' David said when he finally reached him, then lowered his voice. 'Dare I ask why you are here?'

'We thought we'd come and see where you worked, and to meet that lovely girl of yours again.'

'And?'

'We want you to take us to see Max and the brothers.'

'Ah, I'm not sure they will allow civilians into the camp.'

'Thought of that. I've got my uniform in the car, and your mother can be my secretary.'

David ran a hand over his eyes, trying to hide his

amusement. 'Which uniform? The Home Guard one, or the one with all the gold braid on it?'

His father chuckled. 'The gold braid, of course.'

'That won't be necessary. I'll get you in as you are.'

'Oh, shame, I was looking forward to dressing up again.'

They were both openly laughing now, and out of the corner of his eye he could see Alice studying them with interest. 'Alice.' David beckoned her over. 'Meet my father, Admiral Evans.'

She beamed and shook his hand. 'Alan's told me a lot about you. I can see you are father and son, you are so alike.'

'Alice is going to marry Alan,' David explained.

'Pleased to meet you, my dear. He's a lucky man.'

'Of course he is. I tell him so all the time.'

'Very wise.' Sam kept a perfectly straight expression. 'We men are liable to forget just how lucky we are.'

She nodded. 'Have you come to see where we work? Interesting place, isn't it?'

'It certainly is. What do you do here?'

'Oh, all sorts of things, but they need me for my memory.'

'Really? Good, is it?'

'Pretty good.'

Noting that his father showed no sign of breaking off the conversation with this interesting girl, David touched his arm. 'Dad, if you want to make that trip we had better go.'

'Plenty of time, son.' He turned back to Alice. 'My wife is here. You must come and meet her. Alan is a friend of ours, you know.'

'He told me. I've finished my shift now.'

'Splendid.'

After taking his leave of everyone, they went back to the office and found Ted and Alan there as well. The greetings and chatter filled the small office until Sam called for order.

'David is going to take us to meet the boys, and as much fun as I'm having here, we must get going.'

'Oh, can I come too? Alan is inviting them to our wedding and I haven't met them yet,' Alice said.

'Good idea.' Alan put an arm around Alice. 'Let's all go.'

'Hold it right there,' David ordered. 'There is no way they will allow such a large group into the camp.'

'Why not?' his mother asked. 'The war is over now.'

'They are still prisoners. Repatriation will take some time.' He thought for a moment, and then made for the door. 'Let me check on something first.'

He returned some ten minutes later. 'The wireless room patched me through to the camp, and they are at the farm, so we can all go. If the farmer objects to us descending upon him, then we'll have to see them in stages.'

'Fair enough,' his father agreed. 'Now, I can't get everyone in my car.'

'Kathy and I will go on the bike and you can follow us.'

That was agreed, and they all trooped outside.

'This is crazy,' David muttered as he watched them all pile into his father's car.

'But fun.' She laughed. 'Do you know your mother has already started planning our wedding?'

He groaned. 'I was hoping we could keep it simple.'

'Not a chance.'

'Do you mind?'

She reached up and kissed him gently. 'Of course not. My mother would have been doing the same had she still been with us. Your mother knows that and has stepped in to take over that role, and I'm happy about it.'

'Come on, David, stop gassing,' his father called. 'Let's get this ship out to sea.'

Without further delay they were roaring up the road with the car right behind them.

When they pulled into the farm, David took Kathy with him and ordered everyone else to stay where they were while they spoke to the farmer.

They found him in a greenhouse tending tomato plants and he smiled when he saw them. 'Ah, come to see the boys, have you?'

David then explained why his parents wanted to meet them. 'We also have several more with us, and we would like your permission before descending on you.'

'No problem, lad, bring them all in.' He smiled happily. 'That bloody war is over now, thank heavens. Pardon my language, miss.'

'Don't worry about it,' she told him. 'I work with sailors, remember.'

He grinned. 'The boys are in the field behind the barn

over there. Erik and our girl have taken quite a shine to each other.'

'Do you mind?' Kathy asked.

'Not at all. He's a nice lad, and clever too. I've offered him and his brother a cottage on the farm if they want it. It needs a bit of work done to it, of course, but we can soon put that right if they decide to take it.'

'Gerhard told me and that's kind of you.' David shook the farmer's hand. 'Erik has a lot going for him. There are people willing to give him a home; he's being nurtured by an artist and earning money. I can't see any great obstacles to gaining permission for him to stay here.'

'Glad to hear it. They are nice lads. What about Gerhard and Max?'

'They will be going home to see their families first, but I'll get them back here when they want to come.'

Farmer George nodded and smiled. 'I'll tell the wife to send out something to eat and drink. You can have a party, then.'

'You must let us pay you for the refreshments,' David told him.

'Wouldn't dream of it,' George told him as he walked away, whistling cheerfully.

'You go and warn them that we are coming, Kathy, while I go and get the others.'

As usual, Erik saw her first and came running over. 'Lovely you here. Are you on your own?'

'No, there is a crowd of us and the farmer has given

permission for everyone to come and see you. David has gone to fetch them.' Erik's English had improved, but he still left out words and got things round the wrong way sometimes. However, the important thing was he could now communicate with everyone and understand a lot of what was said. She was proud of the way he had grown into a more confident young man.

Max and Gerhard strolled over to greet her.

'Lots of people coming to see us,' Erik told them. 'Who these people?'

Kathy heard the chatter and turned her head. 'You will soon find out. Here they come.'

Max made a sound of surprise and took off towards the crowd.

'Our captain knows them?' Gerhard asked.

'Two of them are David's parents, and they are the ones who have offered to take you in if David can get you released early. They want to meet you. The other two you have already met, and the girl is my friend.'

'They all want to meet us?' Erik looked rather unsure.

'Don't be concerned,' she told him. 'They are very nice. Look how happy Max is to see them.'

Alice reached them first. 'Wow! Isn't this exciting? Let me guess, you must be the artist, Erik, and you are his brother, Gerhard. Lovely to meet you.' She grasped their hands and shook enthusiastically.

They bowed slightly just as everyone else reached them.

'My parents wanted to meet you,' David told them when the introductions were made.

Jean, who was still holding Max's arm, released him and stepped forward, smiling. 'We are so happy to meet you, and we are all doing our best to get you released into our care until everything is sorted out.'

'So kind.' Erik looked at his brother for help.

'We also hope it can be arranged and are grateful for your kindness.'

'Our pleasure.' Sam glanced at his son. 'Don't take too long about it, David. We need to get these boys out of that camp.'

'I'm working on it, Dad, but these things take time.'

'Why don't you throw your weight around, Admiral?' Max said to him. 'You might be able to speed things up.'

Sam winked. 'Already at it, my boy. Might be retired, but the rank can be useful at times.'

Erik grabbed David's arm, clearly not understanding everything. 'He really admiral? You not joking?'

'Oh, don't take any notice of that. He was also a corporal in the Home Guard.'

'You . . . you were what?' Max could hardly speak for laughing.

'A corporal,' Sam replied with a smirk. 'It was fun.'

That brought another howl of laughter from Max, and he slapped David on the back. 'He hasn't changed at all, has he?'

'Not one tiny bit. In fact, I think he's got worse with age.'

The sound of the van approaching caught their attention and the farmer, his wife and daughter got out and began unloading it. George came across with a huge smile on his face and he and his family were introduced to everyone. 'We could hear your laughter from way back. Help us set this up and we can have a real party.'

The atmosphere was relaxed and friendly as they all sat round eating, drinking and laughing. Max and the brothers were proudly showing the photos the major had sent them of their families.

With everyone occupied, David touched Kathy's arm, and they moved a little away from the group, so they could talk. 'That's a good scene, isn't it?'

'It certainly is. When I look at that I can hardly remember how angry I was when I first joined the Wrens. Then one day I was face-to-face with a traumatised boy from a U-boat, and everything changed for me as my anger drained away.' She took his arm and leant against him. 'Because of the kind of work you did I was forced to face up to what had happened. Coming to work for you was a blessing – in more ways than one, though I didn't realise it at the time. However, some things will never be forgotten, will they?'

'No, and some things should be remembered.' David smiled down at her. 'But now we have a new life to carve out for ourselves, and we are going to need the same determination to succeed as we've shown during these years of war.'

Kathy nodded towards the group and smiled wistfully. 'It's been an incredible time, hasn't it? There has been grief and anger, sadness and laughter, and enemies have become friends.'

He bent his head and kissed her gently. 'When we get back we must put in for our discharge. We've wasted enough time, and I want us to marry as soon as possible. There is a future waiting for us – waiting for all of us, friends and enemies alike.'

BERYL MATTHEWS was born in London but now lives in a small village in Hampshire. As a young girl her ambition was to become a professional singer, but the need to earn a wage drove her into an office, where she worked her way up from tea girl to credit controller. After retiring she joined a Writers' Circle in hopes of fulfilling her dream of becoming a published author. With her first book published at the age of seventy-one, she has since written over twenty novels.

To discover more great books and to
place an order visit our website at
allisonandbusby.com

Don't forget to sign up to our free newsletter at
allisonandbusby.com/newsletter
for latest releases, events and exclusive offers

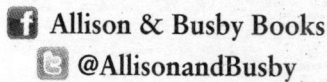 **Allison & Busby Books**
@AllisonandBusby

You can also call us on
020 3950 7834
for orders, queries
and reading recommendations

Friends and Enemies

446 "Since the rebellion . . . taken Richmond": SPC to Richard C. Parsons, July 20, 1862, reel 21, Chase Papers.
446 "The house seemed . . . you were gone": SPC to KCS, June 24, 1862, reel 21, Chase Papers.
446 many long letters: SPC to KCS, June 24, 25, 29, and 30, July 1, 2 and 4, 1862, reel 21, Chase Papers.
446 "a mark of love and . . . on many points": SPC to KCS, July 6, 1862, reel 21, Chase Papers.
446 "All your letters . . . very good": SPC to KCS, July 4, 1862, reel 21, Chase Papers.
446 concealed her unhappiness . . . "So with us it came": William Sprague to KCS, May 27, 1866, Sprague Papers.
447 "My confidence . . . and so will I": SPC to KCS, July 6, 1862, reel 21, Chase Papers.
447 to visit the McDowells' . . . "will alarm you": Mrs. McDowell, quoted in Phelps, *Kate Chase, Dominant Daughter,* p. 121.
447 "The first necessity . . . of no more": *NYT,* July 7, 1862.
447 "Journals of all . . . instant removal": *NYT,* July 10, 1862.
447 "So you want . . . unaffected wonder": GBM to MEM, [July] 13, [1862], in *Civil War Papers of George B. McClellan,* pp. 354–55.
447 *"the proof* . . . hypocrite & villain": GBM to MEM, July 22, [1862], in ibid., p. 368.
448 "there had been . . . opposition to McClellan": SPL to EBL, July 6, 1862, box 230, folder 7, Blair-Lee Papers, NjP-SC.
448 John Astor . . . "by a signal victory": Entry for July 11, 1862, *Diary of George Templeton Strong,* Vol. III, p. 239.
448 "If we could help . . . any other way": Frederick Law Olmsted to "My Dear Doctor," July 13, 1862, reel 2, Papers of Frederick Law Olmsted, Manuscript Division, Library of Congress.
448 "very fierce crusade . . . the art of war": *NYT,* July 10, 1862.
448 Mary Ellet Cabell . . . "tears to his eyes": Mary Ellet Cabell, quoted in Flower, *Edwin McMasters Stanton,* p. 164.
449 "the baby was dying" . . . on July 10: Christopher Wolcott to Pamphila Stanton Wolcott, July 6, 1862, in Wolcott, "Edwin M. Stanton," p. 157b (quote); Gideon Welles, "The History of Emancipation," *Galaxy* 14 (December 1872), p. 842.
449 his own health began to suffer: Benjamin, "Recollections of Secretary Edwin M. Stanton," *Century* (1887), p. 759.
449 "He unflinchingly . . . out of it": Whitman, *Specimen Days* (1902 edn.), p. 36.
449 "Allow me to assure . . . all your life": AL to Quintin Campbell, June 28, 1862, in *CW,* V, p. 288.
449 Stanton . . . shutting down recruiting offices: Thomas and Hyman, *Stanton,* p. 201; Sears, *George B. McClellan,* p. 180.
449 "a general panic": AL to WHS, June 28, 1862, in *CW,* V, p. 292.
449 Seward devised an excellent solution: AL, "Call for Troops," June 30, 1862, in ibid., p. 294 n1.
450 Seward telegraphed . . . "We fail without it": WHS to EMS, July 1, 1862, *OR,* Ser. 3, Vol. II, p. 186.
450 "The existing law" . . . his own responsibility: EMS to WHS, July 1, 1862, *OR,* Ser. 3, Vol. II, pp. 186–87 (quote p. 186).
450 He set a precedent . . . answered Seward's call: *NR,* August 14, 1862.
450 William Junior . . . "line of march": William H. Seward, Jr., speech before members of the 9th New York Artillery, 1912, box 121, Seward Papers, NRU.
450 Will's enlistment . . . his mother's fragile health: William H. Seward, Jr., to WHS, July 17, 1862, reel 117, Seward Papers.
450 "As it is obvious . . . no objection": FAS to FWS, August 10, 1862, reel 115, Seward Papers.
450 to make a personal visit . . . at Harrison's Landing: *Sun,* Baltimore, Md., July 11, 1862.
451 "The day had" . . . to over 100 degrees: *NYT,* July 12, 1862 (quote); *NYH,* July 11, 1862.
451 the "almost overpowering" heat: GBM to MEM, July 8, [1862], in *Civil War Papers of George B. McClellan,* p. 346.
451 at Harrison's Landing . . . moonlit evening: *NYT,* July 12, 1862; *NYH,* July 11, 1862.
451 great cheers . . . "deck of the vessel": *NYT,* July 11, 1862.
451 "strong frank . . . will be saved": GBM to MEM, July 8, [1862], in *Civil War Papers of George B. McClellan,* p. 346.
451 the "Harrison's Landing" letter: GBM to AL, July 7, 1862, *OR,* Ser. 1, Vol. XI, pp. 73–74.
451 Lincoln "made no comments . . . to me for it": McClellan, *McClellan's Own Story,* p. 487.
452 the president reviewed . . . wounded: Sears, *To the Gates of Richmond,* pp. 344–45; *NYH,* July 11, 1862.
452 "Mr. Lincoln rode . . . stove-pipe hat": *NYT,* July 11, 1862.
452 "entangled . . . has been universal": Rev. Joseph H. Twichell, "Army Memories of Lincoln. A Chaplain's Reminiscences," *The Congregationalist and Christian World,* January 30, 1913, p. 154.
452 "successive booming . . . Saul of Oz": *NYH,* July 11, 1862.
452 "thinned ranks . . . with their struggle": *NYT,* July 12, 1862.
452 "On the way . . . swim in the river": *NYH,* July 11, 1862.
452 "Frank was . . . greatly cheered": EBL to SPL, July 18, 1862, in *Wartime Washington,* ed. Laas, p. 165 n8.
452 summoned General Henry Halleck . . . general in chief: AL, "Order Making Henry W. Halleck General-in-Chief," July 11, 1862, in *CW,* V, pp. 312–13.
452 Halleck's victories . . . widely respected: "Halleck, Henry Wager (1815–1872)," in Sifakis, *Who Was Who in the Union,* p. 172.
453 "I do not know . . . I am a General": GBM to MEM, [July] 10, [1862], in *Civil War Papers of George B. McClellan,* p. 348.
453 Senator Chandler of Michigan . . . "the coward": Entry for June 4, 1862, in *The Diary of Edward Bates, 1859–1866,* p. 260.

453 Lincoln was determined . . . "cajoled out of them": Entry for July 24, 1862, in Browning, *The Diary of Orville Hickman Browning*, Vol. I, p. 563.

453 "much of his . . . crushing the rebellion": Benjamin, "Recollections of Secretary Edwin M. Stanton," *Century* (1887), p. 765.

453 "that all that Stanton . . . the President": Entry for July 14, 1862, in Browning, *The Diary of Orville Hickman Browning*, Vol. I, p. 559.

453 All the government departments had closed down: *NR*, August 7, 1862.

453 "never seen more persons . . . resembled": Entry for August 10, 1862, in French, *Witness to the Young Republic*, p. 405.

453 "the ringing of bells . . . Marine Band": *NYT*, August 7, 1862.

454 " 'Well! Hadn't I' . . . once to the stand": Entry for August 6, 1862, *Chase Papers*, Vol. I, p. 360.

454 "I believe there . . . the Secretary of War": AL, "Address to Union Meeting at Washington," August 6, 1862, in *CW*, V, pp. 358–59.

454 "He is one of . . . ever created": Entry for August 10, 1862, in French, *Witness to the Young Republic*, p. 405.

454 "originality . . . took all hearts": Entry for August 6, 1862, *Chase Papers*, Vol. I, p. 360.

454 The great rally concluded . . . in the Union: *NR*, August 7, 1862.

454 she had begun riding: *NYT*, April 5, 1862.

454 "she was so hid . . . she was there": Mary Hay to Milton Hay, April 13, 1862, in *Concerning Mr. Lincoln*, comp. Pratt, p. 94.

454 "she seemed to be" . . . Soldiers' Home: Entry for June 16, 1862, in French, *Witness to the Young Republic*, p. 400.

454 Soldiers' Home: Matthew Pinsker, *Lincoln's Sanctuary: Abraham Lincoln and the Soldiers' Home* (Oxford and New York: Oxford University Press, 2003); National Park Service, U.S. Department of the Interior, *President Lincoln and Soldiers' Home National Monument*, Special Resource Draft Study (August 2002).

455 "an earthly paradise": Julia Wheelock Freeman, *The Boys in White; The Experience of a Hospital Agent in and Around Washington* (New York: Lange & Hillman, 1870), p. 171.

455 a choice destination for Washingtonians: Pinsker, *Lincoln's Sanctuary*, p. 12.

455 "this quiet and beautiful . . . along the hills": *Iowa State Register*, Des Moines, July 2, 1862.

455 At Mary's urging: Pinsker, *Lincoln's Sanctuary*, pp. 4–5.

455 "We are truly . . . to Cambridge": MTL to Mrs. Charles Eames, July 26, [1862], in Turner and Turner, *Mary Todd Lincoln*, p. 131.

455 For Tad . . . campfire at night: Pinsker, *Lincoln's Sanctuary*, p. 78.

455 the Lincolns could entertain . . . among family and friends: Ibid., pp. 9–10.

455 "helped him . . . attorney in Illinois": Ibid., pp. 15 (quote), 81–82.

456 "daily habit . . . in the District": *Saturday Evening Post*, June 21, 1862.

456 "But for these humane . . . lost her child": Mrs. E. F. Ellet, *The Court Circles of the Republic* (Hartford, Conn.: Hartford Publishing Co., 1869; New York: Arno Press, 1975), p. 526.

456 "little cares . . . into nothing": Walt Whitman to Louisa Whitman, December 29, 1862, in Walt Whitman, *The Wound Dresser: A Series of Letters Written from the Hospitals in Washington During the War of the Rebellion*, ed. Richard Maurice Bucke (Boston: Small, Maynard & Co., 1898; Folcroft, Penn.: Folcroft Library Editions, 1975), p. 48.

456 "nothing of ordinary . . . it used to": Walt Whitman to Louisa Whitman, August 25, 1863, in ibid., p. 104.

456 "to form an immense army": *NYTrib*, July 9, 1862.

456 steamers arrived . . . Ambulances stood by: *NR*, June 30, 1862.

456 a massive project of . . . military hospitals: see *NR*, June 17–23, 1862; *Iowa State Register*, Des Moines, July 9, 1862.

456 Union Hotel Hospital . . . "sup their wine": *NR*, January 9, 1862.

456 "many of the doors . . . could christen it": Louisa May Alcott, *Hospital Sketches* (New York: Sagamore Press, 1957), p. 59.

456 The Braddock House . . . old chairs and desks: Freeman, *The Boys in White*, p. 37.

456 the Patent Office . . . transformed into a hospital ward: *NR*, June 27 and September 2, 1862.

456 "a curious scene . . . pavement under foot": Walt Whitman, quoted in *NYT*, February 26, 1863.

457 the Methodist Episcopal Church on 20th Street: *NR*, June 18, 1862.

457 covering pews . . . laboratory and kitchen: *NR*, June 23, 1862.

457 more than three thousand patients: *NR*, April 11, 1862.

457 baskets of fruit . . . pillows of wounded men: *NYTrib*, August 13, 1862 (quote); Ellet, *The Court Circles of the Republic*, p. 526; AL to Hiram P. Barney, August 16, 1862, in *CW*, V, pp. 377–78.

457 One wounded soldier . . . signature: MTL to "Mrs. Agen," August 10, 1864, in Turner and Turner, *Mary Todd Lincoln*, p. 179.

457 of "commanding stature . . . for it so eagerly": Alcott, *Hospital Sketches*, pp. 89–92, 99–100, 103, 104.

458 "singularly cool . . . (full of maggots)": Walt Whitman to Louisa Whitman, October 6, 1863, in Whitman, *The Wound Dresser*, pp. 123–24.

458 "heap of feet" . . . hospital grounds: Walt Whitman to Louisa Whitman, December 29, 1862, in ibid., p. 48.

458 she found it difficult . . . "wounded occupant": Alcott, *Hospital Sketches*, p. 59.

458 "Death itself . . . such a relief": Walt Whitman to Louisa Whitman, August 25, 1863, in Whitman, *The Wound Dresser*, p. 104.

458 "was so blackened" . . . eventually recovered: Amanda Stearns to her sister, May 14, 1863, reprinted in Amanda Akin Stearns, *The Lady Nurse of Ward E* (New York: Baker & Taylor Co., 1909), pp. 25–26 (quote p. 25).

458 Another youth . . . "on the Judgment Day": Alcott, *Hospital Sketches*, pp. 62–63 (quote p. 63).

458 "If she were worldly wise . . . many journals": Stoddard, *Inside the White House in War Times*, p. 48.

458 "While her sister-women . . . the White House": Ames, *Ten Years in Washington*, p. 237.

458 Mary continued . . . work discreetly: *Chicago Tribune*, July 4, 1872; Mary Elizabeth Massey, *Bonnet Brigades* (New York: Alfred A. Knopf, 1966), p. 44.

459 "our ever-bountiful benefactress & friend": *NR*, December 27, 1861.

459 "an angel of mercy": *NR*, June 27, 1862.

459 Lincoln had asked the legislature: AL, "Message to Congress," March 6, 1862, in *CW*, V, pp. 144–46.

459 "less than one half-day's" . . . border states combined: AL to James A. McDougall, March 14, 1862, in *CW*, V, p. 160.

459 "to surrender . . . the Union dissolved": *NYT*, July 13, 1862.

459 If the rebels . . . lose heart: AL, "Message to Congress," March 6, 1862, in *CW*, V, p. 145.

459 "emancipation in any form . . . the Border States": Editors' note on majority reply to AL, "Appeal to Border State Representatives to Favor Compensated Emancipation," July 12, 1862, in ibid., p. 319 n1.

460 "never doubted . . . to abolish slavery": AL, "Message to Congress," April 16, 1862, in ibid., p. 192.

460 "I trust I am not . . . seem like a dream": Frederick Douglass to CS, April 8, 1862, reel 25, Sumner Papers.

460 As slaves in the District . . . "when they wished": Smith, *Francis Preston Blair*, p. 354.

460 "all but one . . . quarters": EBL to SPL, April 19, 1862, in *Wartime Washington*, ed. Laas, p. 130.

460 Henry . . . the rest of his life: Henry, quoted in Smith, *Francis Preston Blair*, p. 354.

460 Nanny . . . "children are free": EBL to SPL, April 19, 1862, in *Wartime Washington*, ed. Laas, p. 130.

460 a new confiscation bill: "An Act to suppress Insurrection, to punish Treason and Rebellion, to seize and confiscate the Property of Rebels, and for other Purposes," July 17, 1862, in *Statutes at Large, Treaties, and Proclamations of the United States of America*, Vol. 12 (Boston, 1863), pp. 589–92, available through "Chronology of Emancipation During the Civil War," *Freedmen and Southern Society Project*, University of Maryland, College Park, www.history.umd.edu/Freedmen/conact2.htm (accessed April 2004).

460 "It was . . . a dead letter from the start": "Confiscation Act of July 17, 1862," in Mark E. Neely, Jr., *The Abraham Lincoln Encyclopedia* (New York: McGraw-Hill, 1982), p. 68.

460 a "disturbing influence . . . to break anew": CS, quoted in James G. Blaine, *Twenty Years of Congress: From Lincoln to Garfield*, Vol. I (Norwich, Conn.: Henry Bill Publishing Co., 1884), p. 374.

461 "our friends . . . take it at its flood": Entry for July 14, 1862, in Browning, *The Diary of Orville Hickman Browning*, Vol. I, p. 558.

461 "will be an end . . . errors of policy": Henry Cooke to Jay Cooke, July 16, 1862, in Ellis Paxson Oberholtzer, *Jay Cooke: Financier of the Civil War* (Philadelphia: George W. Jacobs & Co., 1907), p. 199.

461 "looked weary . . . in his voice": Entry for July 15, 1862, in Browning, *The Diary of Orville Hickman Browning*, Vol. I, p. 560.

461 the president traveled . . . final days of the term: JGN to TB, July 18, 1862, container 2, Nicolay Papers.

461 an extraordinarily productive session: See Leonard P. Curry, *Blueprint for Modern America: Nonmilitary Legislation of the First Civil War Congress* (Nashville, Tenn.: Vanderbilt University Press, 1968), pp. 101–36, 147–48, 179–97, 244–52.

462 "he had lately begun . . . d'etat for our Congress": Entry for July 21, 1862, *Chase Papers*, Vol. I, p. 348.

462 "I ask Congress . . . lost one advocate": WHS to FAS, July 12, 1862, quoted in Seward, *Seward at Washington . . . 1861–1872*, pp. 115–16.

462 The debates had grown . . . "part in them": Field, *Memories of Many Men*, pp. 264–65.

462 "a moral . . . political wrong": AL, "Sixth Debate with Stephen A. Douglas, at Quincy, Illinois," October 13, 1858, in *CW*, III, p. 254.

462 uses to which slaves were put by the Confederacy: Welles, "History of Emancipation," *Galaxy* (1872), pp. 843, 844; Hendrick, *Lincoln's War Cabinet*, p. 355.

462 emancipation could be considered a military necessity: Welles, "History of Emancipation," *Galaxy* (1872), p. 850.

463 the funeral of Stanton's infant son: *Star*, July 11, 1862.

463 "emancipating the slaves . . . justifiable": Entry for c. July 1862, *Welles diary*, Vol. I (1960 edn.), pp. 70–71.

463 when messengers . . . by the diplomats in attendance: Entry for July 21, 1862, *Chase Papers*, Vol. I, p. 348.

463 all members save the postmaster: Welles, "History of Emancipation," *Galaxy* (1872), p. 844.

464 books in the library: MTL to Benjamin B. French, July 26, [1862], in Turner and Turner, *Mary Todd Lincoln*, pp. 129–30; Seale, *The President's House*, Vol. I, pp. 291–92, 380.

464 "profoundly concerned . . . and slavery": Entry for July 21, 1862, *Chase Papers*, Vol. I, p. 348.

464 Lincoln read several orders . . . "decide the question": Entry for July 21, 1862, ibid., pp. 348–49.

464 another cabinet session; Carpenter painting: Stoddard, *Inside the White House in War Times*, p. 11; entry for July 22, 1862, *Chase Papers*, Vol. I, p. 351.

464 Lincoln took the floor . . . "on the slavery question": Welles, "History of Emancipation," *Galaxy* (1872), p. 844.

464 "had resolved upon . . . their advice": Carpenter, *Six Months at the White House*, p. 21.

464 His draft proclamation . . . "and forever": AL, "Emancipation Proclamation—First Draft," [July 22, 1862], in *CW*, V, p. 337.

464 statistics on slaves in border states and Confederacy: These statistics are based on 1860 census data for the numbers of slaves living in the border slave states that remained in the Union, and the eleven slave states that formed the Confederacy.

465 "fraught with consequences . . . could not penetrate": Welles, "History of Emancipation," *Galaxy* (1872), p. 841.

465 the members were startled . . . "immediate promulgation": EMS memorandum, July 22, 1862, reel 3, Stanton Papers, DLC.

465 Bates's approval . . . cadet at West Point: Introduction, and entries for April 14, 1862, and November 30, 1863, in *The Diary of Edward Bates, 1859–1866*, pp. xv–xvi, 250, 319.

465 his "very decided . . . the white race": Welles, "History of Emancipation," *Galaxy* (1872), pp. 844–45.

466 "among our colored . . . 'which they profess' ": Entry for September 25, 1862, in *The Diary of Edward Bates, 1859–1866*, pp. 263–64.

466 Welles remained silent . . . "intensify the struggle": Memorandum from September 22, 1862, quoted in Welles, "History of Emancipation," *Galaxy* (1872), p. 848.

466 "extreme exercise of war powers": Entry for October 1, 1862, *Welles diary*, Vol. I (1960 edn.), p. 159.

466 Caleb Smith . . . "attack the administration": Usher, *President Lincoln's Cabinet*, p. 17.

466 Blair spoke up . . . "were in vain": Welles, "History of Emancipation," *Galaxy* (1872), p. 847.

467 "beyond anything . . . universal emancipation": EMS memorandum, July 22, 1862, reel 3, Stanton Papers, DLC.

467 "depredation and massacre . . . soon as practicable": Entry for July 22, 1862, *Chase Papers*, Vol. I, p. 351.

467 The bold proclamation . . . "was his specialty": Entry for August 22, 1863, *Welles diary*, Vol. I (1960 edn.), p. 415.

467 "golden moment . . . four thousand years": Christopher Wolcott to Pamphila Stanton Wolcott, July 27, 1862, in Wolcott, "Edwin M. Stanton," p. 158a.

467 Lincoln later maintained . . . "Seward spoke": Carpenter, *Six Months at the White House*, p. 21.

467 a racial war in the South . . . their economic interests: EMS memorandum, July 22, 1862, reel 3, Stanton Papers, DLC.

468 "The public mind . . . to give them effect": WHS to FAS, August 7, 1862, in Seward, *Seward at Washington . . . 1861–1872*, p. 121.

468 "would have been . . . territory was conquered": Carpenter, "A Day with Governor Seward," Seward Papers.

468 "Mr. President . . . *shriek*, on the retreat": WHS, quoted in Carpenter, *Six Months at the White House*, pp. 21–22.

468 "until the eagle . . . about his neck": Carpenter, "A Day with Governor Seward," Seward Papers.

468 Seward's argument . . . met with Lincoln: Francis B. Cutting to EMS, February 20, 1867, reel 11, Stanton Papers, DLC.

468 "The wisdom of . . . the progress of events": AL, quoted in Carpenter, *Six Months at the White House*, p. 22.

469 "with public sentiment . . . nothing can succeed": AL, "First Debate with Stephen A. Douglas at Ottawa, Illinois," August 21, 1858, in *CW*, III, p. 27.

469 On August 14 . . . opportunity among their own people: "Address on Colonization to a Deputation of Negroes," August 14, 1862, in *CW*, V, pp. 371–75.

469 "We were entirely hostile" . . . to the proposal: Edward M. Thomas to AL, August 16, 1862, Lincoln Papers.

469 "are as much the natives . . . to a distant shore": *Liberator*, August 22, 1862.

470 provoked Frederick Douglass: Christopher N. Breiseth, "Lincoln and Frederick Douglass: Another Debate," *Journal of the Illinois State Historical Society* 68, no. 1 (February 1975), pp. 14–15.

470 "ridiculous . . . and bitter persecution": *Douglass' Monthly* (September 1862).

470 the "drop of honey": AL, "Temperance Address," February 22, 1842, in *CW*, I, p. 273.

470 "How much better . . . homes in America!": Entry for August 15, 1862, *Chase Papers*, Vol. I, p. 362.

470 cheap "clap-trap . . . perhaps of both": Entry for August, 1862, in Gurowski, *Diary from March 4, 1861 to November 12, 1862*, pp. 251–52.

470 "The Prayer of Twenty Millions": *NYTrib*, August 20, 1862.

471 seizing the opportunity to begin instructing the public: *NYT*, August 24, 1862.

471 "As to the policy . . . will help the cause": AL to Horace Greeley, August 22, 1862, in *CW*, V, pp. 388–89.

471 "I am sorry . . . than human freedom": FAS to WHS, August 24, 1862, reel 114, Seward Papers.

471 "killed years ago . . . destruction of slavery": WHS, quoted in Carpenter, *Six Months at the White House*, pp. 72–73.

472 no "truly republican . . . a great moral evil": FAS, miscellaneous fragment, reel 197, Seward Papers.

CHAPTER 18: "MY WORD IS OUT"

Page

473 Halleck ordered McClellan . . . Alexandria: Henry W. Halleck to EMS, August 30, 1862, in *OR*, Ser. 1, Vol. XII, Part III, p. 739; John J. Hennessy, *Return to Bull Run: The Campaign and Battle of Second Manassas* (New York: Simon & Schuster, 1993), p. 10.

474 He argued ferociously . . . "disastrous in the extreme": GBM to Henry W. Halleck, August 4, 1862, in *Civil War Papers of George B. McClellan*, pp. 383–84 (quote p. 383).

474 His only hope . . . of his command: GBM to MEM, August 8, [1862], in ibid., p. 388.

474 After delaying . . . until August 24: GBM to Henry W. Halleck, August 12, [1862], in ibid., pp. 390–93; Henry W. Halleck to EMS, August 30, 1862, in *OR*, Ser. 1, Vol. XII, Part III, p. 739.

474 General Lee moved north . . . the combined forces of Lee, Longstreet, and Jackson: Hennessy, *Return to Bull Run*, pp. 50–51, 55, 92–93, 122–23, 136.

474 "What is the stake? . . . *cause also*": WHS to FAS[?], August 21, 1862, quoted in Seward, *Seward at Washington . . . 1861–1872*, p. 124.

474 a comet appeared in the northern sky: *NR*, August 27, 1862.

474 "When beggars die": William Shakespeare, *The Tragedy of Julius Caesar*, Act II, sc. 2.

474 Although McClellan agreed . . . "leave of absence!": Sears, *George B. McClellan*, pp. 252–56; GBM to MEM, August 24, [1862], in *Civil War Papers of George B. McClellan*, p. 404 (quote).

474 "Pope is beaten . . . Washn again": GBM to MEM, August 23, [1862], in *Civil War Papers of George B. McClellan*, p. 400.

474 "the smell of the gunpowder . . . perceptible": *Star*, August 30, 1862.

474 "distant thunder": *NR*, September 1, 1862.

474 gathered on street corners . . . rumors flew: Leech, *Reveille in Washington*, p. 188; entry for September 3, 1862, *Welles diary*, Vol. I (1960 edn.), p. 106.

475 "Stonewall Jackson . . . about equal proportions": *NR*, September 1, 1862.

475 "prepared to stay all night, if necessary": Bates, *Lincoln in the Telegraph Office*, p. 118.

475 He wired various generals . . . news from Manassas: AL to Ambrose Burnside, August 29, 1862, in *CW*, V, p. 398; Lincoln to Herman Haupt, August 29, 1862, in ibid., p. 399; Lincoln to GBM, August 29, 1862 in ibid.; Bates, *Lincoln in the Telegraph Office*, pp. 119–21.

475 The president now had . . . "perfectly safe": GBM to AL, August 29, 1862, Lincoln Papers.

475 John Hay met the president . . . "his own scrape": "[1 September 1862, Monday]," in Hay, *Inside Lincoln's White House*, pp. 36–37.

475 McClellan's delay . . . "my opinion, required": EMS to Henry W. Halleck, August 28, 1862, in *OR*, Ser. 1, Vol. XII, Part III, p. 706; Henry W. Halleck to EMS, August 30, 1862, in ibid., p. 739 (quote).

475 "like throwing water . . . that in writing": SPC, paraphrased in entry for September 1, 1862, *Welles diary*, Vol. I (1960 edn.), p. 102.

475 Stanton volunteered . . . agreement regarding McClellan: Entries for August 29–30, 1862, in *Chase Papers*, Vol. I, pp. 366–67.

476 "Never before . . . sink into contempt": EB to Hamilton Gamble, September 1, 1862, Bates Papers, MoSHi.

476 written in Stanton's distinctive back-sloping script: Entry for September 1, 1862, *Welles diary*, Vol. I (1960 edn.), p. 100.

476 "unwilling to be . . . commanded by General Pope": Flower, *Edwin McMasters Stanton*, pp. 176–77.

476 Smith was persuaded . . . to Blair or anyone else: Entry for August 31, 1862, *Welles diary*, Vol. I (1960 edn.), pp. 93–95. Howard Beale has identified some of the language included in the 1911 edition of Welles's published diary as having been added later to the original manuscript diary. See Beale's emendations in individual diary entries for subsequent changes made in Welles's diary.

476 Stanton had invited Lincoln . . . "glad tidings at sunrise": "[1 September 1862, Monday]," in Hay, *Inside Lincoln's White House*, p. 37.

477 When Welles stopped by . . . "disrespectful to the President": Entry for August 31, 1862, *Welles diary*, Vol. I (1960 edn.), pp. 95–98 (quotes pp. 97–98).

477 "had called us . . . against him": Entry for September 1, 1862, ibid., pp. 101–02.

477 "he knew of no particular" . . . cabal against the president: Entry for August 31, 1862, ibid., p. 98.

477 "about Eight oclock . . . 'I am afraid' ": "[1 September 1862, Monday]," in Hay, *Inside Lincoln's White House*, pp. 37–38.

477 As rumors spread . . . 16,000 casualties: "5 September 1862, Friday," in ibid., p. 38; FWS to WHS, September 1, 1862, quoted in Seward, *Seward at Washington . . . 1861–1872*, p. 126; McPherson, *Battle Cry of Freedom*, p. 532.

478 "Jeff. Davis . . . before the National Capital": *NYT*, August 31, 1862.

478 put the president in an untenable . . . angrier he became: "1 September 1862, Monday," in Hay, *Inside Lincoln's White House*, p. 37.

478 "There is no . . . now to sacrifice": AL, quoted in "5 September 1862, Friday," in ibid., pp. 38–39.

478 When Halleck recommended . . . Lincoln agreed: Entry for September 12, 1862, *Welles diary*, Vol. I (1960 edn.), p. 124; Sears, *George B. McClellan*, p. 260.

478 Bates rewrote the protest . . . he agreed McClellan should go: Entry for September 1, 1862, ibid., pp. 100–03 (quotes); entry for September 1, 1863, in *Chase Papers*, Vol. I, pp. 367–68.

478 gathered at noon . . . messy controversy over McClellan: Entry for September 2, 1862, in *Lincoln Day by Day*, Vol. III, p. 137; entry for September 2, 1862, *Welles diary*, Vol. I (1960 edn.), p. 104 (quote).

479 Jenny was expecting . . . Clara, was dying: Janet W. Seward, "Personal Experiences of the Civil War," box 132, Seward Papers, NRU; FAS to WHS, August 24, September 7, 1862, reel 114, Seward Papers; FAS to WHS, September 10, 1862, reel 116, Seward Papers.

479 When he heard . . . cut his vacation short: Seward, *Seward at Washington . . . 1861–1872*, p. 127.

479 the president was called out: Entry for September 2, 1862, *Welles diary*, Vol. I (1960 edn.), p. 104.

479 "in a suppressed voice . . . prove a national calamity": Ibid., pp. 104–05 (quotes); entry for September 2, 1862, in *Lincoln Day by Day*, Vol. III, p. 137.

479 Stanton, recognizing . . . "a drooping leaf": *Evening Post*, New York, July 13, 1891 (quote); Flower, *Edwin McMasters Stanton*, p. 179.

479 "seemed wrung . . . to hang himself": EB, quoted in footnote to AL, "Meditation on the Divine Will," [September 2, 1862?], in *CW*, V, p. 404 n1.

479 "In great contests . . . it shall not end yet": AL, "Meditation on the Divine Will," [September 2, 1862?], in ibid., pp. 403–04.

479 Seward drove immediately . . . "during his absence": Seward, *Seward at Washington . . . 1861–1872*, p. 127.

480 "What is the use . . . should have known it": WHS, quoted in "[Mid-September 1862?]," in Hay, *Inside Lincoln's White House*, p. 40.

480 Seward turned to history . . . "preserve hopefulness": WHS to FS, c. November 1862, quoted in Seward, *Seward at Washington . . . 1861–1872*, p. 144.

480 Seward did not question . . . "sea of revolution": WHS to FAS, September 20, 1862, quoted in ibid., p. 132.

480 a president had to work: "5 September 1862, Friday," in Hay, *Inside Lincoln's White House*, p. 38.

480 McClellan smugly returned to his old headquarters: FWS to WHS, September 3, 1862, quoted in Seward, *Seward at Washington . . . 1861–1872*, p. 127.

480 "Again I have . . . 'away from us again' ": GBM to MEM, September 5, [1862], in *Civil War Papers of George B. McClellan*, p. 435.

480 crossed the Potomac . . . three cigars: James M. McPherson, *Crossroads of Freedom: Antietam*. Pivotal Moments in American History Series (New York: Oxford University Press, 2002), pp. 98, 104–05, 107–08. For actual "Lost Orders," see "Special Orders, No. 191, Hd Qrs Army of Northern Va, Sept 9th 1862," reel 31, McClellan Papers, DLC.

480 the Marylanders greeted . . . their countryside: GBM to MEM, September 12 and 14, [1862], and GBM to AL, September 13, [1862], in *Civil War Papers of George B. McClellan*, pp. 450, 458, 453.

481 "We are in . . . battle of the age": GBM to MEM, [September] 17, [1862], in ibid., p. 468.

481 casualties higher than D-Day: McPherson, *Battle Cry of Freedom*, p. 544.

481 "Our victory was . . . so completely": GBM to MEM, September 20, [1862], in *Civil War Papers of George B. McClellan*, p. 473.

481 Lincoln was thrilled . . . and allowed Lee to cross: AL to GBM, September 15, 1862, *CW*, V, p. 426; GBM to Henry W. Halleck, September 19 and 20, 1862, in *Civil War Papers of George B. McClellan*, pp. 470, 475.

481 "At last our Generals . . . National crisis": *NYT*, September 18, 1862.

481 "Sept. 17 . . . of its downfall": *NYT*, September 20, 1862.

481 On September 22 . . . "a graver tone": Carpenter, *Six Months at the White House*, p. 24; entry for September 22, 1862, in *Chase Papers*, Vol. I, p. 393 (quote); EMS, quoted by Judge Hamilton Ward in interview in the *Lockport Journal*, May 21, 1893, reprinted in Whipple, *The Story-Life of Lincoln*, p. 421.

481 reminding his colleagues . . . "to my Maker": AL, quoted in entry for September 22, 1862, in *Chase Papers*, Vol. I, pp. 393–94.

482 "there were occasions . . . the Supreme Will": Welles, "History of Emancipation," *Galaxy* (1872), p. 847.

482 not seeking "advice" . . . suggestions on language: AL, paraphrased in entry for September 22, 1862, in *Chase Papers*, Vol. I, p. 394.

482 "made a very emphatic . . . the measure": Welles, "History of Emancipation," *Galaxy* (1872), p. 846.

482 Blair reiterated . . . the fall elections: Entry for September 22, 1862, in *Chase Papers*, Vol. I, p. 395.

482 "maintain . . . present President"?: WHS, quoted in entry for September 22, 1862, in ibid., p. 394.

482 "it was not my way . . . take this ground": AL, quoted in Carpenter, *Six Months at the White House*, pp. 23–24.

482 "I can only trust . . . never forget them": AL, "Reply to Serenade in Honor of Emancipation Proclamation," September 24, 1862, in *CW*, V, p. 438.

482 proceeded to Chase's house . . . "that horrible name": "[24 September 1862, Wednesday]," in Hay, *Inside Lincoln's White House*, p. 41 (quote); entry for September 24, 1862, in *Chase Papers*, Vol. I, p. 399; *NYT*, September 25, 1862.

483 "in the meanest . . . evoke a generous thrill": Entry for September 23, 1862, in Gurowski, *Diary from March 4, 1861 to November 12, 1862*, p. 278.

483 "did not . . . of a single negro": Fessenden, paraphrased in entry for November 28, 1862, in Browning, *The Diary of Orville Hickman Browning*, Vol. I, p. 587.

483 "We shout for joy . . . confide in his word": *Douglass' Monthly* (October 1862).

483 "My word is out . . . take it back": AL, quoted in George S. Boutwell, *Speeches and Papers Relating to the Rebellion and the Overthrow of Slavery* (Boston: Little, Brown, 1867), p. 362.

483 "render eternal . . . the two sections": *The Times* (London), quoted in *NYT*, September 30, 1862.

483 *Richmond Enquirer* charged . . . "plots their death": *Richmond Enquirer*, October 1, 1862, quoted in *Philadelphia Inquirer*, October 6, 1862.

483 "said he had studied . . . than they did": "[24 September 1862, Wednesday]," in Hay, *Inside Lincoln's White House*, p. 41.

483 "be enthusiastically . . . great act of the age": Hannibal Hamlin to AL, September 25, 1862, Lincoln Papers.

483 "while commendation . . . not very satisfactory": AL to Hannibal Hamlin, September 28, 1862, in *CW*, V, p. 444.

483 "Stanton must leave . . . old place to me": GBM to MEM, September 20, [1862], in *Civil War Papers of George B. McClellan*, p. 476.

483 he would resign . . . "a servile insurrection": GBM to MEM, September 25, [1862], in ibid., p. 481.

484 McClellan drafted a letter . . . not to send the letter: Sears, *George B. McClellan*, pp. 326–27.

484 Though Stanton and Chase . . . considered resigning: Entries for September 25 and October 3, 1862, *Welles diary*, Vol. I (1960 edn.), pp. 148–49, 160–61.

484 Lincoln had made . . . relieved from duty: AL, quoted in "25 September 1863, Sunday," in Hay, *Inside Lincoln's White House*, p. 232.

484 Lincoln journeyed . . . early in October: Entry for October 1, 1862, in *Lincoln Day by Day*, Vol. III, p. 143; John G. Nicolay and John Hay, *Abraham Lincoln: A History*, Vol. VI (New York: Century Co., 1917), p. 174.

484 Halleck, fearing . . . "see my soldiers": AL, quoted in "Lincoln Visits the Army of the Potomac," *Lincoln Lore*, no. 1277, September 28, 1953.

484 As the regiments . . . "greatly amused the company": *NYH*, October 5, 1862.

484 accommodations at Antietam: "Lincoln Visits the Army of the Potomac," *Lincoln Lore*, no. 1277, September 28, 1953.

484 his "over-cautiousness": AL to GBM, October 13, 1862, Lincoln Papers.

484 "was very affable . . . very kind personally": GBM to MEM, October 5, [1862], in *Civil War Papers of George B. McClellan*, p. 490.

484 "real purpose . . . advance into Virginia": GBM to MEM, October 2, [1862], in ibid., p. 488.

484 "if I were . . . trivial": AL, "Speech at Frederick, Maryland," October 4, 1862, in *CW*, V, p. 450.

484 "May our children . . . and his compeers": AL, "Second Speech at Frederick, Maryland," October 4, 1862, in ibid., p. 450.

485 Lincoln had Halleck telegraph . . . "roads are good": Henry W. Halleck to GBM, October 6, 1862, in *OR*, Ser. 1, Vol. XIX, Part II, p. 10.

485 found all manner of excuses: GBM to Henry W. Halleck, October 7, 9, 11, and 18, 1862, and GBM to AL, October 17 and 30, 1862, in *Civil War Papers of George B. McClellan*, pp. 493, 495, 499, 502, 516.

485 "Will you pardon me . . . fatigue anything?": AL to GBM, October [25], 1862, in *CW*, V, p. 474.

485 "Our war on rebellion . . . specimen after all": Entry for October 23, 1862, *Diary of George Templeton Strong*, Vol. III, p. 267.

485 an "ill wind" of discontent: WHS to FS, October 1862, quoted in Seward, *Seward at Washington . . . 1861–1872*, pp. 141, 142 (quote p. 141).

485 the midterm November elections . . . "hurt to laugh": Sears, *George B. McClellan*, p. 335; Hendrick, *Lincoln's War Cabinet*, p. 325; AL, quoted in Sandburg, *Abraham Lincoln: The War Years*, Vol. I, p. 611 (quote).

485 "I began . . . I relieved him": AL, quoted in "25 September 1863, Sunday," in Hay, *Inside Lincoln's White House*, p. 232.

485 McClellan received . . . "visible on my face": GBM to MEM, November 7, [1862], in *Civil War Papers of George B. McClellan*, p. 520.

485 "More than a hundred . . . shed in profusion": *National Intelligencer*, Washington, D.C., November 14, 1862.

486 "In parting . . . an indissoluble tie": GBM to the Army of the Potomac, November 7, 1862, in *Civil War Papers of George B. McClellan*, p. 521.

486 choice of Burnside proved unfortunate: Darius N. Couch, "Sumner's 'Right Grand Division,' " in *Battles and Leaders of the Civil War*, Vol. III, Pt. 1, p. 106; Schurz, *Reminiscences*, Vol. II, pp. 397–98.

486 "ten times . . . as he has *head*": Entry for January 1, 1863, Fanny Seward diary, Seward Papers.

486 Fredericksburg Campaign: McPherson, *Battle Cry of Freedom*, pp. 571–72; Spencer C. Tucker, "Fredericksburg, First Battle of," in *Encyclopedia of the American Civil War*, ed. Heidler and Heidler, pp. 774–79.

486 "The courage . . . popular government": AL, "Congratulations to the Army of the Potomac," December 22, 1862, in *CW*, VI, p. 13.

486 "awful arithmetic . . . Confederacy gone": AL, paraphrased in Stoddard, *Inside the White House in War Times*, p. 101.

486 "more depressed . . . [his] life": Entry for December 18, 1862, in Browning, *The Diary of Orville Hickman Browning*, Vol. I, p. 601.

487 Tuesday, December 16 . . . "cause was lost": Fessenden, *Life and Public Services of William Pitt Fessenden*, Vol. I, pp. 231–32 (quote p. 232).

487 Chase had claimed . . . "of the cabinet": Benjamin Wade, paraphrased in entry for December 16, 1862, in Browning, *The Diary of Orville Hickman Browning*, Vol. I, p. 597.

487 had repeatedly griped . . . "salvation of the country": SPC to John Sherman, September 20, 1862, reel 22, Chase Papers (quote); SPC to Zachariah Chandler, September 20, 1862, reel 1, Chandler Papers, DLC.

487 "paralizing influence . . . the President": Boston *Commonwealth*, December 6, 1862, quoted in David Donald, *Charles Sumner and the Rights of Man* (New York: Alfred A. Knopf, 1970), p. 87.

487 "President *de facto* . . . to Uncle Abe's nose": *Chicago Tribune*, quoted in Thomas, *Abraham Lincoln*, p. 352.

487 "controlling influence . . . of the President": Fessenden, *Life and Public Services of William Pitt Fessenden*, Vol. I, p. 232.

487 "should go in . . . dismissal of Mr Seward": Benjamin Wade, paraphrased in entry for December 16, 1862, in Browning, *The Diary of Orville Hickman Browning*, Vol. I, p. 597.

487 "that measures should . . . to the war": Fessenden, *Life and Public Services of William Pitt Fessenden*, Vol. I, p. 234.

487 "a want of confidence . . . from the Cabinet": Senator Grimes, paraphrased in ibid., p. 233.

487 Fessenden asked . . . "on mere rumors": Ibid., p. 235.

487 "had no evidence . . . our cause greatly": Entry for December 16, 1862, in Browning, *The Diary of Orville Hickman Browning*, Vol. I, pp. 597–98.

488 "without entire . . . productive of evil": Fessenden, *Life and Public Services of William Pitt Fessenden*, Vol. I, p. 236.

488 "give time for reflection": Entry for December 16, 1862, in Browning, *The Diary of Orville Hickman Browning*, Vol. I, p. 598.

488 Preston King felt . . . " 'I can't get out' ": Seward, *Seward at Washington . . . 1861–1872*, pp. 146–47 (quotes); entry for December 19, 1862, *Welles diary*, Vol. I (1960 edn.), p. 194.

488 "They wish to . . . impose upon a child": Entry for December 18, 1862, in Browning, *The Diary of Orville Hickman Browning*, Vol. I, p. 600.

488 "disappointed . . . and chagrined": Entry for December 20, 1862, *Welles diary*, Vol. I (1960 edn.), p. 201.

488 Frances had journeyed . . . family for Christmas: Entry for December 22, 1862, Fanny Seward diary, Seward Papers.

489 "Do not come . . . & uncomfortable night": Entry for c. December 18 and 20, 1862, Fanny Seward diary, Seward Papers.

489 Charles Sumner was particularly . . . of the Confederates: Fessenden, *Life and Public Services of William Pitt Fessenden*, Vol. I, p. 242.

489 Republican senators convened . . . December 18: Ibid., pp. 236–38.

489 "I saw in a moment . . . ray of hope": Entry for December 18, 1862, in Browning, *The Diary of Orville Hickman Browning*, Vol. I, p. 600.

490 during a three-hour session: Fessenden, *Life and Public Services of William Pitt Fessenden*, Vol. I, p. 242.

490 Jacob Collamer . . . "purpose and action": Committee of Nine paper, quoted in ibid., p. 239.

490 "in the hands . . . malignant Democrats: Benjamin Wade, paraphrased in ibid., p. 240.

490 "had been disgraced": Ibid., p. 241.

490 "lukewarmness . . . *of him unperceived*": Entry for December 19, 1862, in *The Diary of Edward Bates, 1859–1866*, p. 269.

490 "shocked and grieved . . . confidence and zeal": Entry for December 19, 1862, *Welles diary*, Vol. I (1960 edn.), p. 195.

490 "earnest and sad . . . nor passionate": Entry for December 19, 1862, in *The Diary of Edward Bates, 1859–1866*, p. 269.

490 "expressed his satisfaction . . . interview": Fessenden, *Life and Public Services of William Pitt Fessenden*, Vol. I, pp. 242–43.

490 "he must work it out . . . on the matter": "30 October 1863, Friday," in Hay, *Inside Lincoln's White House*, p. 104.

490 He sent notices . . . and "good feeling": Entry for December 19, 1862, *Welles diary*, Vol. I (1960 edn.), pp. 194–95.

491 "could not afford to lose": Entry for December 19, 1862, in *The Diary of Edward Bates, 1859–1866*, p. 269.

491 "possible for him" . . . was forced to acquiesce: Entry for December 19, 1862, *Welles diary*, Vol. I (1960 edn.), pp. 195–96 (quote p. 195).

491 Lincoln began . . . "a reasonable consideration": Entry for December 20, 1862, ibid., p. 196; Fessenden, *Life and Public Services of William Pitt Fessenden*, Vol. I, p. 243 (quote).

491 "all had acquiesced . . . once decided": Entry for December 20, 1862, *Welles diary*, Vol. I (1960 edn.), p. 196.

491 He went on to defend Seward . . . Emancipation Proclamation: Fessenden, *Life and Public Services of William Pitt Fessenden*, Vol. I, pp. 243–44, 245–46.

491 "the whole Cabinet . . . and energetic action": Entry for December 20, 1862, *Welles diary*, Vol. I (1960 edn.), pp. 196–97.

491 Blair followed . . . "plural Executive": Ibid., p. 197.

491 "had differed much . . . matters of that kind": MB, paraphrased in Fessenden, *Life and Public Services of William Pitt Fessenden*, Vol. I, p. 245.

491 Bates expressed . . . as did Welles: Entry for December 19, 1862, in *The Diary of Edward Bates, 1859–1866*, p. 270.

491 As he contemplated . . . "regard to his Cabinet": Entry for December 20, 1862, *Welles diary*, Vol. I (1960 edn.), p. 199.

492 "he should not have come" . . . that substantially strengthened it: SPC, paraphrased in Fessenden, *Life and Public Services of William Pitt Fessenden*, Vol. I, pp. 244, 246.

492 Neither Stanton nor Smith: Ibid., p. 249.

492 Lincoln asked each . . . would be made: Ibid., pp. 246–49; Nicolay and Hay, *Abraham Lincoln*, Vol. VI, p. 266.

492 When Collamer . . . "He lied": Jacob Collamer, quoted in entry for December 22, 1862, in Browning, *The Diary of Orville Hickman Browning*, Vol. I, p. 603.

492 Lincoln agreed . . . tell the truth!: AL, paraphrased by Robert Todd Lincoln, in Nicolay, *Personal Traits of Abraham Lincoln*, pp. 159–60.

492 Welles paid an early call . . . where he found Stanton: Entry for December 20, 1862, *Welles diary*, Vol. I (1960 edn.), pp. 199–200.

493 "Suppose you . . . be left in it?": EMS, quoted in Seward, *Seward at Washington . . . 1861–1872*, p. 147.

493 Welles told Seward . . . "greatly pleased": Entry for December 20, 1862, *Welles diary*, Vol. I (1960 edn.), p. 200.

493 Monty Blair entered . . . Seward's resignation: Seward, *Seward at Washington . . . 1861–1872*, p. 147.

493 When Welles returned . . . hand in his own resignation: Entry for December 20, 1862, *Welles diary*, Vol. I (1960 edn.), p. 201.

493 Word had already leaked . . . "course of difficulties": Henry Cooke to Jay Cooke, December 20, 1862, in Oberholtzer, *Jay Cooke*, pp. 224, 226 (quotes p. 226).

493 "had been painfully . . . neither of you longer": Entry for December 20, 1862, *Welles diary*, Vol. I (1960 edn.), pp. 201–02.

494 Lincoln wrote a letter . . . "your Departments respectively": AL to WHS and SPC, December 20, 1862, in *CW*, VI, p. 12.

494 "Seward comforts . . . deems a necessity": Entry for December 23, 1862, *Welles diary*, Vol. I (1960 edn.), p. 205.

494 "Yes, Judge . . . end of my bag!": AL, quoted in Seward, *Seward at Washington . . . 1861–1872*, p. 148.

494 "I have cheerfully . . . to your command": WHS to AL, December 21, 1862, Lincoln Papers.

494 "come as soon as possible": Entry for December 22, 1862, Fanny Seward diary, Seward Papers.

494 "Will you allow me . . . than in your cabinet": SPC to AL, December 20, 1862, Lincoln Papers.

494 When Chase received . . . return to the Treasury: SPC to AL, December 22, 1862, Lincoln Papers.

494 "Seward was feeling . . . had been for weeks": Entry for December 23, 1862, *Welles diary*, Vol. I (1960 edn.), p. 205.

494 Seward magnanimously invited . . . Christmas Eve: SPC to FWS, December 24, 1862, reel 24, Chase Papers.

495 "a triumph over . . . drive him out": JGN to TB, December 23, 1862, container 2, Nicolay Papers.

495 Chase declined . . . "his hospitality": SPC to FWS, December 24, 1862, reel 24, Chase Papers.

495 "she regretted" . . . exception of Monty Blair: EBL to SPL, January 14, [1863], in *Wartime Washington*, ed. Laas, p. 231.

495 a visit to a Georgetown spiritualist . . . "had success": Entry for January 1, 1863, in Browning, *The Diary of Orville Hickman Browning*, Vol. I, pp. 608–09.

495 "I do not now see . . . I put it through": "30 October 1863, Friday," in Hay, *Inside Lincoln's White House*, p. 104.

CHAPTER 19: "FIRE IN THE REAR"

Page

497 a "general air of doubt": *NYT*, December 27, 1862.

497 "Will Lincoln's . . . Nobody knows": Entry for December 30, 1862, *Diary of George Templeton Strong*, Vol. III, p. 284.

497 As Frederick Douglass . . . give up ground: *Douglass' Monthly* (October 1862).

497 The final proclamation . . . "upon this act": Allen C. Guelzo, *Lincoln's Emancipation Proclamation: The End of Slavery in America* (New York: Simon & Schuster, 2004), pp. 178–81, 254–60 (quotes p. 260); entry for December 31, 1862, *Welles diary*, Vol. I (1960 edn.), pp. 210–11.

497 On the morning . . . fitful sleep: Quarles, *Lincoln and the Negro*, p. 140; Guelzo, *Lincoln's Emancipation Proclamation*, p. 181.

497 He then met with General Burnside . . . offered to resign: *Conversations with Lincoln*, ed. Charles M. Segal (1961; New Brunswick, N.J., and London: Transaction Publishers, 2002), pp. 232–34 (quote p. 232); Donald, *Lincoln*, pp. 409–11.

498 he would replace Burnside with "Fighting Joe" Hooker: Entry for January 25, 1863, in *Lincoln Day by Day*, Vol. III, p. 165.

498 A West Point graduate . . . at Antietam: "Hooker, Joseph (1814–1879)," in Sifakis, *Who Was Who in the Union*, pp. 199–200.

498 Seward returned . . . for correction: Guelzo, *Lincoln's Emancipation Proclamation*, p. 181.

498 New Year's reception . . . "trimming on the waist": Entry for January 1, 1863, Fanny Seward diary, Seward Papers.

498 "looking like a fairy queen": EBL to SPL, January 1, 1863, in *Wartime Washington*, ed. Laas, p. 224.

498 "Oh how pretty she is": Entry for January 1, 1863, Fanny Seward diary, Seward Papers.

498 the gates to the White House . . . shake the president's hand: Noah Brooks, *Mr. Lincoln's Washington: Selections from the Writings of Noah Brooks, Civil War Correspondent*, ed. P. J. Staudenraus (South Brunswick, N.J.: Thomas Yoseloff, 1967), pp. 58–60.

498 "grievously altered . . . cavernous eyes": Ibid., p. 29.

498 "his blessed . . . People's Levee": Ibid., p. 60.

498 "Oh Mr. French . . . remain until it ended": Benjamin B. French, quoted in Randall, *Mary Lincoln*, p. 320.

499 At Chase's mansion . . . "china, glass, and silver": Brooks, *Mr. Lincoln's Washington*, pp. 61–62.

499 "little, aristocratic" . . . years as a lawyer: Ibid., p. 176.

499 Stanton's salary . . . Ellen's dreams: Thomas and Hyman, *Stanton*, p. 392.

499 At 2 p.m. . . . soon joined him: Guelzo, *Lincoln's Emancipation Proclamation*, p. 182.

499 he "took a pen" . . . put the pen down: Carpenter, *Six Months at the White House*, p. 269.

499 "I never . . . signing this paper": AL quoted in Seward, *Seward at Washington . . . 1861–1872*, p. 151.

499 "If my name . . . soul is in it": Carpenter, *Six Months at the White House*, p. 269.

499 "stiff and numb": Seward, *Seward at Washington . . . 1861–1872*, p. 151.

499 "If my hand trembles . . . 'He hesitated' ": Carpenter, *Six Months at the White House*, p. 269.

499 "slowly and carefully" . . . sent out to the press: Seward, *Seward at Washington . . . 1861–1872*, p. 151.

500 "Has Lincoln played false to humanity?": Entry for January 1, 1863, in Adam Gurowski, *Diary from November 18, 1862 to October 18, 1863*. Vol. II. Burt Franklin: Research & Source Works #229 (New York, 1864; New York: Burt Franklin, 1968), p. 61.

500 At Tremont Temple . . . Anna Dickinson: Frederick Douglass, *Life and Times of Frederick Douglass, Written by Himself* (1893 edn.), reprinted in *Frederick Douglass, Autobiographies*. Library of America Series (New York: Literary Classics of the United States, 1994) p. 790 (quote); *Boston Journal*, January 2, 1863; *Boston Transcript*, January 2, 1863.

500 At the nearby Music Hall . . . Oliver Wendell Holmes: *Boston Journal*, January 2, 1863; *Boston Post*, January 2, 1863; Quarles, *Lincoln and the Negro*, p. 143.

500 "Every moment . . . one other chance": Douglass, *Life and Times of Frederick Douglass*, p. 791.

500 "had absolutely no foundation . . . to the quick": Helm, *The True Story of Mary*, pp. 208–09.

500 Mary had rushed . . . the joyous occasion: MTL to CS, December 30, 1862, in Turner and Turner, *Mary Todd Lincoln*, p. 144.

500 "was becoming agony . . . joy and gladness": Douglass, *Life and Times of Frederick Douglass*, p. 791.

500 "It was a sublime . . . with us, here": Eliza S. Quincy to MTL, January 2, 1863, Lincoln Papers.

500 a crowd of serenaders . . . in securing their freedom: Guelzo, *Lincoln's Emancipation Proclamation*, p. 186; *NYT*, January 3, 1863 (quote).

501 "Whatever partial . . . goes backward": *Boston Daily Evening Transcript*, January 2, 1863.

501 "Strange phenomenon . . . in all future ages": James A. Garfield to Burke Hinsdale, January 6, 1863, quoted in
     Theodore Clarke Smith, *The Life and Letters of James Abram Garfield*. Vol. I: *1831–1877* (New Haven: Yale
     University Press, 1925), p. 266.

501 "Fellow-citizens . . . the latest generation": AL, "Annual Message to Congress," December 1, 1862, in *CW*, V,
     p. 537.

501 "had done nothing . . . will be realized": AL, paraphrased in Joshua F. Speed to WHH, February 7, 1866, in
     HI, p. 197.

501 "discord in the North . . . spirit of the nation": *Louisville Journal*, quoted in *Boston Post*, January 2, 1863.

501 "union and harmony . . . destruction": WHS to FS, September 1862, quoted in Seward, *Seward at Washington
     . . . 1861–1872*, p. 135.

501 "It is my conviction . . . sustained it": AL, quoted in Carpenter, *Six Months at the White House*, p. 77.

502 *"slavery and quiet . . .* by tremendous majorities": Walt Whitman, "Origins of Attempted Secession," *The Com-
     plete Prose Works of Walt Whitman*, Vol. II (New York: G. P. Putnam's Sons/The Knickerbocker Press, 1902),
     p. 155.

502 "A man watches . . . strong enough to defeat the purpose": AL, quoted in Carpenter, *Six Months at the White
     House*, p. 77.

502 Horatio Seymour denounced . . . inaugural message: Guelzo, *Lincoln's Emancipation Proclamation*, p. 187.

502 James Robinson recommended: *NYT*, January 10, 1863.

502 Democratic legislatures . . . "crusade against Slavery": Oliver P. Morton to EMS, February 9, 1863, reel 3,
     Stanton Papers, DLC.

502 "under the subterfuge . . . oppose the War": JGN to TB, January 11, 1863, container 2, Nicolay Papers.

502 The "fire in the rear": AL, quoted in CS to Francis Lieber, January 17, 1863, quoted in Edward L. Pierce,
     Memoir and Letters of Charles Sumner. Vol. IV: *1860–1874* (Boston: Roberts Brothers, 1893), p. 114.

502 Army of the Potomac into winter quarters . . . "Valley Forge of the war": McPherson, *Battle Cry of Freedom*,
     pp. 586–88, 590 (quote).

503 Copperheads: McPherson, *Battle Cry of Freedom*, pp. 493, 591, 593, 600; John C. Waugh, *Reelecting Lincoln:
     The Battle for the 1864 Presidency* (New York: Crown Publishers, 1997), p. 91.

503 "fearfully changed" . . . a piercing shriek: Brooks, *Mr. Lincoln's Washington*, pp. 105–06.

503 "Ought this war" . . . then let her go: Clement L. Vallandigham, "The Constitution—Peace—Reunion," Jan-
     uary 14, 1863, *Appendix to the Congressional Globe*, 37th Cong., 3rd sess. pp. 55, 57–59 (quotes on p. 55).

503 The time had come . . . let her go: Brooks, *Mr. Lincoln's Washington*, p. 70.

503 Saulsbury . . . removed from the Senate floor: Ibid., pp. 87–88.

504 "baneful . . . only for the negro": Andrew H. Foote, paraphrased in entry for January 9, 1863, in Browning,
     The Diary of Orville Hickman Browning, Vol. I, p. 611.

504 Orville Browning, who considered . . . "the government": Entry for January 26, 1863, in ibid., p. 620.

504 "conversed with . . . will re enlist": Entry for January 29, 1863, in ibid., pp. 620–21 (quotes p. 621).

504 "the alarming condition . . . a fixed thing": Entry for January 19, 1863, in ibid., p. 616.

504 "the democrats would soon . . . leave them": Entry for January 26, 1863, in ibid., p. 620.

504 "The resources . . . can be maintained": AL, "To the Workingmen of London," February 2, 1863, in *CW*, VI,
     pp. 88–89.

504 the people's representatives had passed: See Curry, *Blueprint for Modern America*.

504 "the grandest pledge . . . means to prevail": *NYT*, February 20, 1863.

504 "largest popular defeat . . . home of the brave": *NYT*, April 21, 1863.

505 "the greatest popular . . . in Washington": *Daily Morning Chronicle*, Washington, D.C., April 1, 1863.

505 Lincoln was dressed . . . of his father's embrace: Jane Grey Swisshelm, quoted in *St. Cloud [Minn.] Democrat*,
     April 9, 1863, in Frank Klement, "Jane Grey Swisshelm and Lincoln: A Feminist Fusses and Frets," *Abraham
     Lincoln Quarterly* 6 (December 1950), pp. 235–36.

505 Lincoln sent a telegram to Thurlow Weed . . . "and so I sent for you": AL, quoted in Barnes, *Memoir of Thur-
     low Weed*, pp. 434–35.

505 The amount needed was $15,000: Ibid., p. 435; AL to TW, February 19, 1862, in *CW*, VI, pp. 112–13.

505 "to influence . . . Connecticut elections": Entry for February 10, 1863, *Welles diary*, Vol. I (1960 edn.), p. 235.

505 "a stunning blow to the Copperheads": *NYT*, April 8, 1863.

505 "puts the Administration . . . seas to the end": *NYT*, April 9, 1863.

505 "frightened" . . . depress voter sentiment: JH to Mrs. Charles Hay, April 23, 1863, in Hay, *At Lincoln's Side*,
     p. 38.

505 "I rejoiced . . . the War commenced": EMS to Isabella Beecher Hooker, May 6, 1863, in Wolcott, "Edwin M.
     Stanton," p. 160.

505 "The feeling of . . . everywhere manifest": JGN to TB, March 22, 1863, container 2, Nicolay Papers.

505 "The glamour . . . the denunciations": Brooks, *Mr. Lincoln's Washington*, p. 138.

506 when Lincoln engaged . . . *"be crippled"*: Entry for January 17, 1863, Fanny Seward diary, Seward Papers.

506 "Well . . . not one has got there yet": AL, quoted in "Personal," *Daily Morning Chronicle*, Washington, D.C.,
     May 2, 1863.

506 "smoking cigars . . . 'good victuals' ": Brooks, *Mr. Lincoln's Washington*, p. 175.

506 At one dinner party . . . "[had] ever known": Entry for January 28, 1863, *Diary of George Templeton Strong*, Vol.
     III, p. 292.

507 welcome diversion in the telegraph office: Bates, *Lincoln in the Telegraph Office*, pp. 41–42, 143, 190.

507 "Abe was in . . . 'none anywhere else' ": AL, quoted in entry for April 21, 1863, in Dahlgren, *Memoir of John A.
     Dahlgren*, p. 390.

507 "a little after midnight . . . queer little conceits": Entry for April 30, 1864, in Hay, *Inside Lincoln's White House*, p. 194.

507 "Only those . . . heart bleeds": MTL to Mary Janes Welles, February 21, 1863, reel 35, Welles Papers.

507 Mary had gamely resumed . . . "to bear up": MTL to Benjamin B. French, March 10, 1863, in Thomas F. Schwartz and Kim M. Bauer, "Unpublished Mary Todd Lincoln," *Journal of the Abraham Lincoln Association* 17 (Summer 1996), p. 5.

507 "affable and pleasant . . . out of sight": Entry for February 22, 1863, in French, *Witness to the Young Republic*, p. 417.

507 "much shorter . . . his composition": Entry for February 12, 1863, Fanny Seward diary, Seward Papers.

508 In gratitude to Rebecca Pomroy . . . "look their best": Boyden, *Echoes from Hospital and White House*, pp. 131–32.

508 "brilliantly lighted . . . children's children": Pomroy, quoted in ibid., pp. 132–33.

508 Swisshelm had initially . . . "and its cause": Jane Grey Swisshelm, *Half a Century* (Chicago: J. G. Swisshelm, 1880), pp. 236–37 (quotes p. 237).

508 Mary was delighted . . . Nettie Colburn: Nettie Colburn Maynard, *Was Abraham Lincoln a Spiritualist?, or Curious Revelations from the Life of a Trance Medium* (Philadelphia: Rufus C. Hartranft, 1891), p. 83.

508 "very choice spirits . . . agreeable ladies": Joshua F. Speed to AL, October 26, 1863, Lincoln Papers.

508 "Welcome, Mr. Lincoln . . . *I was coming*": Mr. Laurie and AL, quoted in Maynard, *Was Abraham Lincoln a Spiritualist?*, p. 83.

508 The guests settled into . . . "easy chairs of the day": S. P. Kase, quoted in J. J. Fitzgerrell, *Lincoln Was a Spiritualist* (Los Angeles: Austin Publishing Co., 1924), pp. 18–19.

509 "Well, Miss Nettie . . . say to me to-night?": Maynard, *Was Abraham Lincoln a Spiritualist?*, p. 85.

509 There is no evidence that Lincoln . . . "learn the secret": "Lord Colchester—Spirit Medium," *Lincoln Lore*, no. 1497 (November 1962), p. 4.

509 She spoke for an hour . . . "not this wonderful?": S. P. Kase, quoted in Fitzgerrell, *Lincoln Was a Spiritualist*, pp. 20–21.

509 "I have neither . . . I must resume it": SPC to Horace Greeley, January 28, 1863, reel 24, Chase Papers.

509 Chase became physically ill . . . make it through: SPC to Richard C. Parsons, February 16, 1863, reel 25, Chase Papers.

510 his own handsome face . . . every dollar bill: SPC, *"Going Home to Vote." Authentic Speeches of S. P. Chase, Secretary of the Treasury, During His Visit to Ohio, with His Speeches at Indianapolis, and at the Mass Meeting in Baltimore, October, 1863* (Washington, D.C.: W. H. Moore, 1863), p. 25; Brooks, *Mr. Lincoln's Washington*, p. 176.

510 his own strained finances . . . bonds to the public: SPC to Jay Cooke, June 2, 1863, reel 27, Chase Papers.

510 Charles Benjamin . . . quickly make amends: Benjamin, "Recollections of Secretary Edwin M. Stanton," *Century* (1887), p. 759.

510 asked why he disliked . . . "detested it": Entry for April 25, 1863, *Diary of George Templeton Strong*, Vol. III, p. 314.

510 "nervous irritability": E. D. Townsend, *Anecdotes of the Civil War in the United States* (New York: D. Appleton & Co., 1884), p. 136.

510 his asthma . . . consent to seek rest: Benjamin, "Recollections of Secretary Edwin M. Stanton," *Century* (1887), pp. 759–60.

510 he enjoyed reading . . . attitude to the war: Ibid., p. 766; Johnson, "Reminiscences of the Hon. Edwin M. Stanton," *RCHS* (1910), p. 80 (quote).

511 Stanton refused to bring . . . remained at his post: Wolcott, "Edwin M. Stanton," p. 161; Thomas and Hyman, *Stanton*, pp. 165–66.

511 "would rather make" . . . ask Stanton for a favor: JH to JGN, November 25, 1863, quoted in Hay, *At Lincoln's Side*, p. 69.

511 Even when Stanton's own son . . . an official appointment: Johnson, "Reminiscences of the Hon. Edwin M. Stanton," *RCHS* (1910), p. 92.

511 rarely returned to Steubenville . . . for the funeral in Ohio: *NYT*, April 14, 1863; Wolcott, "Edwin M. Stanton," p. 130a.

511 Pamphila's conviction . . . died from overwork: Wolcott, "Edwin M. Stanton," p. 159.

511 the War Department utilize the services . . . "to Mr. Capen": AL, "Memorandum Concerning Francis L. Capen's Weather Forecasts," April 28, 1863, in *CW*, VI, pp. 190–91.

511 warring factions in Missouri . . . "hold of the case": AL to Henry T. Blow, Charles D. Drake and Others, May 15, 1863, in ibid., p. 218.

512 hastily written note to General Franz Sigel . . . "keep it up": AL to Franz Sigel, February 5, 1863, in ibid., p. 93.

512 The story is told: AL, quoted in Pinsker, *Lincoln's Sanctuary*, pp. 52–53.

512 Carl Schurz laid the blame . . . "We parted as better friends than ever": Schurz, *Reminiscences*, Vol. II, pp. 393–96.

513 excursion to Falmouth: Noah Brooks, "A Boy in the White House," *St. Nicholas: An Illustrated Magazine for Young Folks* 10 (November 1882), p. 147; Brooks, *Mr. Lincoln's Washington*, pp. 147–64.

513 "one of the purest . . . in the world": Anson G. Henry to his wife, April 12, 1863, transcribed in "Another Hooker Letter," *Abraham Lincoln Quarterly* 2 (March 1942), pp. 10–11.

513 Bates agreed . . . spring battles began: Entry for April 4, 1863, in *The Diary of Edward Bates, 1859–1866*, p. 288.

513 weather conditions: *Sun*, Baltimore, Md., April 6, 1863; entry for April 4, 1863, in *The Diary of Edward Bates, 1859–1866*, p. 287; Brooks, *Mr. Lincoln's Washington*, p. 51.

513 the steamer *Carrie Martin* . . . of George Washington: Seward, *Reminiscences of a War-Time Statesman and Diplomat*, p. 185; Noah Brooks, *Washington, D.C., in Lincoln's Time*, ed. Herbert Mitgang (Chicago: Quadrangle Books, 1971; Athens, Ga., and London: University of Georgia Press, 1989), p. 51.

513 the escalating storm . . . to the dinner menu: Brooks, "A Boy in the White House," *St. Nicholas* (1882), p. 62.

513 "the chief magistrate . . . firing a shot": Brooks, *Mr. Lincoln's Washington*, pp. 148–49.

513 "at its height" . . . a special train: *Sun*, Baltimore, Md., April 7, 1863 (quote); Brooks, *Mr. Lincoln's Washington*, p. 149.

513 "snow piled in huge . . . over the hills": *NYH*, April 10, 1863 (quotes); Brooks, *Washington, D.C. in Lincoln's Time*, p. 52.

514 Hooker's headquarters . . . 133,000 soldiers: Brooks, *Mr. Lincoln's Washington*, pp. 150–51; Shelby Foote, *The Civil War: A Narrative. Vol. II: Fredericksburg to Meridian* (New York: Random House, 1963: New York: Vintage Books, 1986), p. 235.

514 General Hooker and his accommodations: Entry for April 27, 1863, Fanny Seward diary, Seward Papers; *NYH*, April 10, 1863; Brooks, *Mr. Lincoln's Washington*, p. 150.

514 "I believe you to be . . . give us victories": AL to Joseph Hooker, January 26, 1863, in *CW*, VI, pp. 78–79.

514 was so moved by . . . printed in gold letters: Anson G. Henry to his wife, April 12, 1863, transcribed in "Another Hooker Letter," *ALQ* 2 (1942), p. 11.

514 "That is just such . . . man who wrote it": Joseph Hooker, quoted in Brooks, *Washington, D.C. in Lincoln's Time*, p. 57.

514 Mary's curiosity . . . "pleasant to her": *NYH*, April 10, 1863 (quote); *Star*, April 7, 1863; Brooks, *Mr. Lincoln's Washington*, p. 150.

515 reported badinage between . . . " 'sort of rebel' ": Brooks, *Washington, D.C. in Lincoln's Time*, p. 59.

515 Stormy weather . . . "shafts of wit": Brooks, *Mr. Lincoln's Washington*, p. 150; *NYH*, April 10, 1863 (quote).

515 The roar of artillery . . . "among them": Brooks, *Washington, D.C., in Lincoln's Time*, p. 53; *NYH*, April 11, 1863; Brooks, *Mr. Lincoln's Washington*, p. 153 (quote).

515 his gray cloak . . . faithfully by his side: Brooks, "A Boy in the White House," *St. Nicholas* (1882), p. 62.

515 "And thereby hangs . . . folds of the banners": *NYH*, April 11, 1863.

516 At the review of the infantry . . . "far away": Brooks, *Mr. Lincoln's Washington*, pp. 154, 158–59 (quote).

516 he extended his visit: Ibid., p. 161.

516 "the former stood . . . turn their backs": *NYH*, April 10, 1863.

516 rebel camps across the river . . . stars and bars: Brooks, *Mr. Lincoln's Washington*, pp. 155–56.

516 Union pickets . . . "belonging to friendly armies": Seward, *Seward at Washington . . . 1861–1872*, p. 162 (first quote); *NYH*, April 10, 1863 (last quote).

516 a Confederate officer . . . "politely and retired": Brooks, *Mr. Lincoln's Washington*, p. 156.

516 "It was a saddening . . . should arrive": Ibid., pp. 153–54.

517 issued one final directive . . . *all your men*": AL, quoted in Couch, "Sumner's 'Right Grand Division,' " in *Battles and Leaders of the Civil War*, Vol. III, Pt. I, p. 120.

517 boarded the *Carrie Martin* . . . "flags displayed": *NYH*, April 12, 1863.

517 were defending James S. Pleasants . . . "very bitter": EBL to SPL, April 16, 1863, in *Wartime Washington*, ed. Laas, p. 259 (quotes); Court-martial file of James Snowden Pleasants, file MM-15, entry 15, RG 153, DNA; *Sun*, Baltimore, Md., April 9, 1863.

517 sent the *Peterhoff* . . . to the Navy Department: Van Deusen, *William Henry Seward*, pp. 350–51; Monaghan, *Diplomat in Carpet Slippers*, pp. 303–04.

517 led to rumors of . . . "from the real question": Entries for April 23–28, 1863, *Welles diary*, Vol. I (1960 edn.), pp. 285–87 (quotes p. 287).

518 Montgomery Blair also sided . . . "in the Cabinet": Entry for April 17, 1863, ibid., pp. 274–75 (quote p. 275).

518 "I feel that . . . my present position": SPC to AL, March 2, 1863, Lincoln Papers.

518 This squabble was provoked . . . "my resignation": SPC to AL, May 11, 1863, Lincoln Papers.

518 "Chase's feelings were hurt": AL to Anson G. Henry, May 13, 1863, in *CW*, VI, p. 215.

518 he called at Chase's . . . "I finally succeeded": Field, *Memories of Many Men*, p. 303.

518 $45 million in bonds . . . "as do ours": *NYT*, May 3, 1863.

519 he placed his prickly secretary's third resignation: Riddle, *Recollections of War Times*, p. 273.

519 Blair, meanwhile, resented Chase . . . "private counsellor": Entry for May 10, 1863, in *The Diary of Edward Bates, 1859–1866*, pp. 290–91.

519 the Battle of Chancellorsville: See Stephen W. Sears, *Chancellorsville* (Boston and New York: Houghton Mifflin, 1996); Stanley S. McGowen, "Chancellorsville, Battle of," in *Encyclopedia of the American Civil War*, ed. Heidler and Heidler, pp. 394–98; Foote, *The Civil War*, Vol. II, p. 263.

519 "We have been . . . definite information": JGN to TB, May 4, 1863, container 2, Nicolay Papers.

519 Welles joined Lincoln: Entry of May 4, 1863, *Welles diary*, Vol. I (1960 edn.), p. 291.

519 Bates was particularly tense . . . "dangerous service": Entry for May 5, 1863, in *The Diary of Edward Bates, 1859–1866*, p. 289.

519 Lincoln admitted . . . what was going on: EBL to SPL, May 4, 1863, in *Wartime Washington*, ed. Laas, p. 264.

519 "no reliable . . . does not express them": Entry for May 5, 1863, *Welles diary*, Vol. I (1960 edn.), pp. 292–93.

519 "While I am anxious . . . or discomfort": AL to Joseph Hooker, April 28, 1863, in *CW*, VI, pp. 189–90.

519 "God bless you . . . with despatches": AL to Joseph Hooker, 9:40 a.m. telegram, May 6, 1863, in ibid., p. 199.

520 an unwelcome telegram . . . the order to retreat: Joseph Hooker to AL, May 6, 1863, Lincoln Papers; Sears,

Chancellorsville, p. 492; Darius N. Couch, "The Chancellorsville Campaign," in *Battles and Leaders of the Civil War*, Vol. III, Pt. I, pp. 164 (first quote), 167, 169–71 (second and third quotes p. 171).

520 "I shall never forget . . . of despair": Brooks, *Washington, D.C., in Lincoln's Time*, p. 60.

520 "Had a thunderbolt . . . would again commence": Brooks, *Mr. Lincoln's Washington*, p. 179.

520 "ashen" face . . . " 'will the country say!' ": Brooks, *Washington, D.C., in Lincoln's Time*, p. 61.

520 The president informed Senator Sumner . . . "I know not where": Entry for May 6, 1863, *Welles diary*, Vol. I (1960 edn.), pp. 293–94.

520 "This is the darkest day of the war": JH paraphrasing EMS, quoted in *Lincoln's Third Secretary: The Memoirs of William O. Stoddard*, ed. William O. Stoddard, Jr. (New York: Exposition Press, 1955), p. 173.

520 At the Willard . . . bound for Hooker's headquarters: Brooks, *Mr. Lincoln's Washington*, p. 180.

521 "All accounts agree . . . back into the fray": *NYT*, May 12, 1863.

521 casualties at Chancellorsville: McPherson, *Battle Cry of Freedom*, p. 645; Sears, *Chancellorsville*, pp. 492, 501.

521 death of Stonewall Jackson: James I. Robertson, Jr., "Jackson, Thomas Jonathan," in *Encyclopedia of the American Civil War*, ed. Heidler and Heidler, p. 1065.

521 "Since the death . . . death of Jackson": *Richmond Whig*, May 12, 1863.

521 "If possible" . . . ready to assist Hooker: AL to Joseph Hooker, May 7, 1863, in *CW*, VI, p. 201.

CHAPTER 20: "THE TYCOON IS IN FINE WHACK"

Page

522 General Orders No. 38 . . . tried by a military court: "General Orders, No. 38," Department of the Ohio, April 13, 1863, in *OR*, Ser. 1, Vol. XXIII, Pt II, p. 237.

522 "hurl King Lincoln from his throne": Clement L. Vallandigham speech, May 1, 1863, quoted in Fletcher Pratt, *Stanton: Lincoln's Secretary of War* (New York: W. W. Norton & Co., 1953), p. 289.

522 "The door resisted" . . . a side entrance: *Cincinnati Commercial*, quoted in *Star*, May 9, 1863.

522 found him guilty . . . habeas corpus was denied: Trial of Clement L. Vallandigham, enclosure in Ambrose E. Burnside to Henry W. Halleck, May 18, 1863, and General Orders, No. 68, Headquarters, Department of the Ohio, May 16, 1863, *OR*, Ser. 2, Vol. V, pp. 633–46; McPherson, *Battle Cry of Freedom*, p. 597.

522 the *Chicago Times* . . . the paper down: Entry for June 3, 1863, in Browning, *The Diary of Orville Hickman Browning*, Vol. I, p. 632.

522 While he later admitted . . . uphold Burnside: McPherson, *Battle Cry of Freedom*, p. 597; entry for June 3, 1863, *Welles diary*, Vol. I (1960 edn.), p. 321.

523 Thurlow Weed deplored the arrest: TW to John Bigelow, June 27, 1863, in John Bigelow, *Retrospective of an Active Life*. Vol. II: *1863–1865* (New York: Baker & Taylor Co., 1909), p. 23.

523 Senator Trumbull . . . "government overthrown": Entry for May 17, 1863, in Browning, *The Diary of Orville Hickman Browning*, Vol. I, p. 630.

523 "by a large and honest" . . . the loyal states: Nathaniel P. Tallmadge to WHS, May 24, 1863, Lincoln Papers.

523 Lincoln, searching . . . Confederate lines: Charles F. Howlett, "Vallandigham, Clement Laird," in *Encyclopedia of the American Civil War*, ed. Heidler and Heidler, p. 2012.

523 his Copperhead body . . . "where his heart already was": Schuyler Colfax to AL, June 13, 1863, Lincoln Papers.

523 "general satisfaction . . . power for evil": *NYT*, May 21, 1863.

523 Vallandigham was removed . . . escaped to Canada: McPherson, *Battle Cry of Freedom*, p. 597.

523 Stanton revoked . . . to suppress newspapers: EMS to Ambrose E. Burnside, June 1, 1863, in *OR*, Ser. 2, Vol. V, p. 724; General Orders, No. 91, Headquarters, Department of the Ohio, June 4, 1863, *OR*, Ser. 1, Vol. XXIII, Part II, p. 386.

523 "suppress the . . . of its citizens": Carpenter, *Six Months at the White House*, pp. 156–57.

523 Upon hearing . . . opposed his action: Ambrose E. Burnside to AL, May 29, 1863, Lincoln Papers.

523 Lincoln not only refused . . . "through with it": AL to Ambrose E. Burnside, May 29, 1863, in *CW*, VI, p. 237.

523 "Often an idea . . . from every side": James F. Wilson recollections, quoted in Carl Sandburg, *Abraham Lincoln: The War Years*, Vol. II (New York: Harcourt, Brace & Co., 1936; 1939), p. 308.

524 "It has vigor and ability": Entry of June 5, 1863, *Welles diary*, Vol. I (1960 edn.), p. 323.

524 "we are Struggling . . . in Rhetoric": MB to AL, June 6, 1863, Lincoln Papers.

524 The finished letter . . . "if he shall desert": AL to Erastus Corning and Others, [June 12,] 1863, in *CW*, VI, pp. 260–69 (quotes pp. 264, 266–67).

524 "It is full . . . and conclusive": *NYT*, June 15, 1863.

524 Edward Everett . . . "the step complete": Edward Everett to AL, June 16, 1863, Lincoln Papers.

524 "It is a grand document . . . every citizen": "The President's Letter," June 15, 1863, in William O. Stoddard, *Dispatches from Lincoln's White House: The Anonymous Civil War Journalism of Presidential Secretary William O. Stoddard*, ed. Michael Burlingame (Lincoln and London: University of Nebraska Press, 2002), p. 160.

525 Printed in a great variety . . . 10 million people: Donald, *Lincoln*, pp. 443–44.

525 Welles noted . . . "assistant is present": Entry for June 2, 1863, *Welles diary*, Vol. I (1960 edn.), pp. 319–20 (quote p. 320).

525 Blair, frustrated . . . word with Lincoln: Hendrick, *Lincoln's War Cabinet*, p. 387; entry for May 12, 1863, in *The Diary of Edward Bates, 1859–1866*, p. 292.

525 "At such a time . . . interchange of views": Entry for June 30, 1863, *Welles diary*, Vol. I (1960 edn.), p. 351.

525 "There is now . . . consent of the members": Entry for May 16, 1863, in *The Diary of Edward Bates, 1859–1866*, pp. 292–93.

525 "But how idle . . . furnish the means": SPC to David Dudley Field, June 30, 1863, reel 27, Chase Papers.

525 If he were president . . . "of importance": SPC to James A. Garfield, May 31, 1863, reel 12, Papers of James A. Garfield, Manuscript Division, Library of Congress [hereafter Garfield Papers, DLC].

525 Blair decried . . . of Seward and Stanton: Entry for June 23, 1863, *Welles diary*, Vol. I (1960 edn.), p. 340.

525 Lincoln's unwillingness . . . restore McClellan: Entry for June 26, 1863, ibid., p. 345.

525 In Blair's mind . . . "throat if he could": "19 July 1863, Sunday," in Hay, *Inside Lincoln's White House*, p. 65.

526 Blair's hatred for Stanton . . . military information: Entry for June 30, 1863, *Welles diary*, Vol. I (1960 edn.), p. 352.

526 "Strange, strange . . . Stanton and Seward": Entry for June 15, 1863, ibid., p. 329.

526 Recognizing Blair's desire . . . to get through: For a description of Blair's innovations with the postal service, see chapter 31 of Smith, *The Francis Preston Blair Family in Politics*, Vol. II, pp. 90–111.

526 catch up with his "Neptune" . . . telegraph office: Entry for July 14, 1863, *Welles diary*, Vol. I (1960 edn.), p. 370.

526 When he felt compelled . . . "admirable success": AL to GW, July 25, 1863, in *CW*, VI, p. 349.

526 A particularly bitter . . . "be very mad": AL, quoted in entry for May 26, 1863, *Welles diary*, Vol. I (1960 edn.), p. 313.

527 the humorist Orpheus Kerr . . . "as regards myself": Entry for June 17, 1863, ibid., p. 333.

527 William Rosecrans . . . "to do hastily": AL to William S. Rosecrans, May 20, 1863, in *CW*, VI, p. 224.

527 felt compelled to remove General Samuel Curtis . . . "faithful, and patriotic": AL to Samuel R. Curtis, June 8, 1863, in ibid., p. 253.

527 a note from Governor Gamble . . . "grossly offensive": Hamilton R. Gamble to AL, July 13, 1863, Lincoln Papers.

527 was told "to put it away": "23 July 1863, Thursday," in Hay, *Inside Lincoln's White House*, p. 66.

527 "trying to preserve . . . should offend you": AL to Hamilton R. Gamble, July 23, 1863, Lincoln Papers.

528 Milroy railed about "the . . . hatred" of Halleck: Robert H. Milroy to AL, June 28, 1863, Lincoln Papers. See also Robert H. Milroy to John P. Usher, June 28, 1863, Lincoln Papers.

528 "I have scarcely seen . . . you have split": AL to Robert H. Milroy, June 29, 1863, in *CW*, VI, p. 308.

528 "Truth to speak . . . so, ranks you": AL to William S. Rosecrans, March 17, 1863, in ibid., p. 139.

528 Grant had advanced . . . settled into a siege: Stanley S. McGowen, "Vicksburg Campaign (May–July 1863)," in *Encyclopedia of the American Civil War*, ed. Heidler and Heidler, pp. 2021–25.

528 "Whether Gen. Grant . . . brilliant in the world": AL to Isaac N. Arnold, May 26, 1863, in *CW*, VI, p. 230.

528 Stanton had sent Charles Dana . . . long, detailed dispatches: Bruce Catton, *Grant Moves South*. Vol. I: *1861–1863* (Boston: Little, Brown, 1960; 1988), pp. 388–89; Thomas and Hyman, *Stanton*, p. 267.

528 Requesting that General Banks . . . "should prefer that course": Charles A. Dana to EMS, May 26, 1863, reel 5, Stanton Papers, DLC.

528 In a misguided effort . . . other valuables behind: "General Orders, No. 11," Department of the Tennessee, December 17, 1862, in *OR*, Ser. 1, Vol. XVII, Part II, p. 424. See also USG to Christopher P. Wolcott, December 17, 1862, in ibid., pp. 421–22; D. Wolff & Bros, C. F. Kaskell, and J. W. Kaswell to AL, December 29, 1862, in ibid., p. 506; Bertram Wallace Korn, *American Jewry and the Civil War* (Philadelphia: Jewish Publication Society of America, 1951), pp. 122–23.

529 a delegation of Jewish leaders . . . "have at once": Leaders quoted in Korn, *American Jewry and the Civil War*, pp. 124–25.

529 wrote a note to Halleck: Ibid., p. 125.

529 after assuring Grant . . . "necessary to revoke it": Henry W. Halleck to USG, January 21, 1863, in *OR*, Ser. 1, Vol. XXIV, Part I, p. 9 (quote); Henry W. Halleck to USG, January 4, 1863, in *OR*, Ser. 1, Vol. XVII, Part II, p. 530; Circular, 13th Army Corps, Department of the Tennessee, January 7, 1863, in ibid., p. 544.

529 Elizabeth Blair heard . . . "all the time": EBL to SPL, May 8, 1863, in *Wartime Washington*, ed. Laas, p. 266.

529 Bates was told . . . "bloated" appearance: Entry for May 23, 1863, in *The Diary of Edward Bates, 1859–1866*, p. 293.

529 In Grant's case . . . "idiotically drunk": Murat Halstead to SPC, April 1, 1863, Lincoln Papers.

529 After dispatching investigators to look into: Catton, *Grant Moves South*, Vol. I, pp. 388–89; Jean Edward Smith, *Grant* (New York: Simon & Schuster, 2001), p. 231.

529 A memorable story . . . rest of his generals!: John Eaton, *Grant, Lincoln and the Freedmen: Reminiscences of the Civil War* (New York: Longmans, Green & Co., 1907; New York: Negro Universities Press, 1969), p. 90.

529 Wade and Chandler told Lincoln . . . "in reply": JGN to TB, May 17, 1863, container 2, Nicolay Papers.

530 Seward accompanied . . . his garden: See entries for May 1863, in Fanny Seward diary, Seward House, Auburn, New York.

530 favorite old poplar . . . "stroke of the axe": FAS to WHS, June 5, 1863, reel 114, Seward Papers.

530 Fanny wrote that . . . "very lonely": FS to WHS, June 7, 1863, reel 116, Seward Papers.

530 troubling rumors . . . "when I am there": FAS to WHS, June 5, 1863, reel 114, Seward Papers; FS to WHS, June 7, 1863, reel 116, Seward Papers (quote).

530 Seward noted . . . "an invasion of Washington": WHS to [FAS], June 11, 1863, in Seward, *Seward at Washington . . . 1861–1872*, p. 169.

530 Mary and Tad left . . . Continental Hotel: Entry for June 8, 1863, in *Lincoln Day by Day*, Vol. III, p. 188; MTL to John Meredith Read, June 16, [1863], in Turner and Turner, *Mary Todd Lincoln*, p. 152 n2.

530 Welles spoke with Lincoln . . . "thought best": Entry for June 8, 1863, *Welles diary*, Vol. I (1960 edn.), p. 325.

530 "Think you better . . . ugly dream about him": AL to MTL, June 9, 1863, in *CW,* VI, p. 256.
530 Seward sent a telegram . . . "pic-nic to the Lake": Entry for June 15, 1863, in Johnson, "Sensitivity and Civil War," p. 813.
531 Lee had crossed . . . "adds to our strength": WHS to [FAS], June 15, 1863, in Seward, *Seward at Washington . . . 1861–1872,* pp. 169–70.
531 *"Invasion! . . . in Maryland and Pennsylvania"*: *NYT* headline, June 16, 1863.
531 "It is a matter of choice . . . anything at all": AL to MTL, June 16, 1863, in *CW,* VI, p. 283.
531 "The country, now . . . is wide awake": Entry for June 18, 1863, in French, *Witness to the Young Republic,* p. 423.
531 "something of a panic pervades the city": Entry for June 15, 1863, *Welles diary,* Vol. I (1960 edn.), p. 329.
531 he called out a hundred thousand troops: AL, "Proclamation Calling for 100,000 Militia," June 15, 1863, in *CW,* VI, p. 277.
531 "I should think . . . kindness & Patriotism": Entry for June 18, 1863, in French, *Witness to the Young Republic,* p. 424.
531 the committee charged with . . . "all he could ask for": Stoddard, *Inside the White House in War Times,* p. 117.
531 Lincoln's primary concern . . . "outgeneraled": Brooks, *Mr. Lincoln's Washington,* p. 196.
531 "observed in Hooker . . . taken from other points": Entry for June 28, 1863, *Welles diary,* Vol. I (1960 edn.), p. 348.
531 When Hooker delivered a prickly telegram: Joseph Hooker to Henry W. Halleck, June 27, 1863 (9:00 a.m.), in *OR,* Ser. 1, Vol. XXVII, Part I, p. 59; Hooker to Halleck, June 27, 1863 (3:00 p.m.), in ibid., p. 60; Halleck to Hooker, June 27, 1863 (8:00 p.m.), in ibid., p. 60.
531 Lincoln and Stanton replaced him: Henry W. Halleck to George G. Meade, June 27, 1863, in *OR,* Ser. 1, Vol. XXVII, Part I, p. 61; Meade to Halleck, June 28, 1863, in ibid., pp. 61–62; "Meade, George Gordon (1815–1872)," in Sifakis, *Who Was Who in the Union,* p. 266.
532 "Chase was disturbed . . . cared should appear": SPC to Joseph Hooker, June 20, 1863, quoted in Schuckers, *The Life and Public Services of Salmon Portland Chase,* p. 468; entry of June 28, 1863, *Welles diary,* Vol. I (1960 edn.), p. 348 (quote).
532 "You must have been . . . exceeded mine": SPC to KCS, June 29, 1863, reel 27, Chase Papers.
532 "The turning point . . . such a suspense": JGN to TB, July 5, 1863, container 3, Nicolay Papers.
532 "poor and desultory" . . . in the telegraph office: Bates, *Lincoln in the Telegraph Office,* p. 155.
532 Chandler would "never forget . . . on the wall": Zachariah Chandler, quoted in Browne, *The Every-Day Life of Abraham Lincoln,* pp. 597–98.
532 a dispatch from Meade . . . "at all points": George G. Meade to Henry W. Halleck, July 2, 1863 (8:00 p.m.), in *OR,* Ser. 1, Vol. XXVII, Part I, p. 72.
532 "no reliable advices . . . anxiety prevails": *NYT,* July 3, 1863.
532 a messenger handed . . . "reliable": Entry for July 4, 1863, *Welles diary,* Vol. I (1960 edn.), p. 357.
532 a telegram from Meade . . . after severe losses: George G. Meade to Henry W. Halleck, July 3, 1863, *OR,* Ser. 1, Vol. XXVII, Part I, pp. 74–75.
533 Casualties were later calculated: Richard A. Sauers, "Gettysburg, Battle of," in *Encyclopedia of the American Civil War,* ed. Heidler and Heidler, p. 836.
533 "as being the most . . . covered with the dead": McPherson, *Battle Cry of Freedom,* p. 664; Brooks, *Mr. Lincoln's Washington,* pp. 202, 203 (quotes).
533 a celebratory press release: AL, "Announcement of News From Gettysburg," July 4, 1863, in *CW,* VI, p. 314.
533 "the gloomiest Fourth" . . . Fireworks were set off: Entry for July 4, 1863, Fanny Seward diary, Seward Papers.
533 "The results . . . for the moment at least": Entry for July 6, 1863, *Diary of George Templeton Strong,* Vol. III, p. 330.
533 Grant's forty-six-day siege: McGowen, "Vicksburg Campaign (May–July 1863)," in *Encyclopedia of the American Civil War,* ed. Heidler and Heidler, p. 2026; Foote, *The Civil War,* Vol. II, p. 607.
533 Welles had received . . . dispatch in hand: Entry for July 7, 1863, *Welles diary,* Vol. I (1960 edn.), p. 364; Brooks, *Mr. Lincoln's Washington,* pp. 177 (quote), 201.
533 "executed a double . . . excited as he was then": Brooks, *Washington, D.C., in Lincoln's Time,* p. 82.
533 "caught my hand . . . 'it is great!'": Entry for July 7, 1863, *Welles diary,* Vol. I (1960 edn.), p. 364.
533 "The Father . . . to the sea": AL to James C. Conkling, August 26, 1863, *CW,* VI, p. 409.
533 "The rebel troops" . . . about thirty thousand: Charles A. Dana to EMS, July 5, 1863, reel 5, Stanton Papers, DLC.
534 "I write this now . . . and I was wrong": AL to USG, July 13, 1863, in *CW,* VI, p. 326.
534 a large crowd . . . "the beginning of the end": *NYH,* July 8, 1863.
534 the official bulletins were read . . . "beasts at sunrise": Brooks, *Mr. Lincoln's Washington,* p. 201.
535 Mary's carriage accident: *Star,* July 2, 1863; *NYH,* July 11, 1863; Boyden, *Echoes from Hospital and White House,* pp. 143–44; Pinsker, *Lincoln's Sanctuary,* pp. 102–04, 105–06.
535 "never quite recovered . . . of her fall": Robert Todd Lincoln, quoted in Helm, *The True Story of Mary,* p. 250.
535 "complete his work . . . destruction of Lee's army": AL to Henry W. Halleck, [July 7, 1863], in *CW,* VI, p. 319.
535 both Halleck and Lincoln urged Meade: Henry W. Halleck to George G. Meade, July 8, 1863, *OR,* Ser. 1, Vol. XXVII, Part III, p. 605; note 1 of AL to Henry W. Halleck, [July 7, 1863], in *CW,* VI, p. 319.
535 Robert Lincoln later said . . . "his vindication": "[Robert Todd Lincoln's Reminiscences, Given 5 January 1885]," in Nicolay, *An Oral History of Abraham Lincoln,* pp. 88–89.
535 he nonetheless failed to move . . . "anxious and impatient": "13 July 1863, Monday," in Hay, *Inside Lincoln's White House,* p. 62.
535 he received a dispatch from Meade: "14 July 1863, Tuesday," in ibid., p. 62; Circular, Army of the Potomac,

July 14, 1863, in *OR*, Ser. 1, Vol. XXVII, Part III, p. 690; Sauers, "Gettysburg, Battle of," in *Encyclopedia of the American Civil War*, ed. Heidler and Heidler, p. 836.

535 Stanton was reluctant to share . . . president "was not": Entry for July 14, 1863, *Welles diary*, Vol. I (1960 edn.), p. 370.

536 Lincoln caught up . . . "and discouraged": Entry for July 14, 1863, ibid., p. 371.

536 "Our Army held . . . we did not harvest it": AL, quoted in "19 July 1863, Sunday," in Hay, *Inside Lincoln's White House*, pp. 64–65.

536 his profound gratitude . . . "never sent, or signed": AL to George G. Meade, July 14, 1863, Lincoln Papers.

536 Meade's failure to attack . . . "I might run away": Carpenter, *Six Months at the White House*, pp. 219–20.

536 the draft: Samantha Jane Gaul, "Conscription, U.S.A.," in *Encyclopedia of the American Civil War*, ed. Heidler and Heidler, p. 487.

536 Governor Seymour had told . . . the black man: Governor Horatio Seymour, quoted in John G. Nicolay and John Hay, *Abraham Lincoln: A History*, Vol. VII (New York: Century Co., 1917), p. 17.

536 *Daily News* . . . "kill off Democrats": *New York Daily News*, quoted in ibid., p. 18.

536 A provision in the Conscription Act: Gaul, "Conscription, U.S.A.," in *Encyclopedia of the American Civil War*, ed. Heidler and Heidler, p. 488.

537 "a rich man's war and a poor man's fight": Sandburg, *Abraham Lincoln: The War Years*, Vol. II, p. 362.

537 the first day of the draft proceeded: *NYT*, July 14, 1863; Nicolay and Hay, *Abraham Lincoln*, Vol. VII, p. 18.

537 "Scarcely had two dozen" . . . continued unchecked for five days: *NYT*, July 14, 1863 (quotes); *NYT*, July 16, 1863; Sandburg, *Abraham Lincoln: The War Years*, Vol. II, p. 360; Gaul, "Conscription, U.S.A." and "New York City Draft Riots (13–17 July 1863)," in *Encyclopedia of the American Civil War*, ed. Heidler and Heidler, pp. 488, 1414–15.

537 "the all engrossing topic of conversation": Brooks, *Mr. Lincoln's Washington*, p. 219.

537 "have the power for a week": SPC to William Sprague, July 14, 1863, reel 27, Chase Papers.

537 The mob violence finally ended . . . go forward: *NYT*, July 18, 1863.

537 Auburn's draft . . . "apprehension of a riot": FAS to Augustus Seward, July 20, 1863, reel 115, Seward Papers.

537 she reported that Copperheads . . . riots in New York: FAS to WHS, July 18, 1863, reel 114, Seward Papers.

537 several Irishmen fought . . . the Seward home: FAS to WHS, June 28, 1863, reel 114, Seward Papers; FAS to WHS, July 12, 1863, reel 114, Seward Papers; FAS to FWS, July 23, 1863, reel 115, Seward Papers.

537 Frances awoke one morning . . . "I possessed": Janet W. Seward, "Personal Experiences of the Civil War," Seward Papers, NRU.

538 "Do not give yourself . . . not without benefit": WHS to FAS, July 21, 1863, in Seward, *Seward at Washington . . . 1861–1872*, p. 177.

538 "As to personal injury . . . willing to assist them": FAS to WHS, July 18, 1863, reel 114, Seward Papers.

538 everyone was "somewhat" . . . police force: FAS to FWS, July 23, 1863, reel 115, Seward Papers.

538 "The best of order . . . Our recent victories": *NYT*, July 24, 1863.

538 Seward had predicted . . . "up a long time": WHS to [FAS], July 17, 1863, quoted in Seward, *Seward at Washington . . . 1861–1872*, p. 176.

538 "incitement . . . resist the government": FAS to WHS, July 15, 1863, reel 114, Seward Papers.

538 John Hay learned . . . handling of the situation: "25 July 1863, Saturday," in Hay, *Inside Lincoln's White House*, p. 67.

538 "lost ground . . . best men": John A. Dix to EMS, July 25, 1863, reel 5, Stanton Papers, DLC.

538 "The nation is great . . . in 1850 to 1860!": WHS to [FAS], July 25, 1863, quoted in Seward, *Seward at Washington . . . 1861–1872*, p. 177.

538 "President was in . . . sack Phil-del": "19 July 1863, Sunday," in Hay, *Inside Lincoln's White House*, pp. 64, 306 n80.

539 "A few days having passed . . . a true man": AL to Oliver O. Howard, July 21, 1863, in *CW*, VI, p. 341.

539 the six straight hours . . . power to pardon: JH to JGN, [July 19, 1863], in Hay, *At Lincoln's Side*, p. 45.

539 Hay marveled . . . "instead of shooting him": "18 July 1863, Saturday," in Hay, *Inside Lincoln's White House*, p. 64.

539 Lincoln acknowledged . . . "upon him unawares": Eaton, *Grant, Lincoln and the Freedmen*, p. 180.

539 "overcome by a physical . . . the battle begins": "Conversation with Hon. J. Holt, Washington Oct 29 1875," in Nicolay, *An Oral History of Abraham Lincoln*, p. 69.

539 Rather than fearing . . . deserters were executed: Eaton, *Grant, Lincoln and the Freedmen*, p. 180.

539 "where meanness or cruelty were shown": "18 July 1863, Saturday," in Hay, *Inside Lincoln's White House*, p. 64.

539 the case of a captain . . . "Count Peeper": "[July–August 1863]," in ibid., p. 76.

540 "Men and horses . . . every day": JH to JGN, August 13, 1863, in Hay, *At Lincoln's Side*, p. 50.

540 "The garments cling . . . is over everything": Brooks, *Mr. Lincoln's Washington*, p. 223.

540 "hot, dusty weather . . . discomfort of Washington": EMS to Ellen Stanton, August 25, 1863, quoted in Gideon Stanton, ed., "Edwin M. Stanton" (quotes); Pinsker, *Lincoln's Sanctuary*, pp. 116–17.

540 "Nearly everybody . . . skeddadled from the heat": Brooks, *Mr. Lincoln's Washington*, p. 223.

540 Mary fled the capital . . . through most of August: AL to MTL, August 8, 1863, Lincoln Papers; Turner and Turner, *Mary Todd Lincoln*, pp. 153–54.

540 A correspondent . . . "smiling face": *Boston Journal*, August 10, 1863.

540 Lincoln talked about the heat . . . "distress about it": AL to MTL, August 8, 1863, Lincoln Papers.

540 Only in mid-September . . . with her and with Tad: AL to MTL, September 21 and 22, 1863, in *CW*, VI, pp. 471, 474.

540 Mary understood . . . "to letter writing": MTL to AL, November 2, [1862], in Turner and Turner, *Mary Todd Lincoln*, p. 139.

541 "I wish I could gain . . . put to the test": FAS to WHS, June 17, 1863, reel 114, Seward Papers.
541 "Every day . . . gone to the field": WHS to [FAS], July 25, 1863, quoted in Seward, *Seward at Washington . . . 1861–1872*, p. 177.
541 she despaired when . . . "killed & wounded": FAS to WHS, July 5, 1863, reel 114, Seward Papers.
541 Only with Frances . . . exhaustion: WHS to FAS, June 8, 1863, reel 112, Seward Papers.
541 "Thenceforth . . . constant devotion to business": Robert Todd Lincoln to Dr. J. G. Holland, June 6, 1865, box 6, folder 37, William Barton Collection, Special Collections of the Regenstein Library at the University of Chicago.
541 the Equinox House . . . dining facilities: "From The Beginning," historical pamphlet, Equinox House, Manchester, Vt.
541 Mary climbed a mountain . . . Doubleday and his wife: Randall, *Mary Lincoln*, p. 229; *NYH*, September 1, 1863.
541 "We did again . . . fortunes": William Sprague to KCS, May 27, 1866, Sprague Papers.
542 his immense manufacturing company . . . weekly: "The Rhode Island Spragues," December 5, 1883, unidentified newspaper, KCS vertical file, DWP.
542 "I want to show you . . . undone or destroyed": William Sprague to KCS, May 1, 1863, Sprague Papers.
542 "The Gov and Miss Kate . . . into their fold": William Sprague to Hiram Barney, May 18, 1863, Salmon Portland Chase Collection, Historical Society of Pennsylvania, Philadelphia [hereafter Chase Papers, Phi.].
542 "The business . . . lost its identity": William Sprague to KCS, June 16, 1863, Sprague Papers.
542 "a wilderness, a blank": William Sprague to KCS, July 1, 1863, Sprague Papers.
542 He kept her miniature . . . "strong a hold": William Sprague to KCS, June 3, 7 and 8, 1863, Sprague Papers (quotes from June 7 letter).
542 "I am my darling up . . . with the sunshine": William Sprague to KCS, May 21, 1863, Sprague Papers.
542 "I hope my darling . . . morning and adieu": William Sprague to KCS, June 1, 1863, Sprague Papers.
542 Chase opened the discussion . . . "any due to me": SPC to William Sprague, June 6, 1863, reel 27, Chase Papers.
542 "Probably no woman . . . her successes": *Washington Post*, August 1, 1899.
543 "Scarcely a person . . . lent a charm to the whole": FS to LW, February 1, 1863, reel 116, Seward Papers.
543 Kate persuaded William: William Sprague to SPC, May 31, 1863, reel 27, Chase Papers; William Sprague to KCS, June 12, 1863, Sprague Papers; SPC to William Sprague, July 14, 1863, reel 27, Chase Papers.
543 "idea of taking . . . So I yield the point": SPC to William Sprague, July 14, 1863, reel 27, Chase Papers.
543 Chase would continue . . . William would cover: SPC to William Sprague, July 14, 1863, reel 27, Chase Papers; William Sprague to KCS, July 22, 1863, Sprague Papers; Niven, *Salmon P. Chase*, p. 342.
543 "the delicate link . . . united father & daughter": William Sprague to SPC, November 4, 1863, reel 29, Chase Papers.
543 Sprague wisely decided . . . "enduring love": William Sprague to KCS, June 12, 1863, Sprague Papers.
543 "Katie showed me . . . full wealth of her affections": SPC to William Sprague, June 6, 1863, reel 27, Chase Papers.
543 "as much of the pecuniary burden as possible": William Sprague to SPC, May 31, 1863, reel 27, Chase Papers.
543 to divest himself: Belden and Belden, *So Fell the Angels*, pp. 84–85.
543 he informed Jay Cooke . . . "all right-minded men": SPC to Jay Cooke, June 1, 1863, reel 27, Chase Papers.
544 he returned a check . . . "as *be* right": SPC to Jay Cooke, June 2, 1863, reel 27, Chase Papers.
544 Chase joined Kate . . . returned to Washington: Lamphier, *Kate Chase and William Sprague*, p. 54.
544 his only companion . . . "sympathetic way": SPC to Janet Chase Hoyt, August 19, 1863, reel 28, Chase Papers (quote). See also note 2 to published edition of August 19 letter in *The Salmon P. Chase Papers*. Vol. IV: *Correspondence, April 1863–1864*, ed. John Niven (Kent, Ohio, and London: Kent State University Press, 1997), p. 106 n2.
544 He chastised Nettie . . . carelessness pained him: SPC to Janet Chase Hoyt, August 19, 1863, reel 28, Chase Papers.
544 he reprimanded Kate . . . vacation expenses: SPC to KCS, August 19, 1863, reel 28, Chase Papers.
544 a warm correspondence . . . "her letters": Belden and Belden, *So Fell the Angels*, pp. 88–89 (quote p. 89).
544 Mrs. Eastman described . . . "of his own idolatry?": Charlotte S. Eastman to SPC, July 19, 1863, reel 27, Chase Papers.
544 "What a sweet letter" . . . attend to the president: SPC to Charlotte S. Eastman, August 22, 1863, reel 28, Chase Papers.
545 "The Tycoon is in fine whack . . . where he is": JH to JGN, August 7, 1863, in Hay, *At Lincoln's Side*, p. 49.
545 Hay had a good sense of humor . . . "peal of fun": Stoddard, *Inside the White House in War Times*, pp. 93–94.
545 Hay accompanied the president: August 9, 1863, photograph of AL, in Philip B. Kunhardt, Jr., Philip B. Kunhardt III, and Peter W. Kunhardt, *Lincoln: An Illustrated Biography* (New York: Alfred A. Knopf, 1992), p. 216.
545 "very good spirits": "9 August 1863, Sunday," in Hay, *Inside Lincoln's White House*, p. 70.
545 Rigidly posed . . . unsmiling portrait: Kunhardt, et al., *Lincoln*, p. 216.
545 required to sit . . . "Don't move a muscle!": George Sullivan, *Mathew Brady: His Life and Photographs* (New York: Cobblehill Books, 1994), pp. 17–18 (quote p. 18).
545 "contrived grinning . . . become obligatory": James Mellon, ed., *The Face of Lincoln* (New York: Viking Press, 1979), pp. 13–14.
546 "the rebel power . . . to disintegrate": "9 August 1863, Sunday," in Hay, *Inside Lincoln's White House*, p. 70.
546 pleasant outings . . . "sent me to bed": "23 August 1863, Sunday," in ibid., pp. 75–76 (quote p. 76); *Washington Post*, August 3, 1924; Pinsker, *Lincoln's Sanctuary*, p. 115.

546 "I see the President . . . on K Street": Whitman, *Specimen Days* (1971 edn.), p. 26.
546 "The President and I . . . the season is over": EMS to Ellen Stanton, August 25, 1863, quoted in Gideon Stanton, ed., "Edwin M. Stanton."
546 Stanton finally joined his wife . . . the Soldiers' Home: Thomas and Hyman, *Stanton*, p. 284.
546 typically wide-ranging . . . "party to oppose a war": "13 August 1863, Thursday," in Hay, *Inside Lincoln's White House*, pp. 72–73 (quote); Pamela Scott and Antoinette J. Lee, *Buildings of the District of Columbia*. Buildings of the United States Series (New York and Oxford: Oxford University Press, 1993), pp. 119, 128; *"Progress of Civilization,"* Architect of the Capitol website, www.aoc.gov/cc/art/pediments/prog_sen_r.htm (accessed November 2004).
546 tour of upstate New York . . . picnic on the lake: Philip Van Doren Stern, *When the Guns Roared: World Aspects of the American Civil War* (Garden City, N.Y.: Doubleday & Co., 1965), p. 230; Seward, *Seward at Washington . . . 1861–1872*, pp. 186–87.
547 "All seemed . . . themselves very much": FAS to Augustus Seward, August 27, 1863, reel 115, Seward Papers.
547 "When one comes really . . . to like in him": Lord Lyons to Lord Russell, quoted in Stern, *When the Guns Roared*, p. 231.
547 "Hundreds of factories . . . and canals": Seward, *Seward at Washington . . . 1861–1872*, p. 186.
547 European shipbuilders . . . not be delivered: Van Deusen, *William Henry Seward*, pp. 352–56, 361; entries for August 12, 29, September 18, 25, 1863, *Welles diary*, Vol. I (1960 edn.), pp. 399, 429, 435–37, 443.
547 "The White House . . . health of the nation": Dispatch of August 31, 1863, in Stoddard, *Dispatches from Lincoln's White House*, p. 166.

CHAPTER 21: "I FEEL TROUBLE IN THE AIR"

Page

548 180,000 soldiers . . . black males: Eric Foner, *Reconstruction: America's Unfinished Revolution, 1863–1877* (New York: Harper & Row, 1988; 1989), p. 8.
548 Emancipation Proclamation flatly declared . . . "United States": AL, "Emancipation Proclamation," January 1, 1863, in *CW*, VI, p. 30.
548 Stanton authorized . . . and other Northern states: Quarles, *Lincoln and the Negro*, p. 156; Dudley Taylor Cornish, *The Sable Arm: Black Troops in the Union Army, 1861–1865* (Lawrence: University Press of Kansas, 1956; 1987), p. 105.
549 the war would not be won . . . "suppressing the rebels": *Douglass' Monthly* (August 1862).
549 He wrote stirring appeals . . . many other cities: Blight, *Frederick Douglass' Civil War*, pp. 157–59.
549 "Why should a colored . . . that claim respected": *Douglass' Monthly* (April 1863).
549 thousands of Bostonians . . . high-ranking military officials: *Boston Daily Evening Transcript*, May 28, 1863.
549 "No single regiment . . . admirable marching": Ibid.
549 He urged Banks . . . the enlisting process: AL to Nathaniel P. Banks, March 29, 1863, in *CW*, VI, p. 154; AL to David Hunter, April 1, 1863, in ibid., p. 158; AL to USG, August 9, 1863, in ibid., p. 374.
549 "The colored population . . . rebellion at once": AL to Andrew Johnson, March 26, 1863, in ibid., pp. 149–50.
549 Chase . . . "nearly two years ago": SPC to James A. Garfield, May 31, 1863, reel 12, Garfield Papers, DLC.
550 a series of obstacles . . . losing their freedom or their lives: Benjamin Quarles, *Frederick Douglass*. Studies in American Negro Life Series (Associated Publishers, 1948; New York: Atheneum, 1970), pp. 209–10; Quarles, *Lincoln and the Negro*, pp. 167, 169, 173–74, 177.
550 "this is no time . . . to embrace it": *Douglass' Monthly* (August 1863).
550 they earned great respect . . . "bravery and steadiness": Cornish, *The Sable Arm*, pp. 142–43 (quote p. 143).
550 "dooming to death . . . negro troops": *NYTrib*, reprinted in *Liberator*, May 15, 1863.
550 As word of the unique . . . swiftly diminishing: James M. McPherson, *The Negro's Civil War: How American Blacks Felt and Acted During the War for Union* (New York: Pantheon Books, 1965; New York: Ballantine Books, 1991), pp. 176, 179.
550 "What has Mr. Lincoln . . . responsible for them": *Douglass' Monthly* (August 1863).
550 "When I plead . . . rulers at Washington": Frederick Douglass to Major G. L. Stearns, August 1, 1863, reprinted in ibid.
550 he asked Halleck . . . "placed at hard labor": AL, "Order of Retaliation," July 30, 1863, in *CW*, VI, p. 357.
551 The order was "well-written . . . became impossible": Entry for August 4, 1863, in Gurowski, *Diary from November 18, 1862 to October 18, 1863*, pp. 292–93.
551 Douglass agreed . . . "required to act": Douglass to Stearns, August 1, 1863, in *Douglass' Monthly* (August 1863).
551 the lack of "fair play" . . . to the president: Douglass, *Life and Times of Frederick Douglass*, pp. 784–85.
551 "tumult of feeling": Frederick Douglass, quoted in the *Washington Post*, February 13, 1888.
551 "I could not know . . . an interview altogether": Douglass, *Life and Times of Frederick Douglass*, p. 785.
551 a large crowd in the hallway . . . into the office: *Liberator*, January 29, 1864; Philip S. Foner, *Frederick Douglass* (New York: Citadel Press, 1950; repr. 1964), p. 216.
551 "I was never more . . . Abraham Lincoln": Douglass, *Life and Times of Frederick Douglass*, p. 785.
551 The president was seated . . . "began to rise": Douglass, "Lincoln and the Colored Troops," in *Reminiscences of Abraham Lincoln*, ed. Rice, p. 316.
551 Douglass hesitantly began . . . "glad to see you": Douglass, *Life and Times of Frederick Douglass*, p. 786.
551 Lincoln's warmth . . . "Abraham Lincoln": Frederick Douglass to George L. Stearns, August 12, 1863 (photo-

copy), container 53, Papers of Frederick Douglass, Manuscript Division, Library of Congress [hereafter Douglass Papers, DLC].

551 Douglass laid before . . . "very apparent sympathy": Douglass, "Lincoln and the Colored Troops," in *Reminiscences of Abraham Lincoln*, ed. Rice, p. 317.

551 "Upon my ceasing . . . not suspected him": Douglass to Stearns, August 12, 1863, Douglass Papers, DLC.

551 it "seemed a necessary . . . at all as soldiers": Douglass, *Life and Times of Frederick Douglass*, p. 787.

552 "in the end they shall . . . as white soldiers": AL quoted in Douglass, "Lincoln and the Colored Troops," in *Reminiscences of Abraham Lincoln*, ed. Rice, p. 318.

552 "he would sign . . . commend to him": Douglass, *Life and Times of Frederick Douglass*, p. 787.

552 Lincoln's justification . . . "killed for negroes": Douglass to Stearns, August 12, 1863, Douglass Papers, DLC.

552 "once begun . . . humane spirit": Douglass, *Life and Times of Frederick Douglass*, p. 787.

552 he had read a recent speech . . . "retreated from it": *Liberator*, January 29, 1864.

552 "as though I could . . . his shoulder": Douglass, "Lincoln and the Colored Troops," in *Reminiscences of Abraham Lincoln*, ed. Rice, p. 325.

552 "The manner of" . . . in the Mississippi Valley: Douglass, *Life and Times of Frederick Douglass*, pp. 787–88 (quote); Quarles, *Lincoln and the Negro*, pp. 168, 172.

552 The War Department followed up . . . commission was not included: Quarles, *Lincoln and the Negro*, p. 169.

552 "I knew too much . . . mark of my rank": Douglass, *Life and Times of Frederick Douglass*, p. 788.

553 "Perhaps you may like . . . I felt big there!": *Liberator*, January 29, 1864.

553 Conkling had invited . . . loyal Unionists: AL to James C. Conkling, August 26, 1863, in *CW*, VI, p. 406.

553 False rumors circulated: *NYT*, August 8 and 13, 1863.

553 "Ah! I'm glad" . . . he bade him good night: Stoddard, *Inside the White House in War Times*, pp. 129–30.

554 "deceptive and groundless . . . they have strove to hinder it": AL to James C. Conkling, August 26, 1863, in *CW*, VI, pp. 407–10.

554 Lincoln continued to refine . . . public duties: "23 August 1863, Sunday," in Hay, *Inside Lincoln's White House*, p. 76.

554 "You are one of the best . . . very slowly": AL to James C. Conkling, August 27, 1863, in *CW*, VI, p. 414.

554 An immense crowd . . . "the country calls": *Illinois State Journal*, Springfield, Ill., September 2, 1863.

554 he was furious to see . . . around the country: John W. Forney to AL, September 3, 1863, Lincoln Papers.

555 "I am mortified . . . How did this happen?": AL to James C. Conkling, September 3, 1863, in *CW*, VI, p. 430.

555 When a petitioner tried . . . "obvious to any one": AL to D. M. Leatherman, September 3, 1863, in ibid., p. 431.

555 a message arrived from Conkling . . . "the next day": James C. Conkling to AL, September 4, 1863, Lincoln Papers.

555 "Disclaiming the arts . . . wants to discuss": *NYTrib*, September 3, 1863.

555 "The most consummate . . . which needs driving": *NYT*, September 7, 1863.

555 The *Philadelphia Inquirer* . . . "continue to write": *Philadelphia Inquirer*, September 5, 1863.

555 "His last letter . . . logicians of all schools": JH to JGN, September 11, 1863, in Hay, *At Lincoln's Side*, p. 54.

555 the *New York Times* also commended . . . "their faith in him": *NYT*, September 7, 1863.

556 "I know the people . . . on the ground": JH to JGN, September 11, 1863, in Hay, *At Lincoln's Side*, p. 54.

556 Seward came back . . . the diplomatic corps: WHS to Charles Francis Adams, August 25, 1863, quoted in Seward, *Seward at Washington . . . 1861–1872*, p. 188.

556 to celebrate his seventieth . . . "good as I deserve": Entry for September 4, 1863, in *The Diary of Edward Bates, 1859–1866*, pp. 305–06.

556 his ten-day visit . . . "perhaps more missed": Entry for September 11, 1863, *Welles diary*, Vol. I (1960 edn.), p. 431.

556 Lincoln and Stanton had hoped . . . "blow to the rebellion": EMS to William S. Rosecrans, July 7, 1863, in *OR*, Ser. 1, Vol. XXIII, Part II, p. 518.

556 Rosecrans delivered . . . "victory at Chattanooga": JH to JGN, September 11, 1863, in Hay, *At Lincoln's Side*, p. 54.

556 "unexpectedly appeared . . . of [the] Chicamauga": Charles A. Dana to EMS, September 12, 1863, reel 5, Stanton Papers, DLC.

556 battle of Chickamauga: See Dave Powell, "Chickamauga, Battle of," in *Encyclopedia of the American Civil War*, ed. Heidler and Heidler, pp. 427–31.

556 "Chicamauga is as fatal . . . as Bull Run": Charles A. Dana to EMS, September 20, 1863, reel 6, Stanton Papers, DLC.

557 Union casualties: Entry for September 20, 1862, in Long, *The Civil War Day by Day*, p. 412.

557 "We have met with . . . scattered troops there": William S. Rosecrans to Henry W. Halleck, September 20, 1863, in *OR*, Ser. 1, Vol. XXX, Part I, pp. 142–43.

557 the dispatches reached him . . . "awake and watchful": Entry for September 21, 1863, *Welles diary*, Vol. I (1960 edn.), p. 438.

557 wandered into Hay's room . . . "air before it comes": "[27 September 1863, Sunday]," in Hay, *Inside Lincoln's White House*, p. 85.

557 Lincoln telegraphed Mary . . . "see you and Tad": AL to MTL, September 21, 1863, in *CW*, VI, p. 471.

557 Mary responded . . . plans to do so: MTL to AL, September 22, 1863, quoted in Helm, *The True Story of Mary*, p. 215.

557 proved "less unfavorable . . . feared": Entry for September 22, 1863, in *Chase Papers*, Vol. I, p. 449 (quote); Charles A. Dana to EMS, September 20, 1863, in *OR*, Ser. 1, Vol. XXX, Part I, p. 193.

557 Thomas's corps had held . . . than the Federals: Powell, "Chickamauga, Battle of," in *Encyclopedia of the American Civil War*, ed. Heidler and Heidler, p. 430.

557 "still remains in . . . to twenty days": Charles A. Dana to EMS, September 23, 1863, reel 6, Stanton Papers, DLC.

557 Stanton came up with . . . dispatched messengers: Flower, *Edwin McMasters Stanton*, p. 203.

557 Chase had just retired . . . and his entire army: Entry for September 23, 1863, in *Chase Papers*, Vol. I, p. 450.

557 John Hay was sent to the Soldiers' Home . . . back to the War Department: "[27 September 1863, Sunday]," in Hay, *Inside Lincoln's White House*, p. 86 (quotes); John G. Nicolay and John Hay, *Abraham Lincoln: A History*, Vol. VIII (New York: Century Co., 1917), p. 112.

557 "I have invited . . . serious for jokes": Entry for September 23, 1863, in *Chase Papers*, Vol. I, pp. 450–52 (quotes); Flower, *Edwin McMasters Stanton*, p. 203.

558 "he had fully considered . . . with excellent arguments": Entry for September 23, 1863, in *Chase Papers*, Vol. I, p. 452.

558 Stanton immediately sent an orderly . . . "make a few figures": W. H. Whiton recollections, quoted in Gorham, *Life and Public Services of Edwin M. Stanton*, Vol. I, pp. 123–24.

558 "I can complete . . . given my consent": McCallum, EMS, and AL, quoted in Flower, *Edwin McMasters Stanton*, p. 204.

558 "Colonel McCallum . . . I will approve them": AL, quoted in W. H. Whiton recollections, quoted in Gorham, *Life and Public Services of Edwin M. Stanton*, Vol. I, pp. 124–25.

558 Stanton worked . . . stop to resupply: EMS to J. T. Boyle, September 23, 1863, in *OR*, Ser. 1, Vol. XXIX, Part I, p. 147; EMS to R. P. Bowler, September 24, 1863, in ibid., p. 153; Daniel Butterfield to Oliver O. Howard, September 26, 1863, in ibid., p. 160; W. P. Smith to EMS, September 26, 1863, in ibid., p. 161; Flower, *Edwin McMasters Stanton*, pp. 204–06. For documentation of Stanton's efforts to move the 11th and 12th Army Corps to the Army of the Cumberland, see *OR*, Ser. 1, Vol. XXIX, Part 1, pp. 146–95.

559 The first train left Washington . . . arrived in Tennessee: W. P. Smith to EMS, September 26, 1863, in *OR*, Ser. 1, Vol. 29, Part I, p. 161; Flower, *Edwin McMasters Stanton*, pp. 205–06.

559 Monitoring reports . . . agree to leave his post: Flower, *Edwin McMasters Stanton*, pp. 205–07; W. P. Smith to EMS, September 26, 1863, in *OR*, Ser. 1, Vol. XXIX, Part I, p. 162.

559 "It was an extraordinary . . . the twentieth century": McPherson, *Battle Cry of Freedom*, p. 675.

559 Dana's reports . . . troops had lost confidence: Charles A. Dana to EMS, September 30, 1863, in *OR*, Ser. 1, Vol. XXX, Part I, p. 204.

559 Stanton telegraphed Grant . . . discussing the overall military situation: Grant, *Personal Memoirs of U.S. Grant*, pp. 315–16.

559 the general departed for Chattanooga . . . Lookout Mountain: Ibid., pp. 320–51; James H. Meredith, "Chattanooga Campaign" and "Lookout Mountain, Battle of," in *Encyclopedia of the American Civil War*, ed. Heidler and Heidler, pp. 411–15, 1216–18.

559 "would have been a terrible disaster": Grant, *Personal Memoirs of U.S. Grant*, p. 318.

559 "The country does . . . nights work": Entry for September 23, 1863, in *Chase Papers*, Vol. I, p. 453.

560 affectionately call his "Mars": Bates, *Lincoln in the Telegraph Office*, p. 400.

560 "esteem and affection . . . French comic opera": Benjamin, "Recollections of Secretary Edwin M. Stanton," *Century* (1887), pp. 768, 760–61.

560 "No two men were . . . a necessity to each other": *New York Evening Post*, July 13, 1891.

560 "in dealing with the public . . . than his heart": A. E. Johnson, opinion cited in Bates, *Lincoln in the Telegraph Office*, p. 389.

560 the story of a congressman . . . "step over and see him": Julian, *Political Recollections, 1840 to 1872*, pp. 211–12.

561 "remarkable passages . . . at Cincinnati": EMS, quoted in Parkinson to Beveridge, May 28, 1923, container 292, Beveridge Papers, DLC.

561 "Few war ministers . . . for Mr. Lincoln": "The Late Secretary Stanton," *Army and Navy Journal*, January 1, 1870, p. 309.

561 When Stanton was eighteen . . . near death from cholera: Wolcott, "Edwin M. Stanton," p. 36.

561 he insisted on including . . . to stand guard: Joseph Buchanan and William Stanton Buchanan, quoted in Flower, *Edwin McMasters Stanton*, pp. 39, 40.

561 *Oh! Why should the spirit* . . . : William Knox, "Mortality," quoted in Bruce, "The Riddle of Death," in *The Lincoln Enigma*, p. 135.

561 He could recite from memory . . . "in the English language": Carpenter, *Six Months at the White House*, p. 59.

561 *The mossy marbles rest*: Oliver Wendell Holmes, "The Last Leaf," in *The Poetical Works of Oliver Wendell Holmes*, Vol. I (Boston and New York: Houghton Mifflin, 1892), p. 4.

562 he had written . . . "he should be honored?": EMS, "Our Admiration of Military Character Unmerited," 1831, reel 1, Stanton Papers, DLC.

562 an army of more than 2 million men: Margaret E. Wagner, Gary W. Gallagher, and Paul Finkelman, eds., *The Library of Congress Civil War Desk Reference* (New York: Grand Central Press/Simon & Schuster, 2002), p. 376.

562 "There could be no greater . . . to eternity": EMS, quoted in Gideon Stanton, ed., "Edwin M. Stanton."

562 "Doesn't it strike you . . . flowing all about me?": AL quoted in Louis A. Warren, *Lincoln's Youth: Indiana Years, Seven to Twenty-one, 1816–1830* (New York: Appleton Century Crofts, 1959), p. 225 n29.

562 an audience to a group of Quakers: AL to Eliza P. Gurney, September 4, 1864, in *CW*, VII, p. 535.

562 "If I had had . . . still governs it": AL, quoted in Eliza P. Gurney, copy of interview with AL, [October 26, 1862], Lincoln Papers.

562 "On principle . . . no mortal could stay": AL to Eliza P. Gurney, September 4, 1864, in *CW*, VII, p. 535.

563　Stanton still wrote . . . " 'our love in two' ": EMS to SPC, March 7, 1863, Chase Papers, Phi.

563　Stanton would ask Chase to stand: EMS to SPC, December 30, 1863, reel 30, Chase Papers.

563　"It is painful . . . after concurrence, action": SPC to George Wilkes, August 27, 1863, reel 28, Chase Papers.

563　Radicals insisted . . . both the Union and emancipation: Foner, *Reconstruction*, pp. 35–50, 60–62.

564　"standard-bearer . . . of the Radicals": Brooks, *Mr. Lincoln's Washington*, p. 236.

564　Chase's desire . . . proclaim his campaign: Ibid., p. 237.

564　he wrote hundreds of letters . . . Lincoln administration: Hendrick, *Lincoln's War Cabinet*, p. 400.

564　"I should fear nothing . . . management of the War": SPC to Edward D. Mansfield, October 18, 1863, reel 29, Chase Papers.

564　"If I were myself . . . man should be had": SPC to William Sprague, November 26, 1863, reel 30, Chase Papers.

564　He was thrilled . . . on another candidate: Horace Greeley to SPC, September 29, 1863, reel 28, Chase Papers.

565　"first choice . . . should receive it": Edward Jordan to SPC, October 27, 1863, reel 29, Chase Papers.

565　Governor Dennison alerted him . . . "like a beaver": "17 October 1863, Saturday, New York," in Hay, *Inside Lincoln's White House*, p. 92.

565　Seward cautioned . . . "for Mr. Chase": TW note, quoted in "28 November 1863, Saturday," in ibid., p. 119.

565　Samuel Cox . . . "New England States": "24 December 1863, Thursday," in ibid., p. 132.

565　A Pennsylvanian politician . . . "out of both eyes": "25 October 1863, Sunday," in ibid., p. 100.

565　John Hay learned . . . *Independent* to his side: "28 November 1863, Saturday," in ibid., p. 120.

565　"Chase's mad hunt after the Presidency": "29 October 1863, Thursday," in ibid., p. 103.

565　"plowing corn . . . make his department go": "[July–August 1863]," in ibid., pp. 78, 313 n143.

565　Lincoln agreed . . . "very bad taste": AL, quoted in "18 October 1863, Sunday," in ibid., p. 93.

565　"was sorry . . . that it ought to": "29 October 1863, Thursday," in ibid., p. 103.

565　Lincoln's friends . . . "President's interests": Eaton, *Grant, Lincoln and the Freedmen*, p. 176.

565　let "Chase have . . . what he asks": "29 October 1863, Thursday," in Hay, *Inside Lincoln's White House*, p. 103.

565　a "frank, guileless . . . for the first one": Leonard Swett to WHH, January 17, 1866, in *HI*, pp. 168, 164.

566　After criticizing . . . "So I still work on": SPC to James Watson Webb, November 7, 1863, reel 29, Chase Papers.

566　"all along clearly . . . from New Orleans": AL, quoted in "18 October 1863, Sunday," in Hay, *Inside Lincoln's White House*, p. 93.

566　"Chase would try . . . spot he can find": "29 October 1863, Thursday," in ibid., p. 103.

566　the people of Missouri . . . extinguish slavery: AL to Charles D. Drake and Others, October 5, 1863, in *CW*, VI, pp. 499–504; Foner, *Reconstruction*, pp. 41–42.

566　Governor Gamble worried . . . a conservative partisan: Hamilton R. Gamble to AL, October 1, 1863, Lincoln Papers.

567　He was accused . . . guise of military necessity: AL to Charles D. Drake and Others, October 5, 1863, in *CW*, VI, p. 500; "Conversation with Hon. M. S. Wilkinson, May 22 1876," in Nicolay, *An Oral History of Abraham Lincoln*, pp. 59–60; Williams, *Lincoln and the Radicals*, p. 299.

567　a delegation of radicals . . . "not to alienate them": "29 September 1863, Tuesday," in Hay, *Inside Lincoln's White House*, pp. 88–89 (quote); Williams, *Lincoln and the Radicals*, p. 299.

567　"these Radical men . . . side with the Radicals": AL, paraphrased in "10 December 1863, Thursday," in Hay, *Inside Lincoln's White House*, p. 125.

567　"they are nearer . . . set Zionwards": AL, quoted in "28 October 1863, Wednesday," in ibid., p. 101.

567　resented the radicals' demand . . . "short statutes of limitations": "10 December 1863, Thursday," in ibid., p. 125.

567　"So intense and fierce . . . saddest features of the times": Entry for September 29, 1863, *Welles diary*, Vol. I (1960 edn.), p. 448.

567　"show that . . . powerful as they may be": AL, quoted in "29 September 1863, Tuesday," in Hay, *Inside Lincoln's White House*, pp. 88–89.

568　an invitation to spend the evening: EB to J. O. Broadhead, October 24, 1863, Broadhead Papers, MoSHi.

568　"surprised and mortified . . . as traitors": EB to Hamilton R. Gamble, October 10, 1863, Bates Papers, MoSHi (quote); entry for September 30, 1863, in *The Diary of Edward Bates, 1859–1866*, p. 308.

568　Bates should hardly be . . . if he were to decide to run against Lincoln: Hamilton R. Gamble to EB, October 17, 1863, Bates Papers, MoSHi.

568　meeting with the Missourians . . . "instead of wind": "30 September 1863, Wednesday," in Hay, *Inside Lincoln's White House*, p. 89.

568　Lincoln listened attentively . . . remove him from command: AL to Charles D. Drake and Others, October 5, 1863, in *CW*, VI, pp. 500 (quotes), 503.

568　"The President never . . . his candid logic": "30 September 1863, Wednesday," in Hay, *Inside Lincoln's White House*, pp. 89–90.

568　Lincoln emerged . . . "as he supposed": Entry for September 30, 1863, in *The Diary of Edward Bates, 1859–1866*, p. 308.

568　"whoever commands . . . or conservatives": AL to Charles D. Drake and Others, October 5, 1863, in *CW*, VI, p. 504.

569　he wrote to remind . . . "injury to the Military": AL to John M. Schofield, October 1, 1863, in ibid., p. 492.

569　leaning toward . . . "conflicting elements": "13 December 1863, Sunday," in Hay, *Inside Lincoln's White House*, p. 127.

569　he decided to replace him with Rosecrans: "Rosecrans, William Starke (1819–1898)," and "Schofield, John McAllister (1831–1906)," in Sifakis, *Who Was Who in the Union*, pp. 342, 355.

569 Before an overflowing crowd . . . Jefferson Davis himself: Speech by Frank Blair, reprinted in *Missouri Republican*, St. Louis, September 27, 1863.

569 The *Liberator* criticized . . . "which he advocates": *Roxbury Journal*, quoted in *Liberator*, October 16, 1863.

570 "not let even . . . share of his resentment": EBL to SPL, [October 24, 1863], in *Wartime Washington*, ed. Laas, p. 316.

570 He wrote a letter to Monty . . . "skill and usefulness": AL to MB, November 2, 1863, in *CW*, VI, p. 555.

570 a gentle letter of reprimand . . . "would not cure the bite": AL to James M. Cutts, Jr., October 26, 1863, in ibid., p. 538, and note.

570 Chase again intervened . . . eligibility to vote: Niven, *Salmon P. Chase*, p. 339.

570 voiced his opposition at Rockville: Speech of Montgomery Blair, reprinted in the *Star*, October 5, 1863.

571 it aroused deep hostility . . . Blair from his cabinet: Smith, *The Francis Preston Blair Family in Politics*, Vol. II, pp. 241–43, 248; Williams, *Lincoln and the Radicals*, pp. 298, 303.

571 Lincoln refused to support . . . "against him": "22 October 1863, Thursday," in Hay, *Inside Lincoln's White House*, p. 97.

571 Noah Brooks attended a mass rally . . . "utterances": Brooks, *Mr. Lincoln's Washington*, pp. 246–48.

571 Chase was a featured . . . his "fossil theories": Ibid., pp. 247–49.

571 Chase was elated . . . *"a Cardinal principle"*: SPC to Horace Greeley, October 31, 1863, reel 29, Chase Papers.

571 Worried that Lincoln's . . . "were producing logical results": Leonard Swett to WHH, January 17, 1866, in *HI*, pp. 164–65.

572 "the most truly progressive . . . struggles with them": John W. Forney, quoted in "31 December 1863, Thursday," in Hay, *Inside Lincoln's White House*, p. 135.

CHAPTER 22: "STILL IN WILD WATER"

Page

573 Lincoln was visibly unsettled . . . his presidential race: Entry for October 14, 1863, *Welles diary*, Vol. I (1960 edn.), p. 470.

573 Civil liberties was also . . . instituted conscription: William C. Davis, *Look Away! A History of the Confederate States of America* (New York: Free Press, 2002), pp. 174–76, 226.

573 Toombs accused . . . "tide of despotism": Burton J. Hendrick, *Statesmen of the Lost Cause: Jefferson Davis and His Cabinet* (New York: Literary Guild of America, 1939), p. 417.

573 concerned about Ohio: Waugh, *Reelecting Lincoln*, pp. 14–15.

573 Lincoln was disheartened . . . "to the country": Entry for October 14, 1863, *Welles diary*, Vol. I (1960 edn.), p. 470.

573 In Pennsylvania . . . "of the United States": McPherson, *Battle Cry of Freedom*, p. 685.

574 the Woodward campaign . . . "voice & my vote": GBM to Charles J. Biddle, October 12, 1863, in *Civil War Papers of George B. McClellan*, p. 559.

574 took steps to ensure . . . return home to vote: Waugh, *Reelecting Lincoln*, p. 16.

574 If the president granted . . . Union ticket: SPC, *"Going Home to Vote,"* p. 22; Niven, *Salmon P. Chase*, p. 336.

574 the journalist Whitelaw Reid: Niven, *Salmon P. Chase*, p. 336; Hendrick, *Lincoln's War Cabinet*, p. 401.

574 Chase in Columbus . . . "misfortunes averted": SPC, *"Going Home to Vote,"* p. 4.

574 "I come not to speak . . . and without exceptions": Ibid., pp. 5, 13.

575 In public squares . . . "turn to Ohio": *Daily Ohio State Journal*, Columbus, Ohio, October 13, 1863; SPC, *"Going Home to Vote,"* p. 8 (quote).

575 begged his audiences . . . "sixty-five days in the year": SPC, *"Going Home to Vote,"* p. 8.

575 Lincoln took up his usual post: Waugh, *Reelecting Lincoln*, p. 14.

575 a welcome telegram . . . was counted: SPC to AL, October 14, 1863, Lincoln Papers.

575 By 5 a.m. . . . to 100,000: Browne, *The Every-Day Life of Abraham Lincoln*, p. 603; Waugh, *Reelecting Lincoln*, p. 14.

575 *"Glory to God . . . saved the Nation"*: Browne, *The Every-Day Life of Abraham Lincoln*, p. 603.

575 "All honor . . . foe at the ballot-box": EMS to John W. Forney, *NYT*, October 15, 1863.

575 found him "in good spirits": Entry for October 14, 1863, *Welles diary*, Vol. I (1960 edn.), p. 470.

575 "No man knows . . . till he has had it": AL, quoted in James B. Fry, in *Reminiscences of Abraham Lincoln by Distinguished Men of His Time*, ed. Allen Thorndike Rice (New York: North American Publishing Co., 1886), p. 390.

575 "all right" . . . a good secretary: AL, quoted in "18 October 1863, Sunday," in Hay, *Inside Lincoln's White House*, p. 93.

576 "I'm afraid . . . of the presidency": Entry for October 17, 1863, in *The Diary of Edward Bates, 1859–1866*, p. 310.

576 "That visit to the west . . . saved my country": Entry for October 20, 1863, in ibid., p. 311.

576 "it is of the nature . . . with its victim": Edward Bates to James O. Broadhead, October 24, 1863, Broadhead Papers, MoSHi.

576 had "warped" . . . party behind him: Entry for August 22, 1863, *Welles diary*, Vol. I (1960 edn.), p. 413.

576 were moderate compared to the scathing indictments: See Smith, *The Francis Preston Blair Family in Politics*, Vol. II, pp. 234–37.

576 "I little imagined . . . me deeply": SPC to Edward D. Mansfield, October 18, 1863, reel 29, Chase Papers.

576 "The late election" . . . unfit for active duty: James H. Baker to SPC, November 7, 1863, reel 29, Chase Papers.

576 "To him, more than . . . system of slavery": *Liberator,* November 13, 1863.

576 *Liberator* maintained . . . "again acting President": *Liberator,* November 13, 1863.

577 the relationship between the two . . . "gave it new light": Seward, *Seward at Washington . . . 1861–1872,* p. 197.

577 "They say, Mr. President . . . as a Governor?": WHS and AL, quoted in ibid., pp. 193–94.

577 a proclamation . . . "tranquillity and Union": AL, "Proclamation of Thanksgiving," October 3, 1863, in *CW,* VI, p. 497 (quote); Seward, *Seward at Washington . . . 1861–1872,* p. 194.

577 Lincoln told Nicolay . . . "whole of that letter": December 8, 1863 memorandum, container 3, Nicolay Papers.

578 Seward assured Lincoln . . . "will collapse": Seward, *Seward at Washington . . . 1861–1872,* p. 196.

578 Seward left for Auburn . . . short periods of time: See Seward family correspondence in October 1863 on reels 112, 114, and 115 of Seward Papers, and FAS to Anna (Wharton) Seward, November 17, 1863, reel 115, Seward Papers.

578 The previous spring . . . his intelligence safely: William H. Seward, Jr., "Reminiscences of Lincoln," *Magazine of History* 9 (February 1909), pp. 105–06.

578 he delivered a speech . . . "will perish with it": WHS, quoted in Williams, *Lincoln and the Radicals,* p. 301.

578 "as in religion . . . whole United States": WHS, quoted in Seward, *Seward at Washington . . . 1861–1872,* p. 195.

579 arousing the wrath . . . "always be open to him": WHS, quoted in Williams, *Lincoln and the Radicals,* p. 301.

579 Lincoln telegraphed . . . "How is your son?": AL to WHS, November 3, 1863, in *CW,* VI, p. 562.

579 "Thanks . . . majority in the state": WHS to AL, November 3, 1863, Lincoln Papers.

579 a 30,000 majority: Seward, *Seward at Washington . . . 1861–1872,* p. 195.

579 "the Copperhead . . . and humbled": "8 November 1863, Sunday," in Hay, *Inside Lincoln's White House,* p. 109.

579 invitations to the Chase-Sprague wedding: See Niven, *Salmon P. Chase,* p. 342.

579 a diamond tiara worth $50,000: Ibid., p. 343.

579 "about the bridal *trousseau* . . . Millionaire Wedding": *NYT,* November 18, 1863.

579 "to realize" . . . undivided attention: SPC to William Sprague, October 31, 1863, reel 29, Chase Papers.

579 Sprague reassured Chase . . . "and generation": William Sprague to SPC, November 4, 1863, reel 29, Chase Papers.

580 Hay recounted . . . *The Pearl of Savoy:* "22 October 1863, Thursday," in Hay, *Inside Lincoln's White House,* p. 98.

580 The play revolves . . . Marie goes mad: Gaetano Donizetti, *The Pearl of Savoy: A Domestic Drama in Five Acts. French's Standard Drama.* Acting Edition No. 337 (New York: S. French, [1864?]). *The Pearl of Savoy* was an adaptation of Donizetti's *Linda de Chamounix.*

580 "was a coldly calculated . . . father and politics": See J. P. Cullen, "Kate Chase: Petticoat Politician," *Civil War Times Illustrated* 2 (May 1963), p. 15.

580 "in her eyes . . . upon her affections": Perrine, "The Dashing Kate Chase," *Ladies' Home Journal* (1901), p. 11.

580 "wholly innocent . . . several millions": *Daily Eagle,* Brooklyn, N.Y., November 14, 1863.

580 "Miss Kate has . . . sufficient for both": Entry for May 19, 1863, *Welles diary,* Vol. I (1960 edn.), p. 306.

580 Henry Adams . . . as Jephthah's daughter: Ross, *Proud Kate,* p. 121. The tale of Jephthah's daughter is in Judges 11:30–40.

581 "Memory has been busy . . . found a lodgment there": KCS diary, November 11, 1868, Sprague Papers.

581 In the hours before . . . proceeded inside: *Daily Morning Chronicle,* Washington, D.C., November 13, 1863.

581 Monty Blair, who refused . . . "of the occasion": EBL to SPL, November 12, [1863], in *Wartime Washington,* ed. Laas, p. 319.

581 Lord Lyons . . . and Robert C. Schenck: *Daily Morning Chronicle,* Washington, D.C., November 13, 1863; Perrine, "The Dashing Kate Chase," *Ladies' Home Journal* (1901), pp. 11–12; "12 November 1863, Thursday," in Hay, *Inside Lincoln's White House,* p. 111.

581 "Much anxiety" . . . and without Mrs. Lincoln: *Daily Morning Chronicle,* Washington, D.C., November 13, 1863.

581 "bow in reverence . . . *Chase & daughter*": MTL to Simon Cameron, June 16, [1866], in Turner and Turner, *Mary Todd Lincoln,* p. 370.

581 Mary's absence . . . "presidential party": Brooks, *Mr. Lincoln's Washington,* pp. 260–61.

582 "a gorgeous white velvet" . . . specifically for the occasion: *Daily Morning Chronicle,* Washington, D.C., November 13, 1863 (quote); Brooks, *Mr. Lincoln's Washington,* p. 261; Ross, *Proud Kate,* p. 140.

582 "Chase was . . . newly made wife": Brooks, *Mr. Lincoln's Washington,* p. 261.

582 A lavish meal . . . midnight: *Daily Morning Chronicle,* Washington, D.C., November 13, 1863.

582 "a very brilliant . . . had *arrived*": "12 November 1863, Thursday," in Hay, *Inside Lincoln's White House,* p. 111.

582 The young couple left the next morning: *NYT,* November 18, 1863.

582 "Your letter . . . how welcome it was": SPC to KCS, November 18, 1863, reel 29, Chase Papers.

582 "My heart is full . . . perfect honor & good faith": SPC to William Sprague, November 26, 1863, reel 30, Chase Papers.

583 He had been asked . . . would speak: David Wills to AL, November 2, 1863, Lincoln Papers.

583 Lincoln told his cabinet . . . could not spare the time: Entry for December 1863, *Welles diary,* Vol. I (1960 edn.), p. 480; SPC to KCS, November 18, 1863, reel 29, Chase Papers; entry for November 19, 1863, in *The Diary of Edward Bates, 1859–1866,* p. 316.

583 "extremely busy . . . public expectation": Lamon, *Recollections of Abraham Lincoln,* p. 173.

583 Stanton had arranged . . . "the gauntlet": AL to EMS, [November 17, 1863], in *CW*, VII, p. 16 and note.

583 The day before . . . "half of his speech": James Speed quoted in John G. Nicolay, "Lincoln's Gettysburg Address," *Century* 47 (February 1894), p. 597.

583 Various accounts suggest . . . "a makeshift desk": George D. Gitt, quoted in Wilson, *Intimate Memories of Lincoln*, p. 476.

583 Others swear . . . on an envelope: See Garry Wills, *Lincoln at Gettysburg: The Words That Remade America* (New York: Simon & Schuster, 1992), p. 27.

583 Nicolay . . . and humorous stories: Nicolay, "Lincoln's Gettysburg Address," *Century* (1894), p. 601.

583 he was escorted . . . and Edward Everett: David Wills to AL, November 1, 1863, Lincoln Papers.

583 "All the hotels . . . of Gettysburgh immortal": *NYT*, November 21, 1863.

584 He came to the door . . . "say nothing at all": AL, "Remarks to Citizens of Gettysburg, Pennsylvania," November 18, 1863, in *CW*, VI, pp. 16–17.

584 Lincoln sent a servant: Frank L. Klement, "The Ten Who Sat in the Front Row on the Platform During the Dedication of the Soldiers' Cemetery at Gettysburg," *Lincoln Herald* 88 (Winter 1985), p. 108.

584 A telegram arrived . . . Tad was better: EMS to AL, November 18 and 19, 1863, Lincoln Papers.

584 the crowd surged once . . . "part of the human race": WHS, quoted in Seward, *Seward at Washington . . . 1861–1872*, p. 201 (quote); *NYT*, November 21, 1863.

584 the convivial secretary . . . "men of this generation": Entry for November 22, 1863, in French, *Witness to the Young Republic*, p. 434.

584 He wanted to talk . . . and retiring: Klement, "The Ten Who Sat," *Lincoln Herald* (1985), p. 108; Wills, *Lincoln at Gettysburg*, p. 31; entry for November 22, 1863, in French, *Witness to the Young Republic*, p. 434.

584 The huge, boisterous crowd . . . "thousand more": Entry for November 22, 1863, in French, *Witness to the Young Republic*, p. 434.

584 made his final revisions: Nicolay, "Lincoln's Gettysburg Address," *Century* (1894), pp. 601, 602.

584 a chestnut horse . . . three cabinet officers: Sandburg, *Abraham Lincoln: The War Years*, Vol. II, p. 466.

585 Seward, riding . . . "homemade gray socks": Henry Clay Cochrane, quoted in ibid.

585 An audience . . . between Everett and Seward: Klement, "The Ten Who Sat," *Lincoln Herald* (1985), p. 106.

585 "leaned from one side . . . of his right hand": Gitt, quoted in Wilson, *Intimate Memories of Lincoln*, p. 478.

585 Another member . . . to his pocket: Monaghan, *Diplomat in Carpet Slippers*, p. 341.

585 "could not be surpassed by mortal man": Entry for November 22, 1863, in French, *Witness to the Young Republic*, p. 435.

585 "Seldom has a man . . . not like an orator": Klement, "The Ten Who Sat," *Lincoln Herald* (1985), p. 108.

585 "flutter and motion . . . an empty house": Gitt, quoted in Wilson, *Intimate Memories of Lincoln*, p. 478.

585 steel-rimmed spectacles . . . at his pages: Sandburg, *Abraham Lincoln: The War Years*, Vol. II, p. 468.

585 "He had spent . . . supreme principle": Wills, *Lincoln at Gettysburg*, p. 120.

585 "all this quibbling . . . created equal": AL, "Speech at Chicago, Illinois," July 10, 1858, in *CW*, II, p. 501.

585 "the central idea . . . govern themselves": AL, quoted in "7 May 1861, Tuesday," in Hay, *Inside Lincoln's White House*, p. 20.

586 "Four score and seven . . . shall not perish from the earth": AL, "Address Delivered at the Dedication of the Cemetery at Gettysburg, November 19, 1863; Edward Everett Copy," in *CW*, VII, p. 21.

586 "the assemblage . . . there came applause": Gitt, quoted in Wilson, *Intimate Memories of Lincoln*, p. 479.

586 he turned to Ward Lamon . . . "disappointed": Lamon, *Recollections of Abraham Lincoln*, p. 173.

586 "I should be glad . . . in two minutes": Edward Everett to AL, November 20, 1863, Lincoln Papers.

587 Zachariah Chandler . . . tardiness on emancipation: Bruce Tap, "Chandler, Zachariah," in *Encyclopedia of the American Civil War*, ed. Heidler and Heidler, pp. 398–99.

587 "Your president . . . & hold him": Zachariah Chandler to Lyman Trumbull, quoted in Williams, *Lincoln and the Radicals*, p. 179.

587 Having read in the press . . . "buried three days": Zachariah Chandler to AL, November 15, 1863, Lincoln Papers.

587 "My dear Sir . . . wreck the country's cause": AL to Zachariah Chandler, November 20, 1863, in *CW*, VII, pp. 23–24.

588 a mild case of smallpox: Entry for December 2, 1863, in French, *Witness to the Young Republic*, p. 439; entry for December 1863, *Welles diary*, Vol. I (1960 edn.), p. 480.

588 "Yes, it is a bad . . . that calls": *NYT*, December 18, 1863.

588 "the greatest question . . . practical statesmanship": "31 July 1863, Friday," in Hay, *Inside Lincoln's White House*, p. 69.

588 everyone assumed . . . of his divided party: Brooks, *Mr. Lincoln's Washington*, p. 271.

588 John Hay was present . . . "highly satisfactory": "[9 December 1863, Wednesday]," in Hay, *Inside Lincoln's White House*, pp. 121–22.

588 Radicals were thrilled . . . "acts of Congress": AL, "Annual Message to Congress," December 8, 1863, in *CW*, VII, p. 51.

588 "He makes Emancipation . . . of reconstruction": CS to Orestes A. Brownson, December 27, 1863, in *Selected Letters of Charles Sumner*, Vol. II, p. 209.

588 "God bless Old Abe . . . in the President": "[9 December 1863, Wednesday]," in Hay, *Inside Lincoln's White House*, p. 122.

588 had written a letter to Nathaniel Banks . . . "included in the plan": AL to Nathaniel P. Banks, in *CW*, VI, p. 365.

589 He offered full pardons . . . remain as they were: AL, "Proclamation of Amnesty and Reconstruction," December 8, 1863, in *CW*, VII, pp. 54–56.

589 Conservatives hailed . . . as it wished: EBL to SPL, December 8, 1863, in *Wartime Washington*, ed. Laas, p. 325.

589 "theory is identical . . . different nomenclature": CS to Orestes A. Brownson, December 27, 1863, in *Selected Letters of Charles Sumner*, Vol. II, pp. 216–17.

589 Lincoln assured . . . "otherwise would": AL, "Annual Message to Congress," December 8, 1863, in *CW*, VII, p. 52.

589 would devastate Confederate morale: Foner, *Reconstruction*, pp. 36–37.

589 When the Blairs . . . "of modern times": Brooks, *Mr. Lincoln's Washington*, p. 273.

589 "is the great man . . . clearly than anybody": "[9 December 1863, Wednesday]," in Hay, *Inside Lincoln's White House*, p. 122.

589 Judd called . . . "was Mr. Chase": Norman Judd and AL, quoted in "[9 December 1863, Wednesday]," in Hay, *Inside Lincoln's White House*, p. 124.

590 Chase had obstinately . . . perpetuate emancipation: SPC to AL, November 25, 1863, Lincoln Papers.

590 "more positive . . . is not to be had": SPC to Henry Ward Beecher, December 26, 1863, reel 30, Chase Papers.

590 he detected a more hopeful . . . surprisingly well: AL, "Annual Message to Congress," December 8, 1863, in *CW*, VII, pp. 49–50.

590 invited his sister-in-law . . . "and left him alone": David Davis, quoted in *Daily Picayune*, New Orleans, March 14, 1897.

590 Emilie had been living . . . through Union lines: Helm, *The True Story of Mary*, p. 220.

590 "I am totally at a loss . . . secure a pass?": John L. Helm to Mrs. Robert S. Todd, October 11, 1863, quoted in ibid., p. 219.

591 Lincoln personally issued . . . "to Kentucky": AL to Lyman B. Todd, October 15, 1863, in *CW*, VII, p. 517.

591 When Emilie arrived . . . explaining the dilemma: Helm, *The True Story of Mary*, pp. 220–21.

591 "Send her to me": AL, quoted in ibid., p. 221.

591 was received at the White House . . . Confederate Army: Emilie Todd Helm diary [hereafter Helm diary], quoted in ibid., pp. 221–22.

591 "Often the boundaries . . . chose sides": John W. Shaffer, *Clash of Loyalties: A Border County in the Civil War* (Morgantown: West Virginia University Press, 2003), p. 2.

591 they carefully avoided mention . . . "into other channels": Helm diary, quoted in Helm, *The True Story of Mary*, p. 224.

591 Mary did her utmost: Helm diary, quoted in ibid., pp. 222–23.

591 "He comes to me . . . most of the time": MTL, quoted in Helm diary, in ibid., p. 227.

592 "the scape-goat . . . thrill in her voice": MTL, quoted in Helm diary, in ibid., pp. 225, 227.

592 he confided her presence . . . "it known": Entry for December 14, 1863, in Browning, *The Diary of Orville Hickman Browning*, Vol. I, p. 651.

592 invited Emilie to join them: Helm, *The True Story of Mary*, p. 228.

592 Lincoln had personally . . . restore his spirits: Edgcumb Pinchon, *Dan Sickles: Hero of Gettysburg and "Yankee King of Spain"* (Garden City, N.Y.: Doubleday, Doran & Co., 1945), pp. 203–04.

592 Mary also considered . . . merriment: MTL to Sally Orne, [December 12, 1869], in Turner and Turner, *Mary Todd Lincoln*, pp. 533–34.

592 Senator Harris turned . . . "and Manassas": Helm diary, quoted in Helm, *The True Story of Mary*, p. 229.

592 Mary's face "turned . . . assistance in the matter": Helm diary, quoted in ibid., pp. 227, 229–31.

593 prompted Emilie to leave: Helm diary, quoted in ibid., p. 231.

593 "Oh, Emilie . . . hideous nightmare?": MTL, quoted in Helm diary, ibid., p. 226.

593 he took Nicolay and Hay . . . about the play: "[18 December 1863]," in Hay, *Inside Lincoln's White House*, p. 128; *Daily Morning Chronicle*, Washington, D.C., December 19, 1863.

593 "in fine spirits": Entry for December 15, 1863, *Welles diary*, Vol. I (1960 edn.), p. 485.

593 returned to Ford's . . . Bayard Taylor: "[18 December 1863]," in Hay, *Inside Lincoln's White House*, p. 128; *Daily Morning Chronicle*, Washington, D.C., December 18 and 19, 1863.

593 a peculiarly pleasant dream . . . the next day: "23 December 1863," in Hay, *Inside Lincoln's White House*, p. 132.

593 Seward entertained . . . "cloud of smoke": Seward, *Seward at Washington . . . 1861–1872*, p. 206.

593 Bates's children: See introduction, entries for May 28; June 5 and 20; July 1; November 15, 22, 25, and 30; December 16, 19 and 22, 1863, *The Diary of Edward Bates, 1859–1866*, pp. xv–xvi, 294, 295, 299, 315, 319, 320–21, 323.

594 After forty years . . . word against him: Entry for September 4, 1863, in *The Diary of Edward Bates, 1859–1866*, p. 306.

594 he attended a funeral . . . "and die soon": Entry for December 25, 1863, in ibid., p. 324.

594 Edgar's return . . . "on earth forever": Entry for December 25, 1863, *Welles diary*, Vol. I (1960 edn.), p. 494.

594 "The year closes . . . the future than now": Entry for December 31, 1863, ibid., pp. 499–500.

594 the birth of a new baby girl . . . baptismal celebration: EMS to SPC, December 30, 1863, reel 30, Chase Papers.

594 He shared with the men . . . "guests of the nation": *NYT*, December 29, 1863.

594 Lincoln invited Stanton . . . Point Lookout: AL to EMS, December 26, 1863, in *CW*, VII, p. 95 (quote); *NYTrib*, December 29, 1863.

594 He had heard that . . . Confederate strongholds: Thomas and Hyman, *Stanton*, p. 309; "28 December 1863, Monday," in Hay, *Inside Lincoln's White House*, p. 134.

595 "Oh! dying year! . . . brighter hopes dawn": Entry for December 31, 1863, in Adam Gurowski, *Diary: 1863–'64–'65*, Vol. III. Burt Franklin: Research & Source Works #229 (Washington, D.C., 1866; New York: Burt Franklin, 1968), p. 57.

595 "a tall . . . polish of appearance": Entry for February 24, 1861, Charles Francis Adams diary, reel 76.

595 "sphere of civilization": Entry for March 8, 1861, Charles Francis Adams diary, reel 76.

595 no "heroic qualities": Entry for February 21, 1861, Charles Francis Adams diary, reel 76.

595 "not equal . . . of his position": Entry for August 16, 1861, Charles Francis Adams diary, reel 76.

595 At a festive dinner . . . "to one great purpose": Charles Francis Adams, quoted in *NR*, February 2, 1864.

595 "foremost American . . . in his time": "Lowell, James Russell," in *Dictionary of American Biography*, Vol. VI, ed. Dumas Malone (New York: Charles Scribner's Sons, 1933), p. 458.

595 "Never did a President . . . still in wild water": James Russell Lowell, "The President's Policy," *North American Review* 98 (January 1864), pp. 241–43, 249, 254–55.

596 "very excellent . . . over-much credit": Entry for January 5, 1864, *Welles diary*, Vol. I (1960 edn.), p. 504.

CHAPTER 23: "THERE'S A MAN IN IT!"

Page

597 New Year's Day . . . scattered the clouds: Brooks, *Mr. Lincoln's Washington*, pp. 273–74 (quote); *Star*, January 1, 1864; *NR*, January 2, 1864.

597 "Murfreesboro . . . excel these": *NR*, January 1, 1864.

597 "We have a right . . . weathered the gale": *NR*, January 13, 1864.

598 "The instinct of all . . . danger is over": Dispatch of January 18, 1864, in Stoddard, *Dispatches from Lincoln's White House*, p. 203.

598 the traditional New Year's reception: Entry for January 1, 1864, in *Lincoln Day by Day*, Vol. III, p. 231; dispatch of January 4, 1864, in Stoddard, *Dispatches from Lincoln's White House*, p. 199.

598 "a human kaleidoscope . . . petitioners": *NR*, January 2, 1864.

598 *"public-opinion baths* . . . and duty": Carpenter, *Six Months at the White House*, pp. 281–82.

598 "European democrats . . . American a custom": Dispatch of January 4, 1864, in Stoddard, *Dispatches from Lincoln's White House*, p. 199.

598 Lincoln "appeared to be . . . word or two": *NR*, January 2, 1864.

598 Mary Lincoln "never looked better" . . . velvet dress: Brooks, *Mr. Lincoln's Washington*, pp. 274–75 (quote p. 275).

598 "We seem to have . . . cared about it": FWS, quoted in Seward, *Seward at Washington . . . 1861–1872*, p. 207.

598 The winter social calendar . . . of cabinet officers: *NR*, January 19, 1864.

599 "grace and elegance": *NR*, January 26, 1864.

599 "who with such . . . once a week": *NR*, January 16, 1864.

599 "observed of all observers": *NR*, January 2, 1864.

599 "one of the most lovable women": Entry for January 3, 1864, in French, *Witness to the Young Republic*, p. 443.

599 "frosty . . . a very close examination": Brooks, *Mr. Lincoln's Washington*, p. 275.

599 Mary found it necessary . . . "human tide": Stoddard, *Inside the White House in War Times*, p. 49; *NR*, January 2, 1864.

599 ill dressed . . . their carpetbags: *NR*, January 13, 1864.

599 "the lace curtains . . . as a man's hand": Brooks, *Mr. Lincoln's Washington*, p. 253 (quote); B. B. French to Charles R. Train, January 5, 1863, p. 181, Vol. 14, reel 7; French to John H. Rice, March 7, 1864, p. 313, Vol. 14, reel 7; French to Rice, June 16, 1864, pp. 375–76, Vol. 14, reel 7, M371, RG 42, DNA.

600 would inaugurate "the fashionable 'season' ": *NR*, January 6, 1864.

600 visiting members . . . "with their families": *NYT*, January 8, 1864.

600 "not so largely attended as usual": *NYH*, January 13, 1864.

600 she was "disappointed": Entry for January 14, 1864, in French, *Witness to the Young Republic*, p. 443.

600 The Sewards hosted . . . "most brilliant": *NR*, January 26, 1864 (first quote); *NR*, January 15, 1864 (second quote); *NYT*, January 26, 1864 (third quote); *Star*, January 26, 1864.

600 a pleasant evening . . . "relief from care": Seward, *Seward at Washington . . . 1861–1872*, p. 208.

600 Mary could not relinquish . . . and supporters: Anson G. Henry to Isaac Newton, April 21, 1864, Lincoln Papers.

600 Mary's anger . . . "a patriot": Keckley, *Behind the Scenes*, pp. 127–29 (quotes pp. 128, 129).

600 and crossed out . . . "Schleswig-Holstein difficulty": JGN to JH, January 18, 1864, in Nicolay, *With Lincoln in the White House*, p. 124.

600 directed her wrath . . . "night or two": JGN to JH, January 29, 1864, in ibid., p. 125.

601 dinner "was pleasant . . . off very well": Entry for January 22, 1864, *Welles diary*, Vol. I (1960 edn.), p. 512.

601 unable to share . . . "merry-making at a funeral": GW to Edgar T. Welles, February 14, 1864, reel 22, Welles Papers.

601 "the old secession" . . . stars of every occasion: Dispatch of February 6, 1864, in Stoddard, *Dispatches from Lincoln's White House*, pp. 206–07 (quote p. 206).

601 Ulric . . . expert waltzer: Stoddard, *Inside the White House in War Times*, p. 128.

601 Fernando Wood . . . "personal intercourse": Dispatch of February 1, 1864, in Stoddard, *Dispatches from Lincoln's White House*, p. 205.

601 Mary Lincoln sent . . . "to believe it": MTL to Daniel E. Sickles, February 6, 1864, in Turner and Turner, *Mary Todd Lincoln*, pp. 167–68; see also note 3 of MTL to Sickles.

601 when Emilie . . . Martha Todd White: See note 1 to JGN to Benjamin F. Butler, April 19, 1864, Lincoln Papers.

602 Lincoln issued a pass: On the subject of Martha Todd White's dealings with the Lincolns, see JGN to Butler, April 19, 1864; Butler to JGN, April 21, 1864, Lincoln Papers.

602 "Here . . . of your master": Undated newspaper article pasted in JGN to Butler, April 19, 1863, container 28, Butler Papers; newspaper reports of Martha Todd White's statements to General Butler, quoted in Butler to JGN, April 21, 1864, Lincoln Papers.

602 he directed Nicolay to ascertain the facts: JGN to Butler, April 19, 1863, container 28, Butler Papers.

602 Butler replied . . . untoward had been found: Butler to JGN, April 21, 1864, Lincoln Papers.

602 Nicolay used Butler's letter: JGN to Butler, April 28, 1864; JGN to Horace Greeley, April 25, 1864; Greeley to JGN, April 26, 1864, Lincoln Papers. For an example of rebuttal issued, see *NYTrib*, April 27, 1864.

602 Butler was surprised . . . so "silly": Butler to JGN, April 21, 1864, Lincoln Papers.

602 Nor did he want . . . sustain the rebel cause: O. Stewart to AL, April 27, 1864, Lincoln Papers.

602 Browning requested a favor . . . "very good humor": Entry for February 6, 1894, in Browning, *The Diary of Orville Hickman Browning*, Vol. I, p. 659.

602 he had visited . . . Owen Lovejoy: Entry for February 6, 1864, in *Lincoln Day by Day*, Vol. III, p. 238.

602 "the best friend [he] had in Congress": AL, quoted in Carpenter, *Six Months at the White House*, p. 18.

602 suffering from a debilitating liver and kidney ailment: *NYT*, March 28, 1864; Edward Magdol, *Owen Lovejoy: Abolitionist in Congress* (New Brunswick, N.J.: Rutgers University Press, 1967), pp. 400, 402–03.

602 "This war is eating . . . live to see the end": AL, quoted in Carpenter, *Six Months at the White House*, p. 17.

603 a fire alarm rang . . . his brother, Willie: Robert W. McBride, *Personal Recollections of Abraham Lincoln* (Indianapolis: Bobbs-Merrill, 1926), pp. 29–30, 44–46 (quotes pp. 44–45); *Star*, February 11, 1864; *Daily Morning Chronicle*, Washington, D.C., February 11, 1864.

603 A coachman . . . setting the fire: *Star*, February 11, 1864; JGN to JH, February 10, 1864, in Nicolay, *With Lincoln in the White House*, p. 126.

603 instructed him to consult . . . "have it rebuilt": Commissioner B. B. French to John H. Rice, February 11, 1863, pp. 295–96, Vol. 14, reel 7, M371, RG 42, DNA (quote); *Star*, February 11, 1864.

603 "carefully veiled . . . a hopeless one": McClure, *Abraham Lincoln and Men of War-Times*, p. 136.

603 Friends of Chase . . . biographical sketch: Niven, *Salmon P. Chase*, p. 358.

603 "no matter how . . . flimsy political trick": William Orton to SPC, January 6, 1864, in *Chase Papers*, Vol. IV, p. 247.

604 "malignant denunciations": SPC to AL, January 13, 1864, reel 30, Chase Papers.

604 twenty-five long letters . . . inspirational book: Chase's series of autobiographical letters to John T. Trowbridge began on December 27, 1863, and ended on March 22, 1864, see Chase Papers; [John T. Trowbridge], *The Ferry-Boy and the Financier, by a Contributor to the "Atlantic"* (Boston: Walker, Wise, & Co., 1864).

604 An excerpt appeared: J. T. Trowbridge, "The First Visit to Washington," *Atlantic Monthly* 13 (April 1864), pp. 448–57.

604 "So far . . . otherwise than I have": SPC to J. W. Hartwell, February 2, 1864, reel 31, Chase Papers.

604 "I think of you . . . you are—where?": SPC to Charlotte S. Eastman, February 1, 1864, reel 31, Chase Papers.

604 Susan Walker . . . "bluestocking": Niven, *Salmon P. Chase*, pp. 97 (quote), 203–04.

604 "*I wish* you could come . . . you enough": SPC to Susan Walker, January 23, 1864, reel 31, Chase Papers.

605 the public announcement . . . held a large interest: Niven, *Salmon P. Chase*, pp. 357, 359–60; Blue, *Salmon P. Chase*, p. 222.

605 "eating a man's bread . . . the same time": David Davis, quoted in King, *Lincoln's Manager*, p. 213.

605 Chase busied himself lining up support: Hart, *Salmon P. Chase*, pp. 309–10.

605 "gratified . . . should he be reelected": SPC to Flamen Ball, February 2, 1864, reel 31, Chase Papers.

605 "lamented the . . . distinct feeler": Entry for February 3, 1864, *Welles diary*, Vol. I (1960 edn.), pp. 520–21.

605 "immeasurably" . . . to any other candidate: Entry for March 22, 1864, in *The Diary of Edward Bates, 1859–1866*, p. 350.

606 "fair plump lady . . . altogether the advantage": Entry for February 19, 1864, *Welles diary*, Vol. I (1960 edn.), p. 528.

606 the Pomeroy Committee . . . "available candidate": "The Pomeroy Circular," quoted in Schuckers, *The Life and Public Services of Salmon Portland Chase*, pp. 499–500.

606 Pomeroy circular was leaked to the press: J. M. Winchell, quoted in *NYT*, September 15, 1874.

606 "No sensible man . . . if it killed me": David Davis, quoted in King, *Lincoln's Manager*, p. 215.

606 "had no knowledge . . . entire confidence": SPC to AL, February 22, 1864, Lincoln Papers.

606 the circular's author . . . "would sustain": J. M. Winchell, quoted in *NYT*, September 15, 1874.

607 He understood the political . . . "*enemies*": Entry for February 13, 1864, in *The Diary of Edward Bates, 1859–1866*, p. 333.

607 acknowledged receipt . . . "time to do so": AL to SPC, February 23, 1864, reel 31, Chase Papers.

607 "Its recoil . . . than Lincoln": Entry for February 22, 1864, *Welles diary*, Vol. I (1960 edn.), p. 529.

607 "It is unworthy . . . of this movement": *NYT*, February 24, 1864.

607 the effect of the circular . . . Chase's prospects: JGN to TB, February 28, 1864, container 3, Nicolay Papers.

607 In state after state . . . Lincoln's renomination: *NYT*, February 24, 1864; Fitz Henry Warren to TW, March 25, 1864, Lincoln Papers.

607 Pomeroy's home state . . . support for Lincoln: W. W. H. Lawrence to Abel C. Wilder and James H. Lane, February 15, 1864, Lincoln Papers.

607 the "long list . . . degree with Abraham Lincoln": *NYT*, February 29, 1864.

607 *Harper's Weekly* . . . "had been blinded": *Harper's Weekly*, March 5, 1864, p. 146.

608 "The masses . . . earnest and honest": Entry for January 3, 1864, in Gurowski, *Diary: 1863–'64–'65*, p. 60.

608 The fatal blow: Niven, *Salmon P. Chase*, p. 361.

608 "brought matters ... of the gravest character": Richard C. Parsons to SPC, March 2, 1864, reel 32, Chase Papers.

608 to answer Chase's ... "occasion for a change": AL to SPC, February 29, 1864, reel 31, Chase Papers.

608 In a public letter ... "given to my name": SPC to James C. Hall, March 5, 1864, reel 32, Chase Papers.

608 Chase told his daughter ... "welfare of the country": SPC to Janet Chase Hoyt, March 15, 1864, reel 32, Chase Papers.

609 "It proves only ... openly resisted": Entry for March 9, 1864, in *The Diary of Edward Bates, 1859–1866*, p. 345.

609 Leonard Grover estimated ... "a hundred times": Leonard Grover, "Lincoln's Interest in the Theater," *Century* 77 (April 1909), p. 944.

609 "It gave him ... seen by the audience": Noah Brooks, "Personal Reminiscences of Lincoln," *Scribners Monthly* 15 (March 1878), p. 675.

609 "the drama ... entire relief": Stoddard, *Inside the White House in War Times*, p. 191.

609 At a performance ... "Hal's time": Ibid., p. 107.

610 developments with gaslight ... onto the stage: Mary C. Henderson, "Scenography, Stagecraft, and Architecture in the American Theatre: Beginnings to 1870," in Don Wilmeth and Christopher Bigsby, eds., *The Cambridge History of American Theatre*. Vol. I: *Beginnings to 1870* (New York: Cambridge University Press, 1998), p. 415.

610 "To envision nineteenth-century ... intimate space": Levine, *Highbrow / Lowbrow*, pp. 26, 24–25.

610 Frances Trollope complained ... "and whiskey": Trollope, *Domestic Manners of the Americans*, p. 102.

610 The years surrounding ... Charlotte Cushman: Garff B. Wilson, *Three Hundred Years of American Drama and Theatre: From Ye Bear and Ye Cubb to Hair* (Englewood Cliffs, N.J.: Prentice-Hall, 1973), p. 144.

610 "she was not ... vitality of her presence": *NYTrib*, February 19, 1876.

610 Seward and Miss Cushman ... at the Seward home: Van Deusen, *William Henry Seward*, p. 338.

611 a close relationship with young Fanny: See Fanny Seward diary, Seward Papers; FAS to CS, June 10, 1858, reel 17, Sumner Papers.

611 "Imagine me ... use in the world": FS to FAS, February 11, 1864, reel 116, Seward Papers.

611 "the greatest man" ... outside their family: Charlotte Cushman, quoted in entry for October 14, 1864, Fanny Seward diary, Seward Papers.

611 Lincoln made his way ... purpose of her visit: Charlotte Cushman to [WHS], July 9, 1861, Lincoln Papers.

611 "Perhaps the best ... at criticism": AL to James H. Hackett, August 17, 1863, in *CW*, VI, p. 392.

611 Hackett shared ... "without much malice": On the dissemination of Lincoln's letter to Hackett, see note 1 to AL to James H. Hackett, August 17, 1863, in ibid., p. 393; James H. Hackett to AL, October 22, 1863, Lincoln Papers; AL to James H. Hackett, November 2, 1863, in *CW*, VI, pp. 558–59 (quote p. 558).

612 recalled bringing ... "pleasant interval" from his work: William Kelley, in *Reminiscences of Abraham Lincoln*, ed. Rice (1886 edn.), pp. 264–67, 270.

612 "Edwin Booth has done ... any other man": Lucia Gilbert Calhoun, "Edwin Booth," *Galaxy* 7 (January 1869), p. 85.

612 captivated audiences ... generation: Richard Lockridge, *Darling of Misfortune: Edwin Booth, 1833–1893* (New York: Century Co., 1932; New York: Benjamin Blom, 1971), pp. 14, 24, 38–39, 56, 78–79, 81; *Harper's New Monthly Magazine* 22 (April 1861), p. 702; E. C. Stedman, "Edwin Booth," *Atlantic Monthly* 17 (May 1866), p. 589.

612 Lincoln and Seward attended ... *Merchant of Venice*: Entries for February 19, 25, 26; March 2, 4, and 10, 1864, in *Lincoln Day by Day*, Vol. III, pp. 241–45; *NR*, March 3, 5, and 10, 1864; Grover, "Lincoln's Interest in the Theater," *Century* (1909), p. 946.

612 Booth came to dinner ... "want of body in wine": Entry for March 1864, Fanny Seward diary, Seward Papers.

613 anticipating Booth's *Hamlet* ... "upon the stage": Carpenter, *Six Months at the White House*, pp. 49–51 (quote p. 51).

613 "laugh ... ' "Midsummer Night's Dream" ' ": Ibid., p. 150.

613 Chase and Bates considered ... "Satanic diversion": Hendrick, *Lincoln's War Cabinet*, p. 10.

613 Stanton came only once ... Tad loved the theater: Grover, "Lincoln's Interest in the Theater," *Century* (1909), pp. 946, 944–45.

614 Tad would laugh ... "seeing clearly why": "24 April 1864, Sunday," in Hay, *Inside Lincoln's White House*, p. 188.

614 "felt at home" ... actually appeared in a play: Grover, "Lincoln's Interest in the Theater," *Century* (1909), p. 945.

614 who broke down in tears ... and the Taft boys: Bayne, *Tad Lincoln's Father*, p. 201.

614 arrived in the nation's capital: Brooks, *Mr. Lincoln's Washington*, p. 290.

614 Congress had revived ... the Western armies: Smith, *Grant*, pp. 284, 286, 293, 294.

614 He walked into the Willard ... the accommodations: Smith, *Grant*, p. 289; Brooks D. Simpson, *Ulysses S. Grant: Triumph Over Adversity, 1822–1865* (Boston and New York: Houghton Mifflin, 2000), pp. 258–59.

614 Grant took his son ... and took a bow: Brooks, *Mr. Lincoln's Washington*, p. 290 (quotes); Smith, *Grant*, p. 289.

614 walked over to the White House ... "a tone of familiarity": Horace Porter, *Campaigning with Grant* (New York: Century Co., 1897; New York: Konecky & Konecky, 1992), pp. 18–19.

615 "a degree of awkwardness": Entry for March 9, 1864, *Welles diary*, Vol. I (1960 edn.), p. 538.

615 Lincoln referred him to Seward: Smith, *Grant*, pp. 289–90; entry for March 9, 1864, *Welles diary*, Vol. I (1960 edn.), p. 538–39.

615 "laces were torn ... much mixed": Brooks, *Mr. Lincoln's Washington*, p. 290.

615 Seward rapidly maneuvered ... see his face: Carpenter, *Six Months at the White House*, p. 56.

615 "He blushed ... and over his face": *NYH*, March 12, 1864.

615 "his warmest campaign during the war": Carpenter, *Six Months at the White House*, p. 56.

615 The president . . . "walk it abreast": Porter, *Campaigning with Grant*, p. 20.

615 Grant wanted nothing more . . . "presidential chair": J. Russell Jones recollections, quoted in Tarbell, *Life of Abraham Lincoln*, Vol. II (1917 edn.), pp. 187–88.

615 made their way back . . . Grant wrote out his statement: Smith, *Grant*, p. 290; Memorandum, March 9, 1864, container 3, Nicolay Papers.

616 "quite embarrassed . . . difficult to read": Memorandum, March 9, 1864, container 3, Nicolay Papers.

616 went upstairs to talk . . . assistance was needed: Grant, *Personal Memoirs of U.S. Grant*, p. 370.

616 Grant journeyed . . . " '*show*' business!": Carpenter, *Six Months at the White House*, p. 57.

616 "trappings and . . . canopy of heaven": Elihu Washburne, quoted in Blaine, *Twenty Years of Congress*, p. 510.

616 his preference for pork . . . "in spasms": *NYT*, March 31, 1864.

616 "was done exactly . . . into history": McFeely, *Grant*, p. 152.

617 "unusually backward" . . . end of the month: Entry for May 1, 1864, in *The Diary of Edward Bates, 1859–1866*, p. 363.

617 "stormy and inclement . . . of the Old Dominion": Dispatch of April 11, 1864, in Stoddard, *Dispatches from Lincoln's White House*, p. 219.

617 "the toughest snowstorm . . . ever I saw him": Entry for March 23, 1864, in French, *Witness to the Young Republic*, p. 447.

617 "as pleasant and funny" . . . Saturday levee: Benjamin B. French to Pamela Prentiss French, April 10, 1864, transcription, reel 10, French Family Papers, DLC.

617 he strolled into John Hay's room . . . " 'is of me' ": "24 April 1864, Sunday," in Hay, *Inside Lincoln's White House*, p. 188.

617 "a beleaguered nation . . . was never bright": J. G. Randall, *The Civil War and Reconstruction* (1937; Boston: D. C. Heath & Co., 1953), pp. 670, 347.

617 "real suffering . . . in the social scale": *NYT*, July 7, 1864.

617 Food riots had broken out . . . vandalized: Randall, *The Civil War and Reconstruction*, p. 670; Emory M. Thomas, *The Confederate Nation, 1861–1865*. New American Nation Series (New York: Harper & Row, 1979), pp. 199–206.

617 Davis's health gradually . . . isolated himself: Davis, *Jefferson Davis*, pp. 539–40, 551–53.

618 The "tramp" of his feet: Entry for May 8, 1864, in Mary Chesnut, *Mary Chesnut's Civil War*, ed. C. Vann Woodward (New Haven: Yale University Press, 1981), p. 601.

618 Washington was filled . . . were imminent: Dispatch of May 2, 1864, in Stoddard, *Dispatches from Lincoln's White House*, p. 223.

618 "beginning to feel . . . generally been failures": JGN to TB, May 1, 1864, container 3, Nicolay Papers.

618 Lincoln wrote him a letter . . . "dignity at once": "30 April 1864, Saturday," in Hay, *Inside Lincoln's White House*, p. 192.

618 "entire satisfaction . . . power to give": AL to USG, April 30, 1864, in *CW*, VII, p. 324.

618 "been astonished . . . fault is not with you": USG to AL, May 1, 1864, Lincoln Papers.

618 the Army . . . from the James River: Michael Korda, *Ulysses S. Grant: The Unlikely Hero*. Eminent Lives Series (New York: HarperCollins, 2004), p. 97.

618 "This concerted movement . . . in numbers": "30 April 1864, Saturday," in Hay, *Inside Lincoln's White House*, p. 193.

618 great "solicitude . . . great advantages": Entry for May 1, 1864, in Browning, *The Diary of Orville Hickman Browning*, Vol. I, p. 668.

619 the Wilderness: E. M. Law, "From the Wilderness to Cold Harbor," in *Battles and Leaders of the Civil War*, Vol. IV, Pt. I, p. 122; McFeely, *Grant*, p. 167; Gordon C. Rhea, *The Battle of the Wilderness, May 5–6, 1864* (Baton Rouge and London: Louisiana State University Press, 1994), pp. 27, 51, 142, 163, 178, 193.

619 climb over the dead . . . "three and four deep": *NYT*, May 15, 1864.

619 "a nightmare of inhumanity": McFeely, *Grant*, p. 165.

619 86,000 Union and Confederate casualties: Table of casualties, Noah Andre Trudeau, *Bloody Roads South: The Wilderness to Cold Harbor, May–June 1864* (Boston: Little, Brown, 1989), p. 341.

619 "The world has never seen . . . never will again": USG to Julia Dent Grant, May 13, 1864, in *The Papers of Ulysses S. Grant*. Vol. X: *January 1–May 31, 1864*, ed. John Y. Simon (Carbondale and Edwardsville: Southern Illinois University Press, 1982), p. 444.

619 "always regretted . . . was ever made": Grant, *Personal Memoirs of U. S. Grant*, p. 462.

619 as steamers reached the city . . . "torture and pain": Brooks, *Mr. Lincoln's Washington*, pp. 320, 323 (quotes).

619 Judge Taft was present . . . others limping along: Entry for May 11, 1864, Taft diary.

619 As each steamer landed . . . "and manly": Brooks, *Mr. Lincoln's Washington*, p. 323.

619 Elizabeth Blair fled . . . "for my nerves": EBL to SPL, May 30, 1864, in *Wartime Washington*, ed. Laas, p. 386.

619 "The carnage has been unexampled": Entry for May 15, 1864, in *The Diary of Edward Bates, 1859–1866*, p. 366.

619 "it seems to myself . . . battle of the war": WHS, diplomatic circular of May 16, 1864, quoted in Seward, *Seward at Washington . . . 1861–1872*, p. 219.

619 "The intense anxiety . . . for mental activity": Entry for May 17, 1864, *Welles diary*, Vol. II, p. 33.

619 "more nervous and anxious . . . and disaster": JGN to TB, May 15, 1864, container 3, Nicolay Papers.

620 nights when Lincoln did not sleep: Entry for May 7, 1864, *Welles diary*, Vol. II, p. 25.

620 "met him . . . his breast": Carpenter, *Six Months at the White House*, p. 30.

620 made time . . . an opera: Grover, "Lincoln's Interest in the Theater," *Century* (1909), p. 947; entry for May 18, 1864, in *Lincoln Day by Day*, Vol. III, p. 259; Schuyler Colfax, *Life and Principles of Abraham Lincoln* (Philadelphia: Jas. B. Rodgers, 1865), p. 12.

620 "People may think . . . it will kill me": AL, quoted in Colfax, *Life and Principles of Abraham Lincoln*, p. 12.

620 "I saw [Lincoln] walk . . . and anxious scrutiny": Colfax in *Reminiscences of Abraham Lincoln*, ed. Rice (1886 edn.), pp. 337–38.

620 "any other General . . . that wins": "9 May 1864, Monday," in Hay, *Inside Lincoln's White House*, p. 195.

620 Lincoln hugged and kissed . . . "no turning back": Henry E. Wing, *When Lincoln Kissed Me: A Story of the Wilderness Campaign* (New York: Eaton & Mains, and Cincinnati: Jennings & Graham, 1913), pp. 12–13, 38–39.

620 "I propose to fight it out . . . all summer": USG to EMS, May 11, 1864, in *Papers of Ulysses S. Grant*, Vol. X, p. 422.

620 Lincoln's face lit up . . . "the secret" to the army's fortunes: *NYT*, May 18, 1864.

621 Chase grew restless . . . retained the hope: Niven, *Salmon P. Chase*, p. 364.

621 Weed had repeatedly warned . . . Treasury employees: JGN to AL, March 30, 1864; TW to AL, March 25, 1864; W. W. Williams to TW, March 25, 1864, Lincoln Papers.

621 corrupt Treasury agents . . . "inevitably sink": TW to FWS, June 2, 1864, reel 84, Seward Papers.

621 Frank Blair had resigned . . . Treasury agent: Leonard B. Wurthman, Jr., "Frank Blair: Lincoln's Congressional Spokesman," *Missouri Historical Review* LXIV (April 1970), pp. 278–79, 284–86; "Charges Against a Member," April 23, 1864, *Congressional Globe*, 38th Cong., 1st sess., pp. 1827–29; Parrish, *Frank Blair*, p. 192.

621 he began by calmly . . . for the presidency: FB remarks before the House of Representatives, April 23, 1864, *Congressional Globe*, 38th Cong., 1st sess., pp. 1828–32 (quote p. 1829).

622 Elizabeth Blair . . . "revenge is suicide": EBL to SPL, April 23 and June 13, 1864, in *Wartime Washington*, ed. Laas, pp. 369, 392.

622 "mendacious slanders": Thomas Heaton to SPC, April 29, 1864, reel 33, Chase Papers.

622 "violent and injudicious . . . with discretion": Entry for April 28, 1864, *Welles diary*, Vol. II, p. 20.

622 told about the speech . . . "approval of the President": Riddle, *Recollection of War Times*, pp. 267, 268.

622 He considered Frank Blair . . . "did while here": James A. Garfield to J. Harrison Rhodes, April 28, 1864, quoted in Smith, *The Life and Letters of James Abram Garfield*, Vol. I, p. 376.

622 Chase told Riddle . . . "perfectly satisfied": Riddle, *Recollection of War Times*, pp. 268, 270–76.

623 "in the midst . . . actual din of battle": Brooks, *Mr. Lincoln's Washington*, p. 325.

623 the National Union Convention: Ibid., pp. 332–33. According to Brooks, twenty-three states "were represented without contest," and the contested delegations of Missouri and Tennessee were allowed to vote. Unofficial representatives from Confederate states and the territories attended but were not included on the official roll.

623 David Davis . . . "no one is necessary": David Davis to AL, June 2, 1864, Lincoln Papers.

624 Horace Greeley . . . "so heavy investments": Horace Greeley, quoted in *Conversations with Lincoln*, ed. Segal, pp. 320–21.

624 "popular instinct . . . the popular will": William Dennison, et al., to AL, June 14, 1864, Lincoln Papers.

624 "the country at large . . . but Lincoln's": Brooks, *Washington, D.C., in Lincoln's Time*, p. 140.

624 gathered in Cleveland's: Waugh, *Reelecting Lincoln*, pp. 177–80.

624 with a platform . . . "among the soldiers": Resolutions of the "Radical Democracy" party platform, quoted in *NYT*, June 1, 1864.

624 in the telegraph office . . . "four hundred men": Bates, *Lincoln in the Telegraph Office*, pp. 194–95 (quote p. 195).

624 "renomination . . . the odd bits of gossip": Brooks, *Washington, D.C., in Lincoln's Time*, p. 141.

625 was initially confronted . . . "short-haired women": Clark E. Carr, quoted in Waugh, *Reelecting Lincoln*, p. 192.

625 the radicals had tacitly . . . unanimous: Ibid., pp. 195, 196.

625 the tumultuous applause . . . "defense of their country": "Platform of the Union National Convention," quoted in note 1 of AL, "Reply to the Committee Notifying Lincoln of His Renomination," June 9, 1864, in *CW*, VII, pp. 381–82.

625 "The enthusiasm . . . Lincoln was spoken": Brooks, *Mr. Lincoln's Washington*, p. 335.

625 "a purge of any" . . . platform in full: Sixth plank of Union Convention platform, paraphrased in Waugh, *Reelecting Lincoln*, p. 193.

625 "Harmony was . . . their kerchiefs": *NR*, June 9, 1864.

625 his towering presence . . . allotted to a single state: Waugh, *Reelecting Lincoln*, pp. 199–200; Brooks, *Mr. Lincoln's Washington*, p. 326.

626 Weed had initially supported . . . the victorious Johnson: Thomas, *Abraham Lincoln*, p. 429.

626 "Stanton's theory . . . the United States": Albert E. H. Johnson, quoted in *New York Evening Post*, July 13, 1891.

626 a clerk handed him a dispatch . . . "a President?": AL, quoted in Carpenter, *Six Months at the White House*, p. 163.

626 "the cart before the horse": *NR*, June 9, 1864.

626 The embarrassed operator . . . "on my return": AL, quoted in Carpenter, *Six Months at the White House*, p. 163.

626 a committee appointed . . . of his nomination: Ibid., p. 166; entry for June 9, 1864, in *Lincoln Day by Day*, Vol. III, p. 263.

626 did not assume . . . " 'when crossing streams' ": AL, "Reply to Delegation from the National Union League," June 9, 1864, in *CW*, VII, pp. 383–84 (quote p. 384).

626 the Ohio delegation . . . "under his command": AL, "Response to a Serenade by the Ohio Delegation," June 9, 1864, in ibid., p. 384.

626 "nothing could defeat . . . like to die of": *NYT*, June 13, 1864.

CHAPTER 24: "ATLANTA IS OURS"

Page

627 "Our troops have . . . but little": Entry for June 20, 1864, *Welles diary*, Vol. II, pp. 54–55.

627 "The immense slaughter . . . sickens us all": Entry for June 2, 1864, ibid., p. 44.

627 "steady courage": Dispatch of June 6, 1864, in Stoddard, *Dispatches from Lincoln's White House*, p. 234.

628 nearly lost his life at Cold Harbor: Janet W. Seward, "Personal Experiences of the Civil War," Seward Papers, NRU.

628 "I cannot yet . . . a holy cause": FAS to William H. Seward, Jr., May 20, 1864, reel 115, Seward Papers.

628 a "righteous" conflict . . . Mexican War: FAS to Augustus Seward, May 15, 1864, reel 115, Seward Papers.

628 "so nervous . . . all night with terror": EBL to SPL, June 19, [1864], in *Wartime Washington*, ed. Laas, p. 394.

628 "grave & anxious": EBL to SPL, June 21, 1864, in ibid., p. 395.

628 if Frank were taken . . . "are politically": EBL to SPL, June 22, 1864, in note 2 of EBL to SPL, June 21, 1864, in ibid., p. 396.

628 Welles was pained . . . "unfit for any labor": Entry for July 20, 1864, *Welles diary*, Vol. II, p. 82.

628 the Great Central Fair in Philadelphia: William Thompson, "Sanitary Fairs of the Civil War," *Civil War History* 4 (March 1958), p. 60; *NR*, June 16, 1864.

628 "miracles as many . . . world of magic": Unknown observer, quoted in Thompson, "Sanitary Fairs of the Civil War," *CWH* 4 (1958), p. 60.

628 Lincoln, Mary, and Tad left: Entry for June 16, 1864, in *Lincoln Day by Day*, Vol. III, p. 265.

628 they were escorted . . . "in Philadelphia": *NR*, June 16 and 17, 1864 (quote June 17).

629 "War, at the best . . . until that time": AL, "Speech at Great Central Sanitary Fair, Philadelphia, Pennsylvania," June 16, 1864, in *CW*, VII, pp. 394, 395.

629 his own "intense anxiety . . . his post here": Entry for June 20, 1864, *Welles diary*, Vol. II, p. 55.

629 Accompanied by Tad . . . of June 20: Entry for June 20, 1864, in *Lincoln Day by Day*, Vol. III, p. 266.

629 "came down from . . . all who met him": Porter, *Campaigning with Grant*, pp. 217, 218.

629 "plain and substantial . . . hero of Vicksburg": *NYH*, June 25, 1864.

629 Lincoln conversed . . . "three capital jokes": Sylvanus Cadwallader, *Three Years with Grant: As Recalled by War Correspondent Sylvanus Cadwallader*, ed. Benjamin P. Thomas (New York: Alfred A. Knopf, 1956), p. 232.

629 Grant suggested a ride . . . "met him on all sides": Porter, *Campaigning with Grant*, p. 218 (quote); *NR*, June 24, 1864.

630 "a long and lingering look": *NYH*, June 25, 1864.

630 passed a brigade . . . "spontaneous outburst": Cadwallader, *Three Years with Grant*, p. 233.

630 "and his voice . . . if he had inherited it": Porter, *Campaigning with Grant*, pp. 222–23.

630 General Grant took Lincoln aside . . . "but I will go in": USG, quoted in entry for June 26, 1864, in Browning, *The Diary of Orville Hickman Browning*, Vol. I, p. 673.

630 "sunburnt and . . . position and good spirits": "23 June 1864, Thursday," in Hay, *Inside Lincoln's White House*, p. 210.

630 regular Friday cabinet meeting . . . "the General and army": Entry for June 24, 1864, *Welles diary*, Vol. II, p. 58.

631 project his own renewed hope . . . "as a commander": *NYTrib*, June 25, 1864.

631 "of the condition . . . terms of confidence": *Philadelphia Inquirer*, June 25, 1864.

631 "Having hope . . . your goals": Daniel Goleman, *Emotional Intelligence* (New York: Bantam Books, 1995), p. 87. Goleman quotes C. R. Snyder in the third quote.

631 "We are today . . . within a year": Brooks, *Mr. Lincoln's Washington*, p. 343.

631 John Cisco . . . own presidential hopes: John G. Nicolay and John Hay, *Abraham Lincoln: A History*, Vol. IX (New York: Century Co., 1917), p. 91.

631 Lincoln told Chase . . . for Maunsell Field: SPC to AL, June 27, 1864, Lincoln Papers.

631 Field was serving . . . "executive character": Chittenden, *Recollections of President Lincoln* (1901 edn.), pp. 371, 374.

632 Chase awoke the morning after . . . to the Ephesians: Entry for June 28, 1864, in *Chase Papers*, Vol. I, pp. 465–66.

632 "Stand therefore . . . righteousness": Ephesians 6:14.

632 "I can not" . . . on another nominee: AL to SPC, June 28, 1864, in *CW*, VII, pp. 412–13.

632 Chase wrote an immediate request: SPC to AL, June 28, 1864, Lincoln Papers.

632 He telegraphed Cisco . . . three months: SPC to John J. Cisco, June 28, 1864, reel 34, Chase Papers; entry for June 28, 1864, in *Chase Papers*, Vol. I, p. 467.

632 "The difficulty . . . open revolt": AL to SPC, June 28, 1864, in *CW*, VII, pp. 413–14.

632 He began his letter . . . "my resignation": John J. Cisco to SPC, June 28, 1864; SPC to AL, June 29, 1864, Lincoln Papers.

633 "I opened it . . . I did not long reflect": AL, quoted in Field, *Memories of Many Men*, pp. 301–02.

633 "You have been acting . . . I will go": "30 June 1864, Thursday," in Hay, *Inside Lincoln's White House*, p. 213.

633 "Your resignation . . . with the public service": AL to SPC, June 30, 1864, in *CW*, VII, p. 419.

633 Lincoln called John Hay . . . the opening prayer: "30 June 1864, Thursday," in Hay, *Inside Lincoln's White House*, p. 212.

633 Lincoln's penitent request . . . he was needed: Field, *Memories of Many Men*, p. 303.

633 After breakfast . . . it had been accepted: *Chase Papers*, Vol. I, pp. 469–70 (quotes p. 470).

634 spoke of "mutual embarrassment": AL to SPC, June 30, 1864, in *CW*, VII, p. 419.

634 "I had found . . . fitness of selection": Entry for June 30, 1864, in *Chase Papers*, Vol. I, p. 470.

634 "his full armor of noble sentiments": Nicolay and Hay, *Abraham Lincoln*, Vol. IX, p. 84.

634 "The Senators were struck" . . . vehement protest: Brooks, *Washington, D.C., in Lincoln's Time*, p. 119.

634 "Fessenden was frightened . . . was mad": AL, quoted in "30 June 1864, Thursday," in Hay, *Inside Lincoln's White House*, p. 213.

634 Lincoln listened patiently . . . "meet each other": Brooks, *Washington, D.C., in Lincoln's Time*, pp. 119–120 (quotes p. 120).

634 Chase had declined to attend: Entry for June 24, 1864, *Welles diary*, Vol. II, p. 58.

634 "unendurable . . . the last straw": Brooks, *Washington, D.C., in Lincoln's Time*, pp. 120, 121.

634 "very nervous & cut up": "30 June 1864, Thursday," in Hay, *Inside Lincoln's White House*, p. 214.

634 Chittenden was equally . . . "thoroughly miserable": AL, quoted in Chittenden, *Recollections of President Lincoln* (1901 edn.), pp. 377–79 (quotes pp. 378–79).

635 Lincoln paused . . . "loftier motives than any man": Ibid., pp. 379–80.

635 a similar remark . . . "of good will": Entry for June 30, 1864, in *Chase Papers*, Vol. I, p. 471.

635 "the great magician . . . financier of his century": *Chicago Tribune*, July 3, 1864.

635 "Mr. Chase is . . . Webster and Calhoun": *NYTrib*, July 1, 1864.

635 he received a telegram . . . reasons of health: David Tod to AL, June 30, 1864, Lincoln Papers.

635 "laid awake . . . public men": Carpenter, *Six Months at the White House*, p. 182.

635 By morning . . . William Pitt Fessenden: Chittenden, *Recollections of President Lincoln* (1901 edn.), p. 381.

635 "First . . . of many radicals": "1 July 1864, Friday," in Hay, *Inside Lincoln's White House*, p. 216.

636 Lincoln handed Hay . . . "at once to the Senate": AL, quoted in "1 July 1864, Friday," in ibid., p. 215.

636 Lincoln greeted Fessenden . . . would kill him: William Pitt Fessenden, quoted in Fessenden, *Life and Public Services of William Pitt Fessenden*, Vol. I, pp. 315–16.

636 "If you decline . . . the nomination": AL, quoted in "1 July 1864, Friday," in Hay, *Inside Lincoln's White House*, p. 216.

636 "Telegrams came pouring . . . the most miserable": William Pitt Fessenden to his cousin, quoted in Fessenden, *Life and Public Services of William Pitt Fessenden*, Vol. I, p. 320.

636 "Very well . . . save your country": EMS, quoted in ibid., p. 321.

636 As he was driven . . . "danger to the country": William Pitt Fessenden to Justice Tenney, quoted in ibid., pp. 317–18.

636 "He is a man . . . personal integrity": *Chicago Tribune*, July 2, 1864.

636 "He is honest . . . Republican Senators": EBL to SPL, July 2, 1864, in *Wartime Washington*, ed. Laas, p. 398.

637 "I am the most popular man in my country": William Pitt Fessenden, in Fessenden, *Life and Public Services of William Pitt Fessenden*, Vol. I, p. 326.

637 "So my official life closes": Entry for June 30, 1864, in *Chase Papers*, Vol. I, p. 471.

637 the oppressive heat of Washington . . . "are wilting": Entry for July 31, 1864, in *The Diary of Edward Bates, 1859–1866*, p. 392.

637 "laid broad foundations" . . . was still unfinished: Entry for June 30, 1864, in *Chase Papers*, Vol. I, p. 471.

637 Blair and Bates called . . . "as a blessing": Entry for June 30, 1864, *Welles diary*, Vol. II, pp. 62–63 (quote p. 63).

637 "the courage and candor to admit his errors": Entry for March 23, 1864, ibid., p. 545.

637 "his jokes are . . . destitute of wit": Entry for March 22, 1864, ibid., p. 545.

637 "a vague feeling . . . to be cordial": Entry for June 30, 1864, in *The Diary of Edward Bates, 1859–1866*, p. 381.

637 "dropped off . . . every body else": FPB to FB, July 4, 1864, quoted in Smith, *The Francis Preston Blair Family in Politics*, Vol. II, p. 271.

637 Seward, unlike . . . "first day of the Administration": WHS to FAS, [July] 2, 1864, quoted in Seward, *Seward at Washington . . . 1861–1872*, p. 230.

637 he noted sadly . . . "since my resignation": Entry for July 13, 1864, in *Chase Papers*, Vol. I, p. 479.

637 If Chase believed . . . he was mistaken: SPC to EMS, June 30, 1864, in Warden, *Private Life and Public Services*, p. 618.

637 Chase searched for reasons . . . "hostile to me": Entry for July 4, 1864, in *Chase Papers*, Vol. I, p. 476.

638 "The root . . . a joke out of this war": SPC to Whitelaw Reid, quoted in Albert Bushnell Hart, *Salmon P. Chase*. American Statesmen Series (Boston and New York: Houghton Mifflin, 1899), p. 318.

638 To Kate . . . "cannot finish what I began": SPC to KCS, July 3, 1864, reel 34, Chase Papers.

638 whose marriage to William . . . "the balance of power": Lamphier, *Kate Chase and William Sprague*, p. 78.

638 "Can it be . . . even with far less material wealth": Entry for November 4, 1868, KCS diary, Sprague Papers (quotes); Lamphier, *Kate Chase and William Sprague*, pp. 74, 84–85.

639 occasionally loathing . . . "learned to submit": Entry for November 11, 1868, KCS diary, Sprague Papers.

639 Chase witnessed a fight . . . her first child: Entry for September 9, 1864, in *Chase Papers*, Vol. I, p. 501 (quote); Belden and Belden, *So Fell the Angels*, pp. 135–36, 144.

639 The Wade-Davis bill: H. R. 244, 38th Cong., 1st sess. ("Wade-Davis Bill"), in *The Radical Republicans and Reconstruction, 1861–1870*, ed. Harold Hyman. American Heritage Series (Indianapolis and New York: Bobbs-Merrill, 1967), pp. 128–34.

639 In a written proclamation . . . single, inflexible system: AL, "Proclamation Concerning Reconstruction," July 8, 1864, in *CW*, VII, p. 433.

640 he likened the Wade-Davis . . . "fit the bedstead": Brooks, *Washington, D.C., in Lincoln's Time*, pp. 156–57.

640 Lincoln understood . . . "fixed within myself": "4 July 1864, Monday," in Hay, *Inside Lincoln's White House*, pp. 218–19.

640 Wade and Davis published . . . manifesto against him: "The Wade-Davis Manifesto, August 5, 1864," in *The Radical Republicans and Reconstruction, 1861–1870*, ed. Hyman, pp. 137–47.

640 He was not surprised by . . . "that can befall a man": Brooks, *Washington, D.C. in Lincoln's Time*, p. 156.

640 The rumors alarmed . . . eager to get started: EBL to SPL, July 6, 1864, in *Wartime Washington*, ed. Laas, p. 400.

640 In a letter to Frank . . . "a remote future": FPB to FB, July 4, 1864, quoted in Smith, *The Francis Preston Blair Family in Politics*, Vol. II, p. 272.

640 admonitions concerned Monty . . . the Pennsylvania countryside: EBL to SPL, July 6, 1864, in *Wartime Washington*, ed. Laas, p. 400.

640 tried to convince her mother . . . "pulled to pieces": EBL to SPL, July 14, 1864, in ibid., p. 403.

641 Grant's decision . . . General Lew Wallace: John Henry Cramer, *Lincoln Under Enemy Fire: The Complete Account of His Experiences During Early's Attack on Washington* (Baton Rouge: Louisiana State University Press, 1948), pp. 2–8.

641 Wallace understood . . . prepared itself for attack: Seward, *Seward at Washington . . . 1861–1872*, p. 231.

641 "The battle lasted . . . superior numbers": Seward, 9th N.Y. Artillery speech, 1912, Seward Papers, NRU.

641 Will's horse . . . have been captured: Seward, *Seward at Washington . . . 1861–1872*, pp. 244–45.

641 Seward spent a tense . . . he had not been captured: Letter to FAS, quoted in Seward, *Seward at Washington . . . 1861–1872*, p. 233 (quote); Lew Wallace to Henry W. Halleck, July 9, 1864, *OR*, Ser. 1, Vol. XXXVII, Part II, p. 145.

641 "God be praised for the safety of our boy": FAS to WHS, July 11, 1864, reel 114, Seward Papers.

641 "With the help . . . rejoining the forces": Seward, *Seward at Washington . . . 1861–1872*, pp. 231–32.

641 Falkland mansion . . . "top to bottom": Mr. Turton, quoted in *National Intelligencer*, reprinted from the *Daily Morning Chronicle*, Washington, D.C., July 16, 1864.

642 "blackened ruin": EBL to SPL, August 5, 1864, quoted in note 2 of EBL to SPL, July 16, 1864, in *Wartime Washington*, ed. Laas, p. 405.

642 the soldiers scattered papers . . . "great frolic" on the lawn: EBL to SPL, July 16 and 31, [1864], in ibid., pp. 404, 413 (quotes).

642 "perfect saturnalia": EBL to SPL, July 31, [1864], in ibid., p. 413.

642 Breckinridge made them . . . "side of the Mts.": EBL to SPL, July 16 and 31, [1864], in ibid., pp. 404, 413 (quote).

642 He explained . . . "refuge & of rest": EBL to SPL, July 16, [1864], in ibid., p. 405.

642 "made more fuss . . . came back to us": EBL to SPL, July 16, [1864], in ibid., pp. 404–05.

642 In his initial panic . . . during the crisis: Thomas and Hyman, *Stanton*, pp. 319–20.

642 "all convalescents . . . and rifle-pits": Henry W. Halleck to George Cadwalader, July 9, 1864, *OR*, Ser. 1, Vol. XXXVII, Part II, p. 153.

642 "in a pleasant and confident humor": "12 July 1864, Tuesday," in Hay, *Inside Lincoln's White House*, p. 222.

642 "in the least concerned . . . force in our front": "11 July 1864, Monday," in ibid., p. 221.

643 "exhibits none . . . on former occasions": Entry for July 11, 1864, *Welles diary*, Vol. II, p. 72.

643 drove together . . . "were not *frightened*": Entry for July 11, 1864, Taft diary.

643 allowing the residents of Washington . . . "troops to the south": Seward, *Reminiscences of a War-Time Statesman and Diplomat*, p. 246.

643 "Before even the first . . . direction of Washington": Jubal A. Early, "The Advance on Washington in 1864. Letter from General J. A. Early," *Southern Historical Society Papers*, Vol. IX, January–December 1881 (Richmond, Va.: Southern Historical Society; Wilmington, N.C.: Broadfoot Publishing Co., Morningside Bookshop, 1990), p. 306.

643 "to be exceedingly . . . impregnable": Jubal Anderson Early, *War Memoirs: Autobiographical Sketch and Narrative of the War Between the States*, ed. Frank E. Vandiver. Civil War Centennial Series (Bloomington: Indiana University Press, 1960), p. 390.

643 at Fort Stevens: Benjamin Franklin Cooling, *Jubal Early's Raid on Washington, 1864* (Baltimore: Nautical & Aviation Publishing Co. of America, 1989), pp. 117–55.

643 "The President evinced . . . standing upon it": Cramer, *Lincoln Under Enemy Fire*, p. 30.

643 "Get down" . . . unusual incident: Oliver Wendell Holmes, Jr., quoted in ibid., p. 22.

643 "was exciting and wild . . . to have occurred": Entry for July 12, 1864, *Welles diary*, Vol. II, pp. 75–76.

644 "an egregious blunder": Charles A. Dana, *Recollections of the Civil War* (New York: Collier Books, 1963), p. 205.

644 Welles knew . . . appeared "contemptible": Entry for July 13, 1864, *Welles diary*, Vol. II, p. 76.

644 "Mrs. Lincoln . . . away as they did!": Carpenter, *Six Months at the White House*, pp. 301–02 (quote p. 302).

644 "I am informed . . . dismissed from the cabinet": Henry W. Halleck to EMS, July 13, 1864, Lincoln Papers.

644 "Whether the remarks . . . shall be dismissed": EMS to AL, July 14, 1864, Lincoln Papers; AL to EMS, July 14, 1864, in *CW*, VII, pp. 439–40 (quote).

645 "It would greatly pain . . . now or hereafter": AL, "Memorandum Read to Cabinet," [July 14?], 186[4], in *CW*, VII, p. 439.

645 Learning that Ben Butler . . . "civilians on either side": MB to Benjamin F. Butler, August 10, 1864, in *Private and Official Correspondence of Gen. Benjamin F. Butler During the Period of the Civil War*. Vol. V: *August 1864–March 1868* (Norwood, Mass.: Plimpton Press, 1917), p. 32 (quote); Cooling, *Jubal Early's Raid on Washington, 1864*, pp. 152–53.

645 "The loss is . . . is unrelieved[?]": MB to R. A. Sloane, July 21, 1864, reel 22, Blair Family Papers, DLC.

645 "The month of August" . . . throughout the North: Brooks, *Lincoln Observed, Civil War Dispatches of Noah Brooks*, ed. Michael Burlingame (Baltimore, Md., and London: Johns Hopkins University Press, 1998), p. 129.

645 mid-July call for five hundred thousand additional volunteers: *NYT*, July 19, 1864.

645 "dissatisfaction . . . with the colors flying": Ibid.

645 An ingenious attempt: See Dorothy L. Drinkard, "Crater, Battle of the (30 July 1864)," in *Encyclopedia of the American Civil War*, ed. Heidler and Heidler, p. 517; McPherson, *Battle Cry of Freedom*, pp. 758–60.

646 "Piled on top . . . frightened sheep": Brooks, *Lincoln Observed*, p. 130.

646 "It was the saddest . . . again to have": USG to Henry W. Halleck, August 1, 1864, *OR*, Ser. 1, Vol. XL, Part I, p. 17.

646 "less however from the result . . . of the future": Entry for August 2, 1864, *Welles diary*, Vol. II, p. 92.

646 he admitted feeling . . . "of our generals": Entry for August 1, 1864, in *The Diary of Edward Bates, 1859–1866*, p. 392.

646 he met with Grant at Fort Monroe: *NYH*, August 3, 1864.

646 dispatched General Philip Sheridan . . . "troops go also": USG to Henry W. Halleck, August 1, 1864, *OR*, Ser. 1, Vol. XXXVII, Part II, p. 558.

646 "This, I think, is exactly right": AL to USG, August 3, 1864, in *CW*, VII, p. 476.

646 "a long and very pleasant . . . both in time": Benjamin B. French to Henry F. French, August 9, 1864, typescript copy, reel 10, French Family Papers, DLC.

646 "much wretchedness . . . in the land": Entry for August 4, 1864, *Welles diary*, Vol. II, p. 93.

646 "The People are wild for Peace": TW to WHS, August 22, 1864, Lincoln Papers.

646 *"two Ambassadors . . . for a peace"*: William C. Jewett to Horace Greeley, July 5, 1864, Lincoln Papers.

646 Urging the president . . . "doing great harm": Horace Greeley to AL, July 7, 1864, Lincoln Papers.

647 commissioned Horace Greeley . . . escort them to Washington: AL to Horace Greeley, July 9, 1864, in *CW*, VII, p. 435.

647 dispatched John Hay to join Greeley: "[ca. 21 July 1864]," in Hay, *Inside Lincoln's White House*, pp. 224–25; "[after 22 July 1864]," in ibid., p. 228; entry for July 18, 1864, in *Lincoln Day by Day*, Vol. III, p. 273.

647 "To Whom it may concern . . . collateral points": AL, "To Whom It May Concern," July 18, 1864, in *CW*, VII, p. 451.

647 the two envoys . . . to stop the war: "[after 22 July 1864]," in Hay, *Inside Lincoln's White House*, p. 228.

647 He hoped the failed mission . . . of freeing the slaves: Eaton, *Grant, Lincoln and the Freedmen*, p. 176; Nicolay and Hay, *Abraham Lincoln*, Vol. IX, pp. 193–94.

647 "are told . . . an impossibility": TW to WHS, August 22, 1864, Lincoln Papers.

647 Swett felt compelled . . . situation was hopeless: Leonard Swett to his wife, September 8, 1864, quoted in Tarbell, *The Life of Abraham Lincoln*, Vol. II (—: S. S. McClure Co., 1895; New York Doubleday & McClure Co., 1900), p. 202.

647 were mystified . . . "his Cabinet": Entry of August 17, 1864, *Welles diary*, Vol. II, p. 109.

648 "I am in active . . . of the Constitution": Henry J. Raymond to AL, August 22, 1864, Lincoln Papers.

648 "I confess that I . . . prosperity to the country": "The Interview between Thad Stevens & Mr. Lincoln as related by Col R. M. Hoe," compiled by JGN, container 10, Nicolay Papers.

648 asked all cabinet members . . . a successful conclusion: "11 November 1864, Friday," in Hay, *Inside Lincoln's White House*, pp. 247–48.

648 "This morning . . . possibly save it afterwards": AL, "Memorandum Concerning His Probable Failure of Re-election," August 23, 1864, in *CW*, VII, p. 514.

648 "was considering" . . . would lend his hand: Eaton, *Grant, Lincoln and the Freedmen*, pp. 173–75 (quotes pp. 173, 175).

649 Douglass met with . . . "within our boundaries": Douglass, *Life and Times of Frederick Douglass*, pp. 796–97.

649 Douglass promised to confer: Frederick Douglass to AL, August 29, 1864, Lincoln Papers.

649 Randall had hand-delivered . . . "Democrats may stand": Charles D. Robinson to AL, August 7, 1864, Lincoln Papers.

650 Lincoln shared a draft: Frederick Douglass to Theodore Tilton, October 15, 1864, in *The Life and Writings of Frederick Douglass*, Vol. III, ed. Foner, p. 423.

650 "To me it seems . . . matter of policy": AL to Charles D. Robinson, [August] 1864, Lincoln Papers.

650 "as it seems you would . . . made the offer supposed": AL to Charles D. Robinson, August 17, 1864, Lincoln Papers.

650 Douglass saw clearly . . . "do you serious damage": Frederick Douglass to Theodore Tilton, October 15, 1864, in *The Life and Writings of Frederick Douglass*, Vol. III, ed. Foner, p. 423.

650 a messenger informed Lincoln . . . "my friend Douglass": AL, quoted in Douglass, "Lincoln and the Colored Troops," in *Reminiscences of Abraham Lincoln*, ed. Rice, p. 320.

650 "suppress his excitement . . . men in America": Eaton, *Grant, Lincoln and the Freedmen*, pp. 175, 176.

651 "The President was free . . . reminiscences of the past": "Interview with Alexander W. Randall and Joseph T. Mills," August 19, 1864, quoted from the diary of Joseph T. Mills, State Historical Society of Wisconsin, Madison, in *CW*, VII, pp. 506–08 (quotes); Pinsker, *Lincoln's Sanctuary*, p. 158.

651 Lincoln permanently shelved the draft: Note 1 of AL to Charles D. Robinson, August 17, 1864, in *CW*, VII, p. 501.

651 Raymond's suggestion . . . "by peaceful modes": AL to Henry J. Raymond, August 24, 1864, in ibid., p. 517.

652 "slept undisturbed" . . . biography of Lincoln: Nicolay and Hay, *Abraham Lincoln*, Vol. IX, p. 221.

652 "a sort of political Bull Run": JGN to TB, August 28, 1864, container 3, Nicolay Papers.

652 "ever present and companionable": Entry for August 19, 1864, *Welles diary*, Vol. II, p. 112.

652 Mary and Tad . . . Vermont: AL to MTL, August 31, September 8 and September 11, 1864, in *CW*, VII, pp. 526, 544, 547.

652 but did not feel he should . . . "than another arises": WHS to FAS, August 27, 1864, quoted in Seward, *Seward at Washington . . . 1861–1872*, p. 241.

652 "the signs of discontent . . . all to disappear": WHS to home, August 16, 1864, quoted in ibid., p. 240.

652 "firm and hopeful": WHS to FAS, August 27, 1864, quoted in ibid., p. 241.

652 Welles observed . . . "an understanding": Entry for August 19, 1864, *Welles diary*, Vol. II, p. 112.

652 the sight of a disabled soldier: Benjamin, "Recollections of Secretary Edwin M. Stanton," *Century* (1887), p. 761.

652 Lincoln invited Raymond . . . "utter ruination": JGN to JH, August 25, 1864, in Nicolay, *With Lincoln in the White House*, p. 152.

652 chairing a meeting . . . mobilize the party: Leonard Swett to his wife, September 8, 1864, quoted in Tarbell, *The Life of Abraham Lincoln*, Vol. II (1900 edn.), pp. 202–03.

652 "the turning-point . . . we are saved": JGN to JH, August 25, 1864, in Nicolay, *With Lincoln in the White House*, p. 152.

653 Nicolay was relieved . . . "encouraged and cheered": JGN memoranda, quoted in Nicolay and Hay, *Abraham Lincoln*, Vol. IX, p. 221.

653 Noting that the members . . . "for the Union party": *NYT*, August 27, 1864.

653 "I happen temporarily . . . an inestimable jewel": AL, "Speech to One Hundred Sixty-sixth Ohio Regiment," August 22, 1864, in *CW*, VII, p. 512.

653 "giants in the . . . of the opposition": JGN to JH, August 25, 1864, in Nicolay, *With Lincoln in the White House*, p. 152.

654 "we have had nothing . . . change all this": Noah Brooks to JGN, August 29, 1864, Lincoln Papers.

654 "They have a peace . . . to rest upon": Waugh, *Reelecting Lincoln*, p. 89.

654 "It was noticeable" . . . virtual silence: Noah Brooks to JGN, August 29, 1864, Lincoln Papers.

654 "His partisans are united . . . their own choice": Brooks, *Mr. Lincoln's Washington*, p. 368.

654 "was expected . . . surrender and abasement": Entry for September 2, 1864, *Diary of George Templeton Strong*, Vol. III, p. 479.

654 the platform declared . . . "cessation of hostilities": "The Democratic National Platform of 1864 (August 29 1864)," in *Encyclopedia of the American Civil War*, ed. Heidler and Heidler, p. 2375.

654 Strong predicted . . . "on such terms": Entry for September 2, 1864, *Diary of George Templeton Strong*, Vol. III, p. 480.

654 "Atlanta is ours, and fairly won": William T. Sherman to Henry W. Halleck, September 3, 1864, *OR*, Ser. 1, Vol. XXXVIII, Part V, p. 777.

655 Lincoln to order that one hundred guns: AL, "Order for Celebration of Victories at Atlanta, Georgia, and Mobile, Alabama," September 3, 1864, in *CW*, VII, p. 532.

655 "Atlanta is ours . . . are ours now": *NYT*, September 5, 1864.

655 the departing Confederates . . . "of military value": McPherson, *Battle Cry of Freedom*, p. 774.

655 "Glorious news . . . event of the war": Entry for September 3, 1864, *Diary of George Templeton Strong*, Vol. III, pp. 480–81.

655 Seward received the news . . . at his house to celebrate: Seward, *Seward at Washington . . . 1861–1872*, p. 242.

655 the crowd swelled . . . "effective speeches": *NYT*, September 6, 1864.

655 the twin victories . . . "perish and leave no root": WHS, quoted in Seward, *Seward at Washington . . . 1861–1872*, pp. 242–44.

655 "For a man of not very" . . . the upcoming campaign: Entry for September 10, 1864, *Welles diary*, Vol. II, p. 140.

656 "This intelligence will . . . on a peace platform": Entry for September 3, 1864, ibid., pp. 135–36.

656 Peace Democrats threatened . . . "their support": Clement L. Vallandigham to GBM, September 4, 1864, reel 36, McClellan Papers, DLC.

656 six drafts . . . midnight on September 8: *Civil War Papers of George B. McClellan*, p. 588; GBM to MEM, [September 9, 1864], ibid., p. 597.

656 He began with a nod . . . "brethren had been in vain": GBM to the Democratic Nomination Committee, September 8, 1864, in *Civil War Papers of George B. McClellan*, pp. 595–96.

656 "We are going to win . . . unite on Mr. Lincoln": Theodore Tilton to JGN, September 6, 1864, Lincoln Papers.

656 believed that God . . . "nearly capsized it": Leonard Swett to his wife, September 8, 1864, quoted in Tarbell, *The Life of Abraham Lincoln*, Vol. II (1900 edn.), p. 203.

656 "conspiracy against Mr. Lincoln collapsed": TW to WHS, September 10, [1864], Lincoln Papers.

657 "to weaken the President . . . now support Lincoln": Entry for September 10, 1864, *Welles diary*, Vol. II, pp. 140–41.

657 Chase stopped en route . . . "judgment of history?": Entry for September 13, 1864, in *Chase Papers*, Vol. I, p. 502.

657 "Mr. Chase had a long . . . at the north": EBL to SPL, September 16, 1864, in *Wartime Washington*, ed. Laas, p. 429.

657 Chase accompanied Stanton . . . with Lincoln: Entry for September 16, 1864, in *Chase Papers*, Vol. I, pp. 503–04.

657 "I have been . . . demonstrative": SPC to KCS, September 17, 1864, reel 35, Chase Papers.

657 "wronged and hurt . . . fidelity to his Administration": Entry for September 17, 1864, in *Inside Lincoln's Cabinet: The Civil War Diaries of Salmon P. Chase*, ed. David Donald (New York: Longmans, Green, 1954), p. 255.

657 "conviction that . . . in securing it": SPC to KCS, September 17, 1864, reel 35, Chase Papers.

657 He traveled . . . before overflowing crowds: Entries for September 24–November 11, 1864, in *Chase Papers*, Vol. I, pp. 507–10.

658 the state elections . . . previous year: JGN to TB, September 11, 1864, container 3, Nicolay Papers; *NYT*, September 13, 1864.

658 "Three weeks ago . . . confident of success": JGN to TB, September 11, 1864, container 3, Nicolay Papers.

658 Philip Sheridan . . . of Early's army: McPherson, *Battle Cry of Freedom*, p. 777.
658 "shouting of Clerks" . . . news became known: Entry for September 20, 1864, in *Chase Papers*, Vol. I, p. 506.
658 "This will do much . . . loving men": Entry for September 20, 1864, *Welles diary*, Vol. II, p. 151.
658 Blair was aware . . . his resignation to Lincoln: MB to Mary Elizabeth Blair, September 23, 1864, quoted in Smith, *The Francis Preston Blair Family in Politics*, Vol. II, p. 288.
658 his father had repeated . . . "an avowed enemy": FPB to FB, quoted in EBL to SPL, September 24, [1864], in *Wartime Washington*, ed. Laas, p. 433.
658 Henry Wilson warned Lincoln . . . "account of the Blairs": Henry Wilson to AL, September 5, 1864, Lincoln Papers.
658 Monty Blair detested Stanton . . . "a thief": "26 September 1864, Monday," in Hay, *Inside Lincoln's White House*, p. 233.
659 "interchanged words for weeks": Entry for August 11, 1864, *Welles diary*, Vol. II, p. 102.
659 when the opportunity arose . . . stayed in the race: William Frank Zornow, *Lincoln & the Party Divided* (Norman: University of Oklahoma Press, 1954), pp. 144–47.
659 Frémont announced his withdrawal: *NYT*, September 23, 1864.
659 "You have generously . . . connection therewith": AL to MB, September 23, 1864, in *CW*, VIII, p. 18. For Blair's resignation letter, see MB to AL, September 23, 1864, Lincoln Papers.
659 Blair was surprised . . . "yielded to that": Entry for September 23, 1864, *Welles diary*, Vol. II, pp. 156–57.
659 Blair had been . . . "irritating bickerings": Addition to entry for September 23, 1864, ibid., p. 158 n1.
659 "In parting with Blair . . . discriminating and correct": Entry for September 23, 1864, ibid., p. 157.
660 "the removal of . . . befallen the Cabinet": Entry for September 27, 1864, ibid., p. 161.
660 did not consider . . . straight-speaking colleague: Entry for August 2, 1864, ibid., p. 93.
660 "I think Mr. Lincoln . . . *malign influences*": Entry for September 23, 1864, in *The Diary of Edward Bates, 1859–1866*, p. 413.
660 "an unnecessary mortification . . . best all around": MB to Mary Elizabeth Blair, September 23, 1864, quoted in Smith, *The Francis Preston Blair Family in Politics*, Vol. II, p. 288.
660 "In my opinion . . . the reelection of Lincoln": FPB to FB, quoted in EBL to SPL, September 24, [1864], in *Wartime Washington*, ed. Laas, p. 433.
660 "somewhat mortifying . . . a penny to make": FB to FPB, September 30, 1864, Lincoln Papers.
660 hearing the noble . . . "fine manly bearing": EBL to SPL, September 24, [1864], in *Wartime Washington*, ed. Laas, p. 434.
660 Monty insisted . . . "father to the President": MB, quoted in *Chicago Tribune*, October 1, 1864.
661 "very handsomely and is doing his utmost": "26 September 1864, Monday," in Hay, *Inside Lincoln's White House*, p. 233.
661 "a grand central rallying point": "11 October 1864, Tuesday," in Hay, *Inside Lincoln's White House*, p. 240.
661 Lincoln made his . . . chief of the telegraph office: Bates, *Lincoln in the Telegraph Office*, pp. 276–77; Charles A. Dana, "Lincoln and the War Department," *Reminiscences of Abraham Lincoln*, ed. Rice, p. 278.
661 Lincoln took from his pocket . . . "a new passage": Dana, "Lincoln and the War Department," in *Reminiscences of Abraham Lincoln*, ed. Rice (1909 edn.), p. 278. "Petroleum Vesuvius Nasby" was the pseudonym of David Ross Locke.
661 "immensely amusing": "11 October 1864, Tuesday," in Hay, *Inside Lincoln's White House*, p. 239.
661 "I shall never forget . . . such frivolous jests": Dana, "Lincoln and the War Department," in *Reminiscences of Abraham Lincoln*, ed. Rice (1909 edn.), pp. 278–79. Dana's recollection is that this episode occurred while Lincoln was waiting for the results of the November presidential election. Other sources, however, suggest that it probably occurred while a larger crowd waited in the telegraph office for results of the state elections in October. Given that Stanton was ill and remained at home during November elections, Dana has probably confused the two dates.
662 the news from Ohio . . . Republican majority: Waugh, *Reelecting Lincoln*, p. 335.
662 In Indiana . . . congressional seats: AL to USG, October 12, 1864, in *CW*, VIII, p. 45.
662 Lincoln sent a telegram . . . "does it stand now?": AL to Simon Cameron, October 11, 1864, in ibid., p. 43.
662 No answer was received . . . "ominous": "11 October 1864, Tuesday," in Hay, *Inside Lincoln's White House*, p. 240.
662 the margin was so close . . . claim a slight margin: Waugh, *Reelecting Lincoln*, p. 336.
662 "Seward was quite exultant . . . has ever known": Entry for October 13, 1864, *Welles diary*, Vol. II, p. 176.
662 Two nights after . . . 117 to 114: Bates, *Lincoln in the Telegraph Office*, pp. 277–79, 282.
662 "the moral effect . . . greatly impaired": McClure, *Abraham Lincoln and Men of War-Times*, p. 202.
662 voters in Maryland . . . making the difference: Waugh, *Reelecting Lincoln*, p. 354.
662 "Most heartily . . . upon the event": AL, "Response to a Serenade," October 19, 1864, in *CW*, VIII, p. 52.
663 "I had rather have . . . cleaned up effectually": AL, quoted in Brooks, *Lincoln Observed*, p. 138.
663 "We are as certain . . . the sun shines": *New York World*, October 14, 1864.
663 "a quarter-million" . . . deposit in their hometowns: William C. Davis, *Lincoln's Men: How President Lincoln became Father to an Army and a Nation* (New York: Free Press, 1999), pp. 214 (quote), 211.
663 had wired General Sherman . . . "no sense, an order": AL to William T. Sherman, September 19, 1864, in *CW*, VIII, p. 11.
663 Stanton followed up . . . "re-election of Mr. Lincoln": Dana, *Recollections of the Civil War* (1963 edn.), p. 227.
664 Weed alerted . . . New Yorkers ready to vote: TW to FWS, October 10, 1864, reel 85, Seward Papers.
664 Lincoln asked Welles . . . "to gather votes": Entry for October 11, 1864, *Welles diary*, Vol. II, p. 175.
664 "I would rather be . . . elected without it": Ida M. Tarbell, *A Reporter for Lincoln: Story of Henry E. Wing, Soldier and Newspaperman* (New York: The Macmillan Company, 1927), p. 70.

664 "before this morning's . . . ceaseless strife": *NYT*, November 8, 1864.

664 "dark and rainy . . . entirely alone": Brooks, *Washington, D.C., in Lincoln's Time*, p. 195.

664 the tenth time . . . beginning of the country: WHS, "Perseverance in War. Auburn, November 7, 1864," in *Works of William H. Seward*, Vol. V, p. 505.

664 Fessenden was in New York . . . with a fever: Brooks, *Washington, D.C., in Lincoln's Time*, p. 195; Brooks, *Mr. Lincoln's Washington*, p. 385.

664 "I am just enough . . . of Tad's quick-wittedness": Brooks, *Washington, D.C., in Lincoln's Time*, p. 196.

665 As the clock struck . . . a supper of fried oysters: "8 November 1864, Tuesday" in *Inside Lincoln's White House*, pp. 243–46.

665 Lincoln's victory was assured . . . separated by about 400,000 votes: Waugh, *Reelecting Lincoln*, p. 354.

666 the results were far better . . . of U.S. senators: Zornow, *Lincoln & the Party Divided*, p. 198.

666 It was after 2 a.m. . . . "tops of their voices": Pratt, *Stanton*, p. 391.

666 "the verdict of the people . . . no dispute": Brooks, *Washington, D.C., in Lincoln's Time*, p. 197.

666 the soldier vote . . . seven out of every ten soldiers: Waugh, *Reelecting Lincoln*, p. 354.

666 the Confederacy was obviously . . . Napoleon would win: Davis, *Lincoln's Men*, p. 210.

666 "The men had come . . . the term implied": Corporal Leander Stillwell, quoted in ibid., p. 226.

CHAPTER 25: "A SACRED EFFORT"

Page

667 immense crowd . . . second-floor window: Brooks, *Washington, D.C., in Lincoln's Time*, p. 200.

667 "undesirable strife . . . a possibility": AL, "Response to a Serenade," November 10, 1864, in *CW*, VIII, p. 101.

667 "in an exceedingly . . . frame of mind": Brooks, *Washington, D.C., in Lincoln's Time*, p. 200.

668 "we will all come . . . United States": WHS, "The Assurance of Victory," November 10, 1864, *Works of William H. Seward*, Vol. V, pp. 513–14.

668 "I advise you . . . my foreign relations": Brooks, *Washington, D.C., in Lincoln's Time*, pp. 200–01.

668 symbolized the animosity . . . the cabinet: William C. Harris, *Lincoln's Last Months* (Cambridge, Mass., and London: Belknap Press of Harvard University Press, 2004), p. 83.

668 Welles even acknowledged . . . "amicable": Entry for November 26, 1864, *Welles diary*, Vol. II, p. 185.

668 Stanton was sounding . . . Reconstruction: Entry for November 25, 1864, ibid., p. 179.

668 asserted that Seward . . . had outlived: *NYT*, November 29, 1864.

668 "His confidence in Seward is great": Entry for September 27, 1864, *Welles diary*, Vol. II, p. 160.

668 "spends more or less . . . the President": Entry for October 1, 1864, ibid., p. 166.

668 "of the gravest . . . and adviser": Entry for July 22, 1864, ibid., p. 84.

669 plan to foster . . . "by contribution": H. P. Livingston to AL, November 14, 1864, Lincoln Papers; AL to WHS, November 17, 1864, endorsement on Livingston to AL, ibid.; WHS to AL, November 17, 1864, endorsement on Livingston to AL, ibid. (quote).

669 Seward had long since . . . "by the President": Seward, *Seward at Washington . . . 1846–1861*, p. 528.

669 "Henceforth . . . of the human race": WHS, quoted in Seward, *Seward at Washington . . . 1861–1872*, p. 250.

669 "looked older . . . long one, perhaps": Benjamin, "Recollections of Secretary Edwin M. Stanton," *Century* (1887), pp. 758, 759–60.

669 letter to Chase . . . "labor and care": EMS to SPC, November 19, 1864, quoted in Thomas and Hyman, *Stanton*, p. 334.

669 unwritten code . . . "felt it necessary": Thomas and Hyman, *Stanton*, p. 390.

669 president's assent . . . "interfere with him": Flower, *Edwin McMasters Stanton*, pp. 369–70.

670 pressed by relatives . . . "circumspection": AL to EMS, March 18, 1864, in *CW*, VII, pp. 254–55.

670 Stanton replied . . . "promptly obeyed": EMS to AL, March 19, 1864, Lincoln Papers.

671 Lincoln looked . . . "his friends": Carpenter, *Six Months at the White House*, p. 172.

671 clerk recalled . . . "wail of anguish": William H. Whiton, quoted in Flower, *Edwin McMasters Stanton*, pp. 418–19.

671 group of Pennsylvania . . . "have to be done": EMS and AL, quoted in Thomas and Hyman, *Stanton*, p. 387.

671 "I send this . . . in this blunder": AL to USG, September 22, 1864, in *CW*, VIII, p. 17.

672 "his firmness . . . into arrogance": Alonzo Rothschild, *Lincoln, Master of Men: A Study in Character* (Boston and New York: Houghton Mifflin, 1906), p. 231.

672 "hard to vote . . . is a ruffian": Entry for September 17, 1864, in *Diary of George Templeton Strong*, Vol. III, p. 489.

672 "Go home . . . be found guilty": Carpenter, *Six Months at the White House*, p. 246.

672 "Folks come up . . . don't know 'em!": AL, quoted in Rothschild, *Lincoln, Master of Men*, p. 285.

672 discreet New Englander . . . "political gossip": Entry for August 31, 1864, *Welles diary*, Vol. II, p. 131.

672 *Times* of London . . . "first class power": *NR*, January 7, 1865.

673 Bates had contemplated . . . "to your age": Barton Bates to EB, May 13, 1864, Bates Papers, MoSHi.

673 prospect of going home . . . "god's blessing": Entry for May 29, 1864, *The Diary of Edward Bates, 1859–1866*, p. 371.

673 Bates believed . . . "as long as I live": EB to AL, November 24, 1864, Lincoln Papers.

673 first months as Attorney General . . . military matters: Entry for December 31, 1861, *The Diary of Edward Bates, 1859–1866*, pp. 218–19; entry for January 10, 1862, ibid., pp. 223–26.

674 deliver a legal opinion . . . "and clothing": EB to AL, July 14, 1864, *OR*, Ser. 3, Vol. IV, pp. 490–93 (quote p. 493).

674 Abolitionists applauded: Entry for May 26, 1864, *The Diary of Edward Bates, 1859–1866*, p. 371.

674 citizenship issue . . . of the United States: Frank J. Williams, "Attorney General Bates and Attorney President Lincoln," R. Gerald McMurtry Lecture, Lincoln Museum, Fort Wayne, Ind., September 23, 2000, author's collection; Cain, *Lincoln's Attorney General*, pp. 222–23.

674 "Though esteemed . . . constitutional interpretation": *Daily Morning Chronicle*, Washington, D.C., December 4, 1864, quoted in *The Diary of Edward Bates, 1859–1866*, p. 430.

674 reveals frustration . . . "no subordination": Entry for October 1, 1861, ibid., p. 196.

674 General Butler . . . arrests in Norfolk: Entry for August 4, 1864, ibid., pp. 393–94.

675 "chief fear . . . easy good nature": Entry for February 13, 1864, ibid., p. 334.

675 troubled at the start . . . "sure to prevail": EB, quoted in Carpenter, *Six Months at the White House*, pp. 68–69.

675 each of his colleagues . . . "affable and kind": Entry for December 2, 1864, *The Diary of Edward Bates, 1859–1866*, p. 429.

675 Bates left . . . "with regret": Entry for November 30, 1864, ibid., p. 428.

675 forever connected . . . "when I am gone": Poem, quoted in entry for October 13, 1864, ibid., p. 419.

675 "My Cabinet . . . would have to be heeded": AL, quoted in Titian J. Coffey, "Lincoln and the Cabinet," in *Reminiscences of Abraham Lincoln*, ed. Rice (1909 edn.), p. 197.

675 Holt declined the offer . . . "personal character": Joseph Holt to AL, December 1, 1864, Lincoln Papers.

676 "I appoint you . . . come on at once": AL to James Speed, in *CW*, VIII, p. 126.

676 "Will leave tomorrow for Washington": James Speed to AL, December 1, 1864, Lincoln Papers.

676 "I am a . . . everywhere forever": James Speed, quoted in Gary Lee Williams, "James and Joshua Speed: Lincoln's Kentucky Friends" (Ph.D. diss., Duke University, 1971), p. 137.

676 "We are less now but true": James Speed to AL, November 25, 1864, quoted in ibid., p. 138.

676 "a man I know . . . ought to know him well": AL, quoted in Coffey, "Lincoln and the Cabinet," in *Reminiscences of Abraham Lincoln*, ed. Rice (1909 edn.), p. 197.

676 Had it been . . . "freely and publicly": David Herbert Donald, *"We Are Lincoln Men": Abraham Lincoln and His Friends* (New York: Simon & Schuster, 2003), p. 38.

676 "You will find . . . by a big office": AL, quoted in Coffey, "Lincoln and the Cabinet," in *Reminiscences of Abraham Lincoln*, ed. Rice (1909 edn.), p. 197.

677 only position . . . "Stanton ever desired": Wolcott, "Edwin M. Stanton," p. 162.

677 "You have been wearing . . . owes it to you": Robert Grier to EMS, October 13, 1864, Stanton Papers, DLC.

677 Ellen Stanton . . . "subject tomorrow": Entry for October 16, 1864, in Browning, *The Diary of Orville Hickman Browning*, Vol. I, p. 687–88.

677 Matthew Simpson . . . "I will do it": AL, quoted in Gideon Stanton, ed., "Edwin M. Stanton."

677 Grant worried . . . stay at his post: Thomas and Hyman, *Stanton*, p. 337.

677 Stanton informed . . . "among candidates": Edwards Pierrepont to AL, November 24, 1864, Lincoln Papers.

677 He "felt that . . . higher ambition": Wolcott, "Edwin M. Stanton," p. 162.

677 "The country cannot . . . fame already": Henry Ward Beecher to EMS, November 30, 1864, quoted in ibid., p. 163.

678 "Often, in dark hours . . . fresh hope": EMS to Henry Ward Beecher, December 4, 1864, quoted in ibid., pp. 163–64.

678 Welles told Lincoln . . . "suppose he would": Entry for November 26, 1864, *Welles diary*, Vol. II, p. 182.

678 taken his son's . . . personal blow: Entry for September 27, 1864, ibid., p. 161.

678 "I beg you to indulge . . . of that Bench": FPB to AL, October 20, 1864, quoted in Smith, *The Francis Preston Blair Family in Politics*, Vol. II, pp. 298–99.

678 "Chase and his friends . . . Chief-Justiceship": MTL, quoted in "If All the Rest Oppose," in *Conversations with Lincoln*, ed. Segal, p. 360.

679 "had been tried . . . stood by him": FPB to John A. Andrew, quoted in ibid., p. 360.

679 "a crowning and retiring honor": Entry for November 22, 1864, *The Diary of Edward Bates, 1859–1866*, p. 428.

679 had "personally solicited": Entry for October 18, 1864, in Browning, *The Diary of Orville Hickman Browning*, Vol. I, p. 688.

679 "If not overborne . . . to private life": Entry for November 22, 1864, *The Diary of Edward Bates, 1859–1866*, pp. 427–28.

679 "Of Mr. Chase's . . . not hesitate a moment": AL, quoted in John G. Nicolay and John Hay, *Abraham Lincoln: A History*, Vol. IX (New York: Century Co., 1890), p. 394.

679 similar comment . . . "life to the Bench": Schuyler Colfax, quoted in Blue, *Salmon P. Chase*, p. 245.

679 "Now, I know . . . men can tell me": Noah Brooks, "Personal Reminiscences of Lincoln," *Scribner's Monthly* 15 (March 1878), p. 677.

679 "we have stood . . . fitness for the office": AL, quoted in Blue, *Salmon P. Chase*, pp. 244–45.

680 Oblivious to Stanton's . . . "life & work": SPC to EMS, October 13, 1864, *Chase Papers*, Vol. IV, p. 434.

680 "I have something . . . will be satisfied": AL and John B. Alley, quoted in John B. Alley, in *Reminiscences of Abraham Lincoln*, ed. Rice (1886 edn.), pp. 581–82.

680 Lincoln later told Senator Chandler . . . "nominated Chase": Entry for December 15, 1864, *Welles diary*, Vol. II, p. 196.

680 "Probably no other . . . of the President": JGN to TB, December 8, 1864, container 3, Nicolay Papers.

680 got the official word . . . "or office": SPC to AL, December 6, 1864, Lincoln Papers.

680 "overflowing with . . . 'So help me God' ": Brooks, *Washington, D.C., in Lincoln's Time*, pp. 175–76.

681 "I hope the President . . . in the court": Entry for December 6, 1864, *Welles diary*, Vol. II, p. 193.

681 Within hours . . . first black barrister: John S. Rock to CS, December 17, 1864, enclosed in CS to SPC, December 21, 1864, in *Selected Letters of Charles Sumner*, Vol. II, ed. Palmer, p. 259 n1 (quote); entry for January 21, 1865, *Chase Papers*, Vol. I, p. 519.

681 Sumner stood before . . . "of this Court": CS, quoted in Quarles, *Lincoln and the Negro*, p. 232.

681 Rock stepped forward . . . "of a great people": *Harper's Weekly*, February 25, 1865.

681 "has been quite . . . with good feeling": MTL to Mercy Levering Conkling, November 19, [1864], in Turner and Turner, *Mary Todd Lincoln*, p. 187.

682 she had been terrified . . . "run in debt": Keckley, *Behind the Scenes*, pp. 147, 149–50 (quotes).

682 exposed her . . . could not curtail: "Mary Todd Lincoln's Unethical Conduct as First Lady," appendix 2, in Hay, *At Lincoln's Side*, pp. 185–205.

682 "Here is the carriage . . . many questions": Entry for December 14, 1864, Taft diary.

682 new dress . . . "kid gloves": Entry for July 3, 1873, Browning diary, quoted in appendix 2, in Hay, *At Lincoln's Side*, p. 187.

682 "I can neither . . . your acting thus": MTL to Ruth Harris, December 28, [1864], in Turner and Turner, *Mary Todd Lincoln*, p. 196.

682 Newspaper reports . . . "tasteful decoration": *NR*, January 10, 1865.

682 "Mrs. Lincoln was . . . throughout": *NR*, February 17, 1865.

683 "Overcoats . . . for safe-keeping": *NR*, January 6, 1865.

683 "a more general . . . and themselves": *NR*, January 10, 1865.

683 "*I* was pleased . . . *two* school boys": MTL to Sally Orne, [December 12, 1869], quoted in Turner and Turner, *Mary Todd Lincoln*, p. 534.

683 lingering grief . . . favorite rooms: Entry for March 31, 1864, Benjamin B. French journal, reel 2, French Family Papers, DLC.

683 "darling Boy! . . . *far* from being": MTL to Hannah Shearer, November 20, 1864, in Turner and Turner, *Mary Todd Lincoln*, p. 189.

683 Lincoln wrote to General Grant . . . "encumbered": AL to USG, January 19, 1865, in *CW*, VIII, p. 223.

684 Grant replied . . . "Military family": USG to AL, January 21, 1865, Lincoln Papers.

684 Stationed at Grant's . . . "of the nation": Porter, *Campaigning with Grant*, pp. 388–89.

684 "passing time and accumulating years": Entry for January 1, 1865, *Welles diary*, Vol. II, p. 218.

684 last surviving . . . buried in Ohio: Entry for January 1, 1865, *Chase Papers*, Vol. I, p. 511.

684 Chase wrote to . . . New Year's reception: SPC to AL, January 2, 1865, Lincoln Papers.

684 "Without your note . . . bereavement": AL to SPC, January 2, 1865, in *CW*, VIII, p. 195.

684 "a great contrast . . . in good spirits": Entry for January 1, 1865, Taft diary.

684 "Our joy . . . Confederacy were numbered": Hugh McCullough, quoted in Thomas and Hyman, *Stanton*, p. 342.

684 "*anxious* . . . than to acquiesce": AL to William T. Sherman, December 26, 1864, in *CW*, VIII, p. 181.

685 "We have destroyed . . . for six months": FB to FPB, December 16, 1864, quoted in Smith, *The Francis Preston Blair Family in Politics*, Vol. II, p. 180.

685 also paid tribute . . . "great light": AL to William T. Sherman, December 26, 1864, in *CW*, VIII, p. 182.

685 telegram announcing . . . "candle in his hand": Bates, *Lincoln in the Telegraph Office*, pp. 316–17 (quotes p. 317).

685 Fort Fisher . . . "rebels from abroad": *NR*, January 17, 1865 (quote); *NR*, January 18, 1865.

685 at the cabinet . . . "President was happy": Entry for January 17, 1865, *Welles diary*, Vol. II, p. 227.

685 Stephens considered . . . "or Atlanta": Alexander H. Stephens, *A Constitutional View of the Late War Between the States*, Vol. II (Philadelphia: National Publishing Company, 1870), p. 619.

685 nearly every other . . . munitions and supplies: Ibid., p. 620.

685 was in Savannah . . . "delivered to [him]": EMS to AL, quoted in *NR*, January 18, 1865.

685 journeyed to North Carolina . . . "the *real* Stanton": Mrs. Rufus Saxton, quoted in Flower, *Edwin McMasters Stanton*, p. 420.

686 confer with Sherman . . . "*criminal* dislike": Sherman, *Memoirs of General W. T. Sherman*, pp. 604–07; Henry W. Halleck to William Sherman, December 30, 1865, *OR*, Ser. 1, Vol. XLIV, p. 836 (quote).

686 Sherman countered . . . "our substance": William T. Sherman to SPC, January 11, 1865, in *The Salmon P. Chase Papers*, Vol. 5: *Correspondence, 1865–1873*, ed. John Niven (Kent, Ohio, and London, England: Kent State University Press, 1998), pp. 6–7.

686 "Special Field Orders . . . tillable ground": Sherman, *Memoirs of General W. T. Sherman*, p. 609; Special Field Orders, No. 15, Headquarters, Military Division of the Mississippi, January 16, 1865, *OR*, Ser. I, Vol. XLVII, Part II, pp. 60–62.

686 Freedmen's Bureau . . . the South: Foner, *Reconstruction*, pp. 68–69.

686 "A question might . . . all the evils": AL, "Response to a Serenade," February 1, 1865, in *CW*, VIII, p. 254.

686 previous spring . . . party lines: "Thirteenth Amendment," in Neely, *The Abraham Lincoln Encyclopedia*, p. 308.

686 annual message . . . bipartisan unity: AL, "Annual Message to Congress," December 6, 1864, in *CW*, VIII, p. 149.

687 "I have sent for you . . . border state vote": AL, quoted by James S. Rollins, "The King's Cure-All for All Evils," in *Conversations with Lincoln*, ed. Segal, pp. 363–64.

687 assigned two . . . "procure those votes": AL, quoted in John B. Alley, in *Reminiscences of Abraham Lincoln*, ed. Rice (1886 edn.), pp. 585–86.

687 powers extended . . . in New York: "Thirteenth Amendment," in Neely, *The Abraham Lincoln Encyclopedia*, p. 308.

687 Elizabeth Blair noted . . . several members: EBL to SPL, January 31, 1865, in *Wartime Washington*, ed. Laas, p. 469.

687 Ashley learned . . . "the more resolute": AL, quoted in JGN memorandum, January 18, 1865, in Nicolay, *With Lincoln in the White House*, pp. 171, 257 n11.

688 leader of the . . . "political associates": Blaine, *Twenty Years of Congress*, p. 537.

688 Democrats who considered changing: Harris, *Lincoln's Last Months*, p. 128.

688 "We are like whalers . . . into eternity": AL, quoted in John G. Nicolay and John Hay, *Abraham Lincoln: A History*, Vol. X (New York: Century Co., 1890), p. 74.

688 Rumors circulated . . . "have failed": AL and James M. Ashley correspondence, quoted in James M. Ashley to WHH, November 23, 1866, in *HI*, pp. 413–14.

688 "never before . . . within hearing": *Address of Hon. J. M. Ashley, before the Ohio Society of New York*, February 19, 1899 (privately published), p. 21.

688 Chief Justice Chase . . . foreign ministries: Brooks, *Washington, D.C., in Lincoln's Time*, pp. 185–86; *Address of Hon. J. M. Ashley*, p. 21.

689 McAllister . . . "Southern Confederacy": Brooks, *Washington, D.C., in Lincoln's Time*, p. 186.

689 brought forth applause . . . "without a murmur": Alexander Coffroth, quoted in Carl Sandburg, *Abraham Lincoln: The War Years*, Vol. IV (New York: Harcourt, Brace & Company, 1939), p. 10.

689 "Hundreds of tally" . . . votes short: *Address of Hon. J. M. Ashley*, pp. 23–24.

689 Colfax stood . . . "Resolution has passed": Brooks, *Washington, D.C., in Lincoln's Time*, pp. 186–87.

689 five Democrats . . . would have lost: Harris, *Lincoln's Last Months*, p. 132.

689 "For a moment . . . ever heard before": Brooks, *Washington, D.C., in Lincoln's Time*, p. 187.

689 "Before the members . . . had passed": Arnold, *The Life of Abraham Lincoln*, p. 365.

689 Ashley brought . . . "great honor": EMS, quoted in Flower, *Edwin McMasters Stanton*, p. 190.

689 "The passage . . . emancipation proclamation": Arnold, *The Life of Abraham Lincoln*, pp. 365–66.

689 "The occasion was . . . They will do it": AL, "Response to a Serenade," February 1, 1865, in *CW*, VIII, p. 254.

689 legislatures in twenty . . . had spoken: "Thirteenth Amendment," in Neely, *The Abraham Lincoln Encyclopedia*, p. 308.

690 "And to whom . . . to Abraham Lincoln!": William Lloyd Garrison, quoted in Nicolay and Hay, *Abraham Lincoln*, Vol. X, p. 79n.

690 remained unconvinced . . . a pass: AL, pass for FPB, December 28, 1864, Lincoln Papers.

690 proceeding on . . . "without reserve": FPB to Jefferson Davis, December 30, 1864, Lincoln Papers.

690 arrived in Richmond . . . "around him": *NR*, January 19, 1865.

690 "Oh you Rascal . . . to see you": EBL to SPL, January 16, 1865, in *Wartime Washington*, ed. Laas, p. 463.

690 "might be the dreams . . . in his prayers": FPB, memorandum of conversation with Jefferson Davis [January 12, 1865], Lincoln Papers.

690 his proposal . . . allied against the French: FPB, address made to Jefferson Davis [January 12, 1865], Lincoln Papers.

691 Davis agreed . . . "a Foreign Power": FPB, memorandum of conversation with Jefferson Davis [January 12, 1865], Lincoln Papers.

691 Davis agreed to send . . . "two Countries": Jefferson Davis to FPB, January 12, 1865, Lincoln Papers.

691 Lincoln consulted . . . immediately agreed: EMS, quoted in Flower, *Edwin McMasters Stanton*, p. 257.

691 "You may say . . . one common country": AL to FPB, January 18, 1865, in *CW*, VIII, pp. 220–21.

691 Davis called a cabinet . . . Campbell: Davis, *Jefferson Davis*, p. 590.

691 flag of truce . . . the commissioners: *Philadelphia Inquirer*, February 3, 1865.

691 "By common consent . . . a gala day": *NYH*, February 4, 1865.

691 "harbingers of peace . . . common sentiment": *NR*, February 3, 1865.

691 "It was night . . . throughout the country": Stephens, *A Constitutional View of the Late War*, pp. 597–98.

692 Seward headed south . . . "sincere liberality": AL to WHS, January 31, 1865, in *CW*, VIII, p. 250.

692 "convinced" . . . meet with them personally: USG to EMS, February 1, 1865, Lincoln Papers.

692 "Induced by a despatch of Gen. Grant": AL to WHS, February 2, 1865, in *CW*, VIII, p. 256.

692 "Say to the gentlemen . . . can get there": AL to USG, February 2, 1865, in ibid.

692 a single valet . . . Annapolis: *NYH*, February 3, 1865.

692 "supposed to be" . . . little past ten: *NYH*, February 5, 1865.

692 Lincoln joined Seward . . . *River Queen*: *NYT*, February 6, 1865.

692 saloon of . . . "streamers and flags": Stephens, *A Constitutional View of the Late War*, p. 599; *NYT*, February 6, 1865 (quote).

693 Stephens opened . . . "Sections of the country?": Stephens, *A Constitutional View of the Late War*, p. 599.

693 "was altogether . . . was written or read": Seward, *Seward at Washington . . . 1861–1872*, p. 260.

693 "steward, who came" . . . agreement on any issue: Stephens, *A Constitutional View of the Late War*, pp. 619, 600–01, 612, 613, 609, 617.

694 radicals had worked . . . excoriated him: Brooks, *Washington, D.C., in Lincoln's Time*, p. 202.

694 "the leading members . . . will dishonor us": *NYT*, February 3, 1865.

694 Both branches . . . on the proceedings: Brooks, *Washington, D.C., in Lincoln's Time*, pp. 203–04.

694 Stanton worried . . . "serve their purpose": Bates, *Lincoln in the Telegraph Office*, p. 338.

694 Lincoln's report . . . "given to Seward": Brooks, *Lincoln Observed*, pp. 162–63.

694 "as the reading . . . President Lincoln": Brooks, *Washington, D.C., in Lincoln's Time*, pp. 207, 208.

694 "Indeed . . . than Abraham Lincoln": *Harper's Weekly*, February 25, 1865.

695 employed the failed . . . slavery intact: *Richmond Dispatch*, February 7, 1865, quoted in Nicolay and Hay, *Abraham Lincoln*, Vol. X, p. 130.

695 "I can have . . . element of my nature!": Jefferson Davis, quoted in *NR*, February 13, 1865.

695 drafted a proposal . . . "executive control": AL, "To the Senate and House of Representatives," February 5, 1865, in *CW*, VIII, pp. 260–61.

695 unanimous disapproval . . . "adverse feeling": Entry for February 6, 1865, *Welles diary*, Vol. II, p. 237.

695 Usher believed . . . "assault on the President": J. P. Usher, quoted in Nicolay, *An Oral History of Abraham Lincoln*, p. 66.

695 Stanton had long maintained . . . "compensation for slaves": Flower, *Edwin McMasters Stanton*, p. 258.

695 Fessenden declared . . . "come from us": William Pitt Fessenden, quoted in Francis Fessenden, *Life and Public Services of William Pitt Fessenden*, Vol. II (Boston and New York: Houghton, Mifflin, 1907), p. 8.

695 sum he proposed . . . "approved the measure": J. P. Usher, quoted in Nicolay, *An Oral History of Abraham Lincoln*, p. 66.

696 Sherman had headed north . . . on February 17: Entry for February 17, 1865, in Long, *The Civil War Day by Day*, pp. 639–40.

696 Stanton ordered . . . "parts of the city": *NR*, February 22, 1865.

696 "cheerful . . . brightest day in four years": Entry for February 22, 1865, *Welles Diary*, Vol. II, p. 245.

696 "more depressed" . . . in the four years: Entry for February 23, 1865, in *The Diary of Orville Hickman Browning*, Vol. II, 1865–1881, ed. Theodore Calvin Pease and James G. Randall; *Collections of the Illinois State Historical Library*, Vol. XXII (Springfield: Illinois State Historical Library, 1933), p. 8.

696 low spirits . . . "brigand, and pirate": Jonathan Truman Dorris, *Pardon and Amnesty Under Lincoln and Johnson: The Restoration of the Confederates to Their Rights and Privileges, 1861–1898* (Chapel Hill: University of North Carolina Press, 1953), pp. 76–78 (quote p. 77).

696 "I had to stand . . . out of my mind yet": Henry P. H. Bromwell, quoted in *Recollected Words of Abraham Lincoln*, ed. Don E. Fehrenbacher and Virginia Fehrenbacher (Stanford, Calif.: Stanford University Press, 1996), p. 41.

697 he would "not receive . . . seven o'clock p.m.": *NR*, March 2, 1865.

697 "The hopeful condition" . . . the capital: *NR*, March 1, 1865.

697 so overcrowded . . . "found for them": *NR*, March 3, 1865.

697 Douglass decided . . . "of other citizens": Douglass, *Life and Times of Frederick Douglass*, p. 803.

697 visited Chase's . . . "a strange thing": Ibid., pp. 799–800.

697 steady rain . . . foreign ministries: Brooks, *Washington, D.C., in Lincoln's Time*, pp. 210–11; Brooks, *Mr. Lincoln's Washington*, pp. 418, 420 (quote).

697 "One ambassador . . . feet on the floor": Brooks, *Mr. Lincoln's Washington*, p. 421.

697 Johnson rose . . . "extraordinarily red": Brooks, *Washington, D.C., in Lincoln's Time*, p. 211.

697 "in a state of manifest . . . a petrified man": Brooks, *Mr. Lincoln's Washington*, pp. 422, 423.

698 "All this is . . . drunk or crazy": Entry for March 4, 1865, *Welles diary*, Vol. II, p. 252.

698 Dennison . . . "serene as summer": Brooks, *Mr. Lincoln's Washington*, pp. 423–24.

698 "emotion on . . . revisiting the Senate": Entry for March 4, 1865, *Welles diary*, Vol. II, p. 252.

698 Lincoln listened . . . harangue to end: Brooks, *Mr. Lincoln's Washington*, p. 423.

698 his eyes shut: Marquis de Chambrun [Charles Adolphe Pineton], "Personal Recollections of Mr. Lincoln," *Scribner's* 13 (January 1893), p. 26.

698 "You need not . . . a drunkard": AL, as quoted by Hugh McCullough in *Recollected Words of Abraham Lincoln*, p. 320.

698 audience proceeded . . . "glory and light": Brooks, *Mr. Lincoln's Washington*, pp. 424, 425 (quote).

698 an auspicious omen . . . Freedom: Brooks, *Washington, D.C., in Lincoln's Time*, pp. 213, 20–21.

698 "Both read the same . . . this terrible war": AL, "Second Inaugural Address," March 4, 1865, in *CW*, VIII, p. 333. For a thorough discussion of Lincoln's Second Inaugural Address, see Ronald C. White, *Lincoln's Greatest Speech: The Second Inaugural* (New York: Simon & Schuster, 2002).

699 "the eloquence of the prophets": Chambrun, "Personal Recollections of Mr. Lincoln," *Scribner's*, p. 27.

699 "Fondly do we hope . . . with all nations": AL, "Second Inaugural Address," March 4, 1865, in *CW*, VIII, pp. 332–33.

699 "as he became . . . Church member": Leonard Swett to WHH, January 17, 1866, in *HI*, pp. 167–68.

699 crowd cheered . . . drew to a close: *Boston Daily Evening Transcript*, March 4, 1865.

699 "the largest crowd . . . been here yet": JGN to TB, March 5, 1865, container 3, Nicolay Papers.

699 president was . . . five thousand people: *Star*, March 6, 1865.

699 "It was a grand . . . every 4 minutes": Entry for March 5, 1865, in French, *Witness to the Young Republic*, p. 466.

700 "On reaching the door . . . you liked it!": Douglass, *Life and Times of Frederick Douglass*, pp. 803–04.

700 his own assessment . . . "Almighty and them": AL to TW, March 15, 1865, *CW*, VIII, p. 356.

700 *New York World* . . . "statesmanship": *New York World*, March 6, 1865, quoted in Harris, *Lincoln's Last Months*, p. 149.

700 *Tribune* charged . . . chance for peace: *NYTrib*, March 6, 1865, quoted in Harris, p. 150.

701 "That rail-splitting . . . keynote of this war": Charles Francis Adams, Jr., to Charles Francis Adams, Sr., quoted in Harris, *Lincoln's Last Months*, p. 148.

701 London *Spectator* . . . "village lawyer": London *Spectator*, March 25, 1865, quoted in *Lincoln As They Saw Him*, ed. Herbert Mitgang (New York and Toronto: Rinehart & Company, Inc., 1956), pp. 447, 446.

701 Arnold overheard . . . Seward himself: Harris, *Lincoln's Last Months*, p. 148.

701 "The President's . . . position in history": Arnold, *The Life of Abraham Lincoln*, pp. 404–05.

701 "He has called . . . sickening to the heart": *Charleston [S.C.] Mercury*, January 10, 1865, reprinted in *Liberator*, March 3, 1865.

701 "it was always plain . . . judicious and appropriate": Charles A. Dana, quoted in Hay, "Life in the White House in the Time of Lincoln," *Century* (1890), p. 36.

CHAPTER 26: THE FINAL WEEKS

Page

702 "he was in mind . . . all-sufficing strength": Hay, "Life in the White House in the Time of Lincoln," *Century* (1890), p. 37.

703 "a tired spot": Brooks, *Mr. Lincoln's Washington*, p. 161.

703 avoid the thousands . . . "Egyptian locusts": JGN to TB, March 5, 1865, in Nicolay, *With Lincoln in the White House*, p. 175.

703 "The bare thought . . . *crush* me": AL, quoted in Carpenter, *Six Months at the White House*, p. 276.

703 "they don't want . . . must see them": AL, quoted in Hay, "Life in the White House in the Time of Lincoln," *Century* (1890), p. 33.

703 "I think now . . . *nineteen* enemies": AL, quoted in Carpenter, *Six Months at the White House*, p. 276.

703 hope that consul . . . wished to help: AL to WHS, March 6, 1865, *CW*, VIII, p. 337.

703 "at all times . . . of public trusts": AL to Winfield Scott and others, March 1, 1865, *CW*, VIII, p. 327.

704 Fessenden had been assured . . . "with regret": Fessenden, *Life and Public Services of William Pitt Fessenden*, Vol. I, pp. 365, 367 (quote).

704 "I desire gratefully . . . this great people": William Pitt Fessenden to AL, quoted in Fessenden, *Life and Public Services of William Pitt Fessenden*, Vol. I, p. 366.

704 he was nervous . . . "never sorry": Hugh McCulloch, *Men and Measures of Half a Century: Sketches and Comments* (New York: Charles Scribner's Sons, 1888; 1900), pp. 193–94.

704 intended to replace Usher: "Usher, John Palmer," in Neely, *The Abraham Lincoln Encyclopedia*, p. 317.

704 Hay was particularly adept . . . "his influence": William Leete Stone, quoted by Michael Burlingame, in introduction to Hay, *Inside Lincoln's White House*, p. xiii.

704 Nicolay functioned . . . and New York: Donald, *"We Are Lincoln Men,"* p. 209.

704 Hay was chosen . . . reconstruction of Florida: "Hay, John Milton," in Neely, *The Abraham Lincoln Encyclopedia*, p. 149.

705 had come to believe . . . "the hand of God": JH to JGN, August 7, 1863, in Hay, *At Lincoln's Side*, p. 49 (quote); "Hay, John Milton," in Neely, *The Abraham Lincoln Encyclopedia*, p. 149.

705 If the "patent . . . blinking eyes": JH to WHH, September 5, 1866, in *HI*, p. 332.

705 contemplating the purchase of a newspaper: Nicolay, *Lincoln's Secretary*, p. 224.

705 Mary had enlisted . . . Noah Brooks: Anson G. Henry to his wife, March 13, 1865, in *Concerning Mr. Lincoln*, comp. Pratt, p. 117.

705 tried to talk . . . any such discussion: JGN to TB, quoted in Nicolay, *Lincoln's Secretary*, p. 223.

705 Seward found . . . dissenting vote: *NR*, quoted in ibid., p. 224.

705 position paid . . . start married life: JGN to TB, March 12, 1865, quoted in ibid., p. 225.

706 Hay had recognized . . . "personal preeminence": "Hay's Reminiscences of the Civil War," in Hay, *At Lincoln's Side*, p. 129.

706 arranged for Hay . . . for another month: JH to Charles Hay, March 31, 1865, in Hay, *At Lincoln's Side*, p. 103.

706 "It will be . . . at the same time": JGN to TB, quoted in Nicolay, *Lincoln's Secretary*, p. 227.

706 "We are having . . . laid aside": MTL to Abram Wakeman, March 20, [1865], in Turner and Turner, *Mary Todd Lincoln*, pp. 205–06.

706 note to Sumner . . . "familiar to me": MTL to CS, March 23, 1865, in ibid., p. 209.

706 "an emotional temperament . . . heart would break": Helm, *The True Story of Mary*, p. 32.

706 an incident . . . "giving me up the key": Carpenter, *Six Months at the White House*, pp. 91–92.

707 "so full of life . . . little sprite": *NYTrib*, July 17, 1871.

707 Grant had issued . . . "to be asked": *The Personal Memoirs of Julia Dent Grant (Mrs. Ulysses S. Grant)*, ed. John Y. Simon (New York: G. P. Putnam's Sons, 1975), p. 141.

707 "Can you not . . . would do you good": USG to AL, March 20, 1865, Lincoln Papers.

707 Fox was not happy . . . "making the journey": John S. Barnes, "With Lincoln from Washington to Richmond in 1865," Part 1, *Appleton's* 9 (June 1907), p. 519.

707 ordered John Barnes . . . "very funny terms": Ibid., pp. 517–20.

708 presidential party . . . Wharf at Sixth Street: Entry for March 23, 1865, in *Lincoln Day by Day*, Vol. III, p. 322.

708 Stanton had been laid up . . . minutes after: Thomas and Hyman, *Stanton*, p. 350.

708 "a hurricane swept over the city": *Star*, February 15, 1896.

708 "terrific squalls . . . and its driver": *NYH*, March 24, 1865.

708 "while down the river . . . great violence": *Star*, February 15, 1896.

708 Stanton went . . . "at Point Lookout": EMS to AL, March 23, 1865, Lincoln Papers.

708 Tad raced around . . . "delicious fish": William H. Crook, "Lincoln as I Knew Him," *Harper's Monthly* 115 (May/June 1907), p. 46.

709 "loved so well": MTL to Francis B. Carpenter, November 15, [1865], in Turner and Turner, *Mary Todd Lincoln*, p. 284.

709 "it was after . . . headquarters at the top": Crook, "Lincoln as I Knew Him," *Harper's Monthly* (1907), p. 46.

709 Robert Lincoln . . . "was awaiting": *Personal Memoirs of Julia Dent Grant*, p. 142.

709 men went into . . . talked late into the night: Crook, "Lincoln as I Knew Him," *Harper's Monthly* (1907), pp. 46, 47.

709 While the Lincolns . . . original line: Shelby Foote, *The Civil War: A Narrative.* Vol. III: *Red River to Appomattox* (New York: Random House, 1958; New York: Vintage Books, 1986), pp. 838, 840–45.

710 walked up the bluff . . . "ruin of homes": Barnes, "With Lincoln from Washington to Richmond in 1865," Part 1, *Appleton's* (1907), pp. 521–22.

710 "I am here . . . states—1600": AL to EMS, March 25, 1865, *CW*, VIII, p. 374.

710 Stanton replied . . . " 'further off' ": EMS to AL, March 25, 1865, Lincoln Papers.

710 Lincoln's presence . . . "of their triumphs": *NYH*, March 28, 1865.

710 Lincoln seemed . . . "anecdotes": Porter, *Campaigning with Grant*, p. 407.

710 "Mr. President . . . old grudge against England to stand": USG and AL, quoted in Porter, *Campaigning with Grant*, pp. 408–9.

711 Porter's naval flotilla . . . "Come along!": Barnes, "With Lincoln from Washington to Richmond in 1865," Part 1, *Appleton's* (1907), pp. 522–23.

711 ambulance carrying . . . "ark of refuge": Porter, *Campaigning with Grant*, pp. 413–14 (quotes p. 414).

712 saw the attractive . . . "shocked and horrified": Adam Badeau, quoted in Foote, *The Civil War*, Vol. III, p. 847.

712 "was always that . . . impressed by it": John S. Barnes, "With Lincoln from Washington to Richmond in 1865," Part II, *Appleton's* (1907), p. 743.

712 had no desire . . . irrational outburst: Randall, *Mary Lincoln*, pp. 372–74.

712 Sherman was on his way . . . final push: William T. Sherman to Isaac N. Arnold, November 28, 1872, in Arnold, *The Life of Abraham Lincoln*, p. 421.

712 "their hands locked" . . . *River Queen:* Porter, *Campaigning with Grant*, pp. 417–18, 419.

712 greeted Sherman . . . depend upon the actions: William T. Sherman to Isaac N. Arnold, November 28, 1872, in Arnold, *The Life of Abraham Lincoln*, pp. 421–22.

713 long talk with Lincoln . . . "their shops": Sherman, *Memoirs of General W. T. Sherman*, p. 682.

713 "Let them have . . . to the laws": AL, quoted in David D. Porter, *Incidents and Anecdotes of the Civil War* (New York: D. Appleton and Company, 1886), p. 314.

713 privately wished . . . "goodness, than any other": Sherman, *Memoirs of General W. T. Sherman*, pp. 682–83.

713 walked to the railroad . . . "bless you all!": AL, quoted in Porter, *Campaigning with Grant*, pp. 425–26.

714 "I think . . . the wisest course": Entry for March 30, 1865, *Welles diary*, Vol. II, p. 269.

714 "We presume . . . palpable to be doubted": *NYTrib*, March 30, 1865.

714 "change of air & rest": MTL to CS, March 23, 1865, in Turner and Turner, *Mary Todd Lincoln*, p. 209.

714 "to escape the . . . pressure of visitors": *Philadelphia Inquirer*, March 24, 1865.

714 underscore his directive . . . "own hands": EMS to USG, March 3, 1865, *CW*, VIII, pp. 330–31.

714 "I begin to feel . . . little had been done": AL to EMS, March 30, 1865, ibid., p. 377.

714 "I hope you will . . . All well here": EMS to AL, March 31, 1865, ibid., p. 378 n1.

715 accompanied Mary . . . was well: Entry for April 1, 1865, in *Lincoln Day by Day*, Vol. III, p. 324; Randall, *Mary Lincoln*, p. 374.

715 "overwhelmingly charming . . . astounding person": Carl Schurz to his wife, April 2, 1865, in Schurz, *Intimate Letters of Carl Schurz, 1841–1869*, pp. 326–27.

715 "the flash of the cannon . . . in his that night": *Through Five Administrations: Reminiscences of Colonel William H. Crook, Body-Guard to President Lincoln*, ed. Margarita Spalding Gerry (New York and London: Harper & Brothers, 1910), p. 47.

715 broken through Petersburg's . . . and Richmond: Foote, *The Civil War*, Vol. III, pp. 876–80.

715 Lincoln received . . . "12,000 prisoners": AL to MTL, April 2, 1865, *CW*, VIII, p. 384.

715 Lincoln had moved . . . "a foot sideways": AL, quoted in Porter, *Incidents and Anecdotes of the Civil War*, pp. 284–85.

716 "a comfortable . . . yard in front": Porter, *Campaigning with Grant*, p. 449.

716 battlefields, littered . . . "lines of sadness": *Through Five Administrations*, ed. Gerry, p. 48.

716 "dismounted in the street" . . . strolled by: Porter, *Campaigning with Grant*, pp. 450, 451.

716 Grant surmised . . . "and cut him off": Grant, *Personal Memoirs of U. S. Grant*, p. 559.

716 back at City Point . . . "nightmare is gone": AL, quoted in Porter, *Incidents and Anecdotes of the Civil War*, p. 294.

716 in his customary pew . . . "retreating that evening": Davis, *Jefferson Davis*, p. 603; Jefferson Davis to Varina Davis, quoted in Robert McElroy, *Jefferson Davis: The Unreal and the Real* (New York and London: Harper & Brothers, 1937; New York: Smithmark, 1995), p. 454 (quote).

716 "Thereupon . . . all eyes in the house": *NYTrib*, April 8, 1865.

716 Summoning his cabinet . . . west to Danville: Davis, *Jefferson Davis*, p. 604.

716 small fire . . . "three-quarters of a mile": Charles A. Dana to EMS, April 6, 1865, *OR*, Ser. 1, Vol. XLVI, Part III, p. 594.

717 All the public buildings . . . were destroyed: *NYTrib*, April 8, 1865.

717 leaving only . . . the Spotswood Hotel: Charles A. Dana to EMS, April 6, 1865, *OR*, Ser. 1, Vol. XLVI, Part III, p. 594.

717 "Here is . . . Richmond has fallen": Bates, *Lincoln in the Telegraph Office*, pp. 360–61.

717 "spread by a thousand mouths": *Star*, April 3, 1865.

717 "almost by magic . . . fullness of their joy": Brooks, *Washington, D.C.*, in *Lincoln's Time*, p. 219.

717 "wept as children . . . vows of friendship": *NYH*, April 4, 1865.

717 crowd called for Stanton . . . "his emotion": *Star*, February 15, 1896.
717 "gratitude to Almighty . . . with their blood": EMS, quoted in Brooks, *Washington, D.C., in Lincoln's Time*, p. 220.
717 "so overcome by emotion . . . speak continuously": Ibid.
717 Seward . . . "Secretary of War as this": WHS, quoted in ibid., p. 221.
717 crowd erupted . . . "loud and lusty" cheers: *NR*, April 3, 1865.
717 "beaming" Stanton . . . "The Star Spangled Banner": *NYTrib*, April 4, 1865.
717 "The demand seemed . . . press to supply": *Star*, April 3, 1865.
717 One hundred *Herald* . . . section of the city: *NYH*, April 4, 1865.
718 EXTRA! . . . first to enter the city: *NR*, April 3, 1865.
718 eight hundred guns, fired at Stanton's order: Brooks, *Mr. Lincoln's Washington*, p. 431.
718 dinner at Stanton's house: Thomas and Hyman, *Stanton*, p. 353.
718 "if there were to be . . . of the danger": James Speed to Joseph H. Barrett, 1885 September 16, Lincoln Collection, Lincoln Miscellaneous Manuscripts, Box 9, Folder 66, Special Collections, Research Center, University of Chicago Library.
718 tried to keep Lincoln . . . "the same condition": EMS to AL, April 3, 1865, Lincoln Papers.
718 Lincoln was already . . . Richmond the next day: AL to EMS, April 3, 1865, *CW*, VIII, p. 385.
718 At 8 a.m. . . . historic journey to Richmond: Barnes, "With Lincoln from Washington to Richmond in 1865," Part II, *Appleton's* (1907), p. 746.
718 channel approaching . . . "and touched them": *Through Five Administrations*, ed. Gerry, pp. 51–52.
718 "Here we were . . . well to be humble": AL, quoted in Porter, *Incidents and Anecdotes of the Civil War*, pp. 294–95.
719 Lincoln was surrounded . . . "hereafter enjoy": Ibid., p. 295.
719 men stood up . . . "and from the water-side": Ibid., pp. 296–97.
719 crowd trailed Lincoln . . . easily visible: Ibid., p. 299.
719 "walking with his usual . . . in everything": Thomas Thatcher Graves, "The Occupation," Part II of "The Fall of Richmond," in *Battles and Leaders of the Civil War*, Vol. IV, Pt. II, p. 727 (quote); Porter, *Incidents and Anecdotes of the Civil War*, p. 299; *Through Five Administrations*, ed. Gerry, p. 53.
719 Lincoln's bodyguard . . . along the route: *Through Five Administrations*, ed. Gerry, p. 54.
719 occupied the stucco mansion . . . glass of water: Barnes, "With Lincoln from Washington to Richmond in 1865," Part II, *Appleton's* (1907), pp. 748–49.
719 bottle of whiskey . . . "condition for the Yankees": *Through Five Administrations*, ed. Gerry, p. 55.
719 toured the mansion . . . "interested in everything": Graves, "The Occupation," in *Battles and Leaders of the Civil War*, Vol. IV, Pt. II, p. 728.
719 met with the members . . . troops from the war: J. G. Randall and Richard N. Current, *Lincoln the President: The Last Full Measure*, originally published as Vol. 4 of *Lincoln the President* (New York: Dodd, Mead, 1955; Urbana: University of Illinois Press, 1991), pp. 353–56; AL to Godfrey Weitzel, April 6, 1865, *CW*, VIII, p. 389.
720 Confederate statehouse . . . greatly relieved: Porter, *Incidents and Anecdotes of the Civil War*, pp. 302–03.
720 "nothing short of miraculous . . . go in peace": *Through Five Administrations*, ed. Gerry, p. 54.
720 all the public buildings . . . "one blaze of glory": Brooks, *Mr. Lincoln's Washington*, p. 434.
720 "the entire population . . . of lighted candles": *NR*, April 5, 1865.
720 he told Welles . . . "schemes are his apology": Entry for April 5, 1865, *Welles diary*, Vol. II, p. 275.
720 Fanny and her friend . . . horses bolted: Seward, *Seward at Washington . . . 1861–1872*, p. 270 (quote); entry for April 5, 1865, in Johnson, "Sensitivity and Civil War," p. 867; *NR*, April 6, 1865.
720 "swinging the driver . . . a cat by the tail": *NR*, April 6, 1865.
720 Fred and Seward jumped . . . consciousness: Seward, *Seward at Washington . . . 1861–1872*, p. 270 (quote); entry for April 5, 1865, in Johnson, "Sensitivity and Civil War," pp. 867–68; Verdi, "The Assassination of the Sewards," *The Republic* (1873), p. 290.
720 "The horses tore" . . . his broken body: Entry for April 5, 1865, in Johnson, "Sensitivity and Civil War," pp. 867–68.
721 "blood streaming from his mouth": Verdi, "The Assassination of the Sewards," *The Republic* (1873), p. 290.
721 delirious with pain . . . his side for hours: Entry for April 5, 1865, in Johnson, "Sensitivity and Civil War," pp. 868, 869.
721 Stanton sent . . . "presence here is needed": EMS to AL, April 5, 1865, Lincoln Papers.
721 Lincoln advised Grant . . . return to Washington: AL to USG, April 6, 1865, *CW*, VIII, p. 388.
721 Mary and her invited . . . "arrive at City Point": MTL to EMS, April 6, 1865, in Turner and Turner, *Mary Todd Lincoln*, p. 214 (quote); Foote, *The Civil War*, Vol. III, p. 903; Keckley, *Behind the Scenes*, p. 163.
721 Stanton informed . . . "remaining at City Point": EMS to MTL, April 6, 1865, Lincoln Papers.
721 he sent word . . . "clear and spirits good": EMS to AL, April 6, 1865, Lincoln Papers.
721 Mary's party arrived . . . bulletins, all positive: Chambrun, "Personal Recollections of Mr. Lincoln," *Scribner's* (1893), p. 27.
721 "His whole appearance . . . had been attained": James Harlan, quoted in Foote, *The Civil War*, Vol. III, P874r. 903.
721 "it was impossible . . . much less of vanity": Chambrun, "Personal Recollections of Mr. Lincoln," *Scribner's* (1893), p. 28.
722 telegram from Sheridan . . . "Lee will surrender": Phil Sheridan to USG, quoted in AL to EMS, April 7, 1865, *CW*, VIII, p. 389.
722 "Let the *thing* be pressed": AL to USG, April 7, 1865, *CW*, VIII, p. 392.

722 Julia Grant . . . "that we be not judged": *Personal Memoirs of Julia Dent Grant*, p. 149; Chambrun, "Personal Recollections of Mr. Lincoln," *Scribner's* (1893), p. 33 (quote).

722 "he gave orders . . . the great oaks": Chambrun, "Personal Recollections of Mr. Lincoln," *Scribner's* (1893), p. 29 (quote); Keckley, *Behind the Scenes*, p. 169.

722 "an old country . . . quiet place like this": AL, quoted in Arnold, *The Life of Abraham Lincoln*, p. 435.

722 observed a turtle . . . shared "a happy laugh": Keckley, *Behind the Scenes*, p. 170.

722 visited injured soldiers . . . "no more fighting": Chambrun, "Personal Recollections of Mr. Lincoln," *Scribner's* (1893), pp. 30, 33–34.

722 came to say farewell . . . "floating palace": Keckley, *Behind the Scenes*, pp. 171–72.

723 asked them to play . . . "upon literary subjects": Chambrun, "Personal Recollections of Mr. Lincoln," *Scribner's* (1893), pp. 34, 35.

723 "a beautiful quarto . . . in his hands": Edward L. Pierce, *Memoir and Letters of Charles Sumner*, Vol. IV (London: Sampson Low, Marston and Co., 1893), p. 235.

723 passages from *Macbeth* . . . *touch him further*: William Shakespeare, *Macbeth*, Scene II, in *The Riverside Shakespeare*, 2nd edn., Vol. II (Boston and New York: Houghton Mifflin, 1997), p. 1373; Chambrun, "Personal Recollections of Mr. Lincoln," *Scribner's* (1893), p. 35.

723 "how true a description . . . the same scene": Chambrun, "Personal Recollections of Mr. Lincoln," *Scribner's* (1893), p. 35.

723 ominous selection . . . "in continual dread": Speed to Barrett, September 16, 1885, University of Chicago Library.

723 "that the people know . . . without fear": AL, quoted in Thomas and Hyman, *Stanton*, p. 395.

723 passed by Mount Vernon . . . "would again reappear": Chambrun, "Personal Recollections of Mr. Lincoln," *Scribner's* (1893), pp. 35, 32.

724 He had observed . . . "in ruined Richmond": *Through Five Administrations*, ed. Gerry, p. 59.

724 "It was in the evening . . . injuries and the shock": Seward, *Seward at Washington . . . 1861–1872*, pp. 271, 270.

724 his face "so marred . . . patient and uncomplaining": FAS to LW, quoted in ibid., p. 271.

724 "The extreme sensitiveness . . . from the door": Seward, ibid., p. 271.

724 Lincoln entered the room . . . "the end, at last": WHS and AL, quoted in ibid., p. 271.

724 stretched out . . . "satisfied at the labor": Seward, *Seward at Washington . . . 1861–1872*, p. 271; entry for April 9, 1865, in Johnson, "Sensitivity and Civil War," p. 872 (quotes).

725 saw that Seward . . . got up and left the room: Seward, *Seward at Washington . . . 1861–1872*, p. 272.

725 telegram from Grant . . . "proposed by myself": USG to EMS, April 9, 1865, *OR*, Ser. 1, Vol. XLVI, Part III, p. 663.

725 "the President hugged him with joy": *Star*, February 15, 1896.

725 close to 10 p.m. . . . "first time in my life": Entry for April 9, 1865, in Johnson, "Sensitivity and Civil War," p. 871.

725 Both Grant and Lee . . . "dignified in defeat": Jay Winik, *April 1865: The Month That Saved America* (New York: HarperCollins, 2001), p. 193.

725 Grant had sent a note . . . "effusion of blood": USG to Robert E. Lee, April 7, 1865, *OR*, Ser. 1, Vol. XLVI, Part III, p. 619.

725 Lee refused to accept . . . ready to surrender: McPherson, *Battle Cry of Freedom*, p. 848.

725 dressed for the historic . . . "deep, red silk": Douglas Southall Freeman, *R. E. Lee: A Biography*, Vol. IV (New York: Charles Scribner's Sons, 1936), p. 118.

725 imprisoned before . . . "my best appearance": Robert E. Lee, quoted in ibid., p. 118.

725 terms of surrender . . . "properly exchanged": USG to Robert E. Lee, April 9, 1865, quoted in Grant, *Personal Memoirs of U.S. Grant*, p. 581.

725 "the thought occurred to me" . . . twenty-five thousand men: Grant, *Personal Memoirs of U.S. Grant*, pp. 581–83.

726 tried to speak . . . "tears came into his eyes": Freeman, *R. E. Lee*, Vol. IV, p. 144.

726 "Men, we have fought . . . best I could for you": Robert E. Lee, quoted in ibid.

726 "each side of . . . as ever, General Lee!": Charles Blackford, quoted in ibid. pp. 146, 147.

726 "a great boom . . . laid down its arms": Brooks, *Washington, D.C., in Lincoln's Time*, p. 223.

726 "The nation seems . . . terminates the Rebellion": Entry for April 10, 1865, *Welles diary*, Vol. II, p. 278.

726 several thousand gathered . . . "people cheered": *National Intelligencer*, Washington, D.C., April 11, 1865, quoted in *CW*, VIII, p. 393 n1.

726 planning a speech . . . "dribble it all out": AL, "Response to Serenade," *National Intelligencer* version, April 10, 1865, *CW*, VIII, p. 393.

726 If he said something . . . "not to make mistakes": AL, "Response to Serenade," *NR* version, April 10, 1865, *CW*, VIII, p. 394.

726 finally appeared . . . "waving their handkerchiefs": *NR*, April 11, 1865.

727 "I am very greatly . . . with its performance": AL, "Response to Serenade," *National Intelligencer* version, April 10, 1865, *CW*, VIII, p. 393.

727 "it is good to show the rebels . . . hear it again": Chambrun, "Personal Recollections of Mr. Lincoln," *Scribner's* (1893), p. 34.

727 tune followed "Dixie" . . . "in high good-humor": *Through Five Administrations*, ed. Gerry, p. 62 (quote); *National Intelligencer*, April 11, 1865, in *CW*, VIII, pp. 393–94 n1.

727 "If possible . . . than last Monday": MTL to CS, April 10, 1865, in Turner and Turner, *Mary Todd Lincoln*, p. 216.

727 exhilaration was evident . . . "qu'en pensez vous?": MTL to CS, April 11, 1865, in ibid., p. 217.

727 Illuminated once again . . . miles around: Brooks, *Washington, D.C., in Lincoln's Time*, p. 225.

727 "Bonfires blazed . . . rockets were fired": *NYTrib*, April 12, 1865.

727 decorating the front . . . "and evergreens": *Star*, February 15, 1896.

727 a second-story window . . . "of a different character": Brooks, *Washington, D.C., in Lincoln's Time*, pp. 226–27.

727 "the greatest question . . . practical statesmanship": "31 July 1863, Friday," in Hay, *Inside Lincoln's White House*, p. 69.

728 acknowledged that in Louisiana . . . "by smashing it?": AL, "Last Public Address," April 11, 1865, *CW*, VIII, pp. 403–04.

728 John Wilkes Booth . . . passion for the rebels' cause: Lockridge, *Darling of Misfortune*, p. 111.

728 evolved a plan to kidnap . . . not ready to yield: Michael W. Kauffman, *American Brutus: John Wilkes Booth and the Lincoln Conspiracies* (New York: Random House, 2004), pp. 134, 211–12.

728 "Our cause being almost . . . great must be done": Text of John Wilkes Booth diary, available through Abraham Lincoln research website, http://members/aol.com/RVSNorton1/Lincoln52.html (accessed May 2005).

728 Two other conspirators . . . "put him through": John Wilkes Booth, quoted in Donald, *Lincoln*, p. 588.

728 Curiously . . . "God knows what is best": Lamon, *Recollections of Abraham Lincoln*, pp. 116–18.

729 Fehrenbacher is persuasive . . . confused: Commentary on Lamon recollection, *Recollected Words of Abraham Lincoln*, ed. Fehrenbacher and Fehrenbacher, p. 293.

729 While radicals . . . control of the seceded states: Pierce, *Memoir and Letters of Charles Sumner*, Vol. IV, p. 236; SPC to AL, April 12, 1865, Lincoln Papers.

729 "a large majority of the people": *NYH*, quoted in Harris, *Lincoln's Last Months*, p. 216.

729 "Reunion . . . in the minds of men": Brooks, *Washington, D.C., in Lincoln's Time*, p. 228.

729 "there must be . . . robber bands and guerillas": Entry for April 13, 1865, *Welles diary*, Vol. II, p. 279.

729 Lincoln had hoped . . . "their own work": Ibid.

729 "that to place . . . bring trouble with Congress": A. E. H. Johnson, quoted in Flower, *Edwin McMasters Stanton*, p. 272.

729 Stanton insisted . . . "absolutely null and void": EMS, quoted in ibid., p. 271.

729 Speed expressed his accord . . . with Lincoln: Williams, "James and Joshua Speed," p. 148.

730 confessed to Welles . . . tremendously: Gideon Welles, "Lincoln and Johnson," *Galaxy* 13 (April 1872), p. 524.

730 "doubted the policy . . . correct it if he had": Entry for April 13, 1865, *Welles diary*, Vol. II, pp. 279–80.

730 telegram from Campbell . . . originally discussed: John A. Campbell to Godfrey Weitzel, April 7, 1865, *CW*, VIII, pp. 407–08 n1.

730 Lincoln walked over . . . "any specific acts": A. E. H. Johnson, quoted in Flower, *Edwin McMasters Stanton*, p. 272.

730 Lincoln stood up . . . "safe-return to their homes": AL to Godfrey Weitzel, April 12, 1865, *CW*, VIII, p. 407 (quote); EMS, in Flower, *Edwin McMasters Stanton*, p. 271.

730 "that . . . was exactly right": Ibid.

730 "As we reached . . . 'candles from my department' ": *Personal Memoirs of Julia Dent Grant*, pp. 153, 154.

731 received a delightful note . . . "drive with me!": MTL to Mary Jane Welles, July 11, 1865, in Turner and Turner, *Mary Todd Lincoln*, p. 257.

731 "We are rejoicing . . . glorious victories": MTL to James Gordon Bennett, [April 13, 1865], in ibid., p. 219.

731 "charming time . . . into a lad of sixteen": MTL to Abram Wakeman, April 13, [1865], in ibid., p. 220.

731 told Sumner . . . a visit with General Grant: MTL to CS, [April] 13, [1865], in ibid., p. 219.

731 "Well, my son . . . for a long while": Keckley, *Behind the Scenes*, pp. 137–38.

731 Grant arrived . . . this event would be favorable: Entry for April 14, 1865, *Welles diary*, Vol. II, pp. 282–83.

732 Stanton had drafted . . . "asked me to read it": EMS, quoted in Flower, *Edwin McMasters Stanton*, p. 301.

732 cabinet concurred . . . two separate states: Entry for April 14, 1865, *Welles diary*, Vol. II, p. 281; Nicolay and Hay, *Abraham Lincoln*, Vol. X (1890 edn.), p. 284.

732 "he thought it providential . . . harmony and union": Gideon Welles, "Lincoln and Johnson," *Galaxy* 13 (April 1872), p. 526.

732 "Didn't our Chief . . . hair and whiskers": Speed to Barrett, September 16, 1885, Lincoln Collection, University of Chicago Library.

732 Lincoln seemed "more cheerful . . . at home and abroad": EMS to Charles Francis Adams, April 15, 1865, Telegrams Sent by the Secretary of War, pp. 185–186, December 27, 1864–April 20, 1865, Telegrams Collected by the Office of the Secretary of War (Bound) (National Archives Microfilm Publication M-473, reel 88), Records of the Office of the Secretary of War, RG 107, DNA.

732 "spoke very kindly . . . of the Confederacy": EMS to John A. Dix, April 15, 1865, *OR*, Ser. 1, Vol. XLVI, Part III, p. 780.

732 "in marked degree . . . distinguished him": EMS to Charles Francis Adams, April 15, 1865 (M-473, reel 88), RG 107, DNA.

732 "a conspicuous . . . best to let him run": Dana, *Recollection of the Civil War* (1996 edn.), pp. 273–74.

733 She had never seen . . . " 'been very miserable' ": MTL to Francis B. Carpenter, November 15, [1865], in Turner and Turner, *Mary Todd Lincoln*, pp. 284–85.

733 "he spoke of his old . . . riding the circuit": Arnold, *The Life of Abraham Lincoln*, pp. 429–30.

733 hoped to travel . . . back home to Illinois: MTL interview, [September 1866], in *HI*, p. 359; Randall, *Mary Lincoln*, p. 382.

733 group of old friends . . . "to dinner at once": Tarbell, *The Life of Abraham Lincoln*, Vol. II (1900 edn.), p. 235.

734 met with Noah Brooks . . . "its pleasures": AL, quoted in Hollister, *Life of Schuyler Colfax*, p. 252.

734 invited Colfax to join . . . that night: Ibid., p. 253.

734 "more hopeful . . . nearly so with gold": Brooks, *Mr. Lincoln's Washington*, p. 443.
734 *Republican* had announced . . . box that night: *NR*, April 14, 1865.
734 Julia Grant . . . asked to be excused: Grant, *Personal Memoirs of U. S. Grant*, p. 592; *Personal Memoirs of Julia Dent Grant*, p. 155.
734 The Stantons also declined: Thomas and Hyman, *Stanton*, p. 395.
734 "unwilling to encourage . . . poker over his arm": Bates, *Lincoln in the Telegraph Office*, p. 367.
734 "I suppose it's time . . . would rather stay": AL, quoted in Hollister, *Life of Schuyler Colfax*, p. 253.
734 "It has been advertised . . . disappoint the people": AL, quoted in *Through Five Administrations*, p. 67.
735 Booth had devised a plan . . . assassinate the president: Kauffman, *American Brutus*, pp. 212–15.
735 Booth believed he would be . . . "greater tyrant": Text of John Wilkes Booth diary, available through Abraham Lincoln research website, http://members/aol.com/RVSNorton1/Lincoln52.html (accessed May 2005).
735 "Booth knew . . . martyr of Caesar": Kauffman, *American Brutus*, p. 212.
735 slept well the previous . . . "for the first time": Entry for April 14, 1865, in Johnson, "Sensitivity and Civil War," p. 876.
735 "listened with a look . . . the Cabinet meeting": Seward, *Reminiscences of a War-Time Statesman and Diplomat*, p. 258.
735 Fanny's reading . . . how much he enjoyed it: Entry for April 14, 1865, in Johnson, "Sensitivity and Civil War," p. 876.
735 Stanton had stopped by . . . serenading him: Thomas and Hyman, *Stanton*, p. 396.
736 "quiet arrangements" . . . opposite side of the bed: Entry for April 14, 1865, in Johnson, "Sensitivity and Civil War," p. 877.
736 "there seemed nothing unusual . . . presented himself": Seward, *Reminiscences of a War-Time Statesman and Diplomat*, p. 258.
736 Powell told the servant . . . but Fred refused: Verdi, "The Assassination of the Sewards," *The Republic* (1873), p. 293.
736 "stood apparently irresolute . . . pulled the trigger": Seward, *Reminiscences of a War-Time Statesman and Diplomat*, p. 259.
736 last memory Fred would have . . . unconscious: *Cincinnati [Ohio] Commercial*, December 8, 1865.
736 Private Robinson . . . headed toward Seward: Charles F. Cooney, "Seward's Savior: George F. Robinson," *Lincoln Herald* (Fall 1973), p. 93.
736 begging him not to kill . . . "face bending over": Entry for April 14, 1865, in Johnson, "Sensitivity and Civil War," pp. 879–80.
736 large bowie knife . . . "loose on his neck": Verdi, "The Assassination of the Sewards," *The Republic* (1873), p. 291.
736 his only impressions . . . "overcoat is made of": WHS, quoted in *Cincinnati [Ohio] Commercial*, December 8, 1865.
736 Fanny's screams . . . the floor: Entry for April 14, 1865, in Johnson, "Sensitivity and Civil War," p. 880.
737 managed to pull Powell away . . . the right hand: Verdi, "The Assassination of the Sewards," *The Republic* (1873), p. 292.
737 Gus ran for his pistol . . . fled through the city: Seward, *Seward at Washington . . . 1861–1872*, p. 279.
737 lifted Seward onto the bed . . . rooms on the parlor floor: Entry for April 14, 1865, in Johnson, "Sensitivity and Civil War," pp. 882, 884.
737 "He looked like an . . . yes, of one man!": Verdi, "The Assassination of the Sewards," *The Republic* (1873), pp. 291–92.
738 Atzerodt had taken a room . . . "not to kill": Donald, *Lincoln*, p. 596.
738 seated at the bar . . . and never returned: Winik, *April 1865*, p. 226.
738 had attended a dress rehearsal . . . Harry Ford: Kauffman, *American Brutus*, pp. 214, 217.
738 play had started . . . "with a smile and bow": Charles A. Leale, M.D., to Benjamin F. Butler, July 20, 1867, container 43, Butler Papers, DLC.
738 armchair at the center . . . sofa on her left: "Major Rathbone's Affidavit," in J. E. Buckingham, Sr., *Reminiscences and Souvenirs of the Assassination of Abraham Lincoln* (Washington, D.C.: Rufus H. Darby, 1894), pp. 73, 75.
738 "rested her hand . . . situation on the stage": Charles Sabin Taft, "Abraham Lincoln's Last Hours," *Century* 45 (February 1893), p. 634.
738 later recalled . . . "think any thing about it": Randall, *Mary Lincoln*, p. 382.
738 footman delivered a message . . . and fired: Winik, *April 1865*, p. 223; Harris, *Lincoln's Last Months*, p. 224.
739 "As he jumped . . . struck the stage": Taft, "Abraham Lincoln's Last Hours," *Century* 45 (1893), p. 634.
739 "he was suffering . . . he struggled up": Annie F. F. Wright, "The Assassination of Abraham Lincoln," *Magazine of History* 9 (February 9, 1909), p. 114.
739 "his shining dagger . . . it had been a diamond": Leale to Butler, July 20, 1867, container 43, Butler Papers, DLC.
739 shouted . . . "Sic semper tyrannis": Wright, "The Assassination of Abraham Lincoln," *Magazine of History* (1909), p. 114.
739 saw Mary Lincoln . . . "shot the President!": Ibid.
739 Charles Leale . . . pressure on Lincoln's brain: Leale to Butler, July 20, 1867, container 43, Butler Papers, DLC.
739 Charles Sabin Taft . . . boardinghouse: Taft, "Abraham Lincoln's Last Hours," *Century* 45 (1893), p. 635.
739 Joseph Sterling . . . headed for Seward's house: Joseph A. Sterling, quoted in *Star*, April 14, 1918.
740 already gone to bed . . . set forth in the foggy night: Entry for April 14, 1865, *Welles diary*, Vol. II, pp. 283–84.

740 Blood was everywhere . . . floor of the bedroom: Entry for April 14, 1865, in Johnson, "Sensitivity and Civil War," p. 886.

740 "was saturated with blood" . . . he decided to join them: Entry for April 14, 1865, *Welles diary*, Vol. II, pp. 285–86 (quote p. 285).

740 Chase had already retired . . . "a night of horrors": Entries for April 14, 1865, *Chase Papers*, Vol. 1, pp. 528–29.

741 Lincoln had been placed . . . "spare appearance": Entry for April 14, 1865, *Welles diary*, Vol. II, p. 286.

741 "would have killed most men . . . *much vitality*": Entry for April 30, 1865, Taft diary.

741 Mary spent most . . . "overcome by emotion": Entry for April 14, 1865, *Welles diary*, Vol. II, p. 287.

741 "Why didn't he shoot me?" . . . not told, out of fear: Field, *Memories of Many Men*, p. 322.

741 "clean napkins . . . stains on the pillow": Taft, "Abraham Lincoln's Last Hours," *Century* 45 (1893), p. 635.

741 Robert, who had remained . . . "leaving his cheeks": Thomas F. Pendel, *Thirty-Six Years in the White House* (Washington, D.C.: Neale Publishing Company, 1902), pp. 42–43.

741 to summon Tad . . . his father's condition: Leale to Butler, July 20, 1867, container 43, Butler Papers, DLC.

741 Tad and his tutor . . . to see *Aladdin:* M. Helen Palmes Moss, "Lincoln and Wilkes Booth as Seen on the Day of the Assassination," *Century* LXXVII (April 1909), p. 951.

741 decorated with patriotic . . . "shrieking in agony": *NR*, April 15, 1865.

742 "Poor little Tad . . . fell into a sound sleep": Pendel, *Thirty-Six Years in the White House*, p. 44.

742 entire cabinet . . . "heartrending lamentations": *NYH*, April 16, 1865.

742 "there was not a soul . . . love the president": *Star*, February 15, 1896.

742 "While evidently swayed . . . in all things": A. F. Rockwell, quoted in Flower, *Edwin McMasters Stanton*, p. 283.

742 dictated numerous dispatches . . . "wait for the next": *Star*, February 15, 1896.

742 first telegram . . . "in a dangerous condition": Thomas T. Eckert to USG, April 14, 1865, *OR*, Ser. 1, Vol. XLVI, Part III, pp. 744–45.

742 reached Grant . . . "in perfect silence": Porter, *Campaigning with Grant*, p. 499.

742 he had turned "very pale": *Personal Memoirs of Julia Dent Grant*, p. 156.

742 Julia Grant guessed . . . "that could be received": Porter, *Campaigning with Grant*, pp. 499–500.

742 he told Julia . . . "tenderness and magnanimity": *Personal Memoirs of Julia Dent Grant*, p. 156.

743 At 1 a.m., Stanton telegraphed . . . "best detectives": EMS to John H. Kennedy, April 15, 1865, *OR*, Ser. 1, Vol. XLVI, Part III, p. 783.

743 "The wound is mortal . . . is now dying": EMS to John A. Dix, April 15, 1865, 1:30 a.m., *OR*, Ser. 1, Vol. XLVI, Part III, p. 780.

743 "The President continues . . . shot the President": Ibid., 4:10 a.m., p. 781.

743 Shortly after dawn . . . "death-struggle had begun": Entry for April 14, 1865, *Welles diary*, Vol. II, p. 288.

743 "As she entered" . . . sofa in the parlor: Taft, "Abraham Lincoln's Last Hours," *Century* 45 (1893), p. 635.

743 "the town clocks . . . be again resumed": Field, *Memories of Many Men*, p. 325.

743 "Let us pray" . . . everyone present knelt: Leale to Butler, July 20, 1867, container 43, Butler Papers, DLC.

743 At 7:22 a.m. . . . "belongs to the ages": Donald, *Lincoln*, p. 599. As David Donald notes, witnesses thought they heard several variations of Stanton's utterance, including "He belongs to the ages now," "He now belongs to the Ages," and "He is a man for the ages." Donald, *Lincoln*, p. 686, endnote for p. 599 beginning *"to the ages."*

743 "Oh, why did you not . . . he was dying": *NYH*, April 16, 1865.

743 moans could be heard . . . taken to her carriage: Taft, "Abraham Lincoln's Last Hours," *Century* 45 (1893), p. 636; Field, *Memories of Many Men*, p. 326.

743 Stanton's "coolness" . . . streamed down his cheeks: *NYH*, April 16, 1865.

743 "Stanton's grief . . . break down and weep bitterly": Porter, *Campaigning with Grant*, p. 501.

743 "Not everyone knows . . . his honor and yours": JH to EMS, July 26, 1865, in Hay, *At Lincoln's Side*, p. 106.

744 "Is he dead? . . . entire face was distorted": Field, *Memories of Many Men*, p. 327.

744 walked to Seward's house . . . Blair and his father: Entry for April 15, 1865, *Chase Papers*, Vol. I, pp. 529, 530.

744 "with tearful eyes . . . of our side": EBL to SPL, April 15, 1865, in *Wartime Washington*, ed. Laas, p. 495.

744 *Richmond Whig* . . . "South has descended": *Richmond Whig*, quoted in Robert S. Harper, *Lincoln and the Press* (New York: McGraw-Hill, 1951), p. 360.

744 St. Louis . . . comfortable study: Entry for January 27, 1865, *The Diary of Edward Bates, 1859–1866*, p. 443.

744 "the astounding news . . . country and for myself": Entry for April 15, 1865, in ibid., p. 473.

744 News of Lincoln's death . . . "sinking into his mind": Brooks, *Mr. Lincoln's Washington*, pp. 458–59 (quotes p. 459).

745 "The history of governments . . . confidence and regard": "Hay's Reminiscences of the Civil War," in Hay, *At Lincoln's Side*, pp. 128–29.

745 Flags remained . . . "the farewell march": Brooks, *Washington, D.C., in Lincoln's Time*, pp. 271 (quote), 273.

745 nearly two hundred thousand Union soldiers: Smith, *The Francis Preston Blair Family in Politics*, Vol. II, p. 185.

745 "Never in the history . . . shrill call of bugles": Brooks, *Washington, D.C., in Lincoln's Time*, pp. 272–74.

745 "magnificent and imposing spectacle": Entry for May 19, 1865, *Welles diary*, Vol. II, p. 310.

745 "You see in these . . . half a dozen presidents": EMS, quoted in Flower, *Edwin McMasters Stanton*, p. 288.

746 "more and more dim . . . found in every family": AL, "Address Before the Young Men's Lyceum of Springfield, Illinois," January 27, 1838, in *CW*, I, p. 115.

746 "a new birth of freedom . . . perish from the earth": AL, "Address Delivered at the Dedication of the Cemetery at Gettysburg," final text, November 19, 1863, in *CW*, VII, p. 23.

746 second day belonged . . . "with our swords": Sherman, *Memoirs of General W. T. Sherman*, p. 731.

746 All of Washington . . . "All felt this": Entry for April 19, 1865, *Welles diary*, Vol. II, p. 310.

746 "a Cabinet which should . . . than one counsellor": WHS, "The President and His Cabinet," October 20, 1865, *Works of William H. Seward*, Vol. V, p. 527.

747 "I have no doubt . . . greatest man I ever knew": Tribute by General Grant, in Browne, *The Every-Day Life of Abraham Lincoln*, p. 7.
747 "I have more than once . . . Nineteenth Century": Walt Whitman, "November Boughs," *The Complete Prose Works of Walt Whitman*, Vol. III (New York: G. P. Putnam's Sons, Knickerbocker Press, 1902), pp. 206–07.
747 Leo Tolstoy . . . "light beams directly on us": Leo Tolstoy, quoted in *The World*, New York, February 7, 1908.
748 "Every man is said . . . yet to be developed": AL, "Communication to the People of Sangamo County," March 9, 1832, in *CW*, I, p. 8.
748 "he had done nothing . . . that he had lived": AL, paraphrased in Joshua F. Speed to WHH, February 7, 1866, in *HI*, p. 197.
749 "conceived in Liberty . . . all men are created equal": AL, "Address Delivered at the Dedication of the Cemetery at Gettysburg, November 19, 1863; Edward Everett Copy," in *CW*, VII, p. 21.
749 "With malice toward none; with charity for all": AL, "Second Inaugural Address," March 4, 1865, *CW*, VIII, p. 333.

EPILOGUE

Page

751 "night of horrors": Entries for April 14, 1865, *Chase Papers*, Vol. I, p. 529.
751 "vicarious suffering": FAS, in "Miscellaneous Fragments in Mrs. Seward's Handwriting," reel 197, Seward Papers.
751 "the largest . . . woman in America": *New York Independent*, undated, in Seward family scrapbook, Seward House Foundation Historical Association, Inc., Library, Auburn, N.Y.
751 Fanny remained . . . tuberculosis: Taylor, *William Henry Seward*, p. 266.
751 Seward was inconsolable: Van Deusen, *William Henry Seward*, p. 417.
751 "Truly it may . . . mother and daughter": *Washington Republican*, undated, in Seward family scrapbook, Seward House.
751 attempts to mediate . . . radicals in Congress: Van Deusen, *William Henry Seward*, p. 452.
751 "Seward's Folly": Taylor, *William Henry Seward*, p. 278.
751 spent his last years traveling: Ibid., pp. 290–91, 292–94; *NYT*, October 11, 1872.
751 Jenny asked . . . "Love one another": Taylor, *William Henry Seward*, p. 296; Seward, *Seward at Washington . . . 1861–1872*, p. 508 (quote).
751 Thurlow Weed . . . wept openly: Taylor, *William Henry Seward*, p. 296.
751 Stanton's remaining . . . asked for his resignation: Pratt, *Stanton*, p. 452; Thomas and Hyman, *Stanton*, p. 583.
751 Refusing to honor . . . removal order: George C. Gorham, *Life and Public Services of Edwin M. Stanton*, Vol. II (Boston and New York: Houghton, Mifflin, Riverside Press, 1899), p. 444.
751 "barricaded himself": Pratt, *Stanton*, p. 452.
751 taking his meals in the department: Thomas and Hyman, *Stanton*, p. 595.
751 Tenure of Office Act: "Tenure of Office Act," in *The Reader's Companion to American History*, ed. Foner and Garraty, pp. 1,063–64.
752 impeachment failed . . . submitted his resignation: Thomas and Hyman, *Stanton*, p. 608.
752 Grant nominated him . . . "only office": Wolcott, "Edwin M. Stanton," p. 178.
752 short-lived . . . severe asthma attack: *Dictionary of American Biography*, Vol. IX, ed. Dumas Malone (New York: Charles Scribner's Sons, 1935; 1964), p. 520; Thomas and Hyman, *Stanton*, pp. 637–38; Christopher Bates, "Stanton, Edwin McMasters," in *Encyclopedia of the American Civil War*, ed. Heidler and Heidler, p. 1852.
752 "I know that it is . . . he was then": Robert Todd Lincoln to Edwin L. Stanton, quoted in Thomas and Hyman, *Stanton*, p. 638.
752 close-knit family . . . Confederate Army: Cain, *Lincoln's Attorney General*, p. 330.
752 "it was in his social . . . death cannot sever": Address by Colonel J. C. Broadhead, in "Addresses by the Members of the St. Louis Bar on the Death of Edward Bates," Bates Papers, MoSHi.
752 impeachment trial . . . resting with the Democrats: Blue, *Salmon P. Chase*, p. 285.
752 Kate serving . . . derailed his ambitions: *Dictionary of American Biography*, Vol. II, ed. Allen Johnson and Dumas Malone (New York: Charles Scribner's Sons, 1929; 1958), p. 33.
752 switched his allegiance . . . to Horace Greeley: Niven, *Salmon P. Chase*, pp. 447–48.
752 physical condition weakened . . . depression: Ibid., pp. 444, 448–49.
752 "too much of an invalid . . . I were dead": SPC to Richard C. Parsons, May 5, 1873, *Chase Papers*, Vol. V, p. 370.
752 Kate saw her marriage . . . died in poverty: Belden and Belden, *So Fell the Angels*, pp. 297–98, 306–10, 320, 326–27, 348.
753 Frank Blair . . . intemperate denunciations: *Dictionary of American Biography*, Vol. I, ed. Allen Johnson (New York: Charles Scribner's Sons, 1927; 1964), pp. 333–34.
753 died from a fall: *NYT*, July 10, 1875.
753 "his physical vigor . . . of disposition": *Sun*, Baltimore, Md., October 19, 1876.
753 Montgomery served . . . biography of Andrew Jackson: *Dictionary of American Biography*, Vol. I (1964 edn.), p. 340.
753 wrote a series . . . "herculean tasks": Niven, *Gideon Welles*, pp. 576–77 (quote p. 576).
753 perceptive diary . . . streptococcus infection: Ibid., pp. 578, 580.
753 remained friends . . . abridged version: Nicolay, *Lincoln's Secretary*, pp. 301, 342.

753 Shortly before he died ... "overpowering melancholy": William Roscoe Thayer, *The Life and Letters of John Hay* (Boston and New York: Houghton Mifflin, 1929), pp. 405, 407.

753 "each morning ... as an impossibility": MTL to EBL, August 25, 1865, in Turner and Turner, *Mary Todd Lincoln*, p. 268.

753 "precious Tad ... gladly welcome death": MTL to Alexander Williamson, [May 26, 1867], in ibid., p. 422.

753 Tad journeyed ... "beyond his years": *NYTrib*, July 17, 1871.

754 "compression of the heart": Turner and Turner, *Mary Todd Lincoln*, p. 585.

754 "The modest and cordial ... fantastic enterprises": *NYTrib*, July 17, 1871.

754 "It is very hard ... to the contrary": Robert Todd Lincoln to Mary Harlan, quoted in Helm, *The True Story of Mary*, p. 267.

754 erratic behavior ... permanently estranged: Randall, *Mary Lincoln*, pp. 430–34.

754 virtual recluse ... fulfilled at last: Ibid., pp. 442–43.

ILLUSTRATION CREDITS

Numbers in roman type refer to illustrations in the inserts; numbers in *italics* refer to book pages.

Chicago Historical Society: 1, 33, *702*

Abraham Lincoln Presidential Library & Museum: *xx–1*, 2, 3, 4, 5, 13, 19, 22, 23, 26, 29, 31, 32, 35, 36, 39, 44, 46, 47, 48, 49, 51, 55, 62, 63, 72, 73, 74, 76, *170*, *321*, *409*, *445*, *667*

Courtesy of the Department of Rare Books and Special Collections, University of Rochester Library: 6, 7, 9

Seward House, Auburn, New York: 8, 10, 34, 50

From the collection of Louise Taper: 11, 12

Ohio Historical Society: 14, 52

The Saint Louis Art Museum: *60*

Library of Congress: 15, 21, 24, 25, 27, 37, 41, 43, 56, 59, 64, 65, 68, 69, *347*, *377*, *548*

Missouri Historical Society: 16, 17, 18

Picture History: 20, 28, 30, 54, *473*

Western Reserve Historical Society, Cleveland, Ohio: 38

Brown University Library: 40

United States Army Military History Institute: 42

National Archives: 45, 53, 60, 61, 66, 67, 71, 75

Courtesy of J. Wayne Lee: 57, 58

National Portrait Gallery, Smithsonian Institution / Art Resource, New York: 70

Courtesy, American Antiquarian Society: *279*

Civil War Collection, Eastern Kentucky University Archives, Richmond, Kentucky: *323*

White House Historical Association (White House Collection): *597*, *627*

INDEX

Abell, Elizabeth, 55, 56, 93
abolition movement, *see* slaves, slavery
Adams, Charles Francis, 113–14,
126, 193, 250, 257, 259, 263,
268, 283, 288, 289, 304,
309–10, 330, 333, 335, 341,
352, 363–64, 595, 668
Adams, Charles Francis, Jr., 268,
269–70, 274, 282, 302–3, 701
Adams, Henry, 12, 14, 299, 301–2,
580–81
Adams, John, xv, 534
Adams, John Quincy, 38, 111, 113,
119, 130, 141, 266, 387, 491
Aesop's Fables, 51
Alabama, 258, 293
Albany *Atlas and Argus,* 13, 192,
330
Albany Evening Journal, 71, 84, 228,
289
Alcott, Louisa May, 456–58
Allen, Ethan, 151
Alley, John, 680
American Anti-Slavery Society, 111
American Exchange and Review,
603–4
American Party, *see* Know-Nothing
Party
Ames, Mary Clemmer, 401, 458
Anderson, Robert, 297–98, 334, 337,
340, 345, 353–54
Andrew, John, 548, 657
Anthon, John, 32
Antietam, Battle of, 465, 481, 531
Anti-Nebraska Party, 181
anti-slavery movement, *see* slaves,
slavery

"Appeal of the Independent
Democrats in Congress to the
People of the United States,"
161–62, 165
Appleby, Joyce, 38–39
Appomattox Court House, 725
Ariel, 451
Arkansas, 336, 349
Army of Northern Virginia,
Confederate, 725–26
Army of the Cumberland, U.S., 556
Army of the Potomac, U.S., 374,
377–78, 425, 428, 465, 478, 480,
502, 519, 558, 616, 618, 628, 666
in farewell march, 745–46
Lincoln's family visit to, 513–17
Army of the Tennessee, U.S., 502–3
Army of the West, U.S., 746
Army of Virginia, U.S., 473, 478
Arnold, Isaac, 689, 701
Ashbury, Henry, 210
Ashley, James M., 219, 687–89
Ashmun, George, 121, 257, 259, 288,
734
Associated Press, 554, 574
Astor, John, 448
Atlantic Monthly, 604
Atzerodt, George, 735, 738
Auburn, N.Y., 13–14, 253
Freeman affair in, 85–86

Bailey, Gamaliel, 20, 186, 218–19
Bailey, Margaret, 218
Baker, Edward, 89, 107, 121, 328, 402
death of, 380–82
Baker, James, 576
Ball, Flamen, 605